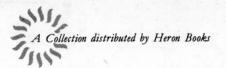 *A Collection distributed by Heron Books*

THE
GREATEST MASTERPIECES
OF
RUSSIAN LITERATURE

MAXIM GORKY

THROUGH
RUSSIA

A BOOK OF STORIES

Translated from the Russian by
C. J. Hogarth
with an Introduction by A. B. Mc Millin

Original Frontispiece by Jean-Pierre Chabrol
Original Illustrations by Lola Fielding

Distributed by
HERON BOOKS

Published by arrangement with
J. M. Dent & Sons Ltd.

13 005 07 R4

Maxim Gorky

INTRODUCTION

"IF there is something great, boundless, vast, painfully gripping and promising which we have been wont to associate with the name of Russia, then it is Gorky whom we must regard as having best expressed all that." Thus wrote Alexander Blok, the great Symbolist poet, effectively chrystallizing the power and fascination of much of his contemporary's work for Russian and non-Russian readers alike. During his lifetime Gorky enjoyed a degree of fame and influence comparable only to that of Count Tolstoy himself, and as with the older writer the reasons for this influence were far from exclusively literary. It was a combination of historical circumstances and innate strength and breadth of character rather than any outstanding gifts as a writer that made Gorky such a significant figure.

Alexei Maximovich Peshkov was born in Nizhny Novgorod (later renamed Gorky) in 1868: the pseudonym Maxim Gorky (in Russian Maxim "the Bitter") was adopted in 1892 when he published his first story. His father was an upholsterer become shipping agent and his mother the daughter of a dyer by the name of Vasily Kashirin. When Gorky was five his father died and so his mother brought him back to the house of the Kashirins in Nizhny. Life in this household with the selfish and mean grandfather and his kind and sensitive old wife is unforgettably described in the first part of Gorky's autobiographical trilogy, *Childhood*. His mother remarried but soon died, whereupon to keep costs down the young Alexei was sent out into the world as an apprentice to a boot maker: this "apprenticeship" turned out to be nothing more than slavish drudgery and for the next ten years Gorky tried a wide variety of employments including that of icon painter (or "God-dauber" as they were known), cook's boy on a river steamer, baker, stevedore, gardener, music hall singer, potboy, store clerk, track layer, rag picker, bird catcher, watchman and lawyer's clerk.

It was on the steamer that he learnt to read: the cook, a drunken ex-soldier, not only taught him his letters but also imbued him with his own tastes which were principally for garishly written blood and thunder stories: one of the first books Gorky read was *The Mysteries of Udolpho*, and for a considerable period his reading was predominantly of this type. This is clearly reflected in his early stories which are marred by a lack of restraint and excessive striving for effect; but although more sober writers like Chekhov and Korolenko urged him to exert greater self discipline, the general public, nurtured as it had been on the solid fare of the nineteenth century realistic tradition and latterly on Chekhov's infinitely subtle but depressing pictures of *fin de siècle* stagnation, welcomed the escapism, delighting in the colour and exuberance of the writing, and choosing to overlook the brashness and lapses of taste.

His first story, *Makar Chudra*, did not appear until 1892, however. At the age of fifteen he had made an unsuccessful attempt to enter a school in Kazan', but, as he wrote later, "it was not the practice at that time to give education free of charge". Four years later after various depressing jobs and feeling the world had no place for him Gorky attempted to shoot himself but only succeeded in piercing a lung, which was, however, to be the cause of his later tuberculosis.

Soon after this he formed a little study circle consisting of a mechanic, carpenter, bookbinder and two telegraphers: they resolved to try the experiment of forming a Tolstoyan colony (it was only later that Gorky was to soundly condemn Tolstoy, Dostoyevsky and, indeed, the nineteenth century as a whole); knowing the Count himself to have a great deal of land they wrote him a remarkably naive letter requesting a small part of it for their project. As no reply was forthcoming Gorky was sent in person, only to be turned away by the Countess after trekking hundreds of miles. This perhaps shows as well as anything how far Gorky's ideas and ideals were from harsh reality at that time. Throughout his life his understanding of the proletariat and petty bourgeoisie whence he had sprung was greater than his comprehension for the intelligentsia—a factor that is reflected in his fiction. It is ironical that not many years later Gorky was to meet Tolstoy as an "equal".

Back in Nizhny a police dossier on him was opened since he persisted in associating with politically suspect people. What made him particularly 'dangerous' was the fact that he was a real worker rather than an intellectual—he was working in a tavern at this time. An investigation failed to reveal anything serious against him, although during the enquiry he "conducted himself with insolence and impertinence". Refused for military service on account of his lung, he spent two years wandering through the whole of Southern Russia: the Donbas, the Ukraine, Bessarabia and the Caucasus. It is his experiences at this time that form the principal content of the collection *Through Russia*.

He finally settled in Tiflis where he wrote for a local newspaper, and published his first story, later obtaining a regular column in a Samara paper, continuing to publish locally and, before long, in the Petersburg press. A collected two-volume edition of his stories in 1898 brought immense popularity. The self-educated orphan had become a celebrity of unparalleled magnitude almost overnight. Meanwhile the police continued to follow his movements, at one stage even detatching a railway carriage in which he was travelling from Petersburg to the Crimea, shunting it off to Podolsk, a provincial town some distance away, to avoid noisy expressions of enthusiasm from crowds waiting to welcome the writer with a banquet in Moscow. The Crimean express then had to make a special stop to pick up Gorky's coach again. His arrest after the 1905 "Bloody Sunday" uprising brought widespread protests both at home and abroad: he was determined to be tried in order to attract attention to the political situation, and it was only by a general amnesty that the authorities were able to avoid this embarrassing problem. The ensuing 'days of freedom' were short lived, and friends soon smuggled him across the Finnish frontier.

Whilst abroad he sought to persuade foreign governments and banks not to make loans to the Russian state, financially ruined as it was by the disastrous war with Japan; at tne same time he wanted to collect money for the revolutionary causes he was supporting at home. Europe, and particularly Germany, received him rapturously, although he was unable to dissuade French bankers from making the loans. The Tsarist government strove vigorously to prevent his entry to the United States, but the State Department upheld the letter of the Constitution and Gorky was admitted. The Russian ambassador then tried a subtler ploy: he revealed and publicised the fact that the writer's travelling companion, Mme Andreyeva, was not in fact his wife. A wave of indignation arose and Gorky found himself on a suitcase in a New York street: fortunately he was rescued by a sympathetic American family who offered him hospitality, but he never forgave America and vented some of his anger in *The City of the Yellow Devil* (1906).

After America Gorky spent seven years on Capri, continuing to write although, curiously enough, very little influenced by his Italian surroundings: in all the time he was there he did not learn a word of Italian. Capri became a place of pilgrimage for Russians abroad—a second *Yasnaya Polyana* in fact, although Gorky was much less aloof and inaccessible than Tolstoy, receiving visitors gladly and replying personally to all of his hundreds of correspondents, many of whom were simple people, some barely literate: one such letter bore the address, 'Switzerland. Isle of Cyprus. Gorky'.

During the First World War Gorky, by now back in Russia, assumed an internationalist position, and in 1917 supported the Bolsheviks, albeit in a rather aloof manner. His personal contacts with Lenin and other leading figures made this possible, and for a considerable period he was the only independent force in the whole of Russia, a unique position which he used to try and protect less favoured fellow writers and other intellectuals; at this stage it was simply a question of saving them from starvation and obtaining scarce necessities like paper and ink, rather than of shielding them from political pressures.

From 1921-4 he lived in Germany and then for four years in Sorrento, finally returning to the Soviet Union in 1929 as the grand old man of Soviet letters. He remained a supporter of the government and its policies to the bitter end, and his death in 1936 was alleged by the public prosecutor to be the result of a Trotskyite plot, but little is known for certain.

Chekhov said, "I think that a time will come when Gorky's works will be forgotten, but it is doubtful that even in a thousand years Gorky, the man, will be forgotten". It is Gorky the man that shines through the stories of *Through Russia*, which were written and published in various journals between 1912 and 1917. This was the period of the great trilogy when most of his autobiographical works were written, and it must be considered the richest of all the veins in Gorky's writing, although it was not especially appreciated during his lifetime: his early popularity with the intelligentsia had waned by this time, although the Bolsheviks and literate proletariat formed an enthusiastic and ever widening readership for his works.

To say that the man shines through is not to imply that Gorky's ego intrudes into the stories: for an autobiographical writer he is exceptionally modest and unobtrusive. What does come across is the value and potential of man as a whole; as Satin exclaims in the play *The Lower Depths*: "*Man*—ther's your truth!... M-a-n! That has a proud ring!" Or again take Ossip's remark at the end of *The Icebreaker*: "The human soul is a winged thing". Gorky reveals an immense interest and love for the infinite variety of humanity, not so much for men as they are, oppressed, brutal and confused, but as the writer believes they could be in other circumstances. In many of the stories the power and beauty of nature symbolising man's true potential is contrasted with his pitiful plight and behaviour. Not that his heroes are stereotyped or in any way over-simplified: Ossip, Gubin, the old man in *The Cemetery*, to take but a few, are very much individual and alive however confused their ideas. Like Tolstoy, Gorky makes considerable use of physical description to reveal a man's character, and like this writer he rarely leaves the reader in doubt as to his own opinions, but he differs from Tolstoy, and indeed all the Russian nineteenth century writers after Gogol, in the saturated style of his writing. Such abundant imagery is quite uncharacteristic of the main stream of Russian realism, and is decidedly variable in quality. Often it is violent to match the undercurrent of the life being described ("at my feet lay a mass of chestnut leaves which resembled the amputated palms of human hands"), sometimes it retains a banality from the writer's early literary experience whilst at other times it rises to heights of great poetic grandeur.

The theme of oppression was far from being a novelty in Russian literature: Pushkin, Gogol, Dostoyevsky and Chekhov had all portrayed 'little men' crushed by their environment, but hitherto the tradition had been principally urban in character, with life in the country tending to be idealised. Gorky again and again contrasts natural beauty with human frailty and ugliness. Where he does take the town as a setting he presents a more detailed picture than had hitherto been seen of the underworld: here, as elsewhere, the strong influence of Dostoyevsky is felt, although Gorky rejected the earlier writer as a false prophet on account of his philosophy of humility and submission.

Through Russia, as the title suggests, offers a broad panorama of life in Russia at the end of the last century. Nowhere is expressed so clearly the sense of hopelessness and frustration felt by the common people at that time; it complements Chekhov's picture of the intelligentsia of the same period. As the ex-soldier in *In a Mountain Defile* says, "Of Russia nothing the least hard or definite can be said, and, indeed, this book conveys the infinite variety of this vast country and its inhabitants". The picture is black, but relieved by man's potential goodness or true self in which the writer deeply believes. Despite "the burden of great and inexorable sorrow with which all life is dowered", all that man really needs is guidance: "in my breast a red flame was smouldering like a living beacon, and leading me to long that some frightened, belated wayfarer should, as it were, sight my little speck of radiancy amid the darkness". For countless thousands of people Gorky became just such a beacon.

A. B. Mc Millin

London, May 1967.

CONTENTS

THE BIRTH OF A MAN

THE year was the year '92, the year of leanness—the scene a spot between Sukhum and Otchenchiri, on the river Kodor, a spot so near to the sea that amid the joyous babble of a sparkling rivulet the ocean's deep-voiced thunder was plainly distinguishable.

Also, the season being autumn, leaves of wild laurel were glistening and gyrating on the white foam of the Kodor like a quantity of mercurial salmon fry. And as I sat on some rocks overlooking the river there occurred to me the thought that, as likely as not, the cause of the gulls' and cormorants' fretful cries where the surf lay moaning behind a belt of trees to the right was that, like myself, they kept mistaking the leaves for fish, and as often finding themselves disappointed.

Over my head hung chestnut trees decked with gold; at my feet lay a mass of chestnut leaves which resembled the amputated palms of human hands; on the opposite bank, where there waved, tanglewise, the stripped branches of a hornbeam, an orange-tinted woodpecker was darting to and fro, as though caught in the mesh of foliage, and, in company with a troupe of nimble titmice and blue tree-creepers (visitors from the far-distant North), tapping the bark of the stem with a black beak, and hunting for insects.

To the left the tops of the mountains hung fringed with dense, fleecy clouds of the kind which presages rain; and these clouds were sending their shadows gliding over slopes green and overgrown with boxwood and that peculiar species of hollow beech-stump which once came near to effecting the downfall of Pompey's host, through depriving his iron-built legions of the use of their legs as they revelled in the intoxicating sweetness of the " mead " or honey which wild bees make from the blossoms of the laurel and the azalea, and travellers still

3

gather from those hollow stems to knead into *lavashi* or thin cakes of millet flour.

On the present occasion I too (after suffering sundry stings from infuriated bees) was thus engaged as I sat on the rocks beneath the chestnuts. Dipping morsels of bread into a potful of honey, I was munching them for breakfast, and enjoying, at the same time, the indolent beams of the moribund autumn sun.

In the fall of the year the Caucasus resembles a gorgeous cathedral built by great craftsmen (always great craftsmen are great sinners) to conceal their past from the prying eyes of conscience. Which cathedral is a sort of intangible edifice of gold and turquoise and emerald, and has thrown over its hills rare carpets silk-embroidered by Turcoman weavers of Shemi and Samarkand, and contains, heaped everywhere, plunder brought from all the quarters of the world for the delectation of the sun. Yes, it is as though men sought to say to the Sun God: " All things here are thine. They have been brought hither for thee by thy people."

Yes, mentally I see long-bearded, grey-headed supermen, beings possessed of the rounded eyes of happy children, descending from the hills, and decking the earth, and sowing it with sheerly kaleidoscopic treasures, and coating the tops of the mountains with massive layers of silver, and the lower edges with a living web of trees. Yes, I see those beings decorating and fashioning the scene until, thanks to their labours, this gracious morsel of the earth has become fair beyond all conception.

And what a privilege it is to be human! How much that is wonderful leaps to the eye—how the presence of beauty causes the heart to throb with a voluptuous rapture that is almost pain!

And though occasions there are when life seems hard, and the breast feels filled with fiery rancour, and melancholy dries and renders athirst the heart's blood, this is not a mood sent us in perpetuity. For at times even the sun may feel sad as he contemplates men, and sees that, despite all that he has done for them, they have done so little in return. . . .

No, it is not that good folk are lacking. It is that they need to be rounded off—better still, to be made anew.

*

Suddenly there came into view over the bushes to my left a

4

file of dark heads, while through the surging of the waves and the babble of the stream I caught the sound of human voices, a sound emanating from a party of " famine people " or folk who were journeying from Sukhum to Otchenchiri to obtain work on a local road then in process of construction.

The owners of the voices I knew to be immigrants from the province of Orlov. I knew them to be so for the reason that I myself had lately been working in company with the male members of the party, and had taken leave of them only yesterday in order that I might set out earlier than they, and, after walking through the night, greet the sun when he should arise above the sea.

The members of the party comprised four men and a woman —the latter a young female with high cheek-bones, a figure swollen with manifest pregnancy, and a pair of greyish-blue eyes that had fixed in them a stare of apprehension. At the present moment her head and yellow scarf were just showing over the tops of the bushes; and while I noted that now it was swaying from side to side like a sunflower shaken by the wind, I recalled the fact that she was a woman whose husband had been carried off at Sukhum by a surfeit of fruit—this fact being known to me through the circumstance that in the workmen's *barraque* where we had shared quarters these folk had observed the good old Russian custom of confiding to a stranger the whole of their troubles, and had done so in tones of such amplitude and penetration that the querulous words must have been audible for five versts around.

And as I had talked to these forlorn people, these human beings who lay crushed beneath the misfortune which had uprooted them f.om their barren and exhausted lands, and blown them, like autumn leaves, towards the Caucasus where nature's luxuriant, but unfamiliar, aspect had blinded and bewildered them, and with its onerous conditions of labour quenched their last spark of courage; as I had talked to these poor people I had seen them glancing about them with dull, troubled, despondent eyes, and heard them say to one another softly, and with pitiful smiles:

" What a country! "

" Aye, that it is!—a country to make one sweat! "

" As hard as a stone it is! "

" Aye, an evil country! "

After which they had gone on to speak of their native haunts, where every handful of soil had represented to them the dust of their ancestors, and every grain of that soil had been watered with the sweat of their brows, and become charged with dear and intimate recollections.

Previously there had joined the party a woman who, tall and straight, had had breasts as flat as a board, and jawbones like the jawbones of a horse, and a glance in her dull, sidelong black eyes like a gleaming, smouldering fire.

And every evening this woman had been wont to step outside the *barraque* with the woman in the yellow scarf, and to seat herself on a rubbish heap, and, resting her cheeks on the palms of her hands, and inclining her head sideways, to sing in a high and shrewish voice:

> Behind the graveyard wall,
> Where fair green bushes stand,
> I'll spread me on the sand
> A shroud as white as snow.
> And not long will it be
> Before my heart's adored,
> My master and my lord,
> Shall answer my curtsey low.

Usually her companion, the woman in the yellow scarf, had, with head bent forward, and eyes fixed upon her stomach, remained silent; but on rare, unexpected occasions she had, in the hoarse, sluggish voice of a peasant, sung a song with the sobbing refrain:

> Ah, my beloved, sweetheart of mine,
> Never again will these eyes seek thine!

Nor amid the stifling blackness of the southern night had these voices ever failed to bring back to my memory the snowy wastes of the North, and the icy, wailing storm-wind, and the distant howling of unseen wolves.

In time the squint-eyed woman had been taken ill of a fever, and removed to the town in a tilted ambulance: and as she had lain quivering and moaning on the stretcher she had seemed still to be singing her little ditty about the graveyard and the sand.

*

The head with the yellow scarf rose, dipped, and disappeared.

After I had finished my breakfast I thatched the honey-pot with some leaves, fastened down the lid, and indolently resumed my way in the wake of the party, my blackthorn staff tip-tapping against the hard tread of the track as I proceeded.

6

The track loomed, a grey, narrow strip, before me, while on my right the restless, dark blue sea had the air of being ceaselessly planed by thousands of invisible carpenters; so regularly did the stress of a wind as moist and sweet and warm as the breath of a healthy woman cause ever-rustling curls of foam to drift towards the beach. Also, careening on to its port quarter under a full set of bellying sails, a Turkish felucca was gliding towards Sukhum; and as it held on its course it put me in mind of a certain pompous engineer of the town who had been wont to inflate his fat cheeks and say: " Be quiet, you, or I will have you locked up!" This man had, for some reason or another, had an extraordinary weakness for causing arrests to be made; and exceedingly do I rejoice to think that by now the worms of the graveyard must have consumed him down to the very marrow of his bones. Would that certain other acquaintances of mine were similarly receiving beneficent attention!

Walking proved an easy task enough, for I seemed to be borne on air, while a chorus of pleasant thoughts, of many-coloured recollections, kept singing gently in my breast—a chorus resembling, indeed, the white-maned billows in the regularity with which now it rose, and now it fell, to reveal in, as it were, soft, peaceful depths the bright, supple hopes of youth, like so many silver fish cradled in the bosom of the ocean.

Suddenly, as it trended seawards, the road executed a half-turn, and skirted a strip of the sandy margin to which the waves kept rolling in such haste. And in that spot even the bushes seemed to have a mind to look the waves in the eyes—so strenuously did they lean across the riband-like path, and nod in the direction of the blue, watery waste, while from the hills a wind was blowing that presaged rain.

*

But hark! From some point among the bushes a low moan arose—the sound which never fails to thrill the soul and move it to responsive quivers!

Thrusting aside the foliage, I beheld before me the woman in the yellow scarf. Seated with her back resting against the stem of a hazel-bush, she had her head sunken deeply between her shoulders, her mouth hideously agape, her eyes staring vaguely before her, her hands pressed to her swollen stomach, her breath issuing with unnatural vehemence, and her abdomen convulsively, spasmodically rising and falling. Meanwhile from her throat were issuing moans which at times caused her yellow teeth to show bare like those of a wolf.

" What is the matter? " I said as I bent over her. " Has anyone assaulted you? "

The only result was that, shuffling bare feet in the sand like a fly, she shook her nerveless hand, and gasped:

" Away, villain! Away with you! "

Then I understood what was the matter, for I had seen a similar case before. Yet for the moment a certain feeling of shyness made me edge away from her a little; and as I did so she uttered a prolonged moan, and her almost bursting eyeballs vented hot, murky tears which trickled down her tense and livid features.

Thereupon I turned to her again, and, throwing down cooking-pot, teapot, and wallet, laid her on her back, and strove to bend her knees upwards in the direction of her body. Meanwhile she sought to repel me with blows on face and breast, and at length rolled on to her stomach. Then, raising herself on all fours, she, sobbing, gasping, and cursing in a breath, crawled away like a bear into a remoter portion of the thicket.

" Beast! " she panted. " Oh, you devil! "

Yet even as the words escaped her lips her arms gave way beneath her, and she collapsed upon her face, with legs stretched out, and her lips emitting a fresh series of convulsive moans.

Excited now to fever pitch, I hurriedly recalled my small store of knowledge of such cases, and, finally, decided to turn her on her back, and, as before, to strive to bend her knees upwards in the direction of her body. Already signs of imminent parturition were not wanting.

" Lie still," I said, " and if you do that it will not be long before you are delivered of the child."

Whereafter, running down to the sea, I pulled up my sleeves, and, on returning, embarked upon my rôle of *accoucheur*.

Scoring the earth with her fingers, uprooting tufts of withered grass, and struggling to thrust them into her mouth, scattering soil over her terrible, inhuman face and bloodshot eyes, the woman writhed like a strip of birch bark in a wood fire. Indeed, by this time a little head was coming into view, and it needed all my efforts to quell the twitchings of her legs, to help the child to issue, and to prevent its mother from thrusting grass down her distorted, moaning throat. Meanwhile we cursed one another: she through her teeth, and I in an undertone: she, I should surmise, out of pain and shame, and I, I feel certain,

8

out of nervousness, mingled with a perfect agony of compassion.

"O Lord!" she gasped with blue lips flecked with foam as her eyes (suddenly bereft of their colour in the sunlight) shed tears born of the intolerable anguish of the maternal function, and her body writhed and twisted as though her frame had been severed in the middle.

"Away, you brute!" was her oft-repeated cry as with her weak hands, hands seemingly dislocated at the wrists, she strove to thrust me to a distance. Yet all the time I kept saying persuasively: "You fool! Bring forth as quickly as you can!" and, as a matter of fact, was feeling so sorry for her that tears continued to spurt from my eyes as much as from hers, and my very heart contracted with pity. Also, never did I cease to feel that I ought to keep saying something: wherefore, I repeated, and again repeated: "Now then! Bring forth as quickly as ever you can!"

*

And at last my hands did indeed hold a human creature in all its pristine beauty. Nor could even the mist of tears prevent me from seeing that that human creature was red in the face, and that, to judge from the manner in which it kept kicking and resisting and uttering hoarse wails (while still bound to its mother by the ligament), it was feeling dissatisfied in advance with the world. Yes, blue-eyed, and with a nose absurdly sunken between a pair of scarlet, rumpled cheeks and lips which ceaselessly quivered and contracted, it kept bawling: "A-a-ah! A-a-ah!"

Moreover, so slippery was it that, as I knelt and looked at it, and laughed with relief at the fact that it had arrived safely, I came near to letting it fall upon the ground: wherefore I entirely forgot what next I ought to have done.

"Cut it!" at length whispered the mother with eyes closed, and features suddenly swollen and resembling those of a corpse. "A knife!" again she whispered with her livid lips. "Cut it!"

My pocket-knife I had had stolen from me in the workmen's *barraque*; but with my teeth I severed the caul, and then the child gave renewed tongue in true Orlovian fashion, while the mother smiled. Also, in some curious fashion the mother's unfathomable eyes regained their colour, and became filled as with blue fire as, plunging a hand into her bodice, and feeling for the pocket, she contrived to articulate with raw and blood-flecked lips:

"I have not a single piece of string or riband to bind the caul with."

Upon that I set to, and managed to produce a piece of riband, and to fasten it in the required position.

Thereafter she smiled more brightly than ever. So radiantly did she smile that my eyes came near to being blinded with the spectacle.

"And now rearrange yourself," I said; "and in the meanwhile I will go and wash the baby."

"Yes, yes," she murmured uneasily. "But be very careful with him—be very gentle."

Yet it was little enough care that the rosy little homunculus seemed to require, so strenuously did he clench his fists, and bawl as though he were minded to challenge the whole world to combat.

"Come, now!" at length I said. "You must have done, or your very head will drop off."

Yet no sooner did he feel the touch of the ocean spray, and begin to be sprinkled with its joyous caresses, than he lamented more loudly and vigorously than ever, and so continued throughout the process of being slapped on the back and breast as, frowning and struggling, he vented squall after squall while the waves laved his tiny limbs.

"Shout, young Orlovian!" said I encouragingly. "Let fly with all the power of your lungs!"

And with that I took him back to his mother. I found her with eyes closed and lips drawn between her teeth as she writhed in the torment of expelling the after-birth. But presently I detected through the sighs and groans a whispered "Give him to me! Give him to me!"

"You had better wait a little," I urged.

"Oh no! Give him to me now!"

And with tremulous, unsteady hands she unhooked the bosom of her bodice, and, freeing (with my assistance) the breast which nature had prepared for at least a dozen children, applied the mutinous young Orlovian to the nipple. As for him, he at once understood the matter, and ceased to send forth further lamentation.

"O pure and holy Mother of God!" she gasped in a long-drawn, quivering sigh as she bent a dishevelled head over the little one, and, between intervals of silence, fell to uttering soft, abrupt exclamations. Then, opening her ineffably beautiful blue eyes, the hallowed eyes of a mother, she raised them towards the azure heavens, while in their depths there was coming and going a flame of joy and gratitude. Lastly, lifting a languid hand, she with a slow movement made the sign of the cross over both herself and her babe.

" Thanks to thee, O purest Mother of God! " she murmured. " Thanks indeed to thee! "

Then her eyes grew dim and vague again, and after a pause (during which she seemed to be scarcely breathing) she said in a hard and matter-of-fact tone:

" Young fellow, unfasten my satchel."

And whilst I was so engaged she continued to regard me with a steady gaze, but when the task was completed she smiled shamefacedly, and on her sunken cheeks and sweat-flecked temples there dawned the ghost of a blush.

" Now," said she, " do you, for the present, go away."

" And if I do so, see that in the meanwhile you do not move about too much."

" No, I will not. But please go away."

So I withdrew a little. In my breast a sort of weariness was lurking, but also in my breast there was echoing a soft and glorious chorus of birds, a chorus so exquisitely in accord with the never-ceasing plash of the sea that for ever could I have listened to it, and to the neighbouring brook as it purled on its way like a maiden engaged in relating confidences about her lover.

Presently the woman's yellow-scarfed head (the scarf now tidily rearranged) reappeared over the bushes.

" Come, come, good woman! " was my exclamation. " I tell you that you must not move about so soon."

And certainly her attitude now was one of utter languor, and she had perforce to grasp the stem of a bush with one hand to support herself. Yet while the blood was gone from her face, there had formed in the hollows where her eyes had been two lakes of blue.

" See how he is sleeping! " she murmured.

And, true enough, the child was sound asleep, though to my eyes he looked much as any other baby might have done, save that the couch of autumn leaves on which he was ensconced consisted of leaves of a kind which could not have been discovered in the far-away forests of Orlov.

" Now, do you yourself lie down awhile," was my advice.

11

" Oh, no," she replied with a shake of her head on its sinuous neck; " for I must be collecting my things before I move on towards——"

" Towards Otchenchiri? "

" Yes. By now my folk will have gone many a verst in that direction."

" And can you walk so far? "

" The Holy Mother will help me."

Yes, she was to journey in the company of the Mother of God. So no more on the point required to be said.

Glancing again at the tiny, inchoate face under the bushes, her eyes diffused rays of warm and kindly light as, licking her lips, she, with a slow movement, smoothed the breast of the little one.

Then I arranged sticks for a fire, and also adjusted stones to support the kettle.

" Soon I will have tea ready for you," I remarked.

" And thankful indeed I shall be," she responded, " for my breasts are dried up."

" Why have your companions deserted you? " I said next.

" They have not deserted me. It was I that left them of my own accord. How could I have exposed myself in their presence? "

And with a glance at me she raised a hand to her face as, spitting a gout of blood, she smiled a sort of bashful smile.

" This is your first child, I take it? "

" It is. . . . And who are you? "

" A man."

" Yes, a man, of course: but are you a *married* man? "

" No, I have never been able to marry."

" That cannot be true."

" Why not? "

With lowered eyes she sat awhile in thought.

" Because, if so, how do you come to know so much about women's affairs? "

This time I *did* lie, for I replied:

" Because they have been my study. In fact, I am a medical student."

" Ah! Our priest's son also was a student, but a student for the Church."

" Very well. Then you know what I am. Now I will go and fetch some water."

Upon this she inclined her head towards her little son, and

12

listened for a moment to his breathing. Then she said with a glance towards the sea:

" I too should like to have a wash, but I do not know what the water is like. What is it? Brackish or salt? "

" No; quite good water—fit for you to wash in."

" Is it really? "

" Yes, really. Moreover, it is warmer than the water of the streams hereabouts, which is as cold as ice."

" Ah! Well, you know best."

Here a shaggy-eared pony, all skin and bone, was seen approaching us at a foot's pace. Trembling, and drooping its head, it scanned us, as it drew level, with a round black eye, and snorted. Upon that its rider pushed back a ragged fur cap, glanced warily in our direction, and again sank his head.

" The folk of these parts are ugly to look at," softly commented the woman from Orlov.

Then I departed in quest of water. After I had washed my face and hands I filled the kettle from a stream bright and lively as quicksilver (a stream presenting, as the autumn leaves tossed in the eddies which went leaping and singing over the stones, a truly enchanting spectacle), and, returning, and peeping through the bushes, perceived the woman to be crawling on hands and knees over the stones, and anxiously peering about, as though in search of something.

" What is it? " I inquired; and thereupon, turning grey in the face with confusion, she hastened to conceal some article under her person, although I had already guessed the nature of the article.

" Give it to me," was my only remark. " I will go and bury it."

" How so? For, as a matter of fact, it ought to be buried under the floor in front of some stove."

" Are we to build a stove *here*—build it in five minutes? " I retorted.

" Ah, I was jesting. But really I would rather not have it buried here, lest some wild beast should come and devour it. . . . Yet it ought to be committed only to the earth."

That said, she, with averted eyes, handed me a moist and heavy bundle: and as she did so she said under her breath, with an air of confusion:

" I beg of you for Christ's sake to bury it as well, as deeply, as you can. Out of pity for my son do as I bid you."

I did as she had requested; and just as the task had been

13

completed I perceived her returning from the margin of the
sea with unsteady gait, and an arm stretched out before
her, and a petticoat soaked to the middle with the sea water.
Yet all her face was alight with inward fire, and as I helped
her to regain the spot where I had prepared some sticks I could
not help reflecting with some astonishment:

" How strong indeed she is! "

Next, as we drank a mixture of tea and honey, she inquired:

" Have you now ceased to be a student? "

" Yes."

" And why so? Through too much drink? "

" Even so, good mother."

" Dear me! Well, your face is familiar to me. Yes, I remember that I noticed you in Sukhum when once you were
arguing with the *barraque* superintendent over the question of
rations. As I did so the thought occurred to me: ' Surely that
bold young fellow must have gone and spent his means on
drink? Yes, that is how it must be.' "

Then, as from her swollen lips she licked a drop of honey,
she again bent her blue eyes in the direction of the bush under
which the slumbering, newly-arrived Orlovian was couched.

" How will he live? " thoughtfully she said with a sigh—
then added to me:

" You have helped me, and I thank you. Yes, my thanks
are yours, though I cannot tell whether or not your assistance
will have helped *him*."

And, drinking the rest of her tea, she ate a morsel of bread,
then made the sign of the cross. And subsequently, as I was
putting up my things, she continued to rock herself to and
fro, to give little starts and cries, and to gaze thoughtfully at
the ground with eyes which had now regained their original
colour. At last she rose to her feet.

" You are not going yet? " I queried protestingly.

" Yes, I must."

" But——"

" The Blessed Virgin will go with me. So please hand me
over the child."

" No, *I* will carry him."

And, after a contest for the honour, she yielded, and we
walked away side by side.

" I only wish I were a little steadier on my feet," she
remarked with an apologetic smile as she laid a hand upon
my shoulder.

14

Meanwhile the new citizen of Russia, the little human being of an unknown future, was snoring soundly in my arms as the sea plashed and murmured, and threw off its white shavings, and the bushes whispered together, and the sun (now arrived at the meridian) shone brightly upon us all.

In calm content it was that we walked; save that now and then the mother would halt, draw a deep breath, raise her head, scan the sea and the forest and the hills, and peer into her son's face. And as she did so even the mist begotten of tears of suffering could not dim the wonderful brilliancy and clearness of her eyes. For with the sombre fire of inexhaustible love were those eyes aflame.

Once, as she halted, she exclaimed:

" O God, O Mother of God, how good it all is! Would that for ever I could walk thus, yes, walk and walk unto the very end of the world! All that I should need would be that thou, my son, my darling son, shouldst, borne upon thy mother's breast, grow and wax strong!"

And the sea murmured and murmured.

THE ICEBREAKER

On a frozen river near a certain Russian town a gang of seven carpenters were hastily repairing an icebreaker which the townsfolk had stripped for firewood.

That year spring happened to be late in arriving, and youthful March looked more like October, and only at noon, and that not on every day, did the pale, wintry sun show himself in the overcast heavens, or, glimmering in blue spaces between clouds, contemplate the earth with a squinting, malevolent eye.

The day in question was the Friday in Holy Week, and, as night drew on, drippings were becoming congealed into icicles half an *arshin* long, and in the snow-stripped ice of the river only the dun hue of the wintry clouds was reflected.

As the carpenters worked there kept mournfully, insistently echoing from the town the coppery note of bells: and at intervals heads would raise themselves, and blue eyes gleam thoughtfully through the same grey fog in which the town lay enveloped, and an axe uplifted would hover a moment in the air as though fearing with its descent to cleave the luscious flood of sound.

Scattered over the spacious river-track were dark pine branches, projecting obliquely from the ice, to mark paths, open spaces, and cracks on the surface; and where they reared themselves aloft these branches looked like the cramped, distorted arms of drowning men.

From the river came a whiff of gloom and depression. Covered over with sodden slush, it stretched with irksome rigidity towards the misty quarter whence blew a languid, sluggish, damp, cold wind.

Suddenly the foreman, one Ossip, a cleanly built, upright little peasant with a neatly curling, silvery beard, ruddy cheeks, and a flexible neck, a man everywhere and always in evidence, shouted:

" Look alive there, my hearties! "

Presently he turned his attention to myself, and smiled insinuatingly.

" Inspector," he said, " what are you trying to poke out of

the sky with that squat nose of yours? And why are you here at all? You come from the contractor, you say?—from Vasili Sergeitch? Well, well! Then your job is to hurry us up, to keep barking out, ' Mind what you are doing, such-and-such gang! ' Yet there you stand—blinking over your task like an object dried stiff! It's not to blink that you're here, but to play the watchdog upon us, and to keep an eye open, and your tongue on the wag. So issue your commands, young cockerel."

Then he shouted to the workmen:

" Now, then! No shirking! Is the job going to be finished to-night, or is it not? "

As a matter of fact, he himself was the worst shirker in the *artel*.[1] True, he was also a first-rate hand at his trade, and a man who could work quickly and well and with skill and concentration; but, unfortunately, he hated putting himself out, and preferred to spend his time in spinning arresting yarns. For instance, on the present occasion he chose the moment when work was proceeding with a swing, when everyone was busily and silently and wholeheartedly labouring with the object of running the job through to the end, to begin in his musical voice:

" Look here, lads. Once upon a time——"

And though for the first two or three minutes the men appeared not to hear him, and continued their planing and chopping as before, the moment came when the soft tenor accents caught and held the men's attention, as they trickled and burbled forth. Then, screwing up his bright eyes with a humorous air, and twisting his curly beard between his fingers, Ossip gave a complacent click of his tongue, and continued measuredly, and with deliberation:

" So he seized hold of the tench, and thrust it back into the cave. And as he turned to proceed through the forest he thought to himself: ' Now I must keep my eyes about me.' And suddenly, from somewhere (no one could have said where), a woman's voice shrieked: ' Elesi-a-ah! Elesi-a-ah! ' "

Here a tall, lanky Morduine named Leuka, with, as surname, Narodetz, a young fellow whose small eyes wore always an expression of astonishment, laid aside his axe, and stood gaping.

" And from the cave a deep bass voice replied: ' Elesi-a-ah! ' while at the same moment the tench sprang from the cave, and, champing its jaws, wriggled and wriggled back to the slough."

[1] Workmen's union.

20

Here an old soldier named Saniavin, a man morose, and a tippler, and a sufferer from asthma and an inexplicable grudge against life in general, croaked out:

" How could your tench have wriggled across dry land if it *was* a fish? "

" Can, for that matter, a fish speak? " was Ossip's good-humoured retort.

All of which inspired Mokei Budirin, a grey-headed *muzhik* of a cast of countenance canine in the prominence of his jaws and the recession of his forehead, and taciturn withal, though not otherwise remarkable, to give slow, nasal utterance to his favourite formula.

" That is true enough," he said.

For never could anything be spoken of that was grim or marvellous or lewd or malicious but Budirin at once re-echoed softly, but in a tone of unshakable conviction: " That is true enough."

Thereafter he would tap me on the breast with his hard and ponderous fist.

Presently work again underwent an interruption through the fact that Yakov Boev, a man who possessed both a stammer and a squint, became similarly filled with a desire to tell us something about a fish. Yet from the moment that he began his narrative everyone declined to believe it, and laughed at his broken verbiage as, frequently invoking the Deity, and cursing, and brandishing his awl, and viciously swallowing spittle, he shouted amid general ridicule:

" Once—once upon a time there lived a man. Yes, other folk before *you* have believed my tale. Indeed, it is no more than the truth that I'm going to tell you. Very well! Cackle away, and be damned! "

Here everyone without exception dropped his work to shout with merriment and clap his hands: with the result that, doffing his cap, and thereby disclosing a silvered, symmetrically shaped head with one bald spot amid its one dark portion, Ossip was forced to shout severely:

" Hi, you Budirin! You've had your say, and given us some fun, and there must be no more of it."

" But I had only just begun what I want to say," the old soldier grumbled, spitting upon the palms of his hands.

Next, Ossip turned to myself.

" Inspector," he began . . .

It is my opinion that, in thus hindering the men from work

21

through his tale-telling, Ossip had some definite end in view. I could not say precisely what that end was, but it must have been the object either of cloaking his own laziness or of giving the men a rest. On the other hand, whenever the contractor was present he, Ossip, bore himself with humble obsequiousness, and continued to assume a guise of simplicity which none the less did not prevent him, on the advent of each Saturday, from inducing his employer to bestow a *pourboire* upon the *artel*.

And though this same Ossip was an *artelui*, and a director of the *artel*, his senior co-members bore him no affection, but, rather, looked upon him as a wag or trifler, and treated him as of no importance. And, similarly, the younger members of the *artel* liked well enough to listen to his tales, but declined to take him seriously, and, in some cases, regarded him with ill-concealed, or openly expressed, distrust.

Once the Morduine, a man of education with whom, on occasions, I held discussions on intimate subjects, replied to a question of mine on the subject of Ossip:

" I scarcely know. Goodness alone knows! No, I do not know anything about him."

To which, after a pause, he added:

" Once a fellow named Mikhailo, a clever fellow who is now dead, insulted Ossip by saying to him: ' Do you call yourself a man? Why, regarded as a workman, you're as lifeless as a doornail, while, seeing that you weren't born to be a master, you'll all your life continue chattering in corners, like a plummet swinging at the end of a string! ' Yes, and that was true enough."

Lastly, after another pause the Morduine concluded:

" No matter. He is not such a bad sort."

My own position among these men was a position of some awkwardness, for, a young fellow of only fifteen, I had been appointed by the contractor, a distant relative of mine, to the task of superintending the expenditure of material. That is to say, I had to see to it that the carpenters did not make away with nails, or dispose of planks in return for drink. Yet all the time my presence was practically useless, seeing that the men stole nails as though I were not even in existence, and strove to show me that among them I was a person too many, a sheer incubus, and seized every opportunity of giving me covert jogs with a beam, and similarly affronting me.

This, of course, made my relations with them highly difficult, embarrassing, and irksome; and though moments occurred when I longed to say something that might ingratiate me, and endeavoured to effect an advance in that direction, the words always failed me at the necessary juncture, and I found myself lying crushed as before under a burdensome sense of the superfluity of my existence.

Again, if ever I tried to make an entry as to some material which had been used, Ossip would approach me, and, for instance, say:

" Is it jotted down, eh? Then let me look at it."

And, eyeing the notebook with a frown, he would add vaguely:

" What a nice hand you write!" (He himself could write only in printing fashion, in the large scriptory characters of the Ecclesiastical Rubric, not in those of the ordinary kind.) " For example, that scoop there—what does *it* say?"

" It is the word ' Good.' "

" ' Good '? But what a slip-knot of a thing! And what are those words *there*, on *that* line?"

" They say, ' Planks, 1 *vershok* by 9 *arshini, 5.*' "

" No, six was the number used."

" No, five."

" Five? Why, the soldier broke one, didn't he?"

" Yes, but never mind—at least it wasn't a plank that was wanted."

" Oh! Well, I may tell you that he took the two pieces to the tavern to get drink with."

Then, glancing into my face with his cornflower-blue eyes and quiet, quizzical smile, he would say without the least confusion as he twisted the ringlets of his beard:

" Put down ' 6.' And see here, young cockerel. The weather has turned wet and cold, and the work is hard, and sometimes folk need to have their spirits cheered and raised with a drop of liquor. So don't you be too hard upon us, for God won't think the more of you for being strict."

And as he thus talked to me in his slow and kindly, but semi-affected, fashion—bespattering me, as it were, with wordy sawdust—I would suddenly grow blind of an eye, and silently show him the corrected figure.

" That's it—that's right. And how fine the figure looks now, as it squats there like a merchant's buxom, comely dame!"

Then he would be seen triumphantly telling his mates of his success; then I would find myself feeling acutely conscious of the fact that everyone was despising me for my complacence, Yes, grown sick beyond endurance with a yearning for some-

23

thing which it could not descry, my fifteen-year-old heart would dissolve in a flood of mortified tears, and there would pass through my brain the despondent, aching thought:

" Oh, what a sad, uncomfortable world is this! How should Ossip have known so well that I should not re-correct the 6 into a 5, or that I should not tell the contractor that the men have bartered a plank for liquor? "

Again, there befell an occasion when the men stole two pounds' weight of five-*vershok* mandrels and bolts.

" Look here," I said to Ossip warningly. " I am going to report this."

" All right," he agreed with a twitch of his grey eyebrows. " Though what such a trifle can matter I fail to see. Yes, go and report every mother's son of them."

And to the men themselves he shouted:

" Hi, boobies! Each of you now stands docked for some mandrels and bolts."

" Why? " was the old soldier's grim inquiry.

" Because you *do* so stand," carelessly retorted the other.

With snarls, thereafter, the men eyed me covertly, until I began to feel that very likely I should not do as I had threatened, and even that so to do might not be expedient.

" But look here," said I to Ossip. " I am going to give the contractor notice, and let all of you go to the devil. For if I were to remain with you much longer I too should become a thief."

Ossip stroked his beard awhile, and pondered. Then he seated himself beside me, and said in an undertone:

" That is true."

" Well? "

" But things are always so. The truth is that it's time you departed. What sort of a watchman, of a checker, are you? In jobs of this kind what a man needs to know is the meaning of property. He needs to have in him the spirit of a dog, so that he shall look after his master's stuff as he would look after the skin which his mother has put on to his own body. But you, you young puppy, haven't the slightest notion of what property means. In fact, were anyone to go and tell Vasili Sergeitch about the way in which you keep letting us off, he'd give it you in the neck. Yes, you're no good to him at all, but just an expense: whereas when a man serves a master he ought, do you understand, to be *profitable* to that master."

He rolled and handed me a cigarette.

"Smoke this," said he, "and perhaps it'll make your brain work easier. If only you had been of a less awkward, uncomfortable nature, I should have said to you, 'Go and join the priests': but, as things are, you aren't the right sort for that—you're too stiff and unbending, and would never make headway even with an abbot. No, you're not the sort to play cards with. A monk is like a jackdaw—he chatters without knowing what he is chattering about, and pays no heed to the root of things, so busy is he with stuffing himself full with the grain. I say this to you with absolute earnestness, for I perceive you to be strange to our ways—a cuckoo that has blundered into the wrong nest."

And, doffing his cap, a gesture which he never failed to execute when he had something particularly important to say, he added humbly and sonorously as he glanced at the grey firmament:

"In the sight of the Lord our ways are the ways of thieves, and such as will never gain of Him salvation."

"And that is true enough," responded Mokei Budirin after the fashion of a clarionet.

From that time forth Ossip of the curly, silvered head, bright eyes, and shadowy soul became an object of agreeable interest for me. Indeed, there grew up between us a species of friendship, even though I could see that a civil bearing towards me in public was a thing that it hurt him to maintain. At all events, in the presence of others he avoided my glance, and his eyes, clear, unsullied, and light blue in tint, wavered unsteadily, and his lips twitched and assumed an artificially unpleasant expression, and he uttered some such speech as:

"Hi, you Makarei, see that you keep your eyes open, and earn your pay, or that pig of a soldier will be making away with more nails!"

But at other times, when we were alone together, he would speak to me kindly and instructively, while his eyes would dance and gleam with a faint, grave, knowing smile, and dart blue rays direct into mine, while for my part, as I listened to his words, I took every one of them to be absolutely true and balanced, despite their strange delivery.

"A man's duty consists in being good," I remarked on one occasion.

"Yes, of course," assented Ossip, though the next moment he veiled his eyes with a smile, and added in an undertone:

"But what do you understand by the term 'good'? In my

opinion, unless virtue be to their advantage, folk spit upon that 'goodness,' that 'honourableness,' of yours. Hence the better plan is to pay folk court, and be civil to them, and flatter and cajole every mother's son of them. Yes, do that, and your 'goodness' will have a chance of bringing you in some return. Not that I do not say that to be 'good,' to be able to look your own ugly jowl in the face in a mirror, is pleasant enough: but, as I see the matter, it is all one to other people whether you be a cardsharper or a priest so long as you're polite, and let down your neighbours lightly. That's what they want." . . .

For my part I never, at that period, grew weary of watching my fellows, for it was my constant idea that some day one of them would be able to raise me to a higher level, and to bring me to an understanding of this unintelligible and complicated existence of ours. Hence I kept asking myself the restless, the importunate question:

" What precisely is the human soul? "

Certain souls, I thought, existed which seemed like balls of copper, for, solid and immovable, they reflected things from their own point of view alone, in a dull and irregular and distorted fashion. And souls, I thought, existed which seemed as flat as mirrors, and, for all intents and purposes, had no existence at all.

And in every case the human soul seemed formless, like a cloud, and as murkily mutable as an imitation opal, a thing which altered according to the colour of what adjoined it.

Only as regarded the soul of the intelligent Ossip was I absolutely at a loss, absolutely unable to reach a conclusion.

Pondering these and similar matters in my mind, I, on the day of which I speak, stood gazing at the river, and at the town under the hill, as I listened to the bells. Rearing themselves aloft like the organ pipes in my favourite Polish-Roman Catholic church, the steeples of the town had their crosses dimly sparkling as though the latter had been stars imprisoned in a murky sky. Yet it was as though those stars hoped eventually to ascend into the purer firmament above the wind-torn clouds that they sparkled; and as I stood watching the clouds glide onward, and momentarily efface, with their shadows, the town's multifarious hues, I marked the fact that although, whenever dark-blue cavities in their substance permitted the beams of the sun to illuminate the buildings below, those buildings' roofs assumed tints of increased cheerfulness, the clouds seemed to glide the faster to veil the beams, while the humid shadows grew more opaque, and the scene darkened as though only for a moment had it assumed a semblance of joy.

The buildings of the town (looking like heaps of muddy snow), the black, naked earth around those buildings, the trees in the gardens, the hummocks of piled-up soil, the dull grey glimmer of the window-panes of the houses—all these things reminded me of winter, even though the misty breath of the northern spring was beginning to steal over the whole.

Presently a young fellow with flaxen hair, a pendent under-lip, and a tall, ungainly figure, by name Mishuk Diatlov, essayed to troll the stanza—

> That morn to him the maiden came,
> To find his soul had fled.

Whereupon the old soldier shouted:

" Hi, you! Have you forgotten the day? "

And even Boev saw fit to take umbrage at the singing, and, threatening Diatlov with his fist, to rap out:

" Ah, *sobatchnia dusha !* " [1]

" What a rude, rough, primitive lot we Russians are! " commented Ossip, seating himself atop of the icebreaker, and screwing up his eyes to measure its fall. " To speak plainly, we Russians are sheer barbarians. Once upon a time, I may tell you, an anchorite happened to be on his travels; and as the people came pressing around him, and kneeling to him, and tearfully beseeching him with the words, ' O holy father, inter-cede for us with the wolves which are devouring our substance! ' he replied: ' Ha! Are you, or are you not, Orthodox Christians? See that I assign you not to condign perdition! ' Yes, angry in very truth he was. Nay, he even spat in the people's faces. Yet in reality he was a kindly old man, for his eyes kept shedding tears equally with theirs."

Twenty *sazheni* below the icebreaker was a gang of barefooted sailors, engaged in hacking out the floes from under their barges; and as they shattered the brittle, greyish-blue crust on the river, the mattocks rang out, and the sharp blades of the ice-cutters gleamed as they thrust the broken fragments under the surface. Meanwhile there could be heard a bubbling of water, and the sound of rivulets trickling down to the sandy margin of the river. And similarly among our own gang was there audible a scraping of planes, and a screeching of saws, and a clattering of iron braces as they were driven into the

[1] " Soul of a dog."

smooth yellow wood, while through all the web of these sounds there ran the ceaseless song of the bells, a song so softened by distance as to thrill the soul, much as though dingy, burdensome labour were holding revel in honour of spring, and calling upon the latter to spread itself over the starved, naked surface of the gradually thawing ground.

At this point someone shouted hoarsely:

" Go and fetch the German. We have not got hands enough."

And from the bank someone bawled in reply:

" Where *is* he? "

" In the tavern. That is where you must go and look for him."

And as they made themselves heard, the voices floated up turgidly into the sodden air, spread themselves over the river's mournful void, and died away.

Meanwhile our men worked with industry and speed, but not without a fault or two, for their thoughts were fixed upon the town and its wash-houses and churches. And particularly restless was Sashok Diatlov, a man whose hair, as flaxen as that of his brother, seemed to have been boiled in lye. At intervals, glancing up-river, this well-built, sturdy young fellow would say softly to his brother:

" It's cracking now, eh? "

And, certainly, the ice had " moved " two nights ago, so that since yesterday morning the river watchmen had refused to permit horsed vehicles to cross, and only a few beadlike pedestrians now were making their way along the marked-out ice paths, while, as they proceeded, one could hear the water slapping against the planks as the latter bent under the travellers' weight.

" Yes, it *is* cracking," at length Mishuk replied with a hoist of his ginger eyebrows.

Ossip too scanned the river from under his hand. Then he said to Mishuk:

" Pah! It is the dry-squeak of the planes in your own hand that you keep hearing, so go on with your work, you son of a beldame. And as for you, Inspector, do you help me to speed up the men instead of burying your nose in your notebook."

By this time there remained only two more hours for work, and the arch of the icebreaker had been wholly sheathed in butter-tinted scantlings, and nothing required to be added to it save the great iron braces. Unfortunately, Boev and Saniavin, the men who had been engaged upon the task of cutting out the sockets for the braces, had worked so amiss, and run their lines

28

so straight, that, when it came to the point, the arms of the braces refused to sink properly into the wood.

"Oh, you cock-eyed fool of a Morduine!" shouted Ossip, smiting his fist against the side of his cap. "Do you call *that* sort of thing work?"

At this juncture there came from somewhere on the bank a seemingly exultant shout of:

"Ah! *Now* it's giving way!"

And almost at the same moment there stole over the river a sort of rustle, a sort of quiet crunching which made the projecting pine branches quiver as though they were trying to catch at something, while, shouldering their mattocks, the barefooted sailors noisily hastened aboard their barges with the aid of rope ladders.

And then curious indeed was it to see how many people suddenly came into view on the river—to see how they appeared to issue from below the very ice itself, and, hurrying to and fro like jackdaws startled by the shot of a gun, to dart hither and thither, and to seize up planks and boathooks, and to throw them down again, and once more to seize them up.

"Put the tools together," Ossip shouted. "And look alive there, and make for the bank."

"Aye, and a fine Easter Day it will be for us on *that* bank!" growled Sashok.

Meanwhile it was the river rather than the town that seemed to be motionless—the latter had begun, as it were, to quiver and reel, and, with the hill above it, to appear to be gliding slowly up stream, even as the grey, sandy bank some ten *sazheni* from us was beginning to grow tremulous, and to recede.

"Run, all of you!" shouted Ossip, giving me a violent push as he did so. Then to myself in particular he added: "Why stand gaping there?"

This caused a keen sense of danger to strike home to my heart, and to make my feet feel as though already the ice was escaping their tread. So, automatically picking themselves up, those feet started to bear my body in the direction of a spot on the sandy bank where the winter-stripped branches of a willow tree were writhing, and whither there were betaking themselves also Boev, the old soldier, Budirin, and the brothers Diatlov. Meanwhile the Morduine ran by my side, cursing vigorously as he did so, and Ossip followed us, walking backwards.

"No, no, Narodetz," he said.

"But, my good Ossip——"

29

" Never mind. What has to be, has to be."

" But, as likely as not, we may remain stuck here for **two days!** "

" Never mind even if we *do* remain stuck here."

" But what of the festival? "

" It will have, for this year at least, to be kept without you."

Seating himself on the sand, the old soldier lit his pipe, and growled:

" What cowards you all are! The bank was only fifteen *sazheni* from us, yet you ran as though possessed! "

" With you yourself as leader," put in Mokei.

The old soldier took no notice, but added:

" What were you all afraid of? Once upon a time Christ Himself, Our Little Father, died."

" And rose again," muttered the Morduine with a tinge of resentment. Which led Boev to exclaim:

" Puppy, hold your tongue! What right have *you* to air your opinions? "

" Besides, this is Good Friday, not Easter Day," the old soldier concluded with severe, didactical mien.

In a gap of blue between the clouds there was shining the March sun, and everywhere the ice was sparkling as though in derision of ourselves. Shading his eyes, Ossip gazed at the dissolving river, and said:

" Yes, it *is* rising—but that will not last for long."

" No, but long enough to make us miss the festival," grumbled Sashok.

Upon this the smooth, beardless face of the youthful Morduine, a face dark and angular like the skin of an unpeeled potato, assumed a resentful frown, and, blinking his eyes, he muttered:

" Yes, here we may have to sit—here where there's neither food nor money! Other folk will be enjoying themselves, but *we* shall have to remain hugging our hungry stomachs like a pack of dogs! "

Meanwhile Ossip's eyes had remained fixed upon the river, for evidently his thoughts were far away, and it was in absentminded fashion that he replied:

" Hunger cannot be considered where necessity impels. By the way, what use are our damned icebreakers? For the protection of barges and such? Why, the ice hasn't the sense to care. It just goes sliding over a barge, and farewell is the word to *that* bit of property! "

"Damn it, but none of us have a barge for property, have we?"

"You had better go and talk to a fool."

"The truth is that the icebreaker ought to have been taken in hand sooner."

Finally, the old soldier made a queer grimace, and ejaculated: "Blockhead!"

From a barge a knot of sailors shouted something, and at the same moment the river sent forth a sort of whiff of cruel chilliness and brooding calm. The disposition of the pine boughs now had changed. Nay, everything in sight was beginning to assume a different air, as though everything were charged with tense expectancy.

One of the younger men asked diffidently, beneath his breath: "Mate Ossip, what are we going to do?"

"What do you say?" Ossip queried absent-mindedly.

"I say, what are we going to do? Just to sit here?"

To this Boev responded, with loud, nasal derision in his tone:

"Yes, my lad, for the Lord has seen fit to prevent you from participating in His most holy festival."

And the old soldier, in support of his mate, extended his pipe towards the river, and muttered with a grin:

"You want to cross to the town, do you? Well, be off with you, and though the ice may give way beneath your feet and drown you, at least you'll be taken to the police-station, and so get to your festival. For that's what you want, I suppose?"

"True enough," Mokei re-echoed.

Then the sun went in, and the river grew darker, while the town stood out more clearly. Ceaselessly the younger men gazed towards the town with wistful, gloomy eyes, though silently they remained where they were.

Similarly I myself was beginning to find things irksome and uncomfortable, as always happens when a number of companions are thinking different thoughts, and contain in themselves none of that unity of will which alone can join men into a direct, uniform force. Rather, I felt as though I could gladly leave my companions and start out upon the ice alone.

Suddenly Ossip recovered his faculties. Rising, then doffing his cap and making the sign of the cross in the direction of the town, he said with a quiet, simple, yet somehow authoritative, air:

31

" Very well, my mates. Go in peace, and may the Lord
go with you! "

" But whither? " asked Sashok, leaping to his feet. " To
the town? "

" Whither else? "

The old soldier was the only one not to rise, as with conviction
he remarked:

" It will result but in our getting drowned."

" Then stay where you are."

Ossip glanced around the party. Then he continued:

" Bestir yourselves! Look alive! "

Upon which all crowded together, and Boev, thrusting the
tools into a hole in the bank, groaned:

" The order ' go ' has been given, so go we *must*, well though
a man in receipt of such an order might ask himself, ' How is
it going to be done? ' "

Ossip seemed, in some way, to have grown younger
and more active, while the habitually shy, though good-
humoured, expression of his countenance was gone from his
ruddy features, and his darkened eyes had assumed an air of
stern activity. Nay, even his indolent, rolling gait had disappeared, and in his step there was more firmness, more
assurance, than had ever before been the case.

" Let every man take a plank," he said, " and hold it in front
of him. Then, should anyone fall in (which God forbid!), the
plank-ends will catch upon the ice to either side of him, and
hold him up. Also, every man must avoid cracks in the ice.
Yes, and is there a rope handy? Here, Narodetz! Reach me
that spirit-level. Is everyone ready? I will walk first, and next
there must come—well, which is the heaviest?—you, soldier,
and then Mokei, and then the Morduine, and then Boev, and
then Mishuk, and then Sashok, and then Makarei, the lightest
of all. And do you all take off your caps before starting, and
say a prayer to the Mother of God. Ha! Here is Old Father
Sun coming out to greet us."

Readily did the men bare their tousled grey or flaxen heads
as momentarily the sun glanced through a bank of thin white
vapour before again concealing himself, as though averse to
arousing any false hopes.

" Now! " sharply commanded Ossip in his new-found voice.
" And may God go with us! Watch my feet, and don't crowd too
much upon one another, but keep, each, at a *sazhen's* distance
or more—in fact, the more the better. Yes, come, mates! "

With which, stuffing his cap into his bosom, and grasping the spirit-level in his hands, Ossip set foot upon the ice with a sliding, cautious, shuffling gait. At the same moment there came from the bank behind us a startled cry of:

" Where are you off to, you fools? "

" Never mind," said Ossip to ourselves. " Come along with you, and don't stand staring."

" You blockheads! " the voice repeated. " You had far better return."

" No, no! come on! " was Ossip's counter-command. " And as you move think of God, or you'll never find yourselves among the invited guests at His holy festival of Eastertide."

Next Ossip sounded a police whistle, which act led the old soldier to exclaim:

" Oh, that's the way, mate! Good! Yes, *you* know what to do. Now notice will have been given to the police on the further bank, and, if we're not drowned, we shall find ourselves clapped in gaol when we get there. However, *I*'m not responsible."

In spite of this remonstrance, Ossip's sturdy voice drew his companions after him as though they had been tied to a rope.

" Watch your feet carefully," once more he cried.

Our line of march was directed obliquely, and in the opposite direction to the current. Also, I, as the rearmost of the party, found it pleasant to note how the wary little Ossip of the silvery head went looping over the ice with the deftness of a hare, and practically no raising of the feet, while behind him there trailed, in wild-goose fashion, and as though tied to a single invisible string, six dark and undulating figures the shadows of which kept making themselves visible on the ice, from those figures' feet to points indefinitely remote. And as we proceeded all of us kept our heads lowered as though we had been descending from a mountain in momentary fear of a false step.

Also, though the shouting in our rear kept growing in volume, and we could tell that by this time a crowd had gathered, not a word could we distinguish, but only a sort of ugly din.

In time our cautious march became for me a mere, mechanical, wearisome task, for on ordinary occasions it was my custom to maintain a pace of greater rapidity. Thus eventually I sank into the semi-conscious condition amid which the soul turns to vacuity, and one no longer thinks of oneself, but, on the contrary, issues from one's personality, and begins to see objects with unwonted clarity, and to hear sounds with unwonted precision. Under my feet the seams in the blue-grey, leaden ice lay full of water, while as for the ice itself, it was blinding in its expansive glitter. even though in places it had come to be either cracked or bulbous, or had ground itself into powder with its own movement, or had become heaped into slushy hummocks of pumice-like sponginess and the consistency of broken glass. And everywhere around me I could discern the chilly, gaping smile of blue crevices which caught at my feet, and rendered the tread of my boot-soles unstable. And ever, as we marched, could the voices of Boev and the old soldier be heard speaking in antiphony, like two pipes being fluted by one and the same pair of lips.

" *I* won't be responsible," said the one voice.

" Nor I," responded the other.

" The only reason why I have come is that I was told to do so. That's all about it."

" Yes, and the same with me."

" One man gives an order, and another man, perhaps a man a thousand times more sensible than he, is forced to obey it."

" Is *any* man, in these days, sensible, seeing what a racket we have to live among? "

By this time Ossip had tucked the skirts of his greatcoat into his belt, while beneath those skirts his legs (clad in grey cloth gaiters of a military pattern) were shuffling along as lightly and easily as springs, and in a manner that suggested that there was turning and twisting in front of him some person whom, though desirous of barring to him the direct course, the shortest route, Ossip successfully opposed and evaded by dint of dodges and deviations to right and left, and occasional turns about, and the execution of dance steps and loops and semi-circles. Meanwhile in the tones of Ossip's voice there was a soft, musical ring that struck agreeably upon the ear, and harmonised to admiration with the song of the bells.

Just when we were approaching the middle of the river's breadth of four hundred *sazheni* there resounded over the surface of the ice a vicious rustle, while a piece of ice slid from under my feet. Stumbling, and powerless to retain my footing, I blundered down upon my knees in helpless astonishment: and then, as I glanced upstream, fear gripped at my throat, deprived me of speech, and darkened all my vision. For the whole substance of the grey ice-core had come to life and begun to heave itself upwards! Yes, the hitherto level surface was thrusting forth sharp angular ridges, and the air seemed full of a strange sound like the trampling of some heavy being over broken glass.

With a quiet trickle there came a swirl of water around me, while an adjacent pine bough cracked and squeaked as though it too had come to life. My companions shouted, and collected into a knot: whereupon, at once dominating and quelling the tense, painful hubbub of sounds, there rang forth the voice of Ossip.

" Mother of God! " he shouted. " Scatter, lads! Get away from one another, and keep each to himself! Now! Courage! "

With that, springing towards us as though wasps had been after him, and grasping the spirit-level as though it had been a weapon, he jabbed it to every side, as though fighting invisible foes, while, just as the quivering town began, seemingly, to glide past us, and the ice at my feet gave a screech and crumbled to fragments beneath me, so that water bubbled to my knees, I leapt up from where I was, and rushed blindly in Ossip's direction.

" Where are you coming to, fool? " was his shout as he brandished the spirit-level. " Stand still where you are! "

Indeed, Ossip seemed no longer to be Ossip at all, but a person curiously younger, a person in whom all that had been familiar in Ossip had become effaced. Yes, the once blue eyes had turned to grey, and the figure added half an *arshin* to its stature as, standing as erect as a newly made nail, and pressing both feet together, the foreman stretched himself to his full height, and shouted with his mouth open to its widest extent:

" Don't shuffle about, nor crowd upon one another, or I'll break your heads! "

Whereafter of myself in particular he inquired as he raised the spirit-level:

" What is the matter with *you*, pray? "

" I am feeling frightened," I muttered in response.

" Feeling frightened of *what*, indeed? "

" Of being drowned."

" Pooh! Just you hold your tongue."

Yet the next moment he glanced at me, and added in a gentler, quieter tone:

" None but a fool gets drowned. Pick yourself up and come along."

Then once more he shouted full-throated words of encouragement to his men; and as he did so his chest swelled, and his head rocked with the effort.

Yet, crackling and cracking, the ice was breaking up: and soon it began slowly to bear us past the town. 'Twas as though some unknown force ashore had awakened, and was striving to tear the banks of the river in two, so much did the portion of the landscape downstream seem to be standing still while the portion level with us seemed to be receding in the opposite direction, and thus causing a break to take place in the middle of the picture.

And soon this movement, a movement agonisingly slow, deprived me of my sense of being connected with the rest of the world, until, as the whole receded, despair again gripped my heart and unnerved my limbs. Roseate clouds were gliding across the sky and causing stray fragments of the ice, which, seemingly, yearned to engulf me, to assume reflected tints of a similar hue. Yes, it was as though the birth of spring had reawakened the universe, and was causing it to stretch itself, and to emit deep, hurried, broken pants that cracked its bones as the river, embedded in the earth's stout framework, revivified the whole with thick, turbulent, ebullient blood.

And this sense of littleness, of impotence, amid the calm, assured movement of the earth's vast bulk weighed upon my soul, and evoked, and momentarily fanned to flame, in me the shameless human question, " What if I should stretch forth my hand and lay it upon the hill and the banks of the river, and say, ' Halt until I come to you!'? "

Meanwhile the bells continued the mournful moaning of their resonant, coppery notes; and that moaning led me to reflect that within two days (on the night of the morrow) they would be pealing a joyous welcome to the Resurrection Feast.

" Oh that all of us may live to hear that sound! " was my unspoken thought.

Before my vision there kept quavering seven dark figures—figures shuffling over the ice, and brandishing planks like oars. And wriggling like a lamprey in front of them was a little old fellow, an old fellow resembling Saint Nicholas the Wonder-worker, an old fellow who kept crying softly, but authoritatively:

" Do not stare about you! "

And ever the river was growing rougher and ruder; ever its backbone was beginning to puiver and flounder like a whale underfoot, with its liquescent body of cold, grey, murky water bursting with increasing frequency from its shell of ice, and lapping hungrily at our feet.

Yes, we were human beings traversing, as it were, a slender pole over a bottomless abyss; and as we walked, the water's soft, *cantabile* plash set me in mind of the depths below, of the infinite time during which a body would continue sinking through dense, chilly bulk until sight faded and the heart stopped beating. Yes, before my mind's eye there arose men drowned, and devoured by crayfish, men with crumbling skulls and swollen features and glassy, bulging eyes and puffy hands and outstretched fingers and palms of which the skin had rotted off with the damp.

The first to fall in was Mokei Budirin. He had been walking next ahead of the Morduine, and, as a man habitually silent and absorbed, proceeding on his way more quietly than the rest. Suddenly something had seemed to catch at his legs, and he had disappeared until only his head and his hands, as the latter clutched at his plank, had been left above-level.

" Run and help him, somebody! " was Ossip's instant cry.
" Yes, but not all of you—just one or two. Help him, I say! "

The spluttering Mokei, however, said to the Morduine and myself:

" No; do you move away, mates, for I shall best help myself. Never you mind."

And, sure enough, he did succeed in drawing himself out on to the ice without assistance. Whereafter he remarked as he shook himself:

" A nice pickle, this, to be in! I might as well have been drowned! "

And, in fact, at the moment he looked, with his chattering teeth and great tongue licking a dripping moustache, precisely like a large, good-natured dog.

Then I remembered how, a month earlier, he had accidentally driven the blade of his axe through the joint of his left thumb, and, merely picking up the white fragment of flesh with the nail turning blue, and scanning it with his unfathomable eyes, had remarked, as though it was he himself that had been at fault:

" How often before I have injured that thumb I could not say. And when once I dislocated it I went on working with it longer than was right. . . . Now I will go and bury it."

With which, carefully wrapping up the fragment in some shavings, he had thrust the whole into his pocket, and bandaged the wounded hand.

Similarly, after that, did Boev, the man next in order behind Mokei, contrive to wrest himself from the grasp of the ice; though, on immersion, he started bawling, " Mates, I shall drown! I am dead already! Help me, help me!" and became so cramped with terror as to be extricated only with great difficulty, while amid the general confusion the Morduine too nearly slipped into the water.

" A narrow shave of saying Vespers to-night with the devils in Hell!" he remarked as he clambered back, and stood grinning with an even more angular and attenuated appearance than usual.

The next moment Boev achieved a second plunge, and screamed, as before, for help.

" Don't shout, you goat of a Yashka!" Ossip exclaimed as he threatened him with the spirit-level. " Why scare people? *I'll* give it you! Look here, lads. Let every man take off his belt and turn out his pockets. Then he'll walk lighter."

Toothed jaws gaped and crunched at us at every step, and vomited thick spittle; at every tenth step their keen blue fangs reached for our lives. Meanwhile the soaked condition of our boots and clothes had rendered us as slimy as though smeared with paste. Also, it so weighed us down as to hinder any active movement, and to cause each step to be taken cautiously, slowly, silently, and with ponderous diffidence.

Yet, soaked though we were, Ossip might verily have known the number of cracks in advance, so smooth and harelike was his progress from floe to floe as at intervals he faced about, watched us, and cried sonorously:

" That's the way to do it, eh?"

Yes, he absolutely played with the river, and though it kept catching at his diminutive form, he always evaded it, circum-vented its movements, and avoided its snares. Nay, capable even of directing its trend did he seem, and of thrusting under our feet only the largest and firmest floes.

" Lads, there is no need to be downhearted," he would cry at intervals.

" Ah, that brave Ossip!" the Morduine once ejaculated. " In very truth is he a man, and no mistake! Just look at him!"

The closer we approached the further shore, the thinner, and the more brittle, did the ice become, and the more liable we to break through it. By this time the town had nearly passed us, and we were bidding fair to be carried out into the Volga, where the ice would still be sound, and, as likely as not, draw us under itself.

" By your leave, we are going to be drowned," the Morduine murmured as he glanced at the blue shadow of eventide on our left.

And simultaneously, as though compassionating our lot, a large floe grounded upon the bank, glided upwards with a cracking and a crashing, and there held fast!

" Run, all of you! " came a furious shout from Ossip. " Hurry up, now! Put your very best legs foremost! "

For myself, as I sprang upon the floe I lost my footing, and, falling headlong, and remaining seated on the hither end of the floe amid a shower of spray, saw five of my seven comrades rush past as, pushing and jostling, they made for the shore. But presently the Morduine turned and halted beside me, with the intention of rendering Ossip assistance.

" Run, you young fools! " the latter exclaimed. " Come! Be off with you! "

Somehow in his face there was now a livid, uncertain air, while his eyes had lost their fire, and his mouth was curiously agape.

" No, mate. Do *you* get up," was my counter-adjuration.

" Unfortunately, I have hurt my leg," he replied with his head bent down. " In fact, I am not sure that I *can* get up."

However, we contrived to raise him and carry him ashore with an arm of his resting on each of our necks. Meanwhile he growled with chattering teeth:

" Aha, you river devils! Drown me if you can! But I've not given you a chance, the Lord be thanked! Hi, look out! The ice won't bear the three of us. Mind how you step, and choose places where the ice is bare of snow. There it's firmer. No, a better plan still would be to leave me where I am."

Next, with a frowning scrutiny of my face, he inquired:

" That notebook of our misdeeds—hasn't it had a wetting and got done for? "

That very moment, as we stepped from the stranded floe (in grounding, it had crushed and shattered a small boat), such part of it as lay in the water gave a loud crack, and, swaying to and fro, and emitting a gurgling sound, floated clear of the rest.

" Ah! " was the Morduine's quizzical comment. " *You* knew well enough what needed to be done."

Wet, and chilled to the bone, though relieved in spirit, we stepped ashore to find a crowd of townspeople in conversation

39

with Boev and the old soldier. And as we deposited our charge under the lea of a pile of logs he shouted cheerfully:

" Mates, Makarei's notebook is done for, soaked through! "

And since the notebook in question was weighing upon my breast like a brick, I pulled it out unseen, and hurled it far into the river with a plop like that of a frog.

As for the Diatlovs, they lost no time in setting out in search of *vodka* in the tavern on the hill, and slapped one another on the back as they ran, and could be heard shouting, " Hurrah, hurrah! "

Upon this a tall old man with the beard of an apostle and the eyes of a brigand muttered:

" Infidels, why disturb peaceful folk like this? You ought to be thrashed! "

Whereupon Boev, who was changing his clothes, retorted:

" What do you mean by ' disturb '? "

" Besides," put in the old soldier, " even though we are Christians like yourself, we might as well have been drowned for all that you did to help us."

" What could we have done? "

Meanwhile Ossip had remained lying on the ground with one leg stretched out at full length, and tremulous hands fumbling at his greatcoat as under his breath he muttered:

" Holy Mother, how wet I am! My clothes, though I have only worn them a year, are ruined for ever! "

Moreover, he seemed now to have shrunken again in stature —to have become crumpled up like a man run over. Indeed, as he lay he seemed actually to be melting, so continuously was his bulk decreasing in size.

But suddenly he raised himself to a sitting posture, groaned, and exclaimed in high-pitched, wrathful accents:

" May the devil take you all! Be off with you to your wash-houses and churches! Yes, be off, for it seems that, as God couldn't keep His holy festival without you, I've had to stand within an ace of death and to spoil my clothes—yes, all that you fellows should be got out of your fix! "

Nevertheless the men merely continued taking off their boots, and wringing out their clothes, and conversing, with sundry gasps and grunts, with the bystanders. So presently Ossip resumed:

" What are you thinking of, you fools? The washhouse is the best place for you, for if the police get you, they'll soon find you a lodging, and no mistake! "

One of the townspeople put in officiously:

" Aye, aye. The police have been sent for."

And this led Boev to exclaim to Ossip:

" Why pretend like that? "

" Pretend? I? "

" Yes—you."

" What do you mean? "

" I mean that it was you who egged us on to cross the river."

" You say that it was I? "

" I do."

" Indeed? "

" Aye," put in Budirin quietly, but incisively. And him the Morduine supported by saying in a sullen undertone:

" It *was* you, mate. By God it was. It would seem that you have forgotten."

" Yes, *you* started all this business," the old soldier corroborated, in dour, ponderous accents.

" Forgotten, indeed? *He ?* " was Boev's heated exclamation. " How can you say such a thing? Well, let him not try to shift the responsibility on to others—that's all! *We*'ll see, right enough, that he goes through with it! "

To this Ossip made no reply, but gazed frowningly at his dripping, half-clad men.

All at once, with a curious outburst of mingled smiles and tears (it would be hard to say which), he shrugged his shoulders, threw up his hands, and muttered:

" Yes, it *is* true. If it please you, it was I that contrived the idea."

" Of *course* it was! " the old soldier cried triumphantly.

Ossip turned his eyes again to where the river was seething like a bowl of porridge, and, letting his eyes fall with a frown, continued:

" In a moment of forgetfulness I did it. Yet how is it that we were not all drowned? Well, you wouldn't understand even if I were to tell you. No, by God, you wouldn't! . . . Don't be angry with me, mates. Pardon me for the festival's sake, for I am feeling uneasy of mind. Yes, I it was that egged you on to cross the river, the old fool that I was! "

" Aha! " exclaimed Boev. " But, had I been drowned, what should you have said *then*? "

In fact, by this time Ossip seemed conscious to the full of the futility and the senselessness of what he had done: and in his state of sliminess, as he sat nodding his head, picking

41

at the sand, looking at no one, and emitting a torrent of remorseful words, he reminded me strongly of a new-born calf.

And as I watched him I thought to myself:

" Where now is the leader of men who could draw his fellows in his train with so much care and skill and authority? "

And into my soul there trickled an uneasy sense of something lacking. Seating myself beside Ossip (for I desired still to retain a measure of my late impression of him), I said to him in an undertone:

" Soon you will be all right again."

With a sideways glance he muttered in reply, as he combed his beard:

" Well, you saw what happened just now. Always do things so happen."

While for the benefit of the men he added:

" That was a good jest of mine, eh? "

The summit of the hill which lay crouching, like a great beast, on the brink of the river was standing out clearly against the fast darkening sky, while a clump of trees thereon had grown black, and everywhere blue shadows of the spring even-tide were coming into view, and looming between the housetops where the houses lay pressed like scabs against the hill's opaque surface, and peering from the moist, red jaws of the ravine which, gaping towards the river, seemed as though it were stretching forth for a draught of water.

Also, by now the rustling and crunching of the ice on the similarly darkening river was beginning to assume a deeper note, and at times a floe would thrust one of its extremities into the bank as a pig thrusts its snout into the earth, and there remain motionless before once more beginning to sway, tearing itself free, and floating away down the river as another such floe glided into its place.

And ever more and more swiftly was the water rising, and washing away soil from the bank, and spreading a thick sediment over the dark-blue surface of the river. And as it did so there resounded in the air a strange noise as of chewing and champ-ing, a noise as though some huge wild animal were masticating, and licking itself with its great long tongue.

And still there continued to come from the town the melan-choly, distance-softened, sweet-toned song of the bells.

Presently the brothers Diatlov appeared descending from the hill with bottles in their hands, and sporting like a couple of joyous puppies, while to intercept them there could be seen advancing along the bank of the river a grey-coated police sergeant and two black-coated constables.

"O Lord!" groaned Ossip as he rubbed his knee.

As for the townsfolk, they had no love for the police, so hastened to withdraw to a little distance, where they silently awaited the officers' approach. Before long the sergeant, a little, withered sort of a fellow with diminutive features and a sandy, stubby moustache, called out in gruff, stern, hoarse, laboured accents:

"So here you are, you rascals!"

Ossip prised himself up from the ground with his elbow, and said hurriedly:

"It was I that contrived the idea of the thing, your Excellency; but pray let me off in honour of the festival."

"What do you say, you——?" the sergeant began, but his bluster was lost amid the swift flow of Ossip's further conciliatory words.

"We are folk of this town," Ossip continued, "who to-night found ourselves stranded on the further bank, with nothing to buy bread with, even though the day after to-morrow will be Christ's day, the day when Christians like ourselves wish to clean themselves up a little, and to go to church. So I said to my mates, 'Be off with you, my good fellows, and may God send that no mishap befall you!' And for this presumptuousness of mine I have been punished already, for, as you can see, I have as good as broken my leg."

"Yes," ejaculated the sergeant grimly. "But if you had been drowned, what then?"

Ossip sighed wearily.

"What then, do you say, your Excellency? Why, then, nothing, with your permission."

This led the officer to start railing at the culprit, while the crowd listened as silently and attentively as though he had been saying something worthy to be heard and heeded, rather than foully and cynically miscalling their mothers.

Lastly, our names having been noted, the police withdrew, while each of us drank a dram of *vodka* (and thereby gained a measure of warmth and comfort), and then began to make for our several homes. Ossip followed the police with derisive eyes: whereafter he leapt to his feet with a nimble, adroit movement, and crossed himself with punctilious piety.

"That's all about it, thank God!" he exclaimed.

"What?" sniggered Boev, now both disillusioned and

astonished. " Do you really mean to say that that leg of yours is better already? Or do you mean that it never was injured at all? "

" Ah! So you wish that it *had* been injured, eh? "

" The rascal of a Petrushka! " the other exclaimed.

" Now," commanded Ossip, " do all of you be off, mates." And with that he pulled his wet cap on to his head.

I accompanied him—walking a little behind the rest. As he limped along he said in an undertone—said kindly, and as though he were communicating a secret known only to himself:

" Whatsoever one may do, and whithersoever one may turn, one will find that life cannot be lived without a measure of fraud and deceit. For that is what life *is*, Makarei, the devil fly away with it! . . . I suppose you're making for the hill? Well, I'll keep you company."

Darkness had fallen, but at a certain spot some red and yellow lamps, lamps the beams of which seemed to be saying, " Come up hither! " were shining through the obscurity.

Meanwhile, as we proceeded in the direction of the bells that were ringing on the hill, rivulets of water flowed with a murmur under our feet, and Ossip's kindly voice kept mingling with their sound.

" See," he continued, " how easily I befooled that sergeant! That is how things have to be done, Makarei—one has to keep folk from knowing one's business, yet to make them think that *they* are the chief persons concerned, and the persons whose wit has put the cap on the whole."

Yet as I listened to his speech, while supporting his steps, I could make little of it.

Nor did I care to make very much of it, for I was of a simple and easy-going nature. And though at the moment I could not have told whether I really liked Ossip, I would still have followed his lead in any direction—yes, even across the river again, though the ice had been giving way beneath me.

And as we proceeded, and the bells echoed and re-echoed, I thought to myself with a spasm of joy:

" Ah, many times may I thus walk to greet the spring! "

While Ossip said with a sigh:

" The human soul is a winged thing. Even in sleep it flies."

*

A winged thing? Yes, and a thing of wonder.

GUBIN

THE place where I first saw him was a tavern wherein, ensconced in the chimney-corner, and facing a table, he was exclaiming stutteringly, " Oh, *I* know the truth about you all! Yes, *I* know the truth about you! " while standing in a semicircle in front of him, and unconsciously rendering him more and more excited with their sarcastic interpolations, were some tradesmen of the superior sort—five in number. One of them remarked indifferently:

" How should you *not* know the truth about us, seeing that you do nothing but slander us? "

Shabby, in fact in rags, Gubin at that moment reminded me of a homeless dog which, having strayed into a strange street, has found itself held up by a band of dogs of superior strength, and, seized with nervousness, is sitting back on its haunches and sweeping the dust with its tail, and, with growls, and occasional barings of its fangs, and sundry barkings, attempting now to intimidate its adversaries, and now to conciliate them. Meanwhile, having perceived the stranger's helplessness and insignificance, the native pack is beginning to moderate its attitude, in the conviction that, though continued maintenance of dignity is imperative, it is not worth while to pick a quarrel so long as an occasional yelp be vented in the stranger's face.

" To whom are you of any use? " one of the tradesmen at length inquired.

" Not a man of us but may be of use."

" To whom, then? " . . .

I had long since grown familiar with tavern disputes concerning verities, and not infrequently seen those disputes develop into open brawls; but never had I permitted myself to be drawn into their toils, or to be set wandering amid their tangles like a blind man negotiating a number of hillocks. Moreover, just before this encounter with Gubin I had arrived at a dim surmise that when such differences were carried to the point of madness and bloodshed they constituted, really,

47

an expression of the unmeaning, hopeless, melancholy life that is lived in the wilder and more remote districts of Russia— of the life that is lived on swampy banks of dingy rivers, and in our smaller and more God-forgotten towns. For it would seem that in such places men have nothing to look for, nor any knowledge of how to look for anything: wherefore they brawl and shout in vain attempts to dissipate despondency. . . .

I myself was sitting near Gubin, but on the other side of the table. Yet this was not because his outbursts and the tradesmen's retorts thereto were a pleasure to listen to, since to me both the one and the other seemed about as futile as beating the air.

" To whom are *you* of use? "

" To himself every man can be useful."

" But what good can one do oneself? " . . .

The windows of the tavern were open, while in the pendent, undulating cloud of blue smoke that the flames of the lamps emitted those lamps looked like so many yellow pitchers floating amid the waters of a stagnant pond. Out of doors there was brooding the quiet of an August night, and not a rustle, not a whisper was there to be heard. Hence as, numbed with melancholy, I gazed at the inky heavens and limpid stars I thought to myself:

" Surely, never were the sky and the stars meant to look down upon a life like this, a life like this? "

Suddenly someone said with the subdued assurance of a person reading aloud from a written document:

" Unless the peasants of Kubarovo keep a watch upon their timber lands, the sun will fire them to-morrow, and then the Birkins' forest also will catch alight."

For a moment the dispute died down. Then, as it were cleaving the silence, a voice said stutteringly:

" Who cares about the significance of the word ' truth '? "

And the words, heavy, jumbled, and clumsy, filled me with despondent reflections. Then again the voices rose—this time in louder and more venomous accents, and with their din recalled to me, by some accident, the foolish lines:

> The gods did give men water
> To wash in, and to drink;
> Yet man has made it but a pool
> In which his woes to sink.

Presently I moved outside and, seating myself on the steps of the veranda, fell to contemplating the dull, blurred windows of the Archpriest's house on the other side of the square, and to watching how black shadows kept flitting to and fro behind their panes as the faint, lugubrious notes of a guitar made themselves heard, and a high-pitched, irritable voice kept repeating at intervals, " Allow me. Pray permit me to speak," and being answered by a voice which intermittently shot into the silence, as into a bottomless sack, the words, " No, do you wait a moment, do you wait a moment."

Surrounded by the darkness, the houses looked stunted like gravestones, with a line of black trees above their roofs that loomed shadowy and cloud-like. Only in the furthest corner of the expanse was the light of a solitary street lamp bearing a resemblance to the disk of a stationary, resplendent dandelion.

Over everything was melancholy. Far from inviting was the general outlook. So much was this the case that, had, at that moment, anyone stolen upon me from behind the bushes and dealt me a sudden blow on the head, I should merely have sunk to earth without attempting to see who my assailant had been.

Often, in those days, was I in this mood, for it clave to me as faithfully as a dog—never did it wholly leave me.

" It was for men like *those* that this fair earth of ours was bestowed upon us! " I thought to myself.

Suddenly, with a clatter, someone ran out of the door of the tavern, slid down the steps, fell headlong at their foot, quickly regained his equilibrium, and disappeared in the darkness after exclaiming in a threatening voice:

" Oh, *I*'ll pay you out! *I*'ll skin you, you damned ——! "

Whereafter two figures that also appeared in the doorway said as they stood talking to one another:

" You heard him threaten to fire the place, did you not? "

" Yes, I did. But why should he want to fire it? "

" Because he is a dangerous rascal."

Presently, slinging my wallet upon my back, I pursued my on-ward way along a street that was fenced on either side with a tall palisade. As I proceeded long grasses kept catching at my feet and rustling drily. And so warm was the night as to render the payment of a lodging fee superfluous; and the more so since in the neighbourhood of the cemetery, where an advanced guard of young pines had pushed forward to the cemetery wall and littered the sandy ground with a carpet of red, dry cones, there were sleeping-places prepared in advance.

Suddenly from the darkness there emerged, to recoil again, a man's tall figure.

" Who is that? Who is it? " asked the hoarse, nervous voice of Gubin in dissipation of the deathlike stillness.

Which said, he and I fell into step with one another. As we proceeded he inquired whence I had come, and why I was still abroad. Whereafter he extended to me, as to an old acquaintance, the invitation:

" Will you come and sleep at my place? My house is near here, and as for work, I will find you a job to-morrow. In fact, as it happens, I am needing a man to help me clean out a well at the Birkins' place. Will the job suit you? Very well, then. Always I like to settle things overnight, as it is at night that I can best see through people."

The " house " turned out to be nothing more than an old one-eyed, hunchbacked washhouse or shanty which, bulging of wall, stood wedged against the clayey slope of a ravine as though it would fain bury itself amid the boughs of the neighbouring arbutus-trees and elders.

Without striking a light, Gubin flung himself upon some mouldy hay that littered a threshold as narrow as the threshold of a dog-kennel, and said to me with an air of authority as he did so:

" I will sleep with my head towards the door, for the atmosphere here is a trifle confined."

And, true enough, the place reeked of elderberries, soap, burnt stuff, and decayed leaves. I could not conceive why I had come to such a spot.

The twisted branches of the neighbouring trees hung motionless athwart the sky, and concealed from view the golden dust of the Milky Way, while across the Oka an owl kept screeching, and the strange, arresting remarks of my companion pelted me like showers of peas.

" Do not be surprised that I should live in a remote ravine," he said. " I, whose hand is against every man, can at least feel lord of what I survey here."

Too dark was it for me to see my host's face, but my memory recalled his bald cranium, and the yellow light of the lamps falling upon a nose as long as a woodpecker's beak, a pair of grey and stubbly cheeks, a pair of thin lips covered by a bristling moustache, a mouth sharp-cut as with a knife, and full of black, evil-looking stumps, a pair of pointed, sensitive, mouse-like ears, and a clean-shaven chin. The last feature in no way consorted with his visage, or with his whole appearance; but at least it rendered him worthy of remark, and enabled one to realise that one had to deal with neither a peasant nor a soldier nor a tradesman, but with a man peculiar to himself. Also, his frame was lanky, with long arms and legs, and pointed knees and elbows. In fact, so like a piece of string was his body that to twist it round and round, or even to tie it into a knot, would, seemingly, have been easy enough.

For awhile I found his speech difficult to follow; wherefore silently I gazed at the sky, where the stars appeared to be playing at follow-my-leader.

" Are you asleep? " at length he inquired.

" No, I am not. Why do you shave your beard? "

" Why do you ask? "

" Because, if you will pardon me, I think your face would look better bearded."

With a short laugh he exclaimed:

" Bearded? Ah, sloven! Bearded, indeed! "

To which he added more gravely:

" Both Peter the Great and Nicholas I. were wiser than you, for they ordained that whosoever should be bearded should have his nose slit, and be fined a hundred roubles. Did you ever hear of that? "

" No."

" And from the same source, from the beard, arose also the Great Schism."

His manner of speaking was too rapid to be articulate, and, in leaving his mouth, his words caused his lips to bare stumps and gums amid which they lost their way, became disintegrated, and issued, as it were, in an incomplete state.

" Everyone," he continued, " knows that life is lived more easily with a beard than without one, since with a beard lies are more easily told—they can be told, and then hidden in the masses of hair. Hence we ought to go through life with our faces naked, since such faces render untruthfulness more difficult, and prevent their owners from prevaricating without the fact becoming plain to all."

" But what about women? "

" What about women? Well, women can always lie to their husbands successfully, but not to all the town, to all the world, to folk in general. Moreover, since a woman's real business in life is the same as that of the hen, to rear young, what can it matter if she *does* cackle a few falsehoods, provided that she be neither a priest nor a mayor nor a *tchinovnik*, and does not possess any authority, and cannot establish laws? For the really important point is that the law itself should not lie, but ever uphold truth pure and simple. Long has the prevalent illegality disgusted me."

The door of the shanty was standing open, and amid the outer darkness, as in a church, the trees looked like pillars, and the white stems of the birches like silver candelabra tipped with a thousand lights, or dimly-seen choristers with faces showing pale above sacramental vestments of black. All my soul was full of a sort of painful restlessness. It was a feeling as though I should live to rise and go forth into the darkness, and offer battle to the terrors of the night; yet ever, as my companion's torrential speech caught and held my attention, it detained me where I was.

" My father was a man of no little originality and character," he went on. " Wherefore none of the townsfolk liked him. By the age of twenty he had risen to be an alderman, yet never to the end could get the better of folk's stubbornness and stupidity, even though he made it his custom to treat all and sundry to food and drink, and to reason with them. No, not even at the last did he attain his due. People feared him because he revolutionised everything, revolutionised it down to the very roots: the truth being that he had grasped the one essential fact that law and order must be driven, like nails, into the people's very vitals."

Mice squeaked under the floor, and on the further side of the Oka an owl screeched, while amid the pitch-black heavens I could see a number of blotches intermittently lightening to an elusive red and blurring the faint glitter of the stars.

" It was one o'clock in the morning when my father died," Gubin continued. " And upon myself, who was seventeen and had just finished my course at the municipal school of Riazan, there devolved, naturally enough, all the enmity that my father had incurred during his lifetime. ' He is just like his sire,' folk said. Also, I was alone, absolutely alone, in the world, since my mother had lost her reason two years before my father's death, and passed away in a frenzy. However, I had an uncle, a retired *unter-officier* who was both a sluggard, a tippler, and a hero (a hero because he had had his eyes shot out at Plevna, and his left arm injured in a manner which had induced paralysis, and his breast adorned with the military cross and a set of medals). And sometimes this uncle of mine would rally me on my learning. For instance, ' Scholar,' he would say, ' what does " tiversia " mean? ' ' No such word exists,' would be my reply, and thereupon he would seize me by the hair, for he was rather an awkward person to deal with. Another factor as concerned making me ashamed of my scholarship was the ignorance of the townspeople in general, and in the end I became the common butt, a sort of ' holy idiot.' "

So greatly did these recollections move Gubin that he rose and transferred his position to the door of the hut, where, a dark blur against the square of blue, he lit a gurgling pipe, and puffed thereat until his long, conical nose glowed. Presently the surging stream of words began again.

" At twenty I married an orphan, and when she fell ill and died childless I found myself alone once more, and without an adviser or a friend. However, still I continued both to live and to look about me. And in time I perceived that life is not lived wholly as it should be."

" What in life is ' not lived wholly as it should be '? "

" Everything in life. For life is mere folly, mere fatuous nonsense. The truth is that our dogs do not bark always at the right moment. For instance, when I said to folk, ' How would it be if we were to open a technical school for girls? ' they merely laughed and replied, ' Trade workers are hopeless drunkards. Already have we enough of them. Besides, hitherto women have contrived to get on *without* education.' And when next I conceived a scheme for instituting a match factory, it befell that the factory was burnt down during its first year of existence, and I found myself once more at a loose end. Next a certain woman got hold of me, and I flitted about her like a martin around a belfry, and so lost my head as to live life as though I were not on earth at all—for three years I did not know even what I was doing, and only when I recovered my senses did I perceive myself to be a pauper, and my all, every single thing that I had possessed, to have passed into *her* white hands. Yes, at twenty-eight I found myself a beggar. Yet I have never wholly regretted the fact, for certainly for a time I lived life as few men ever live it. ' Take my all—take it! ' I used to say to her. And, truly enough, I should never have done much good with my father's fortune, whereas she —well, so it befell. Somehow I think that in those days my opinions must have been different from now—now that I have lost everything. . . . Yet the woman used to say, ' You have *not* lost everything,' and she had wit enough to fit out a whole townful of people."

" This woman—who was she? "

" The wife of a merchant. Whenever she unrobed and said, ' Come! What is this body of mine worth? ' I used to make reply, ' A price that is beyond compute.' . . . So within three years everything that I possessed vanished like smoke. Sometimes, of course, folk laughed at and jibed at me: nor did I ever refute them. But now that I have come to have a better understanding of life's affairs I see that life is not wholly lived as it should be. For that matter, too, I do not hold my tongue on the subject, for that is not my way—still left to me I have a tongue and my soul. The same reason accounts for the fact that no one likes me, but that by everyone I am looked upon as a fool."

" How, in your opinion, ought life to be lived? "

Without answering me at once, Gubin sucked at his pipe until his nose made a glowing red blur in the darkness. Then he muttered slowly:

" How life ought to be lived no one could say exactly. And this though I have given much thought to the subject, and still am doing so."

I found it no difficult matter to form a mental picture of the desolate existence which this man must be leading—this man whom all his fellows both derided and shunned. For at that time I too was bidding fair to fail in life, and had my heart in the grip of ceaseless despondency.

The truth is that of futile people Russia is over-full. Many such I myself have known: and always they have attracted me as strongly and mysteriously as a magnet—always they have struck me more favourably than the provincial-minded majority who live for food and work alone, and put away from them all that could conceivably render their breadwinning difficult, or prevent them from snatching bread out of the hands of their weaker neighbours. For most such folk are gloomy and self-contained, with hearts that have turned to wood, and an outlook that ever reverts to the past: unless, indeed, they be folk of spurious good-nature, an addition to talkativeness, and an apparent *bonhomie* which veils a frigid, grey interior, and conveys an impression of cruelty and greed of all that life contains.

Always, in the end, I have detected in such folk something wintry, something that makes them seem, as it were, to be spending spring and summer in expectation solely of the winter season, with its long nights, and its cold of an austerity which forces one for ever to be consuming food.

Yet seldom among this distasteful and wearisome crowd of wintry folk is there to be encountered a man who has altogether proved a failure. But if he has done so, he will be found to be a man whose nature is of a more thoughtful, a more truly existent, a more clear-sighted cast than that of his fellows— a man who at least can look beyond the boundaries of the trite and commonplace, and whose mentality has a greater capacity for attaining spiritual fulfilment, and is more desirous of doing so, than the mentality of his compeers. That is to say, in such a man óne can always detect a striving for space, as a man who, loving light, carries light in himself.

Unfortunately, all too often is that light only the fugitive phosphorescence of putrefaction: wherefore as one contemplates him one soon begins to realise with bitterness and vexation and disappointment that he is but a sluggard, but a braggart, but one who is petty and weak and blinded with conceit and distorted with envy, but one between whose word and whose deed there gapes a disparity even wider and deeper than the disparity which divides the word from the deed of the man of winter, of the man who, though he be as tardy as a snail, at least is making some way in the world, in contradistinction from the failure who revolves ever in a single spot, like some barren old maid before the reflection in her looking-glass.

Hence, as I listened to Gubin, there recurred to me more than one instance of his type.

"Yes, I have succeeded in observing life throughout," he muttered drowsily as his head sank slowly upon his breast.

And sleep overtook myself with similar suddenness. Apparently that slumber was of a few minutes' duration only, yet what aroused me was Gubin pulling at my leg.

"Get up now," he said. "It is time that we were off."

And as his bluish-grey eyes peered into my face, somehow I derived from their mournful expression a sense of intellectuality. Beneath the hair on his hollow cheeks were reddish veins, while similar veins, bluish in tint, covered with a network his temples, and his bare arms had the appearance of being made of tanned leather.

Dawn had not yet broken when we rose and proceeded through the slumbering streets beneath a sky that was of a dull yellow, and amid an atmosphere that was full of the smell of burning.

"Five days now has the forest been on fire," observed Gubin. "Yet the fools cannot succeed in putting it out."

Presently the establishment of the merchants Birkin lay

before us, an establishment of curious aspect, since it constituted, rather, a conglomeration of appendages to a main
building of ground floor and attics, with four windows facing
on to the street, and a series of underpropping annexes. That
series extended to the wing, and was solid and permanent,
and bade fair to overflow into the courtyard, and through the
entrance-gates, and across the street, and to the very kitchen-
garden and flower-garden themselves. Also, it seemed to have
been stolen piecemeal from somewhere, and at different periods,
and from different localities, and tacked at haphazard on to
the walls of the parent erection. Moreover, all the windows
of the latter were small, and in their green panes, as they
confronted the world, there was a timid and suspicious air,
while, in particular, the three windows which faced upon the
courtyard had iron bars to them. Lastly, there were posted,
sentinel-like, on the entrance-steps two water-butts, as a pre-
caution against fire.

"What think you of the place?" Gubin muttered as he
peered into the well. "Isn't it a barbarous hole? The right
thing would be to pull it down wholesale, and then rebuild it
on larger and less restricted lines. Yet these fools merely go
tacking new additions on to the old."

For awhile his lips moved as in an incantation. Then he
frowned, glanced shrewdly at the structures in question, and
continued softly:

"I may say in passing that the place is *mine*."

"*Yours ?*"

"Yes, mine. At all events, so it used to be."

And he pulled a grimace as though he had got the toothache
before adding with an air of command:

"Come! *I* will pump out the water, and *you* shall carry it
to the entrance-steps and fill the water-butts. Here is a pail,
and here a ladder."

Whereafter, with a considerable display of strength, he set
about his portion of the task, whilst I myself took pail in hand
and advanced towards the steps, to find that the water-butts
were so rotten that, instead of retaining the water, they let
it leak out into the courtyard. Gubin said with an oath:

"Fine masters these—masters who grudge one a groat, and
squander a rouble! What if a fire *were* to break out? Oh, the
blockheads!"

Presently the proprietors in person issued into the courtyard
—the stout, bald Peter Birkin, a man whose face was flushed

even to the whites of his shifty eyes, and, close behind him, like his shadow, Jonah Birkin, a person of sandy, sullen mien, and overhanging brows, and dull, heavy eyes.

"Good day, dear sir," said Peter Birkin thinly, as with a puffy hand he raised from his head a cloth cap, while Jonah nodded, and then, with a sidelong glance at myself, asked in a deep bass voice:

"Who is this young man?"

Large and important like peacocks, the pair then shuffled across the wet yard, and, in so doing, went to much trouble to avoid soiling their polished shoes. Next Peter said to his brother:

"Have you noticed that the water-butts are rotted? Oh, that fine Yakinika! He ought long ago to have been dismissed."

"Who is that young man over there?" Jonah repeated with an air of asperity.

"The son of his father and mother," Gubin replied quietly, and without so much as a glance at the brothers.

"Well, come along," snuffled Peter with a drawling of his vowels. "It is high time that we were moving. It doesn't matter *who* the young man may be."

And with that they slip-slopped across to the entrance-gates, while Gubin gazed after them with knitted brows, and as the brothers were disappearing through the wicket said carelessly:

"The old sheep! They live solely by the wits of their step-mother, and if it were not for her, they would long ago have come to grief. Yes, she is a woman beyond words clever. Once upon a time there were three brothers—Peter, Alexis, and Jonah; but unfortunately Alexis got killed in a brawl. A fine, tall fellow *he* was, whereas these two are a pair of gluttons, like everyone else in this town. Not for nothing do three loaves figure on the municipal arms! Now, to work again! Or shall we take a rest?"

Here there stepped on to the veranda a tall, well-grown young woman in an open pink bodice and a blue skirt who, shading blue eyes with her hand, scanned the courtyard and the steps, and said with some diffidence:

"Good day, Yakov Vasilitch."

With a good-humoured glance in response, and his mouth open, Gubin waved a hand in greeting.

"Good day to *you*, Nadezhda Ivanovna," he replied. "How are you this morning?"

Somehow this made her blush, and cross her arms upon her

ample bosom, while her kindly, rounded, eminently Russian face evinced the ghost of a shy smile. At the same time, it was a face wherein not a single feature was of a kind to remain fixed in the memory, a face as vacant as though nature had forgotten to stamp thereon a single wish. Hence even when the woman smiled there seemed to remain a doubt whether the smile had really materialised.

" How is Natalia Vasilievna? " continued Gubin.

" Much as usual," the woman answered softly.

Whereafter hesitantly, and with downcast eyes, she essayed to cross the courtyard. As she passed me I caught a whiff of raspberries and currants.

Disappearing into the grey mist through a small door with iron staples, she soon reissued thence with a hencoop, and, seating herself on the steps of the doorway, and setting the coop on her knees, took between her two large palms some fluttering, chirping, downy, golden chicks, and raised them to her ruddy lips and cheeks with a murmur of:

" O my little darlings! O my little darlings! "

And in her voice, somehow, there was a note as of intoxication, of abandonment. Meanwhile dull, reddish sunbeams were beginning to peer through the fence, and to warm the long, pointed staples with which it was fastened together, while in a stream of water that was dripping from the eaves, and trickling over the floor of the court, and around the woman's feet, a single beam was bathing and quivering as though it would fain effect an advance to the woman's lap and the hencoop, and, with the soft, downy chicks, enjoy the caresses of the woman's bare white arms.

" Ah, little things! " again she murmured. " Ah, little children of mine! "

Upon that Gubin suddenly desisted from his task of hauling up the bucket, and, as he steadied the rope with his arms raised above his head, said quickly:

" Nadezhda Ivanovna, you ought indeed to have had some children—six at the least! "

Yet no reply came, nor did the woman even look at him.

The rays of the sun were now spreading, smokelike and greyish-yellow, over the silver river. Above the river's calm bed a muslin texture of mist was coiling. Against the nebulous heavens the blue of the forest was rearing itself amid the fragrant, pungent fumes from the burning timber.

Yet still asleep amid its sheltering half-circle of forest was the quiet little town of Miamlin, while behind it, and encompassing it as with a pair of dark wings, the forest in question looked as though it were ruffling its feathers in preparation for further flight beyond the point where, the peaceful Oka reached, the trees stood darkening, overshadowing the water's clear depths, and looking at themselves therein.

Yet, though the hour was so early, everything seemed to have about it an air of sadness, a mien as though the day lacked promise, as though its face were veiled and mournful, as though, not yet come to birth, it nevertheless were feeling weary in advance.

Seating myself by Gubin on some trampled straw in the hut ordinarily used by the watchman of the Birkins' extensive orchard, I found that, owing to the orchard being set on a hillside, I could see over the tops of the apple and pear and fig trees, where their tops hung bespangled with dew as with quicksilver, and view the whole town and its multi-coloured churches, yellow, newly-painted prison, and yellow-painted bank.

And while in the town's lurid, four-square buildings I could trace a certain resemblance to the aces of clubs stamped upon convicts' backs, in the grey strips of the streets I could trace a certain resemblance to a number of rents in an old, ragged, faded, dusty coat. Indeed, that morning all comparisons seemed to take on a tinge of melancholy: the reason being that throughout the previous evening there had been moaning in my soul a mournful dirge on the future life.

With nothing, however, were the churches of the town of which I am speaking exactly comparable, for many of them had attained a degree of beauty the contemplation of which caused the town to assume, throughout, a different, a more pleasing and seductive, aspect. Thought I to myself: " Would that men had fashioned all other buildings in the town as the churches have been fashioned!"

One of the latter, an old, squat edifice the blank windows of which were deeply sunken in the stuccoed walls, was known as the " Prince's Church," for the reason that it enshrined the remains of a local Prince and his wife, persons of whom it stood recorded that " they did pass all their lives in kindly, unchanging love." . . .

The following night Gubin and I chanced to see Peter Birkin's tall, pale, timid young wife traverse the garden on her way to a tryst in the washhouse with her lover, the precentor of the Prince's Church. And as, clad in a simple gown, and barefooted, and having her ample shoulders swathed in an old-gold jacket or shawl of some sort, she crossed the orchard by a path running between two lines of apple-trees, she walked with the unhasting gait of a cat which is crossing a yard after a shower of rain, and from time to time, whenever a puddle is encountered, lifts and shakes fastidiously one of its soft paws. Probably, in the woman's case, this came of the fact that things kept pricking and tickling her soles as she proceeded. Also, her knees, I could see, were trembling, and her step had in it a certain hesitancy, a certain lack of assurance.

Meanwhile, bending over the garden from the warm night sky, the moon's kindly visage, though on the wane, was shining brightly; and when the woman emerged from the shadow of the trees I could discern the dark patches of her eyes, her rounded, half-parted lips, and the thick plait of hair which lay across her bosom. Also, in the moonlight her bodice had assumed a bluish tinge, so that she looked almost phantasmal; and when soundlessly, moving as though on air, she stepped back into the shadow of the trees, that shadow seemed to lighten.

All this happened at midnight, or thereabouts, but neither of us was yet asleep, owing to the fact that Gubin had been telling me some interesting stories concerning the town and its families and inhabitants. As soon, however, as he descried the woman looming like a ghost he leapt to his feet in comical terror—then subsided on to the straw again, contracted his body as though he were in convulsions, and hurriedly made the sign of the cross.

" O Jesus our Lord! " he gasped. " Tell me what that is, tell me what that is! "

" Keep quiet, you," I urged.

Instead, lurching in my direction, he nudged me with his arm. " Is it Nadezhda, think you? " he whispered.

" It is."

" Phew! The scene seems like a dream. Just in the same way, and in the very same place, did her mother-in-law, Petrushka's stepmother, use to come and walk. Yes, it was *just* like this."

Then, rolling over, face downwards, he broke into subdued, malicious chuckles: whereafter, seizing my hand and sawing it up and down, he whispered amid his exultant pants:

" I expect Petrushka is asleep, for probably he has taken

too much liquor at the Bassanov's *smotrini*.[1] Aye, he will be asleep. And as for Jonah, *he* will have gone to Vaska Klochi. So to-night, until morning, Nadezhda will be able to kick up her heels to her heart's content."

I too had begun to surmise that the woman was come thither for purposes of her own. Yet the scene was almost dreamlike in its beauty. It thrilled me to the soul to watch how the woman's blue eyes gazed about her—gazed as though she were ardently, caressingly whispering to all living creatures, asleep or awake:

" O my darlings! O my darlings! "

Beside me the uncouth, broken-down Gubin went on in hoarse accents:

" You must know that she is Petrushka's *third* wife, a woman whom he took to himself from the family of a merchant of Murom. Yet the town has it that not only Petrushka, but also Jonah, makes use of her—that she acts as wife to both brothers, and therefore lacks children. Also has it been said of her that one Trinity Sunday she was seen by a party of women to mis-conduct herself in this garden with a police sergeant, and then to sit on his lap and weep. Yet this last I do not wholly believe, for the sergeant in question is a veteran scarcely able to put one foot before the other. Also, Jonah, though a brute, lives in abject fear of his stepmother."

Here a worm-eaten apple fell to the ground, and the woman paused: whereafter, with head a little raised, she resumed her way with greater speed.

As for Gubin, he continued, unchecked, though with a trifle less animosity—rather as though he were reading aloud a manuscript which he found wearisome:

" See how a man like Peter Birkin may pride himself upon his wealth, and receive honour during his lifetime, yet all the while have the devil grinning over his shoulder! "

Then he, Gubin, kept silence awhile, and merely breathed heavily, and twisted his body about. But suddenly he resumed in a strange whisper:

" Fifteen years ago—no, surely it was longer ago than that? —Madame Nadkin, Nadezhda's mother-in-law, made it her practice to come to this spot to meet her lover. And a fine gallant *he* was! "

Somehow, as I watched the woman creeping along, and

[1] A festival at which a fiancé pays his first visit to the house of the parents of his betrothed.

looking as though she were intending to commit a theft, or as though she fancied that at any moment she might see the plump brothers Birkin issue from the courtyard into the garden and come shuffling ponderously over the darkened ground, with ropes and cudgels grasped in coarse, red hands which knew no pity; somehow, as I watched her, I felt saddened, and paid little heed to Gubin's whispered remarks, so intently were my eyes fixed upon the granary wall as, after gliding along it awhile, the woman bent her head and disappeared through the dark blue of the washhouse door. As for Gubin, he went to sleep with a last drowsy remark of:

" Life is all falsity. Husbands, wives, fathers, children—all of them practise deceit."

In the east portions of the sky were turning to light purple, and other portions to a darker hue, while from time to time I could see, looming black against those portions, coils of smoke the density of which kept being stabbed with fiery spikes of flame, so that the vague, towering forest looked like a hill on the top of which a fiery dragon was crawling about, and writhing, and intermittently raising tremulous, scarlet wings, and as often relapsing into, becoming submerged in, the bank of vapour. And, in contemplating the spectacle, I seemed actually to be able to hear the cruel, hissing din of combat between red and black, and to see pale, frightened rabbits scudding from underneath the roots of trees amid showers of sparks, and panting, half-suffocated birds fluttering wildly amid the branches as further and further afield, and more and more triumphantly, the scarlet dragon unfurled its wings, and consumed the darkness, and devoured the rain-soaked timber.

Presently from the dark, blurred doorway in the wall of the washhouse there emerged a dark figure which went flitting away among the trees, while after it someone called in a sharp, incisive whisper:

" Do not forget. You *must* come."

" Oh, I shall be only too glad! "

" Very well. In the morning the lame woman shall call upon you. Do you hear? "

And as the woman disappeared from view the other person sauntered across the garden, and scaled the fence with a clatter.

That night I could not sleep, but, until dawn, lay watching the burning forest as gradually the weary moon declined, and the lamp of Venus, cold and green as an emerald, came into view over the crosses on the Prince's Church. Indeed was the

latter a fitting place for Venus to illumine if really it had been
the case that the Prince and Princess had " passed their lives
in kindly, unchanging love " !

Gradually the dew cleared the trees of the night darkness,
and caused the damp, grey foliage to smile once more with
aniseed and red raspberry, and to sparkle with the gold of
their mildew. Also, there came hovering about us goldfinches
with their little red-hooded crests, and fussy tomtits in their
cravats of yellow, while a nimble, dark-blue woodpecker scaled
the stem of an apple-tree, and everywhere yellow leaves fluttered
to earth, and, in doing so, so closely resembled birds as to make
it not always easy to distinguish whether a leaf or a tomtit
had glimmered for a moment in the air.

Gubin awoke, sighed, and with his gnarled knuckles gave
his puffy eyes a rub. Then he raised himself upon all-fours,
and, crawling, much dishevelled with sleep, out of the watchman's hut, snuffed the air (a process in which his movements
approximated comically to those of a keen-nosed watch-dog).
Finally he rose to his feet, and, in the act, shook one of the
trees so violently as to cause a bough to shed its burden of ripe
fruit, and disperse the apples hither and thither over the dry
surface of the ground, or cause them to bury themselves among
the long grass. Three of the juiciest apples he duly recovered,
and, after examination of their exterior, probed with his teeth,
while kicking away from him as many of the remainder as he
could descry.

" Why spoil those apples? " I queried.

" Oh, so you are *not* asleep? " he countered with a nod of
his melon-shaped cranium. " As a matter of fact, a few apples
won't be missed, for there are too many of them about. My own
father it was that planted the trees which have grown them."

Then, turning upon me a keen, good-humoured eye, and
chuckling, he added:

" What about that Nadezhda? Ah, she is a clever woman
indeed! Yet *I* have a surprise in store for her and her lover."

" Why should you have? "

" Because I desire to benefit mankind at large " (this was
said didactically, and with a frown). " For, no matter where
I detect evil or underhandedness, it is my duty, I feel it to be
my duty, to expose that evil, and to lay it bare. There exist
people who need to be taught a lesson, and to whom I long to
cry, ' Sinners that you are, do you lead more righteous lives! ' "

From behind some clouds the sun was rising with a disk **as** murky and mournful as the face of an ailing child. It was as though he were feeling conscious that he had done amiss in so long delaying to shed light upon the world, in so long dallying on his bed of soft clouds amid the smoke of the forest fire. But gradually the cheering beams suffused the garden throughout, and evoked from the ripening fruit an intoxicating wave of scent in which there could be distinguished also the bracing breath of autumn.

Simultaneously there rose into the sky, in the wake of the sun, a dense stratum of cloud which, blue and snow-white in colour, lay with its soft hummocks reflected in the calm Oka, and so wrought therein a secondary firmament as profound and impalpable as its original.

" Now then, Makar ! " was Gubin's command, and once more I posted myself at the bottom of the well. About three *sazheni* in depth, and lined with cold, damp mud to above the level of my middle, the orifice was charged with a stifling odour both of rotten wood and of something more intolerable still. Also, whenever I had filled the pail with mud, and then emptied it into the bucket and shouted " Right away ! " the bucket would start swinging against my person and bumping it, as un-willingly it went aloft, and thereafter discharge upon my head and shoulders clots of filth and drippings of water—meanwhile screening, with its circular bottom, the glowing sun and now scarce visible stars. In passing, the spectacle of those stars' waning both pained and cheered me, for it meant that for a companion in the firmament they now had the sun. Hence it was until my neck felt almost fractured, and my spine and the nape of my neck were aching as though clamped in a cast of plaster of paris, that I kept my eyes turned aloft. Yes, any-thing to gain a sight of the stars ! From them I could not remove my vision, for they seemed to exhibit the heavens in a new guise, and to convey to me the joyful tidings that in the sky there was present also the sun.

Yet though, meanwhile, I tried to ponder on something great, I never failed to find myself cherishing the absurd, obstinate apprehension that soon the Birkins would leave their beds, enter the courtyard, and have Nadezhda betrayed to them by Gubin.

And throughout there kept descending to me from above the latter's inarticulate, as it were damp-sodden, observations.

" Another rat ! " I heard him exclaim. " To think that those two fellows, men of money, should neglect for two whole years to clean out their well! Why, what can the brutes have been drinking meanwhile? Look out below, you!"

And once more, with a creaking of the pulley, the bucket would descend—bumping and thudding against the lining of the well as it did so, and bespattering afresh my head and shoulders with its filth. Rightly speaking, the Birkins ought to have cleared out the well themselves!

At length, " Let us exchange places," I cried.

" What is wrong? " inquired Gubin in response.

" Down here it is cold—I can't stand it any longer."

" Gee up!" exclaimed Gubin to the old horse which supplied the leverage power for the bucket: whereupon I seated myself upon the edge of the receptacle and went aloft, where everything was looking so bright and warm as to bear a new and unwontedly pleasing appearance.

So now it was Gubin's turn to stand at the bottom of the well. And soon, in addition to the odour of decay, and a subdued sound of splashing, and the rumblings and bumpings of the iron bucket against its chain, there began to come up from the damp, black cavity a perfect stream of curses.

" The infernal skinflints!" I heard my companion exclaim. " Hullo, here is something! A dog or a baby, eh? The damned old barbarians!"

And the bucket ascended with, among its contents, a sodden and most ancient hat. With the passage of time Gubin's temper grew worse and worse.

" If I *should* find a baby here," next he exclaimed, " I shall report the matter to the police, and get those blessed old brothers into trouble."

Each movement of the leathern-hided, wall-eyed steed which did our bidding was accompanied by a swishing of a sandy tail which had for its object the brushing away of autumn's harbingers, the bluebottles. Almost with the tranquil gait of a religious did the animal accomplish its periodical journeys from the wall to the entrance-gates, and back again; after which it always heaved a profound sigh, and stood with its bony crest lowered.

Presently from a corner of the yard that lay screened behind some rank, pale, withered, trampled herbage a door screeched, and into the yard there issued Nadezhda Birkin, carrying a bunch of keys, and followed by a lady who, elderly and rotund of figure, had a few dark hairs growing on her full and rather haughty upper lip. As the two walked towards the cellar

(Nadezhda being clad only in an under-petticoat, with a chemise half-covering her shoulders, and slippers thrust on to bare feet), I perceived from the languor of the younger woman's gait that she was feeling weary indeed.

"Why do you look at us like that?" her senior inquired of me as she drew level. And as she did so the eyes that peered at me from above the full and, somehow, displaced-looking cheeks hid in them a dim, misty, half-blind expression.

"That must be Peter Birkin's mother-in-law," was my unspoken reflection.

At the door of the cellar Nadezhda handed the keys to her companion, and with a slow step which set her ample bosom swaying, and increased the disarray of the bodice on her round, but broad, shoulders, approached myself, and said quietly:

"Please open the gutter-sluice and let out the water into the street, or the yard will soon be flooded. Oh, the smell of it! What is that thing there? A rat? O *batinshka*, what a horrible mess!"

Her face had about it a drawn look, and under her eyes there were a pair of dark patches, and in their depths the dry glitter of a person who has spent a night of waking. True, it was a face still fresh of hue; yet beads of sweat were standing on the forehead, and her shoulders looked grey and heavy—as grey and heavy as unleavened bread which the fire has coated with a thin crust, yet failed to bake throughout.

"Please, also, open the wicket," she continued. "And, in case a lame old beggar-woman should call, come and tell me. I am the Nadezhda Ivanovna for whom she will inquire. Do you understand?"

From the well, at this point, there issued the words:

"Who is that speaking?"

"It is the mistress," I replied.

"What? Nadezhda? With her I have a bone to pick."

"What did he say?" the woman asked tensely as she raised her dark, thinly pencilled brows, and made as though to go and lean over the well. Independently of my own volition I forestalled what Gubin might next have been going to say by remarking:

"I must tell you that last night he saw you walking in the garden here."

"Indeed?" she ejaculated, and drew herself to her full height. Yet in doing so she blushed to her shoulders, and, clapping plump hands to her bosom, and opening dark eyes to their fullest, said in a hasty and confused whisper as, again paling, and shrinking in stature, she subsided like a piece of pastry that is turning heavy:

" Good Lord! *What* did he see? . . . If the lame woman should call, you must not admit her. No, tell her that she will not be wanted, that I cannot, that I must not—— But see here. Here is a rouble for you. Oh, good Lord!"

By this time even louder and more angry exclamations had begun to ascend from Gubin. Yet the only sound to reach my ears was the woman's muttered whispering, and as I glanced into her face I perceived that its hitherto high-coloured and rounded contours had fallen in, and turned grey, and that her flushed lips were trembling to such an extent as almost to prevent the articulation of her words. Lastly, her eyes were frozen into an expression of pitiful, doglike terror.

Suddenly she shrugged her shoulders, straightened her form, put away from her the expression of terror, and said quietly, but incisively:

" You will not need to say anything about this. Allow me."

And with a swaying step she departed—a step so short as almost to convey the impression that her legs were bound together. Yet while the gait was the gait of a person full of suppressed fury, it was also the gait of a person who can scarcely see an inch in advance.

" Haul away, you! " shouted Gubin.

I hauled him up in a state of cold and wet: whereafter he fell to stamping around the coping of the well, cursing, and waving his arms.

" What have you been thinking of all this time? " he vociferated. " Why, for ever so long I shouted and shouted to you! "

" I have been telling Nadezhda that last night you saw her walking in the garden."

He sprang towards me with a vicious scowl.

" Who gave you leave to do so? " he exclaimed.

" Wait a moment. I said that it was only *in a dream* that you saw her crossing the garden to the washhouse."

" Indeed? And why did you do that? "

Somehow, as, barelegged, and dripping with mud, he stood blinking his eyes at me with a most disagreeable expression, he looked extremely comical.

" See here," I remarked. " You have only to go and tell her husband about her for *me* to go and tell him the same story about your having seen the whole thing in a dream."

" Why? " cried Gubin, now almost beside himself. Presently, however, he recovered sufficient self-possession to grin and ask in an undertone:

" *How much did she give you ?* "

I explained to him that my sole reason for what I had done had been that I pitied the woman, and feared lest the brothers Birkin should do an injury to one who at least ought not to be betrayed. Gubin began by declining to believe me, but eventually, after the matter had been thought out, said:

" Acceptance of money for doing what is right is certainly irregular; but at least is it better than acceptance of money for conniving at sin. Well, you have spoilt my scheme, young fellow. Hired only to clean out the well, I would nevertheless have cleaned out the establishment as a whole, and taken pleasure in doing so."

Then once more he relapsed into fury, and muttered as he scurried round and round the well:

" How *dared* you poke your nose into other people's affairs? Who are *you* in this establishment? "

The air was hot and arid, yet still the sky was as dull as though coated throughout with the dust of summer, and, as yet, one could gaze at the sun's purple, rayless orb without blinking, and as easily as one could have gazed at the glowing embers of a wood fire.

Seated on the fence, a number of rooks were directing intelligent black eyes upon the heaps of mud which lay around the coping of the well. And from time to time they fluttered their wings impatiently, and cawed.

" I got you some work," Gubin continued in a grumbling tone, " and put heart into you with the prospect of employment. And now you have gone and treated me like——"

At this point I caught the sound of a horse trotting towards the entrance-gates, and heard someone shout, as the animal drew level with the house:

" *Your* timber too has caught alight! "

Instantly, frightened by the shout, the rooks took to their wings and flew away. Also, a window-sash squeaked, and the courtyard resounded with sudden bustle—the culinary regions vomiting the elderly lady and the tousled, half-clad Jonah, and an open window the upper half of the red-headed Peter.

" Men, harness up as quickly as possible! " the latter cried, his voice charged with a plaintive note.

And, indeed, he had hardly spoken before Gubin led out a

fat roan pony, and Jonah pulled from a shelter a light buggy or *britchka*. Meanwhile Nadezhda called from the veranda to Jonah:

" Do you first go in and dress yourself! "

The elderly lady then unfastened the gates; whereupon a stunted, oldish *muzhik* in a red shirt limped into the yard with a foam-flecked steed, and exclaimed:

" It is caught in two places—at the Savelkin clearing and near the cemetery! "

Immediately the company pressed around him with groans and ejaculations, and Gubin alone continued to harness the pony with swift and dexterous hands—saying to me through his teeth as he did so, and without looking at anyone:

" That is how those wretched folk *always* defer things until too late."

The next person to present herself at the entrance-gates was a beggar-woman. Screwing up her eyes in a furtive manner, she droned:

" For the sake of Lord Je-e-esus! "

" God will give you alms! God will give you alms! " was Nadezhda's reply as, turning pale, she flung out her arms in the old woman's direction. " You see, a terrible thing has happened —our timber lands have caught fire. You must come again later."

Upon that Peter's bulky form (which had entirely filled the window from which it had been leaning) disappeared with a jerk, and in its stead there came into view the figure of a woman. Said she contemptuously:

" See the visitation with which God has tried us, you men of faint hearts and indolent hands! "

The woman's hair was grey at the temples, and had resting upon it a silken cap which so kept changing colour in the sunlight as to convey to one the impression that her head was bonneted with steel, while in her face, picturesque but dark (seemingly blackened with smoke), there gleamed two pupil-less blue eyes of a kind which I had never before beheld.

" Fools," she continued, " how often have I not pointed out to you the necessity of cutting a wider space between the timber and the cemetery? "

From a furrow above the woman's small, but prominent, nose a pair of heavy brows extended to temples that were silvered over. As she spoke there fell a strange silence amid which, save for the pony's pawing of the mire, no sound mingled with the sarcastic reproaches of the deep, almost masculine voice.

" That again is the mother-in-law," was my inward reflection.

Gubin finished the harnessing—then said to Jonah in the tone of a superior addressing a servant:

" Go in and dress yourself, you object! "

Nevertheless the Birkins drove out of the yard precisely as they were, while the peasant mounted his belathered steed and followed them at a trot, and the elderly lady disappeared from the window, leaving its panes even darker and blacker than they had previously been. Gubin, slip-slopping through the puddles with bare feet, said to me with a sharp glance as he moved to shut the entrance-gates:

" I presume that I can now take in hand the little affair of which you know."

" Yakov! " at this juncture someone shouted from the house.

Gubin straightened himself *à la militaire*.

" Yes, I am coming," he replied.

Whereafter, padding on bare soles, he ascended the steps. Nadezhda, standing at their top, turned away with a frown of repulsion at his approach, and nodded and beckoned to myself.

" What has Yakov said to you? " she inquired.

" He has been reproaching me."

" Reproaching you for what? "

" For having spoken to you."

She heaved a sigh.

"Ah, the mischief-maker! " she exclaimed. " And what is it that he wants? "

As she pouted her displeasure her round and vacant face looked almost childlike.

" Good Lord! " she added. " What *do* such men as he want? "

Meanwhile the heavens were becoming overspread with dark grey cloud, and presaging a flood of autumn rain, while from the window near the steps the voice of Peter's mother-in-law was issuing in a steady stream. At first, however, nothing was distinguishable save a sound like the humming of a spindle.

" It is my mother that is speaking," Nadezhda explained softly. " She'll give it him! Yes, *she* will protect me! "

Yet I scarcely heard Nadezhda's words, so greatly was I feeling struck with the quiet forcefulness, the absolute assurance, of what was being said within the window.

" Enough, enough! " said the voice. " Only through lack of occupation have you joined the company of the righteous."

Upon this I made a move to approach closer to the window; whereupon Nadezhda whispered:

" Whither are you going? You must not listen."

While she was yet speaking I heard come from the window:

" Similarly your revolt against mankind has come of idleness, of lack of an interest in life. To you the world has been wearisome, so, while devising this revolt as a resource, you have excused it on the ground of service of God and love of equity, while in reality constituting yourself the devil's workman."

Here Nadezhda plucked at my sleeve, and tried to pull me away, but I remarked:

" I *must* learn what Gubin has got to say in answer."

This made Nadezhda smile, and then whisper with a confiding glance at my face:

" You see, I have made a full confession to her. I went and said to her: ' Mamenka, I have had a misfortune.' And her only reply as she stroked my hair was, ' Ah, little fool! ' Thus you see that she pities me. And what makes her care the less that I should stray in that direction is that she yearns for me to bear her a child, a grandchild, as an heir to her property."

Next Gubin was heard saying within the room:

" Whensoever an offence is done against the law I——"

At once a stream of impressive words from the other drowned his utterance.

" An offence is not always an offence of moment, since sometimes a person outgrows the law, and finds it too restrictive. No one person ought to be rated against another. For whom alone ought we to fear? Only the God in whose sight *all* of us have erred."

And though in the elderly lady's voice there were weariness and distaste, the words were spoken slowly and incisively. Upon this Gubin tried to murmur something or another, but again his utterance failed to edge its way into his interlocutor's measured periods.

" No great achievement is it," she said, " to condemn a fellow creature. For always it is easy to sit in judgment upon our fellows. And even if a fellow creature be allowed to pursue an evil course unchecked, his offence may yet prove productive of good. Remember how in every case the Saints reached God. Yet how truly sanctified, by the time that they did so reach Him, were they! Let this ever be borne in mind, for we are over-apt to condemn and punish."

" In former days, Natalia Vasilievna, you took away from

me my substance, you took my all. Also, let me recount to you how we fell into disagreement."

" No; there is no need for that."

" Thereafter I ceased to be able to bear the contemplation of myself: I ceased to consider myself as of any value."

" Let the past remain the past. That which must be is not to be avoided."

" Through you, I say, I lost my peace of mind."

Nadezhda nudged me, and whispered with gay malice:

" That is probably true, for they say that once he was one of her lovers."

Then she recollected herself, and, clapping her hands to her face, cried through her fingers:

" O good Lord! What have I said? No, no, you must not believe these tales. They are only slanders, for she is the best of women."

" When evil has been done," continued the quiet voice within the window, " it can never be set right by recounting it to others. He upon whom a burden has been laid should try to bear it. And, should he fail to bear it, the fact will mean that the burden has been beyond his strength."

" It was through you that I lost everything. It was you that stripped me bare."

" But to that which you lost I added movement. Nothing in life is ever lost; it merely passes from one hand to another —from the unskilled hand to the experienced, so that even the bone picked of a dog may ultimately become of value."

" Yes, a bone—that is what *I* am."

" Why should you say that? You are still a man."

" Yes, a man, but a man useful for what? "

" Useful, even though the use may not yet be fully apparent."

To this, after a pause, the speaker added:

" Now, depart in peace, and make no further attempt against this woman. Nay, do not even speak ill of her if you can help it, but consider everything that you saw to have been seen in a dream."

" Ah! " was Gubin's contrite cry. " It shall be as you say. Yet, though I should hate, I could not bear, to grieve you, I must confess that the height whereon you stand is——"

" Is what, O friend of mine? "

" Nothing; save that of all souls in this world you are, without exception, the best."

" Yakov Petrovitch, in this world you and I might have

72

ended our lives together in honourable partnership. And even now, if God be willing, we might do so."

" No. Rather must farewell be said."

All became quiet within the window, except that after a prolonged silence there came from the woman a deep sigh, and then a whisper of, " O Lord! "

Treading softly, like a cat, Nadezhda darted away towards the steps; whereas I, less fortunate, was caught by the departing Gubin in the very act of leaving the neighbourhood of the window. Upon that he inflated his cheeks, ruffled up his sandy hair, turned red in the face like a man who has been through a fight, and cried in strange, querulous, high-pitched accents:

" Hi! What were you doing just now? Long-legged devil that you are, I have no further use for you—I do not intend to work with you any more. So you can go."

At the same moment the dim face, with its great blue eyes, showed itself at the window, and the stern voice inquired:

" What does the noise mean? "

" What does it mean? It means that I do not intend——"

" You must not, if you wish to create a disturbance, do it anywhere but in the street. It must not be created here."

" What is all this? " Nadezhda put in with a stamp of her foot. " What——"

At this point the cook rushed out with a toasting-fork, and militantly ranged herself by Nadezhda's side, exclaiming:

" See what comes of not having a single *muzhik* in the house! "

I now prepared to withdraw, but, in doing so, glanced once more at the features of the elderly lady, and saw that the blue pupils were dilated so as almost to fill the eyes in their entirety, and to leave only a bluish margin. And strange and painful were those eyes—eyes fixed blindly, eyes which seemed to have strayed from their orbits through yielding to emotion and a consequent overstrain, while the apple of the throat had swelled like the crop of a bird, and the sheen of the silken headdress become as the sheen of metal. Involuntarily I thought to myself:

" It is a head that must be made of iron."

By this time Gubin had penitently subsided, and was ex changing harmless remarks with the cook, while carefully avoiding my glance.

" Good day to you, madame," at length I said as I passed the window.

Not at once did she reply, but when she did so she said kindly:

" And good day to *you*, my friend. Yes, I wish you good day."

To which she added an inclination of the head which resembled nothing so much as a hammer which much percussion upon an anvil has wrought to a fine polish.

NILUSHKA

THE timber-built town of Buev, a town which has several times been burnt to the ground, lies huddled upon a hillock above the river Obericha. Its houses, with their many-coloured shutters, stand so crowded together as to form around the churches and gloomy law courts a perfect maze—the streets which intersect the dark masses of houses meandering aimlessly hither and thither, and throwing off alley-ways as narrow as sleeves, and feeling their way along plot-fences and warehouse walls, until, viewed from the hillock above, the town looks as though someone has stirred it up with a stick and dispersed and confused everything that it contains. Only from the point where Great Zhitnaia Street takes its rise from the river do the stone mansions of the local merchants (for the most part German colonists) cut a grim, direct line through the packed clusters of buildings constructed of wood, and skirt the green islands of gardens, and thrust aside the churches: whereafter, continuing its way through Council Square (still running inexorably straight), the thoroughfare stretches to, and traverses, a barren plain of scrub, and so reaches the pine plantation belonging to the Monastery of St. Michael the Archangel where the latter is lurking behind a screen of old red spruces of which the denseness seems to prop the very heavens, and which on clear, sunny days can be seen rising to mark the spot whence the monastery's crosses, like the gilded birds of the forest of eternal silence, scintillate a constant welcome.

At a distance of some ten houses before Zhitnaia Street debouches upon the plain which I have mentioned there begin to diverge from the street, and to trend towards a ravine, and eventually to lose themselves in the latter's recesses, the small, squat shanties with one or two windows apiece which constitute the suburb of Tolmachikha. This suburb, it may be said, had as its original founders the menials of a landowner named Tolmachev—a landowner who, after emancipating his serfs some thirteen years before all serfs were legally emancipated,[1]

[1] In the year 1861.

was, for his action, visited with such bitter revilement that, in dire offence at the same, he ended by becoming an inmate of the monastery, and there spending ten years under the vow of silence, until death overtook him amid a peaceful obscurity born of the fact that the authorities had forbidden his exhibition to pilgrims or strangers.

It is in the very cots originally apportioned to Tolmachev's menials, at the time, fifty years ago, when those menials were converted into citizens, that the present inhabitants of the suburb dwell. And never have they been burnt out of those homes, although the same period has seen all Buev save Zhitnaia Street consumed, and everywhere that one may delve within the township one will be sure to come across undestroyed hearthstones.

The suburb, as I have said, stands at the hither end and on the sloping side of one of the arms of a deep, wooded ravine, with its windows facing towards the ravine's yawning mouth, and affording a view direct to the Mokrīe (certain marshes beyond the Obericha) and the swampy forest of firs into which the dim red sun declines. Further on, the ravine trends across the plain—then bends round towards the western side of the town, and eats away the clayey soil with an appetite which each spring increases, and which, carrying the soil down to the river, is gradually clogging the river's flow, and diverting the muddy water towards the marshes, and converting those marshes into a lagoon outright. The fissure in question is named " The Great Ravine," and has its steep flanks so overgrown with chestnuts and laburnums that even in summer-time its recesses are cool and moist, and so serve as a convenient trysting-place for the poorer lovers of the suburb and the town, and witness their tea-drinkings and frequently fatal quarrels, as well as being used by the more well-to-do for a dumping ground for rubbish of the nature of deceased dogs, cats, and horses.

Pleasantly singing, there scours the bottom of the ravine the brook known as the Zhandarmski Spring, a brook celebrated throughout Buev for its crystal-cold water, which is so icy of temperature that even on a burning day it will make the teeth ache. This water the denizens of Tolmachikha account to be their peculiar property: wherefore they are proud of it, and drink it to the exclusion of any other, and so live to a green old age which in some cases cannot even reckon its years. And by way of a livelihood the men of the suburb indulge in hunting, fishing, fowling, and thieving (not a single artisan proper does the suburb contain, save the cobbler Gorkov—a thin, consumptive skeleton of surname Tchulan); while, as regards the women, they, in winter, sew, and make sacks for Zimmel's mill, and pull tow, and in summer they scour the plantation of the monastery for truffles and other produce, and the forest on the other side of the river for huckleberries. Also, two of the suburb's women practise as fortune tellers, while two others conduct an easy and highly lucrative trade in prostitution.

The result is that the town, as distinguished from the suburb, believes the men of the latter to be one and all thieves, and the women and girls of the suburb to be one and all disreputable characters. Hence the town strives always to restrict and extirpate the suburb, while the suburbans retaliate upon the townsfolk with robbery and arson and murder, while despising those townsfolk for their parsimony, decorum, and avarice, and detesting the settled, comfortable mode of life which they lead.

So poor, for that matter, is the suburb that never do even beggars resort thither, save when drunk. No, the only creatures which resort thither are dogs which subsist no one knows how as predatorily they roam from court to court with tails tucked between their flanks, and bloodless tongues hanging down, and legs ever prepared, on sighting a human being, to bolt into the ravine, or to let down their owners upon subservient bellies in expectation of a probable kick or curse.

In short, every cranny of every cot in the place, with the grimy panes of their windows, and their lathed roofs overgrown with velvety moss, breathes forth the universal, deadly hopelessness induced by Russia's crushing poverty.

In the Tolmachikhans' backyards grow only alders, elders, and weeds. Everywhere docks thrust up heads through cracks in the fences to catch at the legs or the skirts of passers-by, while masses of nettles squeeze their way under fences to sting little children. Apropos, the latter are all thin and hungry, in the highest degree quarrelsome, and addicted to prolonged lamentation. Also, each spring sees a certain proportion of their number carried off by diphtheria, while scarlatina and measles are as epidemic among them as is typhoid among their elders.

Thus the sounds of life most to be heard throughout the suburb are the sounds either of weeping or of mad cursing. In general, however, life in Tolmachikha is lived quietly and lethargically. So much is this the case that in spring even the cats forbear to squall save in crushed and subdued accents.

The only local person to sing is Felitzata; and even she does so only when she is drunk. It may be said that Felitzata is a saucy, cunning procuress, and does her singing in a peculiarly thick and rasping voice which, with many croaks and hiatuses, necessitates much closing of the eyes, and a great protruding of the apple of the throat. Indeed, it is only the women of the place who, turbulently quarrelsome and hysterically noisy, spend most of the day in scouring the streets with skirts tucked up, and never cease begging for pinches of salt or flour or spoonfuls of oil as they rail and screech at and beat their children, and thrust withered breasts into their babies' mouths, and rush and fling themselves about, and bawl in a constant endeavour to right their woebegone condition. Yes, all are dishevelled and dirty, and have wizened, bony faces, and the restless eyes of thieves. Never, indeed, is a woman plump of figure save at the period when she is ill, and her eyes are dim, and her gait is laboured. Yet until they are forty the majority of the women become pregnant with every winter, and on the arrival of spring may be seen walking abroad with large stomachs and blue hollows under the eyes. And even this does not prevent them from working with the same desperate energy as when they are not with child. In short, the inhabitants of the place resemble needles and threads with which some rough, clumsy, and impatient hand is for ever trying to darn a ragged cloth which as constantly parts and rends.

*

The chief person of repute in the suburb is my landlord, one Antipa Vologonov—a little old man who keeps a shop of " odd wares," and also lends money on pledge.

Unfortunately Antipa is a sufferer from a long-standing tendency to rheumatism which has left him bow-legged, and twisted and swollen his fingers to the extent that they will not bend. Hence he always keeps his hands tucked into his sleeves, though seemingly he has the less use for them in that, even when he withdraws them from their shelter, he does so as cautiously as though he were afraid of their becoming dislocated.

On the other hand, he never loses his temper, and he never grows excited.

" Neither of those things suits me," he will say, " for my heart is dilated, and might at any moment fail."

As for his face, it has high cheek-bones· which in places blossom into dark red blotches; an expression as calm as that of the face of a Khirghiz; a chin whence dangle wisps of mingled grey, red, and flaxen hair of a perpetually moist appearance; oblique and ever-changing eyes which are permanently contracted; a pair of thick, parti-coloured eyebrows which cast deep shadows over the eyes; and temples whereon a number of blue veins struggle with an irregular, sparse coating of bristles. Finally, about his whole personality there is something ever variable and intangible.

Also, his gait is irritatingly slow; and the more so owing to his coat, which, of a cut devised by himself, consists, as it were, of cassock, sarafan,[1] and waistcoat in one. As often as not he finds the skirts of the garment cumbering his legs: whereupon he has to stop and give them a kick. And thus it comes about that permanently the skirts are ragged and torn.

" No need for hurry," is his customary remark. " Always, in time, does one win to one's pitch in the market-place."

His speech is cast in rounded periods, and displays a great love for ecclesiastical terms. On the occurrence of one such term, he pauses thereafter as though mentally he were adding to the term a very thick, a very black, full-stop. Yet always he will converse with anyone, and at great length—his probable motive being a desire to leave behind him the reputation of a wise old man.

In his shanty are three windows facing on to the street, and a partition-wall which divides it into two rooms of unequal size. In the larger room, which contains a Russian stove, he himself lives: in the smaller room I have my abode. By a passage the two are separated from a storeroom where, closeted behind a door to which there are a heavy, old-fashioned bolt and many iron and brass screws, Antipa preserves pledges left by his neighbours, such as samovars, ikons, winter clothing and the like. Of this storeroom he always carries the great indented key at the back of the strap which upholds his cloth breeches; and whenever the police call to ascertain whether he is harbouring any stolen goods a long time ensues whilst he is shifting the key round to his stomach, and again a long time whilst he is unfastening it from the belt. Meanwhile he says pompously to the Superintendent or the Deputy Superintendent:

" Never do I take in goods of that kind. Of the truth of what I say, your honour, you have more than once assured yourself in person."

[1] Jacket

81

Also, whenever Antipa sits down the key rattles against the back or the seat of his chair: whereupon he bends his arm with difficulty, and feels to see whether or not the key has come unslung. This I know for the reason that the partition-wall is not so thick but that I can hear his every breath drawn, and divine his every movement.

Of an evening, when the misty sun is slanting across the river towards the auburn belt of pines, and distilling pink vapours from the sombre vista to be seen through the shaggy mouth of the ravine, Antipa Vologonov sets out a squat samovar that is dinted of side, and plated with green oxide on handle, turncock, and spout. Then he seats himself at his table by the window.

At intervals I hear the evening stillness broken by questions put in a tone which implies always an expectation of a precise answer.

" Where is Darika? "

" He has gone to the spring for water." The answer is given whiningly, and in a thin voice.

" And how is your sister? "

" Still in pain."

" Yes? Well, you can go now."

Giving a slight cough to clear his throat, the old man begins to sing in a quavering falsetto:

> Once a bullet smote my breast,
>   And scarce the pang I felt.
> But ne'er the pang could be express'd
>   Which love's flame since hath dealt!

As the samovar hisses and bubbles heavy footsteps resound in the street, and an indistinct voice says:

" He thinks that because he is a Town Councillor he is also clever."

" Yes; such folk are apt to grow very proud."

" Why, all his brains put together wouldn't grease one of my boots! "

And as the voices die away the old man's falsetto trickles forth anew, humming:

" The poor man's anger—— Minika! Hi, you! Come in here, and I will give you a bit of sugar. How is your father getting on? Is he drunk at present? "

" No, sober, for he is taking nothing but *kvas* and cabbage soup."

" And what is he doing for a living? "

" Sitting at the table, and thinking."

" And has your mother been beating him again? "

" No—not again."

" And she—how is she? "

" Obliged to keep indoors."

" Well, run along with you."

Softly there next presents herself before the window Felit-zata, a woman of about forty with a hawk-like gleam in her coldly civil eyes, and a pair of handsome lips compressed into a covert smile. She is well known throughout the suburb, and once had a son, Nilushka, who was the local " God's fool." Also she has the reputation of knowing what is correct procedure on all and sundry occasions, as well as of being skilled in lamentations, funeral rites, and festivities in connection with the musterings of recruits. Lastly she has had a hip broken, so that she walks with an inclination towards the left.

Her fellow women say of her that her veins contain " a drop of gentle blood "; but probably the statement is inspired by no more than the fact that she treats everyone with the same cold civility. Nevertheless there *is* something peculiar about her, for her hands are slender, and have long fingers, and her head is haughtily poised, and her voice has a metallic ring, even though the metal has, as it were, grown dull and rusty. Also, she speaks of everyone, herself included, in the most rough and downright terms, yet terms which are so simple that, though her talk may be disconcerting to listen to, it could never be called obscene.

For instance, once I overheard Vologonov reproach her for not leading a more becoming life.

" You ought to have more self-restraint," said he, " seeing that you are a lady, and also your own mistress."

" That is played out, my friend," she replied. " You see, I have had very much to bear, for there was a time when such hunger used to gnaw at my belly as you would never believe. It was then that my eyes became dazzled with the tokens of shame. So I took my fill of love, as does every woman. And once a woman has become a light-o'-love she may as well doff her shift altogether, and use the body which God has given her. And, after all, an independent life is the best life: so I hawk myself about like a pot of beer, and say, ' Drink of this, anyone who likes, while it still contains liquor.' "

" It makes one feel ashamed to hear such talk," said Vologonov with a sigh.

In response she burst out laughing.

" What a virtuous man! " was her comment upon his remark.

Until now Antipa had spoken cautiously, and in an under-tone, whereas the woman had replied in loud accents of challenge.

" Will you come in and have some tea? " he said next as he leant out of the window.

" No, I thank you. In passing, what a thing I have heard about you! "

" Do not shout so loud. Of what are you speaking? "

" Oh, of *such* a thing! "

" Of *nothing*, I imagine."

" Yes, of *everything*."

" God, who created all things, alone knows everything."

Whereafter the pair whispered together awhile. Then Felit-zata disappeared as suddenly as she had come, leaving the old man sitting motionless. At length he heaved a profound sigh, and muttered to himself:

" Into that Eve's ears be there poured the poison of the asp! . . . Yet pardon me, O God! Yea, pardon me! "

The words contained not a particle of genuine contrition. Rather, I believe, he uttered them because he had a weakness not for words which signified anything, but for words which, being out of the way, were not used by the common folk of the suburb.

*

Sometimes Vologonov knocks at the partition-wall with a superannuated *arshin* measure which has only fifteen *vershoki* of its length remaining. He knocks, and shouts:

" Lodger, would you care to join me in a pot of tea? "

During the early days of our acquaintanceship he regarded me with marked and constant suspicion. Clearly he deemed me to be a police detective. But subsequently he took to scanning my face with critical curiosity; until at length he said with an air of imparting instruction:

" Have you ever read *Paradise Lost and Destroyed*? "

" No " I replied. " Only *Paradise Regained*."

This led him to wag his parti-coloured beard in token that he disagreed with my choice, and to observe:

" The reason why Adam lost Paradise is that he allowed Eve to corrupt him. And never did the Lord permit him to regain it. For who is worthy to return to the gates of Paradise? Not a single human being."

And, indeed, I found it waste of time to dispute the matter, for he merely listened to what I had got to say, and then, without an attempt at refutation, repeated in the same tone as before, and exactly in the same words, his statement that "Adam lost Paradise for the reason that he allowed Eve to corrupt him."

Similarly did women constitute our most usual subject of conversation.

"You are young," once he said, "and therefore a human being bound to find forbidden fruit blocking your way at every step. This because the human race is a slave to its love of sin, or, in other words, to love of the Serpent. Yes, woman constitutes the prime impediment to everything in life, as history has many times affirmed. And first and foremost is she the source of restlessness. 'Charged with poison, the Serpent shall plunge in thee her fangs.' Which Serpent is, of course, our desire of the flesh, the Serpent at whose instigation the Greeks razed towns to the ground, and ravaged Troy and Carthagena and Egypt, and the Serpent which caused an amorous passion for the sister of Alexander Pavlovitch[1] to bring about Napoleon's invasion of Russia. On the other hand, both the Mohammedan nations and the Jews have from earliest times grasped the matter aright, and kept their women shut up in their back premises; whereas *we* permit the foulest of profligacy to exist, and walk hand in hand with our women, and allow them to graduate as female doctors, and to pull teeth, and all the rest of it. The truth is that they ought not to be allowed to advance beyond midwife, since it is woman's business either to serve as a breeding animal or opprobriously to be called *neiskusobrachnaia neviesta*.[2] Yes, woman's business should end there."

Near the stove there ticks and clicks on the grimy wall that is papered with "rules and regulations" and sheets of yellow manuscript the pendulum of a small clock, with, hanging to one of its weights, a hammer and a horseshoe, and, to the other, a copper pestle. Also, in a corner of the room a number of ikons make a glittering show with their silver *appliqué* and the gilded halos which surmount their figures' black visages, while a stove with a ponderous grate glowers out of the window at the greenery in Zhitnaia Street and beyond the ravine (beyond the ravine everything looks bright and beautiful), and the dusty, dimly lighted storeroom across the passage emits a perennial odour of dried mushroom, tobacco leaves, and hemp oil.

---

[1] The Emperor Alexander I.
[2] "Maid who hast never tasted of marriage."

Vologonov stirs his strong, stewed tea with a battered old teaspoon, and says with a sigh as he sips a little:

"All my life I have been engaged in gaining experience; so that now I know most things, and ought to be listened to with attention. Usually folk do so listen to me, but though here and there one may find a living soul, of the rest it may be said: 'In the House of David shall terrible things come to pass, and fire shall consume the spirit of lechery.'"

The words resemble bricks in that they seem, if possible, to increase the height of the walls of strange and extraneous events, and even stranger dramas, which loom for ever around me.

"For example," continues the old man, "why is Mitri Ermolaev Polukonov, our ex-mayor, lying dead before his time? Because he conceived a number of arrogant projects. For example, he sent his eldest son to study at Kazan: with the result that during the son's second year at the University he, the son, brought home with him a curly-headed Jewess, and said to his father: 'Without this woman I cannot live—in her are bound up my whole soul and strength.' Yes, a pass indeed! And from that day forth nothing but misfortune befell, in that Yashka took to drink, the Jewess gave way to repining, and Mitri had to go perambulating the town with piteous invitations to 'come and see, my brethren, to what depths I have sunk!' And though, eventually, the Jewess died of a bloody flux, of a miscarriage, the past was beyond mending, and, while the son went to the bad, and took to drink for good and all, the father 'fell a victim by night to untimely death.' Yes, the lives of two folk were thus undone by 'the thorn-bearing company of Judæa.' Like ourselves, the Hebrew has a destiny of his own. And destiny cannot be driven out with a stick. Of each of us the destiny is unhasting. It moves slowly and quietly, and can never be avoided. 'Wait,' it says. 'Seek not to press onward.'"

As he discourses Vologonov's eyes ceaselessly change colour —now turning to a dull grey, and wearing a tired expression, and now becoming blue, and assuming a mournful air, and now (and most frequently of all) beginning to emit green flashes of an impartial malevolence.

"Similarly, the Kapustins, once a powerful family, came at length to dust—became as nothing. It was a family the members of which were ever in favour of change, and devoted to anything that was new. In fact, they went and set up a piano! Well, of them only Valentine is still on his legs, and he (he is a doctor of less than forty years of age) is a hopeless drunkard, and saturated with dropsy, and fallen a prey to asthma, so that his cancerous eyes protrude horribly. Yes, the Kapustins, like the Polukonovs, may be ' written down as dead.' "

Throughout Vologonov speaks in a tone of unassailable conviction, in a tone implying that never could things happen, never could things have happened, otherwise than as he has stated. In fact, in his hands even the most inexplicable, the most grievous, phenomena of life become such as a law has inevitably decreed.

" And the same thing will befall the Osmukhins," he next remarks. " Let them be a warning to you never to make friends with Germans, and never to engage in business with them. In Russia any housewife may brew beer; yet our people will not drink it—they are more used to spirits. Also, Russian folk like to attain their object in drinking *at once*; and a *shkalik*[1] of vodka will do more to sap wit than five *kruzhki*[2] of beer. Once our people liked uniform simplicity; but now they are become like a man who was born blind, and has suddenly acquired sight. A change indeed! For thirty-three years did Ilya of Murom[3] sit waiting for his end before it came: and all who cannot bide patiently in a state of humility——"

Meanwhile clouds shaped like snow-white swans are traversing the roseate heavens, and disappearing into space, while below them, on earth, the ravine can be seen spread out like the pelt of a bear which the broad shoulders of some fabulous giant have sloughed before taking refuge in the marshes and forest. In fact, the landscape reminds me of sundry ancient tales of marvels, as also does Antipa Vologonov, the man who is so strangely conversant with the shortcomings of human life, and so passionately addicted to discussing them.

For a moment or two he remains silent as sibilantly he purses his lips and drinks some saffron-coloured tea from the saucer which the splayed fingers of his right hand are balancing on their tips. Whereafter, when his wet moustache has been dried, his level voice resumes its speech in tones as measured as those of one reading aloud from the Psalter.

[1] A measure equal to the fortieth part of a *vedro* (2.7 gallons).
[2] A measure equal to 2.16 Imperial pints.
[3] Ilya Murometz, the legendary figure most frequently met with in Russian *bilini* (folk songs), and probably identical with Elijah the Prophet, though credited with many of the attributes proper, rather, to the pagan god Perun the Thunderer.

"Have you noticed a shop in Zhitnaia Street kept by an old man named Asiev? Once that man had ten sons. Six of them, however, died in infancy. Of the remainder the eldest, a fine singer, was at once extravagant and a bookworm: wherefore, whilst an officer's servant at Tashkend, he cut the throats of his master and mistress, and for doing so was executed by shooting. As a matter of fact, the tale has it that he had been making love to his mistress, and then been thrown over in favour of his master once more. And another son, Grigori, after being given a high school education at St. Petersburg, became a lunatic. And another, Alexei, entered the army as a cavalryman, but is now acting as a circus rider, and probably has also become a drunkard. And the youngest son of all, Nikolai, ran away as a boy, and, eventually arriving in Norway with a precious scheme for catching fish in the Arctic Ocean, met with failure through the fact that he had overlooked the circumstance that we Russians have fish of our own and to spare, and had to have his interest assigned by his father to a local monastery. So much for fish of the Arctic Seas! Yet if Nikolai had only waited, if he had only been more patient, he——"

Here Vologonov lowers his voice, and continues with something of the growl of an angry dog:

"I too have had sons, one of whom was killed at Kushka (a document has certified to that effect), another was drowned whilst drunk, three more died in infancy, and only two are still alive. Of these last, I know that one is acting as a waiter in a hotel at Smolensk, while the other, Melenti, was educated for the Church, sent to study in a seminary, induced to abscond and get into trouble, and eventually dispatched to Siberia. There now! Yes, the Russian is what might be called a ' lightweighted ' individual, an individual who, unless he holds himself down by the head, is soon carried off by the wind like a chicken's feather. For we are too self-confident and restless. Before now I myself have been a gull, a man lacking balance: for never does youth realise its own insignificance, or know how to wait."

Dissertations of the kind drop from the old man like water from a leaky pipe on a cold, blustery day in autumn. Wagging his grey beard, he talks and talks, until I begin to think that he must be an evil wizard, and master of this remote, barren, swampy, ravine-pitted region—that he it is who originally planted the town in this uncomfortable, clayey hollow, and has thrown the houses into heaps, and entangled the streets, and wantonly created the town's unaccountably rude and rough and deadly existence, and addled men's brains with disconnected nonsense, and consumed their hearts with a fear of life. Yes, it comes to me that it must be he who during the long six months of winter causes cruel snowstorms from the plain to invade the town, and with frost compresses the buildings of the town until their rafters crack, and stinging cold brings birds to the ground. Lastly, I become seized with the idea that it must be he who, almost every summer, envelops the town in those terrible visitations of heat by night which seem almost to cause the houses to melt.

However, as a rule he maintains complete silence, and merely makes chewing motions with his strong-toothed jaws as he sits wagging his beard from side to side. At such times there is in his eyes a bluish fire like the gleam of charcoal, while his crooked fingers writhe like worms, and his outward appearance becomes sheerly that of a magician of iniquity.

Once I asked him:

" What in particular ought men to wait for? "

For a while he sat clasping his beard, and, with contracted eyes, gazing as at something behind me. Then he said quietly and didactically:

" Some day there will arise a Strange Man who will proclaim to the world the Word to which there never was a beginning. But to which of us is the hour when that Man will arise known? To none of us. And to which of us are known the miracles which that Word will perform? To none of us."

*

Once upon a time there used to glide past the window of my room the fair, curly, wavering, golden head of Nilushka the idiot, a lad looking like a thing which the earth has begotten of love. Yes, Nilushka was like an angel in some sacred picture adorning the southern or the northern gates of an ancient church, as, with his flushed face smeared with wax-smoke and oil, and his light blue eyes gleaming in a cold, unearthly smile, and a frame clad in a red smock reaching to below his knees, and the soles of his feet showing black (always he walked on tiptoe), and his thin calves, as straight and white as the calves of a woman, covered with golden down, he walked the streets.

Sometimes hopping along on one leg, and smiling, and waving his arms, and causing the ample folds and sleeves of his smock

to flutter until he seemed to be moving in the midst of a *nimbus*,
Nilushka would sing in a halting whisper the childish ditty:

> O Lo-ord, pardon me!
> Wo-olves run,
> And do-ogs run,
> And the hunters wait
> To kill the wolves.
> O Lo-ord, pardon me!

Meanwhile he would diffuse a cheering atmosphere of happiness with which no one in the locality had anything in common. For he was ever a lighthearted, winning, essentially pure innocent of the type which never fails to evoke good-natured smiles and kindly emotions. Indeed, as he roamed the streets the suburb seemed to live its life with less clamour, to appear more decent of outward guise, since the local folk looked upon the imbecile with far more indulgence than they did upon their own children, and he was intimate with, and beloved by, even the worst. Probably the reason for this was that the semblance of flight amid an atmosphere of golden dust which was his combined with his straight, slender little figure to put all who beheld him in mind of churches, angels, God, and Paradise. At all events, all viewed him in a manner contemplative, interested, and more than a little deferential.

A curious fact was the circumstance that whenever Nilushka sighted a stray gleam from a piece of glass, or the glitter of a morsel of copper in sunlight, he would halt dead where he was, turn grey with the ashiness of death, lose his smile, and remain dilating to an unnatural extent his clouded and troubled eyes. And so, with his whole form distorted with horror, and his thin hand crossing himself, and his knees trembling, and his smock fluttering around his frail wisp of a body, and his features growing stonelike, he would, for an hour or more, continue to stand, until at length someone laid a hand in his, and led him home.

The tale had it that, born, in the first instance, " soft-headed," he finally lost his reason five years before the period of which I am writing, when a great fire occurred, and that thenceforth anything, save sunlight, that in any way resembled fire plunged him into this torpor of dumb dread. Naturally the people of the suburb devoted to him a great deal of attention.

" There goes God's fool," would be their remark. " It will not be long before he dies and becomes a Saint, and we fall down and worship him."

Yet there were persons who would go so far as to crack rude jests at his expense. For instance, as he would be skipping along, with his childish voice raised in his little ditty, some idler or another would shout from a window, or through the cranny of a fence:

" Hi, Nilushka! Fire! Fire! "

Whereupon the angel-faced imbecile would sink to earth as though his legs had been cut away at the knee from under him, and he would huddle, frantically clutching his golden head in his permanently soiled hands, and exposing his youthful form to the dust, under the nearest house or fence.

Only then would the person who had given him the fright repent, and say with a laugh:

" God in heaven, what a stupid lad this is! "

And, should that person have been asked why he had thus terrified the boy, he would probably have replied:

" Because it is such sport to do so. As a lad who cannot feel things as other human beings do, he inclines folk to make fun of him."

As for the omniscient Antipa Vologonov, the following was his frequent comment on Nilushka:

" Christ also had to walk in terror. Christ also was persecuted. Why so? Because ever He endured in rectitude and strength. Men need to learn what is real and what is unreal. Many are the sins of earth come of the fact that the *seeming* is mistaken for the actual, and that men keep pressing forward when they ought to be waiting, to be proving themselves."

Hence Vologonov, like the rest, bestowed much attention upon Nilushka, and frequently held conversations with him.

" Do you now pray to God," he said once as he pointed to heaven with one of his crooked fingers, and with the disengaged hand clasped his dishevelled, variously coloured beard.

Whereupon Nilushka glanced fearfully at the mysteriously pointing finger, and, plucking sharply at his forehead, shoulders, and stomach with two fingers and a thumb, intoned in thin, plaintive accents:

" Our Father in Heaven——"

" *Which art* in Heaven."

" Yes, in the Heaven of Heavens."

" Ah, well! God will understand. He is the friend of all ' blessed ones.' " [1]

[1] Idiots; since persons mentally deficient are popularly deemed to stand in a peculiarly close relation to the Almighty.

Again, great was Nilushka's interest in anything spherical. Also, he had a love for handling the heads of children; when, softly approaching a group from behind, he would, with his bright, quiet smile, lay slender, bony fingers upon a close-cropped little poll; with the result that the children, not relishing such fingering, would take alarm at the same, and, bolting to a discreet distance, thence abuse the idiot, put out their tongues at him, and drawl in a nasal chorus:

"Nilka, the bottle-neck, the neck without a nape to it!"[1]

Yet their fear of him was in no way reciprocated, nor, for that matter, did they ever assault him, despite the fact that occasionally they would throw an old boot or a chip of wood in his direction—throw it aimlessly, and without really desiring to hit the mark aimed at.

Also, anything circular—for example, a plate or the wheel of a toy—engaged Nilushka's attention, and led him to caress it as eagerly as he did globes and balls. Evidently the rotundity of the object was the point that excited his interest. And as he turned the object over and over, and felt the flat part of it, he would mutter:

"But what about the other one?"

What "the other one" meant I could never divine. Nor could Antipa. Once, drawing the idiot to him, he said:

"Why do you always say 'What about the other one'?"

Troubled and nervous, Nilushka merely muttered some unintelligible reply as his fingers turned and turned about the circular object which he was holding.

"Nothing," at length he replied.

"Nothing of what?"

"Nothing here."

"Ah, he is too foolish to understand," said Vologonov with a sigh as his eyes darkened in meditative fashion.

"Yes, though it may seem foolish to say so," he added, "some people would envy him."

"Why should they?"

"For more than one reason. To begin with, he lives a life free from care—he is kept comfortably, and even held in respect; since no one can properly understand him, and everyone fears him, through a belief that folk without wit, the 'blessed ones of God,' are more especially the Almighty's favourites than persons

---

[1] Probably the attractiveness of this formula lay rather in the rhyming of the Russian words ("Nilka, butilka, bashka bez zatilka!") than in their actual meaning.

possessed of understanding. Only a very wise man could deal with such a matter, and the less so in that it must be remembered that more than one ' blessed one ' has become a Saint, while some of those possessed of understanding have gone—well, have gone whither? Yes, indeed!"

And, thoughtfully contracting the bushy eyebrows which looked as though they had been taken from the face of another man, Vologonov thrust his hands up his sleeves, and stood eyeing Nilushka shrewdly with his intangible gaze.

Never did Felitzata say for certain who the boy's father had been, but at least it was known to me that in vague terms she had designated two men as such—the one a young " survey student," and the other a merchant by name Viporotkov, a man notorious to the whole town as a most turbulent rake and bully. But once when she and Antipa and I were seated gossiping at the entrance-gates, and I inquired of her whether Nilushka's father were still surviving, she replied in a careless way:

" He is so, damn him! "

" Then who is he? "

Felitzata, as usual, licked her faded, but still comely, lips with the tip of her tongue before she replied:

" A monk."

" Ah!" Vologonov exclaimed with unexpected animation. " That, then, explains things. At all events, we have in it an intelligible *theory* of things."

Whereafter he expounded to us at length, and with no sparing of details, the reason why a monk should have been Nilushka's father rather than either the merchant or the young " survey student." And as Vologonov proceeded he grew unwontedly enthusiastic, and went so far as to clench his fists: until presently he heaved a sigh, as though mentally hurt, and said frowningly and reproachfully to the woman:

" Why did you never tell us this before? It was exceedingly negligent of you."

Felitzata looked at the old man with sarcasm and sauciness gleaming in her brown eyes. Suddenly, however, she contracted her brows, counterfeited a sigh, and whined:

" Ah, I was good-looking then, and desired of all. In those days I had both a good heart and a happy nature."

" But the monk may prove to have been an important factor in the question," was Antipa's thoughtful remark.

" Yes, and many another man than he has run after me for his pleasure," continued Felitzata in a tone of reminiscence.

This led Vologonov to cough, rise to his feet, lay his hand upon the woman's claret-coloured sleeve of satin, and say sternly:

"Do you come into my room, for I have business to transact with you."

As she complied she smiled and winked at me. And so the pair departed—he shuffling carefully with his bandy legs, and she watching her steps as though at any moment she might collapse on to her left side.

Thenceforth Felitzata visited Vologonov almost daily; and once during the time of two hours or so that the pair were occupied in drinking tea I heard, through the partition-wall, the old man say in vigorous, level, didactical tones:

"These tales and rumours ought not to be dismissed save with caution. At least ought they to be given the benefit of the doubt. For though all that he says may *seem* to us unintelligible, there may yet be enshrined therein a meaning, such as——"

"You say a meaning?"

"Yes, a meaning which, eventually, will be vouchsafed to you in a vision. For example, you may one day see issue from a dense forest a man of God, and hear him cry aloud: ' Felitzata, O servant of God, O sinner most dark of soul——' "

"What a croaking, to be sure!"

"Be silent! No nonsense! Do you blame yourself rather than sing your own praises. And in that vision you may hear the man of God cry: ' Felitzata, go you forth and do that which one who shall meet you may request you to perform!' And, having gone forth, you may find the man of God to be the monk whom we have spoken of."

"A-a-ah!" the woman drawled with an air of being about to say something more.

"Come, fool!"

"You see——"

"Have I, this time, abused you?"

"No, but——"

"I have an idea that the man of God will be holding a crook."

"Of course," assented Felitzata.

Similarly, on another occasion, did I hear Antipa mutter confidentially to his companion:

"The fact that all his sayings are so simple is not a favourable sign. For, you see, they do not harmonise with the affair in its entirety—in such a connection words should be mysterious, and, so, able to be interpreted in more than one way, seeing that the more meanings words possess, the more are those words respected and heeded by mankind."

" Why so? " queried Felitzata.

" Why so? " re-echoed Vologonov irritably. " Are we not, then, to respect *anyone* or *anything*? Only he is worthy of respect who does not harm his fellows; and of those who do not harm their fellows there are but few. To this point you must pay attention—you must teach him words of variable import, words more abstract, as well as more sonorous."

" But I know no such words."

" I will repeat to you a few, and every night, when he goes to bed, you shall repeat them to *him*. For example, ' Adom ispolneni, pokaites.'[1] And mark that the exact words of the Church be adhered to. For instance, ' Dushënbitzi, pozhaleite Boga, okayannïe,'[2] must be said rather than ' Dushënbitzi, pozhaleite Boga, okayanni,' since the latter, though the shorter form, is also not the correct one. But perhaps I had better instruct the lad myself."

" Certainly that would be the better plan."

So from that time onwards Vologonov fell to stopping Nilushka in the street, and repeating to him something or another in his kindly fashion. Once he even took him by the hand, and, leading him to his room, and giving him something to eat, said persuasively:

" Say this after me. ' Do not hasten, O ye people.' Try if you can say that."

" ' A lantern,' " began Nilushka civilly.

" ' A lantern? ' Yes. Well, go on, and say, ' I am a lantern unto thee——' "

" I want to sing it."

" There is no need for that, though presently you *shall* sing it. For the moment your task is to learn the correct *speaking* of things. So say after me——"

" O Lo-ord, have mercy! " came in a quiet, thoughtful chant from the idiot. Whereafter he added in the coaxing tone of a child:

" We shall all of us have to die."

" Yes, but come, come! " expostulated Vologonov. " What are you blurting out *now*? That much I know without your telling me—always have I known, little friend, that each of us

---

[1] " Do ye people who are filled with venom repent."

[2] " Murderers of the soul, accursed ones, repent ye before God."

is hastening towards his death. Yet your want of understanding exceeds what should be."

" Dogs run——"

" Dogs? Now, enough, little fellow."

" Dogs run like chickens. They run here, in the ravine," continued Nilushka in the murmuring accents of a child of three.

" Nevertheless," mused Vologonov, " even that seeming nothing of his may mean something. Yes, there may lie in it a great deal. Now, say: ' Perdition will arise before him who shall hasten.' "

" No, I want to *sing* something."

With a splutter Vologonov said:

" Truly you are a difficult subject to deal with! "

And with that he fell to pacing the floor with long, thoughtful strides as the idiot's voice cried in quavering accents:

" O Lo-ord, have me-ercy upon us! "

*

Thus the winsome Nilushka proved indispensable to the foul, mean, unhealthy life of the suburb. Of that life he coloured and rounded off the senselessness, the ugliness, the superfluity —he resembled an apple hanging forgotten on a gnarled old worm-eaten tree whence all the fruit and the leaves have fallen until only the branches wave in the autumn wind. Rather, he resembled a sole-surviving picture in the pages of a ragged, soiled old book which has neither a beginning nor an ending, and therefore can no longer be read, is no longer worth the reading, since now its pages contain nothing intelligible.

And as, smiling his gracious smile, the lad's pathetic, legendary figure flitted past the mouldy huts and cracked fences and riotous beds of nettles, there would readily recur to the memory, and succeed one another, visions of some of the finer and more reputable personages of Russian lore—there would file before one's mental vision, in endless sequence, men whose biographies inform us how, in fear for their souls, they left the life of the world, and, hieing them to the forests and the caves, abandoned mankind for the wild things of nature. And at the same time would there recur to one's memory poems concerning the blind and the poor—in particular, the poem concerning Alexei the Man of God, and all the multitude of other fair, but unsubstantial, forms wherein Russia has embodied her sad and terrified soul, her humble and protesting grief. Yet it was a process to depress one almost to the point of distraction.

Once, forgetting that Nilushka was imbecile, I conceived an irrepressible desire to talk with him, and to read him good poetry, and to tell him both of the world's youthful hopes and of my own personal thoughts.

The occasion happened on a day when, as I was sitting on the edge of the ravine, and dangling my legs over the ravine's depths, the lad came floating towards me as though on air. In his hands, with their fingers as slender as a girl's, he was holding a large leaf; and as he gazed at it the smile of his clear blue eyes was, as it were, pervading him from head to foot.

"Whither, Nilushka?" said I.

With a start he raised his head and eyes heavenward. Then timidly he glanced at the blue shadow of the ravine, and extended to me his leaf, over the veins of which there was crawling a ladybird.

"A *bukan*," he observed.

"It is so. And whither are you going to take it?"

"We shall all of us die. I was going to take and bury it."

"But it is alive: and one does not bury things before they are dead."

Nilushka closed and opened his eyes once or twice.

"I should like to sing something," he remarked.

"Rather, do you *say* something."

He glanced at the ravine again—his pink nostrils quivering and dilating; then sighed as though he was weary, and in all unconsciousness muttered a foul expression. As he did so I noticed that on the portion of his neck below his right ear there was a large birthmark, and that, covered with golden down like velvet, and resembling in shape a bee, it seemed to be endowed with a similitude of life, through the faint beating of a vein in its vicinity.

Presently the ladybird raised her upper wings as though she were preparing for flight; whereupon Nilushka sought with a finger to detain her, and, in so doing, let fall the leaf, and enabled the insect to detach itself, and fly away at a low level. Upon that, bending forward with arms outstretched, the idiot went softly in pursuit, much as though he himself were launching his body into leisurely flight, but, when ten paces away, stopped, raised his face to heaven, and, with arms pendent before him, and the palms of his hands turned outwards as though resting on something which I could not see, remained fixed and motionless.

From the ravine there were tending upwards towards the

sunlight some green sprigs of willow, with dull yellow flowers and a clump of grey wormwood, while the damp cracks which seamed the clay of the ravine were lined with round leaves of the "mother-stepmother plant," and round about us little birds were hovering, and from both the bushes and the bed of the ravine there was ascending the moist smell of decay. Yet over our heads the sky was clear, as the sun, now sole occupant of the heavens, declined slowly in the direction of the dark marshes across the river; only above the roofs of Zhitnaia Street could there be seen fluttering about in alarm a flock of snow-white pigeons, while waving below them was the black besom which had, as it were, swept them into the air, and from afar one could hear the sound of an angry murmur, the mournful, mysterious murmur of the town.

Whiningly, like an old man, a child of the suburb was raising its voice in lamentation; and as I listened to the sound it put me in mind of a clerk reading Vespers amid the desolation of an empty church. Presently a brown dog passed us with shaggy head despondently pendent, and eyes as beautiful as those of a drunken woman.

And, to complete the picture, there was standing, outlined against the nearest shanty of the suburb, a shanty which lay at the extreme edge of the ravine—there was standing, face to the sun, and back to the town, as though preparing for flight, the straight, slender form of the boy who, while alien to all, caressed all with the eternally incomprehensible smile of his angel-like eyes. Yes, that golden birthmark so like a bee I can see to this day!

*

Two weeks later, on a Sunday at mid-day, Nilushka passed into the other world. That day, after returning home from late Mass, and handing to his mother a couple of wafers which had been given him as a mark of charity, the lad said:

"Mother, please lay out my bed on the chest, for I think that I am going to lie down for the last time."

Yet the words in no way surprised Felitzata, for he had often before remarked, before retiring to rest:

"Some day we shall all of us have to die."

At the same time, whereas, on previous occasions, Nilushka had never gone to sleep without first of all singing to himself his little song, and then chanting the eternal, universal "Lord, have mercy upon us!" he, on this occasion, merely folded his

98

hands upon his breast, closed his eyes, and relapsed into slumber.

That day Felitzata had dinner, and then departed on business of her own; and when she returned in the evening she was astonished to find that her son was still asleep. Next, on looking closer at him, she perceived that he was dead.

" I looked," she related plaintively to some of the suburban residents who came running to her cot, " and perceived his little feet to be blue: and since it was only just before Mass that I had washed his hands with soap, I remarked the more readily that his feet were become less white than his hands. And when I felt one of those hands I found that it had stiffened."

On Felitzata's face, as she recounted this, there was manifest a nervous expression. Likewise, her features were a trifle flushed. Yet gleaming also through the tears in her languorous eyes there was a sense of relief—one might almost have said a sense of joy.

" Next," continued she, " I looked closer still, and then fell on my knees before the body, sobbing: ' O my darling, whither art thou fled? O God, wherefore hast Thou taken him from me? ' "

Here Felitzata inclined her head upon her left shoulder, contracted her brows over her mischievous eyes, clasped her hands to her breast, and fell into the lament:

> Oh, gone is my dove, my radiant moon!
> O star of mine eyes, thou hast set too soon!
> In darksome depths thy light lies drown'd,
> And time must yet complete its round,
> And the trump of the Second Advent sound,
> Ere ever my——

" Here, you! Hold your tongue! " grunted Vologonov irritably.

For myself, I had, that day, been walking in the forest, until, as I returned, I was brought up short before the windows of Felitzata's cot by the fact that some of the erstwhile turbulent denizens of the suburb were whispering softly together as, with an absence of all noise, they took turns to raise themselves on tiptoe, and, craning their necks, to peer into one of the black window-spaces. Yes, like bees on the step of a hive did they look, and on the great majority of faces, and in the great majority of eyes, there was quivering an air of tense, nervous expectancy.

Only Vologonov was nudging Felitzata, and saying to her in a loud, authoritative tone:

" Very ready are you to weep, but I should like first to hear the exact circumstances of the lad's death."

Thus invited, the woman wiped her eyes with the sleeve of her bodice, licked her lips, heaved a prolonged sigh, and fell to regarding Antipa's red, hardbitten face with the cheerful, unabashed glance of a person who is under the influence of liquor. From under her white head-band there had fallen over her temples and her right cheek a few wisps of golden hair; and indeed, as she drew herself up, and tossed her head and bosom, and smoothed out and stretched the creases in her bodice, she looked less than her years. Everyone now fell to eyeing her in an attentive silence, though not, it would seem, without a touch of envy.

Abruptly, sternly the old man inquired:

" Did the lad ever complain of ill-health? "

" No, never," Felitzata replied. " Never once did he speak of it—never once."

" And he had not been beaten? "

" Oh, how can you ask me such a thing, and especially seeing that, that——? "

" I did not say beaten by *you*."

" Well, I cannot answer for anyone else, but at least had he no mark on his body, seeing that when I lifted the smock I could find nothing save for scratches on legs and back."

Her tone now had in it a new ring, a ring of increased assurance, and when she had finished she closed her bright eyes languidly before heaving a soft, as it were, voluptuous, and, withal, very audible sigh.

Someone here murmured:

" She *did* use to beat him."

" What? "

" At all events she used to lose her temper with him."

This led to the putting of a further dozen or so of leading questions; whereafter Antipa, for a while, preserved a suggestive silence, and the crowd too remained silent, as though it had suddenly been lulled to slumber. Only at long last, and with a clearing of his throat, did Antipa say:

" Friends, we must suppose that God, of His infinite Mercy, has vouchsafed to us here a special visitation, in that, as all of us have perceived, a lad bereft of wit, the same radiant lad whom all of us have known, has here abided in the closest of communion with the Blessed Dispenser of life on earth."

Then I moved away, for upon my heart there was pressing

100

a burden of unendurable sorrow, and I was yearning, oh, so terribly, to see Nilushka once more.

The back portion of Felitzata's cot stood a little sunken into the ground, so that the front portion had its cold window panes and raised sash tilted a trifle towards the remote heavens. I bent my head, and entered by the open door. Near the threshold Nilushka was lying on a narrow chest against the wall. The folds of a dark-red pillow of fustian under the head set off to perfection the pale blue tint of his round, innocent face under its corona of golden curls; and though the eyes were closed, and the lips pressed tightly together, he still seemed to be smiling in his old quiet, but joyous, way. In general, the tall, thin figure on the mattress of dark felt, with its bare legs, and its slender hands and wrists folded across the breast, reminded me less of an angel than of a certain image of the Holy Child with which a blackened old *ikon* had rendered me familiar from my boyhood upwards.

Everything amid the purple gloom was still. Even the flies were forbearing to buzz. Only from the street was there grating through the shaded window the strong, roguish voice of Felitzata as it traced the strange, lugubrious word-pattern:

> With my bosom pressed to the warm, grey earth,
> To thee, grey earth, to thee, O my mother of old,
> I beseech thee, I who am a mother like thee,
> And a mother in pain, to enfold in thy arms
> This my son, this my dead son, this my ruby,
> This my drop of my heart's blood, this my——

Suddenly I caught sight of Antipa standing in the doorway. He was wiping his eyes with the back of his hand. Presently in a gruff and unsteady voice he said:

"It is all very fine for you to weep, good woman, but the present is not the right moment to sing such verses as those —they were meant, rather, to be sung in a graveyard at the side of a tomb. Well, tell me everything without reserve. Important is it that I should know *everything*."

Whereafter, having crossed himself with a faltering hand, he carefully scrutinised the corpse, and at last let his eyes halt upon the lad's sweet features. Then he muttered sadly:

"How extraordinarily he has grown! Yes, death has indeed enlarged him! Ah, well, so be it! Soon I too shall have to be stretching myself out. Oh that it were now!"

Then with cautious movements of his deformed fingers he straightened the folds of the lad's smock, and drew it over the legs. Whereafter he pressed his flushed lips to the hem of the garment.

Said I to him at that moment:

" What is it that you have been wanting of him? Why is it that you have been trying to teach him strange words? "

Straightening himself, and glancing at me with dim eyes, Antipa repeated:

" What is it that I have been wanting of him? " To the repetition he added with manifest sincerity, though also with a self-depreciatory movement of the head:

" To tell the truth, I scarcely know *what* it is that I have been wanting of him. By God I do not. Yet, as one speaking the truth in the presence of death, I say that never during my long lifetime had I so desired aught else. . . . Yes, I have waited and waited for fortune to reveal it to me: and ever has fortune remained mute and tongueless. Foolish was it of me to have expected otherwise, to have expected, for instance, that some day there might occur something marvellous, something unlooked-for."

With a short laugh, he indicated the corpse with his eyes, and continued more firmly:

" Yes, bootless was it to have expected anything from such a source as that. Never, despite one's wishes, was anything possible of acquisition thence. . . . This is usually the case. Felitzata, as a clever woman indeed (albeit one cold of heart), was for having her son accounted a God's fool, and thereby gaining some provision against her old age."

" But you yourself were the person who suggested that? You yourself wished it? "

" I? "

Presently, thrusting his hands up his sleeves, he added dully and brokenly:

" Yes, I *did* wish it. Why not, indeed, seeing that at least it would have brought comfort to the poor people of this place? Sometimes I feel very sorry for them with their bitter, troublous lives—lives which may be the lives of rogues and villains, yet are lives which have produced amongst us a *pravednik*." [1]

All the evening sky was now aflame. Upon the ear there fell the mournful lament:

> When snow has veiled the earth in white,
> The snowy plain the wild wolves tread.
> They wail for the cheering warmth of spring
> As I bewail the bairn that's dead.

[1] A " just person," a human being without sin.

102

Vologonov listened for a moment. Then he said firmly:

"These are mere accesses of impulse which come upon her. And that is only what might be expected. Even as in song or in vice there is no holding her, so remorse, when it has fastened upon such a woman's heart, will know no bounds. I may tell you that on one occasion two young merchants took her, stripped her stark naked, and drove her in their carriage down Zhitnaia Street, with themselves sitting on the seats of the vehicle, and Felitzata standing upright between them—yes, in a state of nudity! Thereafter they beat her almost to death."

As I stepped out into the dark, narrow vestibule, Antipa, who was following me, muttered:

"Such a lament as hers could come only of genuine grief."

We found Felitzata in front of the hut, with her back covering the window. There, with hands pressed to her bosom, and her skirt all awry, she was straining her dishevelled head towards the heavens, while the evening breeze, stirring her fine auburn hair, scattered it promiscuously over her flushed, sharply-defined features and wildly protruding eyes. A bizarre, pitiable, and extraordinary figure did she cut as she wailed in a throaty voice which constantly gathered strength:

> O winds of ice, winds cruel and rude,
> Press on my heart till its throbbings fail!
> Arrest the current of my blood!
> Turn these hot melting tears to hail!

Before her there was posted a knot of women, compassionate contemplators of the singer's distracted, grief-wrought features. Through the ravine's dark opening I could see the sun sinking below the suburb before plunging into the marshy forest and having his disk pierced by sharp, black tips of pine-trees. Already everything around him was red. Already, seemingly, he had been wounded, and was bleeding to death.

THE CEMETERY

In a town of the steppes where I found life exceedingly dull the best and the brightest spot was the cemetery. Often did I use to walk there, and once it happened that I fell asleep on some thick, rich, sweet-smelling grass in a cradle-like hollow between two tombs.

From that sleep I was awakened with the sound of blows being struck against the ground near my head. The concussion of them jarred me not a little, as the earth quivered and tinkled like a bell. Raising myself to a sitting posture, I found sleep still so heavy upon me that at first my eyes remained blinded with unfathomable darkness, and could not discern what the matter was. The only thing that I could see amid the golden glare of the June sunlight was a wavering blur which at intervals seemed to adhere to a grey cross, and to make it give forth a succession of soft creaks.

Presently, however—against my wish, indeed—that wavering blur resolved itself into a little, elderly man. Sharp-featured, with a thick, silvery tuft of hair beneath his under lip, and a bushy white moustache, curled in military fashion, on his upper, he was using the cross as a means of support as, with his disengaged hand outstretched, and sawing the air, he dug his foot repeatedly into the ground, and, as he did so, bestowed upon me sundry dry, covert glances from the depths of a pair of dark eyes.

" What have you got there? " I inquired.

" A snake," he replied in an educated bass voice as with a rugged forefinger he pointed downwards: whereupon I perceived that wriggling on the path at his feet, and convulsively whisking its tail, there was an *echidna*.

" Oh, it is only a grassworm," I said vexedly.

The old man pushed away the dull, iridescent, rope - like thing with the toe of his boot, raised a straw hat in salute, and strode firmly onwards.

" I thank you," I called out: whereupon he replied without looking behind him:

" If the thing really *was* a grassworm, of course there was no danger."

Then he disappeared among the tombstones.

Look·ng at the sky, I perceived the time to be about five o'clock.

The steppe wind was sighing over the tombs, and causing long stems of grass to rock to and fro, and freighting the heated air with the silken rustling of birches and limes and other trees, and leading one to detect amid the humming of summer a note of quiet grief eminently calculated to evoke lofty, direct thoughts concerning life and one's fellow-men.

Veiling, with greenery, grey and white tombstones worn with the snows of winter, crosses streaked with marks of rain, and the wall with which the graveyard was encircled the rank vegetation served to conceal also the propinquity of a slovenly, clamorous town which lay coated with rich, sooty grime amid an atmosphere of dust and smells.

As I set off for a ramble among the tombs and tangled grass I could discern through openings in the curtain of verdure a belfry's gilded cross which reared itself solemnly over crosses and memorials. At the foot of those memorials the sacramental vestment of the cemetery was studded with a kaleidoscopic sheen of flowers over which bees and wasps were so hovering and humming that the grass's sad, prayerful murmur seemed charged with a song of life which yet did not hinder reflections on death. Fluttering above me on noiseless wing were birds the flight of which sometimes made me start, and stand wondering whether the object before my gaze was really a bird or not: and everywhere the shimmer of gilded sunlight was setting the close-packed graveyard in a quiver which made the mounds of its tombs reminiscent of a sea when, after a storm, the wind has fallen, and all the green level is an expanse of smooth, foamless billows.

Beyond the wall of the cemetery the blue void of the firmament was pierced with smoky chimneys of oil-mills and soap factories, the roofs of which showed up like particoloured stains against the darker rags and tatters of other buildings; while blinking in the sunlight I could discern clatter-emitting windows which looked to me like watchful eyes. Only on the nearer side of the wall was a sparse strip of turf dotted over with ragged, withered, tremulous stems, and beyond this, again, lay the site of a burnt building which constituted a black patch of earth-heaps, broken stoves, dull grey ashes, and coal dust. To

heaven gaped the black, noisome mouths of burning-pits wherein the more economical citizens were accustomed nightly to get
rid of the contents of their dustbins; among the tall stems of
steppe grass waved large, glossy leaves of ergot; in the sunlight splinters of broken glass sparkled as though they were
laughing; and from two spots in the dark brown plot which
formed a semicircle around the cemetery there projected, like
teeth, two buildings the new yellow paint of which nevertheless
made them look mean and petty amid the tangle of rubbish,
pigweed, groundsel, and dock.

Indolently roaming hither and thither, a few speckled hens
resembled female pedlars, and some pompous red cockerels a
troupe of firemen; in the orifices of the burning-pits a number
of mournful-eyed, homeless dogs were lying sheltered; among
the shoots of the steppe scrub some lean cats were stalking
sparrows; and a band of children who were playing hide-and-
seek among the orifices above-mentioned presented a pitiful
sight as they went skipping over the filthy earth, and disappearing in the crevices among the piles of heaped-up dirt.

Beyond the site of the burnt-out building there stretched a
series of mean, close-packed huts which, crammed exclusively
with needy folk, stood staring, with their dim, humble eyes of
windows, at the crumbling bricks of the cemetery wall, and
the dense mass of trees which that wall enclosed. Here, in one
such hut, had I myself a lodging, in a diminutive attic which
not only smelt of lamp-oil, but stood in a position to have
wafted to it the least gasp or ejaculation on the part of my
landlord, Iraklei Virubov, a clerk in the local treasury. In
short, I could never glance out of the window at the cemetery
on the other side of the strip of dead, burnt, polluted earth
without reflecting that, by comparison, that cemetery was a
place of sheer beauty, a place of ceaseless attraction.

And ever, that day, as though he had been following me,
could there be sighted among the tombs the dark figure of the
old man who had so abruptly awakened me from slumber; and
since his straw hat reflected the sunlight as brilliantly as the disk
of a sunflower as it meandered hither and thither, I, in my turn,
found myself following *him*, though thinking, all the while, of
Iraklei Virubov. Only a week was it since Iraklei's wife, a thin,
shrewish, long-nosed woman with green and catlike eyes, had
set forth on a pilgrimage to Kiev, and Iraklei had hastened to
import into the hut a stout, squint-eyed damsel whom he
had introduced to me as his " niece by marriage."

" She was baptised Evdokia," he had said on the occasion
referred to. " Usually, however, I call her Dikanka. Pray be
friendly with her, but remember, also, that she is not a person
with whom to take liberties."

Large, round-shouldered, and clean-shaven like a *chef*, Virubov was for ever hitching up breeches which had slipped from a
stomach ruined with surfeits of water-melon. And always
were his fat lips parted as though athirst, and perpetually had
he in his colourless eyes an expression of insatiable hunger.

One evening I overheard a dialogue to the following effect.

" Dikanka, pray come and scratch my back. Yes, between
the shoulder-blades. O-o-oh, that is it. My word, how strong
you are! "

Whereat Dikanka had laughed shrilly. And only when I
had moved my chair, and thrown down my book, had the
laughter and unctuous whispering died away, and given place
to a whisper of:

" Holy Father Nicholas, pray for us unto God! Is the supper
kvas ready, Dikanka? "

And softly the pair had departed to the kitchen—there to
grunt and squeal once more like a couple of pigs. . . .

The old man with the grey moustache stepped over the turf
with the elastic stride of youth, until at length he halted before
a large monument in drab granite, and stood reading the
inscription thereon. Featured not altogether in accordance
with the Russian type, he had on a dark-blue jacket, a turned
down collar, and a black stock finished off with a large bow—
the latter contrasting agreeably with the thick, silvery, as
it were molten chin-tuft. Also, from the centre of a fierce
moustache there projected a long and gristly nose, while over
the grey skin of his cheeks there ran a network of small red
veins. In the act of raising his hand to his hat (presumably
for the purpose of saluting the dead), he, after conning the dark
letters of the inscription on the tomb, turned a sidelong eye
upon myself: and since I found the fact embarrassing, I frowned,
and passed onward, full, still, of thoughts of the street where
I was residing, and where I desired to fathom the mean existence
eked out by Virubov and his " niece."

As usual, the tombs were also being patrolled by Pimesha,
otherwise Pimen Krozootov, a bibulous, broken-down ex-
merchant who used to spend his time in stumbling and falling
about the graves in search of the supposed resting-place of his
wife. Bent of body, Pimesha had a small, bird like face over-

grown with grey down, the eyes of a sick rabbit, and, in general, the appearance of having undergone a chewing by a set of sharp teeth. For the past three years he had thus been roaming the cemetery, though his legs were too weak to support his under-sized, shattered body; and whenever he caught his foot he fell, and for long could not rise, but lay gasping and fumbling among the grass, and rooting it up, and sniffing with a nose as sharp and red as though the skin had been flayed from it. True, his wife had been buried at Novotchevkassk, a thousand versts away, but Pimen refused to credit the fact, and always, on being told it, stuttered with much blinking of his wet, faded eyes: "Natasha? Natasha is here."

Also, there used to visit the spot, well-nigh daily, a Madame Christoforov, a tall old lady who, wearing black spectacles and a plain grey, shroudlike dress that was trimmed with black velvet, never failed to have a stick between her abnormally long fingers. Wizened of face, with cheeks hanging down like bags, and a knot of grey, rather, grey-green, hair combed over her temples from under a lace scarf, and almost concealing her ears, this lady pursued her way with deliberation, and entire assurance, and yielded the path to no one whom she might encounter. I have an idea that there lay buried there a son who had been killed in a roisterers' brawl.

Another habitual visitor was thin-legged, short-sighted Aulic Councillor Praotzev, ex-schoolmaster. With a book stuffed into the pocket of his canvas pea-jacket, a white um-brella grasped in his red hand, and a smile extending to ears as sharp and pointed as a rabbit's, he could, any Sunday after dinner, be seen skipping from tomb to tomb, with his umbrella brandished like a white flag soliciting terms of peace with death.

And, on returning home before the bell rang for Vespers, he would find that a crowd of boys had collected outside his garden wall: whereupon, dancing about him like puppies around a stork, they would fall to shouting in various merry keys:

"The Councillor, the Councillor! Who was it that fell in love with Madame Sukhinikh, and then fell into the pond?"

Losing his temper, and opening a great mouth, until he looked like an old rook which is about to caw, the Councillor would stamp his foot several times, as though preparing to dance to the boys' shouting, and lower his head, grasp his umbrella like a bayonet, and charge at the lads with a panting shout of:

"I'll tell your fathers! Oh, I'll tell your mothers!"

111

THE CEMETERY

As for the Madame Sukhinikh referred to, she was an old beggar-woman who, the year round, and in all weathers, sat on a little bench beside the cemetery wicket, and stuck to it like a stone. Her large face, a face rendered bricklike by years of inebriety, was covered with dark blotches born of frostbite, alcoholic inflammation, sunburn, and exposure to wind, and her eyes were perpetually in a state of suppuration. Never did anyone pass her but she proffered a wooden cup in a suppliant hand, and cried hoarsely, rather as though she were cursing the person concerned:

"Give something for Christ's sake! Give in memory of your kinsfolk there!"

Once an unexpected storm blew in from the steppes, and brought a downpour which, overtaking the old woman on her way home, caused her, her sight being poor, to fall into a pond, whence Praotzev attempted to rescue her, and into which, in the end, he slipped himself. From that day onwards he was twitted on the subject by the boys of the town.

Other frequenters of the cemetery I see before me—dark, silent figures, figures of persons whom still unsevered cords of memory seemed to have bound to the place for the rest of their lives, and compelled to wander, like unburied corpses, in quest of suitable tombs. Yes, they were persons whom life had rejected, and death, as yet, refused to accept.

Also, at times there would emerge from the long grass a homeless dog with large, sullen eyes, eyes startling at once in their intelligence and in their absolute Ishmaelitism; until almost one expected to hear issue from the animal's mouth reproaches couched in human language.

And sometimes the dog would still remain halted in the cemetery as, with tail lowered, it swayed its shelterless, shaggy head to and fro with an air of profound reflection, while occasionally venting a subdued, long-drawn yelp or howl.

Again, among the dense old lime-trees there would be scurrying an unseen mob of starlings and jackdaws whose young would, meanwhile, maintain a soft, hungry piping, a sort of gently persuasive, chirruping chorus: until in autumn, when the wind had stripped bare the boughs, these birds' black nests would come to look like mouldy, rag-swathed heads of human beings which someone had torn from their bodies, and flung into the trees, to hang for ever around the white, sugarloaf-shaped church of the martyred St. Barbara. During that autumn season, indeed, everything in the cemetery's vicinity looked sad

112

and tarnished, and the wind would wail about the place, and
sigh like a lover who has been driven mad through bereave-
ment. . . .

Suddenly the old man halted before me on the path, and,
sternly extending a hand towards a white stone monument
near us, read aloud:

" ' Under this cross there lies buried the body of the respected
citizen and servant of God, Diomid Petrovitch Ussov,' " etc.,
etc.

Whereafter the old man replaced his hat, thrust his hands
into the pockets of his pea-jacket, measured me with eyes dark
in colour, but exceptionally clear for his time of life, and said:

" It would seem that folk could find nothing to say of this
man beyond that he was a ' servant of God.' Now, how can a
' servant ' be worthy of honour at the hand of ' citizens '? "

" Possibly he was an ascetic," was my hazarded conjecture;
whereupon the old man rejoined with a stamp of his foot:

" Then in such case one ought to write——"

" To write what? "

" To write *everything*, in fullest possible detail."

And with the long, firm stride of a soldier my interlocutor
passed onwards towards a more remote portion of the cemetery
—myself walking, this time, beside him. His stature placed
his head on a level with my shoulder only, and caused his straw
hat to conceal his features. Hence, since I wished to look at
him as he discoursed, I found myself forced to walk with head
bent, as though I had been escorting a woman.

" No, that is not the way to do it," presently he continued
in the soft, civil voice of one who has a complaint to present.
" Any such proceeding is a mark of barbarism merely—of a
complete lack of observation of men and life."

With a hand taken from one of his pockets he traced a large
circle in the air.

" Do you know the meaning of that? " he inquired.

" Its meaning is death," was my diffident reply, made with
a shrug of the shoulders.

A shake of his head disclosed to me a keen, agreeable, finely
cut face as he pronounced the following Slavonic words:

" ' Smertü smert vsekonechnïe pogublena bwist.' " [1]

" Do you know that passage? " presently he added.

Yet it was in silence that we walked the next ten paces—he
threading his way along the rough, grassy path at considerable

[1] " Death hath been for ever overthrown by death."

113

speed. Suddenly he halted, raised his hat from his head, and proffered me a hand.

" Young man," he said, " let us make one another's better acquaintance. I am Lieutenant Savva Yalovlev Khorvat, formerly of the State Remount Establishment, subsequently of the Department of Imperial Lands. I am a man who, after never having been found officially remiss, am living in honourable retirement—a man at once a householder, a widower, and a person of hasty temper."

Then, after a pause, he added:

" Vice-Governor Khorvat of Tambov is my brother—a younger brother; he being fifty-five, and I sixty-one, si-i-ixty-one."

His speech was rapid, but as precise as though no mistake was permissible in its delivery.

" Also," he continued, " as a man cognisant of every possible species of cemetery, I am much dissatisfied with *this* one. In fact, never satisfied with such places am I."

Here he brandished his fist in the air, and described a large arc over the crosses.

" Let us sit down," he said, " and I will explain things."

So, after that we had seated ourselves on a bench beside a white oratory, and Lieutenant Khorvat had taken off his hat, and with a blue handkerchief wiped his forehead and the thick, silvery hair which bristled from the knobs of his scalp, he continued:

" Mark you well the word *kladbistché*." [1] Here he nudged me with his elbow—continuing, thereafter, more softly: " In a *kladbistché* one might reasonably look for *kladi*, for treasures of intellect and enlightenment. Yet what do we find? Only that which is offensive and insulting. All of us does it insult, for thereby is an insult paid to all who, in life, are bearing still their ' cross and burden.' You too will, one day, be insulted by the system, even as shall I. Do you understand? I repeat, ' their cross and burden '—the sense of the words being that, life being hard and difficult, we ought to honour none but those who *still* are bearing their trials, or bearing trials for you and me. Now, *these* folk here have ceased to possess consciousness."

Each time that the old man waved his hat in his excitement, its small shadow, bird-like, flew along the narrow path, and

[1] The word, though customarily used for cemetery, means, primarily, a treasure-house.

114

over the cross, and, finally, disappeared in the direction of the town.

Next, distending his ruddy cheeks, twitching his moustache, and regarding me covertly out of boylike eyes, the Lieutenant resumed:

" Probably you are thinking, ' The man with whom I have to deal is old and half-witted.' But no, young fellow; that is not so, for long before *your* time had I taken the measure of life. Regard these memorials. *Are* they memorials? For what do they commemorate as concerns you and myself? They commemorate, in that respect, nothing. No, they are not memorials; they are merely passports or testimonials conferred upon itself by human stupidity. Under a given cross there may lie a Maria, and under another one a Daria, or an Alexei, or an Evsei, or someone else—all ' servants of God,' but not otherwise particularised. An outrage this, sir! For in this place folk who have lived their difficult portion of life on earth are seen robbed of that record of their existences which ought to have been preserved for your and my instruction. Yes, *a description of the life lived by a man* is what matters. A tomb might then become even more interesting than a novel. Do you follow me? "

" Not altogether," I rejoined.

He heaved a very audible sigh.

" It should be easy enough," was his remark. " To begin with, I am *not* a ' servant of God.' Rather, I am a man intelligently, of set purpose, keeping God's holy commandments so far as lies within my power. And no one, not even God, has any right to demand of me more than I can give. That is so, is it not? "

I nodded.

" There! " the Lieutenant cried briskly as, cocking his hat, he assumed a still more truculent air. Then, spreading out his hands, he growled in his flexible bass:

" What is this cemetery? It is merely a place of show."

At this moment, for some reason or another, there occurred to me an incident which involved the figure of Iraklei Virubov, the figure which had carpet slippers on its ponderous feet, thick lips, a greedy mouth, deceitful eyes, and a frame so huge and cavernous that the dapper little Lieutenant could have stepped into it complete.

The day had been a Sunday, and the hour eventide. On the burnt plot of ground some broken glass had been emitting a reddish gleam, shoots of ergot had been diffusing their gloss, children shouting at play, dogs trotting backwards and forwards, and all things, seemingly, faring well, sunken in the stillness of the portion of the town adjoining the rolling, vacant steppe, with, above them, only the sky's level, dull-blue canopy, and, around them, only the cemetery, like an island amidst a sea.

With Virubov, I had been sitting on a bench near the wicket-gate of his hut, as intermittently he had screwed his lecherous eyes in the direction of the stout, ox-eyed lacemaker, Madame Ezhov, who, after disposing of her form on a bank hard by, had fallen to picking lice out of the curls of her eight-year-old Petka Koshkodav. Presently, as swiftly she had rummaged the boy's hair with fingers grown used to such rapid movement, she had said to her husband (a dealer in second-hand articles), who had been seated within doors, and therefore rendered invisible—she had said with oily derision:

" Oh, yes, you bald-headed old devil, you! Of course *you* got your price. Ye-es. Then, fool, you ought to have had a slipper smacked across that Kalmuck snout of yours. Talk of *my* price, indeed! "

Upon this Virubov had remarked with a sigh, and in sluggish, sententious tones:

" To grant the serfs emancipation was a sheer mistake. I am a humble enough servant of my country, yet I can see the truth of what I have stated, since it follows as a matter of course. What ought to have been done is that all the estates of the landowners should have been conveyed to the Tsar. Beyond a doubt that is so. Then both the peasantry and the townsfolk, the whole people, in short, would have had but a single landlord. For never can the people live properly so long as it is ignorant of the point where it stands: and since it loves authority, it loves to have over it an autocratic force, for its control. Always can it be seen seeking such a force."

Then, bending forward, and infusing into each softly uttered word a perfect lusciousness of falsity, Virubov had added to his neighbour:

" Take, for example, the working-woman who stands free of every tie."

" How do *I* stand free of anything? " the neighbour had retorted, in complete readiness for a quarrel.

" Oh, I am not speaking in your despite, Pavlushka, but to your credit," hastily Virubov had protested.

116

" Then keep your blandishments for that heifer, your ' niece,' "
had been Madame Ezhov's response.

Upon this Virubov had risen heavily, and remarked as he
moved away towards the courtyard:

" All folk need to be supervised by an autocratic eye."

Thereafter had followed a bout of choice abuse between his
neighbour and his " niece," while Virubov himself, framed in
the wicket-gate, and listening to the contest, had smacked his
lips as he gazed at the pair, and particularly at Madame Ezhov.
At the beginning of the bout Dikanka had screeched:

" It is my opinion, it is my opinion, that——"

" Don't treat me to any of *your* slop! " the long-fanged Pavla
had interrupted for the benefit of the street in general. And
thus had the affair continued. . . .

Lieutenant Khorvat blew the fag-end of his cigarette from
his mouthpiece, glanced at me, and said with seemingly, a not
over-civil twitch of his bushy moustache:

" Of what are you thinking, if I might inquire?

" I am trying to understand you."

" You ought not to find that difficult," was his rejoinder as
again he doffed his hat, and fanned his face with it. " The
whole thing may be summed up in two words. It is that we lack
respect both for ourselves and for our fellow men. Do you
follow me *now*? "

His eyes had grown once more young and clear, and, seizing
my hand in his strong and agreeably warm fingers, he continued:

" Why so? For the very simple reason that I cannot respect
myself when I can learn nothing, simply nothing, about my
fellows."

Moving nearer to me, he added in a mysterious undertone:

" In this Russia of ours none of us really knows why he has
come into existence. True, each of us knows that he was born,
and that he is alive, and that one day he will die: but which
of us knows the reason why all that is so? "

Through renewed excitement its colour had come back to
the Lieutenant's face, and his gestures became so rapid as to
cause the ring on his finger to flash through the air like the link
of a chain. Also, I was enabled to detect the fact that on the
small, neat wrist under his left cuff there was a bracelet finished
with a medallion.

" All this, my good sir, is because (partially through the fact
that men forget the point, and partially through the fact that
that point fails to be understood aright) the *work* done by a

117

man is concealed from our knowledge. For my own part, I have an idea, a scheme—yes, a scheme—in two words, a, a——"

" N-n-o-u, n-n-o-u! " the bell of the monastery tolled over the tombs in languid, chilly accents.

" —a scheme that every town and every village, in fact, every unit of homogeneous population, should keep a record of the particular unit's affairs, a, so to speak, ' book of life.' Which ' book of life ' should be more than a list of the results of the unit's labour; it should also be a living narrative of the workaday activities accomplished by each member of the unit. Eh? And, of course, the record to be compiled without official interference—solely by the town council or district administration, or by a special ' board of life and works ' or some such body, provided only that the task be not carried out by nominees of the *Government*. And in that record there should be entered everything—that is to say, everything of a nature which ought to be made public—concerning each several man who has lived among us, and has since gone from our midst."

Here the Lieutenant stretched out his hand again in the direction of the tombs.

" My right is it," he added, " to know how those folk there spent their lives. For it is by their labours and their thoughts, and even on the product of their bones, that I myself am now subsisting. You agree, do you not? "

In silence I nodded; whereupon he cried triumphantly:

" Ah! You see, do you? Yes, an indispensable point is it that whatsoever a man may have done, whether good or evil, should be recorded. For example, suppose he has manufactured a stove specially good for heating purposes: record the fact. Or suppose he has killed a mad dog: record the fact. Or suppose he has built a school, or cleansed a dirty street, or been a pioneer in the teaching of sound farming, or striven, by word and deed, his life long, to combat official irregularities: record the fact. Again, suppose a woman has borne ten or fifteen healthy children: record the fact. Yes, and this last with particular care, since the conferment of healthy children upon the country is a work of absolute importance."

Further, pointing to a grey headstone with a worn inscription, he shouted (or almost did so):

" Under that stone lies buried the body of a man who never in his life loved but one woman, but *one* woman. Now, *that* is a fact which ought to have been recorded about him, for it is not merely a string of names that is wanted, but a narrative of

118

deeds. Yes, I have not only a desire, but a *right*, to know the lives which men have lived, and the works which they have performed: and whenever a man leaves our midst we ought to inscribe over his tomb full particulars of the ' cross and burden ' which he bore, as particulars ever to be held in remembrance, and inscribed there both for my benefit and for the benefit of life in general, as constituting a clear and circumstantial record of the given career. Why did that man live? To the question write down, always, the answer in large and conspicuous characters. Eh? "

" Most certainly."

This led the Lieutenant's enthusiasm to increase still more as, for the third time waving. his hand in the direction of the tombs, and mouthing each word, he continued:

" The folk of that town are liars pure and simple, for of set purpose they conceal the particulars of careers, that they may depreciate those careers in our eyes, and, while showing us the insignificance of the dead, fill the living with a sense of similar insignificance, since insignificant folk are the easiest to manage. Yes, it is a scheme thought out with diabolical ingenuity. Yet, for myself—well, try and make me do what I don't *intend* to do ! "

To which, with his face wrinkled with disgust, he added in a tone like a shot from a pistol:

" Machines are we! Yes, machines, and nothing else ! "

Curious was it to watch the old man's excitement as one listened to the strong bass voice amid the stillness of the cemetery. Once more over the tombs there came floating the languid, metallic notes of " N-n-o-u ! N-n-o-u ! "

The oily gloss on the withered grass had vanished, faded, and everything turned dull, though the air remained charged with the spring perfume of the geraniums and stocks and narcissi which encircled some of the graves.

" You see," continued the Lieutenant, " one could not deny that each of us has his value. By the time that one has lived threescore years one perceives that fact very clearly. Never *conceal* things, since every life lived ought to be set in the light, and is capable of being so, in that every man is a workman for the world at large, and constitutes an instructor in good or in evil, and that life, when looked into, constitutes, as a whole, the sum of all the labour done by the aggregate of us petty, insignificant individuals. That is why we ought not to hide away a man's work, but to publish it abroad, and to inscribe on the cross over his tomb his deeds, his services, in their entirety. Yes, however negligible may have been those deeds, those services, hold them up for the perusal of those who can discover good even in what is negligible. *Now* do you understand me?"

"I do," I replied. "Yes, I do."

"Good!"

The bell of the monastery struck two hasty beats — then became silent, so that only the sad echo of its voice remained reverberating over the cemetery. Once more my interlocutor drew out his cigarette-case, silently offered it to myself, and lighted and puffed industriously at another cigarette. As he did so his hands, as small and brown as the claws of a bird, shook a little, and his head, bent down, looked like an Easter egg in plush.

Still smoking, he looked me in the eyes with a self-diffident frown, and muttered:

"Only through the labour of man does the earth attain development. And only by familiarising himself with, and remembering, the past can man obtain support in his work on earth."

In speaking, the Lieutenant lowered his arm; whereupon on to his wrist there slipped the broad golden bracelet adorned with a medallion, and there gazed at me thence the miniature of a fair-haired woman: and since the hand below it was freckled, and its flexible fingers were swollen out of shape, and had lost their symmetry, the woman's fine-drawn face looked the more full of life, and, clearly picked out, could be seen to be smiling a sweet and slightly imperious smile.

"Your wife or your daughter?" I queried.

"My God! My God!" was, with a subdued sigh, the only response vouchsafed. Then the Lieutenant raised his arm, and the bracelet slid back to its resting-place under his cuff.

Over the town the columns of curling smoke were growing redder, and the clattering windows blushing to a tint of pink that recalled to my memory the livid cheeks of Virubov's "niece," of the woman in whom, like her uncle, there was nothing that could provoke one to "take liberties."

Next there scaled the cemetery wall, and stealthily stretched themselves on the ground, so that they looked not unlike the far-flung shadows of the cemetery's crosses, a file of dark, tattered figures of beggars, while on the further side of the slowly darkening greenery a cantor drawled in sluggish, careless accents:

THE CEMETERY

" E-e-ternal me-e——"

" Eternal memory of what? " exclaimed Lieutenant Khorvat with an angry shrug of his shoulders. " Suppose, in his day, a man has been the best cucumber-salter or mushroom-pickler in a given town. Or suppose he has been the best cobbler there, or that once he said something which the street wherein he dwelt can still remember. Would not *that* man be a man whose record should be preserved, and made accessible to my recollection? "

And again the Lieutenant's face wreathed itself in solid rings of pungent tobacco smoke.

Blowing softly for a moment, the wind bent the long stems of grass in the direction of the declining sun, and died away. All that remained audible amid the stillness was the peevish voices of women saying:

" To the left, *I* say."

" Oh, what is to be done, Tanechka? "

Expelling a fresh cloud of tobacco smoke in cylindrical form, the old man muttered:

" It would seem that those women have forgotten the precise spot where their relative or friend happens to lie buried."

As a hawk flew over the sun-reddened belfry-cross the bird's shadow glided over a memorial stone near the spot where we were sitting, glanced off the corner of the stone, and appeared anew beyond it. And the watching of this shadow I somehow found a pleasant diversion.

Went on the Lieutenant:

" *I* say that a graveyard ought to evince the victory of life, the triumph of intellect and of labour, rather than the power of death. However, imagine how things would work out under my scheme. Under it the record of which I have spoken would constitute a history of a town's lite wh ch, if anything, would increase men's respect for their fellows. Yes, such a history as *that* is what a cemetery ought to be. Otherwise the place is useless. Similarly will the past prove useless if it can give us nothing. Yet is such a history ever compiled? If it is, how can one say that events are brought about by, forsooth, ' servants of God '? "

Pointing to the tombs with a gesture as though he were swimming, he paused for a moment or two.

" You are a good man," I said, " and a man who must have lived a good and interesting life."

121

He did not look at me, but answered quietly and thought-fully:

"At least a man ought to be his fellows' friend, seeing that to them he is beholden for everything that he possesses, and for everything that he contains. I myself have lived——"

Here, with a contraction of his brows, he fell to gazing about him, as though he were seeking the necessary word: until, seeming to fail to find it, he continued gravely:

"Men need to be brought closer together, until life shall have become better adjusted. Never forget those who are departed, for anything and everything in the life of a 'servant of God'" may prove instructive and of profound significance."

On the white sides of the memorial-stones the setting sun was casting warm, lurid reflections, until the stonework looked as though it had been splashed with hot blood. Moreover, everything around us seemed curiously to have swelled and grown larger and softer and less cold of outline: the whole scene, though as motionless as ever, appeared to have taken on a sort of bright-red humidity, and deposited that humidity in purple, scintillating quivering dew on the turf's various spikes and tufts. Gradually, also, the shadows were deepening and lengthening, while on the further side of the cemetery wall a cow lowed at intervals, in a gross and drunken fashion, and a party of fowls cackled what seemed to be curses in response, and a saw grated and screeched.

Suddenly the Lieutenant burst into a peal of subdued laughter, and continued to do so until his shoulders shook. At length he said through the paroxysms, as, giving me a push, he cocked his hat boyishly:

"I must confess that, that—that the view which I first took of you was rather a tragic one. You see, when I saw a man lying prone on the grass I said to myself: 'H'm! What is that?' Next I saw a young fellow roaming about the cemetery with a frown settled on his face, and his breeches bulging; and again I said to myself——"

"A book is lying in my breeches pocket," I interposed.

"Ah! Then I understand. Yes, I made a mistake, but a very welcome one. However, as I say, when I first saw you I said to myself: 'There is a man lying near that tomb. Perhaps he has a bullet, a wound, in his temple?' And, as you know——"

He stopped to wink at me with another outburst of soft, good-humoured laughter. Then he continued:

"Nevertheless the scheme of which I have told you cannot really be called a scheme, since it is merely a fancy of my own. Yet I *should* like to see life lived in better fashion."

He sighed, and paused, for evidently he was becoming lost in thought.

"Unfortunately," he continued at last, "the latter is a desire which I have conceived too late. If only I had done so fifteen years ago, when I was filling the post of Inspector of the prison at Usman——"

His left arm stretched itself out, and once more there slid on to his wrist the bracelet. For a moment he touched its gold with a rapid, but careful and delicate, movement—then he restored the trinket to its retreat, rose suddenly, looked about him for a second or two with a frown, and said in dry, brisk tones as he gave his iron-grey moustache an energetic twist:

"Now I must be going."

For a while I accompanied him on his way, for I had a keen desire to hear him say something more in that pleasant, powerful bass of his: but though he stepped past the gravestones with strides as careful and regular as those of a soldier on parade, he failed again to break silence.

Just as we passed the chapel of the monastery there floated forth into the fair evening stillness, from the bars of a window, while yet not really stirring that stillness, a hum of gruff, lazy, peevish ejaculations. Apparently they were uttered by two persons who were engaged in a dispute, since one of them muttered:

"What have you done? What have you done?"

And the other responded carelessly:

"Hold your tongue, now! Pray hold your tongue!"

ON A RIVER STEAMER

THE water of the river was smooth, and dull silver of tint. Also, so barely perceptible was the current that it seemed to be almost stagnant under the mist of the noontide heat, and only by the changes in the aspect of the banks could one realise how quietly and evenly the river was carrying on its surface the old yellow-hulled steamer with the white-rimmed funnel, and also the clumsy barge which was being towed in her wake.

Dreamily did the floats of the paddle-wheels slap the water. Under the planks of the deck the engines toiled without ceasing. Steam hissed and panted. At intervals the engine-room bell jarred upon the ear. At intervals, also, the tiller-chains slid to and fro with a dull, rattling sound. Yet, owing to the somnolent stillness settled upon the river, these sounds escaped, failed to catch, one's attention.

Through the dryness of the summer the water was low. Periodically, in the steam r's bow, a deck hand like a king, a man with a lean, yellow, black-avised face and a pair of languishing eyes, threw overboard a polished log as in tones of melting melancholy he chanted:

Se-em, se-em, shest! [1]

It was as though he were wailing:

Seyem, seyem, a yest—*nishevo* [2]

Meanwhile the steamer kept turning her stearlet-like [3] prow deliberately and alternately towards either bank as the barge yawed behind her, and the grey hawser kept tautening and quivering, and sending out showers of gold and silver sparkles. Ever and anon, too, the captain on the bridge kept shouting hoarsely through a speaking-trumpet:

" About, there! "

Under the stem of the barge a wave ran which, divided into a pair of white wings, serpentined away towards either bank.

---

[1] " Seven, seven, six! " (the depth of water, reckoned in *sazheni* or fathoms).

[2] " Let us eat, let us eat, but to eat there is—*nothing* / "

[3] The stearlet is a fish of the salmon species.

In the meadowed distance peat seemed to be being burnt, and over the black forest there had gathered an opalescent cloud of smoke which suffused also the neighbouring marshes.

To the right the bank of the river towered up into lofty, precipitous, clayey slopes intersected with ravines wherein aspens and birches found shelter.

Everything ashore had about it a restful, sultry, deserted look. Even in the dull blue, torrid sky was there nought save a white-hot sun.

In endless vista were meadows studded with trees—trees sleeping in lonely isolation, and, in places, surmounted with either the cross of a rural church which looked like a day star or the sails of a windmill; while further back from the banks lay the tissue cloths of ripening crops, with, here and there, a human habitation.

Throughout, the scene was indistinct. Everything in it was calm, touchingly simple, intimate, intelligible, grateful to the soul. So much so that as one contemplated the slowly-varying vistas presented by the loftier bank, the immutable stretches of meadowland, and the green, timbered dance-rings where the forest approached the river, to gaze at itself in the watery mirror, and recede again into the peaceful distance; as one gazed at all this one could not but reflect that nowhere else could a spot more simply, more kindly, beautiful be found than these peaceful shores of the great river.

Yet already a few shrubs by the river's margin were beginning to display yellow leaves, though the landscape as a whole was smiling the doubtful, meditative smile of a young bride who, about to bear her first child, is feeling at once nervous and delighted at the prospect.

*

The hour was past noon, and the third-class passengers, languid with fatigue induced by the heat, were engaged in drinking either tea or beer. Seated mostly on the bulwarks of the steamer, they silently scanned the banks, while the deck quivered, crockery clattered at the buffet, and the deck hand in the bows sighed soporifically:

Six! Six! Six-and-a-half!

From the engine-room a grimy stoker emerged. Rolling along, and scraping his bare feet audibly against the deck, he approached the boatswain's cabin, where the said boatswain, a fair-haired, fair-bearded man from Kostroma was standing in the doorway. The senior official contracted his rugged eyes quizzically, and inquired:

" Whither in such a hurry? "

" To pick a bone with Mitka."

" Good! "

With a wave of his black hand the stoker resumed his way, while the boatswain, yawning, fell to casting his eyes about him. On a locker near the companion of the engine-room a small man in a buff pea-jacket, a new cap, and a pair of boots on which there were clots of dried mud was seated.

Through lack of diversion the boatswain began to feel inclined to hector somebody, so cried sternly to the man in question:

" Hi, there, chawbacon! "

The man on the locker turned about—turned nervously, and much as a bullock turns. That is to say, he turned with his whole body.

" Why have you gone and put yourself *there* ? " inquired the boatswain. " Though there is a notice to tell you *not to* sit there, it is there that you must go and sit! Can't you read? "

Rising, the passenger inspected, not the notice, but the locker. Then he replied:

" Read? Yes, I *can* read."

" Then why sit there where you oughtn't to? "

" I cannot see any notice."

" Well, it's hot there anyway, and the smell of oil comes up from the engines. . . . Whence have you come? "

" From Kashira."

" Long from home? "

" Three weeks, about."

" Any rain at your place? "

" No. But why? "

" How come your boots to be so muddy? "

The passenger lowered his head, extended cautiously first one foot, and then the other, scrutinised them both, and replied:

" You see, they are not *my* boots."

With a roar of laughter that caused his brilliant beard to project from his chin, the boatswain retorted:

" I think you must drink a bit."

The passenger said nothing more, but retreated quietly, and with short strides, to the stern. From the fact that the sleeves of his pea-jacket reached far below his wrists it was clear that the garment had originated from the shoulders of another man.

As for the boatswain, on noting the circumspection and diffidence with which the passenger walked, he frowned, sucked at his beard, approached a sailor who was engaged in vigorously scrubbing the brass on the door of the captain's cabin with a naked palm, and said in an undertone:

" Did you happen to notice the gait of that little man there in the light pea-jacket and dirty boots? "

" I did."

" Then see here. Do you keep an eye upon him."

" But why? Is he a bad lot? "

" Something like it, I think."

" I will, then."

At a table near the hatchway of the first-class cabin a fat man in grey was drinking beer. Already he had reached a state of moderate fuddlement, for his eyes were protruding sightlessly, and staring unwinkingly at the opposite wall. Meanwhile a number of flies were swarming in the sticky puddles on the table, or else crawling over his greyish beard and the brick-red skin of his motionless features.

The boatswain winked in his direction, and remarked:

" Half-seas over, *he* is."

" 'Tis his way," a pockmarked, eyebrow-less sailor responded.

Here the drunken man sneezed: with the result that a cloud of flies were blown over the table. Looking at them, and sighing as his companion had done, the boatswain thoughtfully observed:

" Why, he regularly sneezes flies, eh? "

*

The resting-place which I myself had selected was a stack of firewood over the stokehole shoot; and as I lay upon it I could see the hills gradually darkening the water with a mourning veil as calmly they advanced to meet the steamer, while in the meadows a last lingering glow of the sunset's radiance was reddening the stems of the birches, and making the newly mended roof of a hut look as though it were cased in red fustian, and communicating to everything else in the vicinity a semblance of floating amid fire, and effacing all outline, and causing the scene as a whole to dissolve into streaks of red and orange and blue, save where, on a hill above the hut, a black grove of firs stood thrown into tense, keen, and clear-cut relief.

Under a hill a party of fishermen had lit a wood fire, the flames of which could be seen playing upon, and picking out, the white hull of a boat, the dark figure of a man therein, a fishing-net suspended from some stakes, and a woman in a yellow bodice who was sitting beside the fire. Also, amid the golden radiance there could be distinguished a quivering of the leaves on the lower branches of the tree whereunder the woman sat shaded.

All the river was calm, and not a sound occurred to break the stillness ashore, while the air under the awning of the third-class portion of the vessel felt as stifling as during the earlier part of the day. By this time the conversation of the passengers, damped by the shadow of dusk, had merged into a single sound which resembled the humming of bees; and amid it one could not distinguish nor divine who was speaking, nor the subject of discussion, since every word therein seemed disconnected, even though all appeared to be talking amicably, and in order, concerning a common topic. At one moment a suppressed laugh from a young woman would reach the ear; in the cabin a party who had agreed to sing a song of general acceptation were failing to hit upon one, and disputing the point in low and dispassionate accents; and in each such sound there was something vespertinal, gently sad, softly prayer-like.

From behind the firewood near me a thick, rasping voice said in deliberate tones:

" At first he was a useful young fellow enough, and clean and spruce; but lately he has become shabby and dirty, and is going to the dogs."

Another voice, loud and gruff, replied:

" Aha! Avoid the ladies, or one is bound to go amiss."

" The saying has it that always a fish makes for deeper water."

" Besides, he is a fool, and that is worse still. By the way, he is a relative of yours, isn't he? "

" Yes. He is my brother."

" Indeed? Then pray forgive me."

" Certainly: but, to speak plainly, he is a fool."

At this moment I saw the passenger in the buff pea-jacket approach the sally-port, grasp with his left hand a stanchion, and step on to the grating under which one of the paddle-wheels was churning the water to foam. There he stood looking over the bulwarks with a swinging motion akin to that of a bat when, grappling some object or another with its wings, it hangs suspended in the air. The fact that the man's cap was drawn tightly over his ears caused the latter to stick out almost to the point of absurdity.

Presently he turned and peered into the gloom under the

awning, though, seemingly, he failed to distinguish myself reposing on the firewood. This enabled me to gain a clear view of a face with a sharp nose, some tufts of light-coloured hair on cheeks and chin, and a pair of small, muddy-looking eyes. He stood there as though he were listening to something.

All of a sudden he stepped firmly to the sally-port, swiftly unlashed from the iron top-rail a mop, and threw it overboard. Then he set about unlashing a second article of the same species.

" Hi! " I shouted to him. " What are you doing there? "

With a start the man turned round, clapped a hand to his forehead to discover my whereabouts, and replied softly and rapidly, and with a stammer in his voice:

" How is that your business? Get away with you! "

Upon this I approached him, for I was astonished and amused at his impudence.

" For what you have done the sailors will make you pay right enough," I remarked.

He tucked up the sleeves of his pea-jacket as though he were preparing for a fight. Then, stamping his foot upon the slippery grating, he muttered:

" I perceived the mop to have come untied, and to be in danger of falling into the water through the vibration. Upon that I tried to secure it, and failed, for it slipped from my hands as I was doing so."

" But," I remarked in amazement, " my belief is that you *wilfully* untied the mop, to throw it overboard! "

" Come, come! " he retorted. " Why should I have done that? What an extraordinary thing it would have been to do! How could it have been possible? "

Here he dodged me with a dexterous movement, and, re-arranging his sleeves, walked away. The length of the pea-jacket made his legs look absurdly short, and caused me to notice that in his gait there was a tendency to shuffle and hesitate.

Returning to my retreat, I stretched myself upon the firewood once more, inhaled its resinous odour, and fell to listening to the slow-moving dialogue of some of the passengers around me.

" Ah, good sir," a gruff, sarcastic voice began at my side: but instantly a yet gruffer voice intervened with:

" Well? "

" Oh, nothing, except that to ask a question is easy, and to answer it may be difficult."

" True."

From the ravines a mist was spreading over the river.

ON A RIVER STEAMER

At length night fell, and as folk relapsed into slumber the babel of tongues became stilled. The ear, as it grew used to the boisterous roar of the engines and the measured rhythm of the paddle-wheels, did not at first notice the new sound born of the fact that into the sounds previously made familiar there began to intrude the snores of slumberers, and the padding of soft footsteps, and an excited whisper of:

"I said to him—yes, I said: 'Yasha, you must not, you shall not, do this.' "

The banks had disappeared from view. Indeed, one continued to be reminded of their existence only by the slow passage of the scattered fires ashore, and the fact that the darkness lay blacker and denser around those fires than elsewhere. Dimly reflected in the river, the stars seemed to be absolutely motionless, whereas the trailing, golden reproductions of the steamer's lights never ceased to quiver, as though striving to break adrift, and float away into the obscurity. Meanwhile foam like tissue paper was licking our dark hull, while at our stern, and sometimes overtaking it, there trailed a barge with a couple of lanterns in her prow, and a third on her mast, which at one moment marked the reflections of the stars, and at another became merged with the gleams of firelight on one or the other bank.

On a bench under a lantern near the spot where I was lying a stout woman was asleep. With one hand resting upon a small bundle under her head, she had her bodice torn under the armpit, so that the white flesh and a tuft of hair could be seen protruding. Also, her face was large, dark of brow, and full of jowl to a point that caused the cheeks to roll to her very ears. Lastly, her thick lips were parted in an ungainly, corpse-like smile.

From my own position on a level higher than hers I looked dreamily down upon her, and reflected: " She is a little over forty years of age, and (probably) a good woman. Also, she is travelling to visit either her daughter and son-in-law or her son and daughter-in-law, and therefore is taking with her some presents. Also, there is in her large heart much of the excellent and maternal."

Suddenly something near me flashed as though a match had been struck, and, opening my eyes, I perceived the passenger in the curious pea-jacket to be standing near the woman spoken of, and engaged in shielding a lighted match with his sleeve.

Presently he extended his hand and cautiously applied the particle of flame to the tuft of hair under the woman's armpit. There followed a faint hiss, and a noxious smell of burning hair was wafted to my nostrils.

I leapt up, seized the man by the collar, and shook him soundly.

" What are you at? " I exclaimed.

Turning in my grasp, he whispered with a scarcely audible, but exceedingly repulsive, giggle:

" *Haven't* I given her a good fright, eh? "

Then he added:

" Now, let me go! Let go, I say! "

" Have you lost your wits? " I retorted with a gasp.

For a moment or two his blinking eyes continued to glance at something over my shoulder. Then they returned to me, while he whispered:

" Pray let me go. The truth is that, unable to sleep, I conceived that I would play this woman a trick. Was there any harm in that? See, now. She is still asleep."

As I thrust him away his short legs, legs which might almost have been amputated, staggered under him. Meanwhile I reflected:

" No, I was *not* wrong. He *did* of set purpose throw the mop overboard. What a fellow! "

A bell sounded from the engine-room.

" Slow! " someone shouted with a cheerful hail.

Upon that steam issued with such resounding shrillness that the woman awoke with a jerk of her head: and as she put up her left hand to feel her armpit her crumpled features gathered themselves into wrinkles. Then she glanced at the lamp, raised herself to a sitting position, and, fingering the place where the hair had been destroyed, said softly to herself:

" Oh, holy Mother of God! "

Presently the steamer drew to a wharf, and, with a loud clattering, firewood was dragged forth and cast into the stokehole with uncouth, warning cries of " *Tru-us-sha*! " [1]

Over a little town which had its back pressed against a hill the waning moon was rising, and brightening all the black river, and causing it to gather life as the radiance laved, as it were, the landscape in warm water.

Walking aft, I seated myself among some bales, and contem-

[1] The word means ship's hold or stokehole, but here is, probably, equivalent to the English " Heads below! "

plated the town's frontage. Over one end of it rose, tapering like a walking-stick, a factory chimney, while at the other end, as well as in the middle, rose belfries one of which had a gilded steeple, and the other one a steeple either green or blue, but looking black in the moonlight, and shaped like a ragged paint-brush.

Opposite the wharf there was stuck in the wide gable of a two-storied building a lantern which, flickering, diffused but a dull, anæmic light from its dirty panes, while over the long strip of the broken signboard of the building there could be seen straggling, and executed in large yellow letters, the words, "Tavern and ——" No more of the legend than this was visible.

Lanterns were hanging in two or three other spots in the drowsy little town; and wherever their murky stains of light hung suspended in the air there stood out in relief a medley of gables and drab-tinted trees and false windows in white paint, on walls of a dull slate colour.

Somehow I found contemplation of the scene depressing.

Meanwhile the vessel continued to emit steam as she rocked to and fro with a creaking of wood, and a slap-slapping of water, and a scrubbing of her sides against the wharf. At length someone ejaculated surlily:

"Fool, you must be asleep! The winch, you say? Why, the winch is at the stern, damn you!"

"Off again, thank the Lord!" added the rasping voice already heard from behind the bales, while to it an equally familiar voice rejoined with a yawn:

"It's time we *were* off!"

Said a hoarse voice:

"Look here, young fellow. What was it he shouted?"

Hastily and inarticulately, with a great deal of smacking of the lips and stuttering, someone replied:

"He shouted: 'Kinsmen, do not kill me! Have some mercy, for Christ's sake, and I will make over to you everything— yes, everything into your good hands for ever! Only let me go away, and expiate my sins, and save my soul, through prayer. Aye, I will go on a pilgrimage, and remain hidden my life long, to the very end. Never shall you hear of me again, nor see me.' Then Uncle Peter caught him a blow on the head, and his blood splashed out upon me. As he fell I—well, I ran away, and made for the tavern, where I knocked at the door and shouted: 'Sister, they have killed our father!' Upon that she put her

135

head out of the window, but only said: 'That merely means that the rascal is making an excuse for vodka.' . . . Aye, a terrible time it was—was that night! And how frightened I felt! I made, at first, for the garret, but presently thought to myself: 'No; they would soon find me there, and put me to an end as well, for I am the heir direct, and should be the first to succeed to the property.' So I crawled on to the roof, and there lay hidden behind the chimney-stack—sat holding on with arms and legs, while unable to speak for sheer terror."

" What were you afraid of? " a brusque voice interrupted.

" What was I afraid of? "

" At all events, you joined your uncle in killing your father, didn't you? "

" In such an hour one has not time to think—one just kills a man because one can't help oneself, or because it seems so easy to kill."

" True," the hoarser voice commented in dull and ponderous accents. " When once blood has flowed the fact leads to more blood, and if a man has started out to kill, he cares nothing for any reason—he finds good enough the reason which comes first to his hand."

" But if this young fellow is speaking the truth, he had a *business* reason—though, properly speaking, even property ought not to provoke quarrels."

" Similarly one ought not to kill just when one chooses. Folk who commit such crimes should have justice meted out to them."

" Yes, but it is difficult always to obtain such justice. For instance, this young fellow seems to have spent over a year in prison for nothing."

" ' For nothing '? Why, did he not entice his father into the hut, and then shut the door upon him, and throw a coat over his head? He has said so himself. ' For nothing,' indeed! "

Upon this the rapid stream of sobbed, disconnected words which I had heard before from some speaker poured forth anew. Somehow I guessed that it came from the man in the dirty boots as once more he recounted the story of the murder.

" I do not wish to justify myself," he said. " I say merely that, inasmuch as I was promised a reprieve at the trial, I told everything, and was therefore allowed to go free, while my uncle and my brother were sentenced to penal servitude."

" But you *knew* that they had agreed to kill him? "

" Well, it is my idea that at first they intended only to give him a good fright. Never did my father recognise me as his son—always he called me a Jesuit."

The gruffer of the two voices pulled up the speaker.

" To think," it said, " that you can actually talk about it all! "

" Why shouldn't I? My father brought tears to the eyes of many an innocent person."

" A fig for people's tears! If our causes of tears were one and all to be murdered, what would the state of things become? Shed tears, but never blood; for blood is not yours to shed. And even if you should believe your own blood to be your own, know that it is not so, that your blood does *not* belong to you, but to Someone Else."

" The point in question was my father's property. It all shows how a man may live awhile, and earn his living, and then suddenly go amiss, and lose his wits, and even conceive a grudge against his own father. . . . Now I must get some sleep."

Behind the bales all grew quiet. Presently I rose to peer in that direction. The passenger in the buff pea-jacket was sitting huddled up against a coil of rope, with his hands thrust into his sleeves, and his chin resting upon his arms. As the moon was shining straight into his face, I could see that the latter was as livid as that of a corpse, and had its brows drawn down over its narrow, insignificant eyes.

Beside him, and close to my head, there was lying stretched on the top of the coil of rope a broad-shouldered peasant in a short smock and a pair of patched boots of white felt. The ringlets of the wearer's curly beard were thrust upwards, and his hands clasped behind his head, as with ox-like eyes he stared at the zenith where a few stars were shining and the moon was beginning to sink.

At length, in a trumpet-like voice (though he seemed to do his best to soften it) the peasant asked:

" Your uncle is on that barge, I suppose? "

" He is. And so is my brother."

" Yet *you* are here! How strange! "

The dark barge, towed against the steamer's blue-silver wash of foam, was cleaving it like a plough, while under the moon the lights of the barge showed white, and the hull and the prisoners' cage stood raised high out of the water as to our right the black, indentated bank glided past in sinuous convolutions.

From the whole soft, liquescent, fluid scene the impression

which I derived was melancholy. It evoked in my spirit a sense of instability, of a lack of restfulness.

" Why are you travelling? "

" Because I wish to have a word with him."

" With your uncle? "

" Yes."

" About the property? "

" What else? "

" Then look here, my young fellow. Drop it all—both your uncle and the property, and betake yourself to a monastery, and there live and pray. For if you have shed blood, and especially if you have shed the blood of a kinsman, you will stand for ever estranged from all, while, moreover, bloodshed is a dangerous thing—it may at any time come back upon you."

" But the property? " the young fellow asked with a lift of his head.

" Let it go," the peasant vouchsafed as he closed his eyes.

On the younger man's face the down twitched as though a wind had stirred it. He yawned, and looked about him for a moment. Then, descrying myself, he cried in a tone of resentment:

" What are you looking at? And why do you keep following me about? "

Here the big peasant opened his eyes, and, with a glance first at the man, and then at myself, growled:

" Less noise there, you mitten-face! "

As I retired to my nook and lay down I reflected that what the big peasant had said was apposite enough—that the young fellow's face did in very truth resemble an old and shabby woollen mitten.

*

Presently I dreamt that I was painting a belfry, and that, as I did so, huge, goggle-eyed jackdaws kept flying around the belfry's gables, and flapping at me with their wings, and hindering my work: until, as I sought to beat them off, I missed my footing, fell to earth, and awoke to find my breath choking amid a dull, sick, painful feeling of lassitude and weakness, and a kaleidoscopic mist quavering before my eyes till it rendered me dizzy. From my head, behind the ear, a thin stream of blood was trickling.

Rising with some difficulty to my feet, I stepped aft to a

pump, washed my head under a jet of cold water, bound it with my handkerchief, and, returning, inspected my resting-place in a state of bewilderment as to what could have caused the accident to happen.

On the deck near the spot where I had been asleep there was standing stacked a pile of small logs, prepared for the cook's galley; while in the precise spot where my head had rested there was reposing a birch faggot of which the withy-tie had come unfastened. As I raised the fallen faggot I perceived it to be clean and composed of silky loppings of birch-bark which rustled as I fingered them: and, consequently, I reflected that the ceaseless vibration of the steamer must have caused the faggot to become jerked on to my head.

Reassured by this plausible explanation of the unfortunate, but absurd, occurrence of which I have spoken, I next returned to the stern, where there were no oppressive odours to be encountered, and whence a good view was obtainable.

The hour was the turn of the night, the hour of maximum tension before dawn, the hour when all the world seems plunged in a profundity of slumber whence there can be no awakening, and when the completeness of the silence attunes the soul to special sensibility, and when the stars seem to be hanging strangely close to earth, and the morning star, in particular, to be shining as brightly as a miniature sun. Yet already had the heavens begun to grow coldly grey, to lose their nocturnal softness and warmth, while the rays of the stars were drooping like petals, and the moon, hitherto golden, had turned pale, and become dusted over with silver, and moved further from the earth as intangibly the water of the river sloughed its thick, viscous gleam, and swiftly emitted, and withdrew, stray, pearly reflections of the changes occurring in the heavenly tints.

In the east there was rising, and hanging suspended over the black spears of the pine forest, a thin pink mist the sensuous hue of which was glowing ever brighter, and assuming a density ever greater, and standing forth more boldly and clearly, even as a whisper of timid prayer merges into a song of exultant thankfulness. Another moment, and the spiked tops of the pines blazed into points of red fire resembling festival candles in a sanctuary.

Next, an unseen hand threw over the water, drew along its surface, a transparent and many-coloured net of silk. This was the morning breeze, herald of dawn, as with a coating of tissue-like, silvery scales it rippled the river until the eye grew

139

weary of trying to follow the play of gold and mother-of-pearl and purple and bluish-green reflected from the sun-renovated heavens.

Next, like a fan there unfolded themselves the first sword-shaped beams of day, with their tips blindingly white; while simultaneously one seemed to hear descending from an illimitable height a dense sound-wave of silver bells, a sound-wave advancing triumphantly to greet the sun as his roseate rim became visible over the forest like the rim of a cup that, filled with the essence of life, was about to empty its contents upon the earth, and to pour a bounteous flood of creative puissance upon the marshes whence a reddish vapour as of incense was arising. Meanwhile on the more precipitous of the two banks some of the trees near the river's margin were throwing soft green shadows over the water, while gilt-like dew was sparkling on the herbage, and birds were awakening, and as a white gull skimmed the water's surface on level wings the pale shadow of those wings followed the bird over the tinted expanse, while the sun, suspended in flame behind the forest, like the Imperial bird of the fairy-tale, rose higher and higher into the greenish-blue zenith, until silvery Venus, expiring, herself looked like a bird.

Here and there on the yellow strip of sand by the river's margin long-legged snipe were scurrying about. Two fishermen were rocking in a boat in the steamer's wash as they hauled their tackle. Floating from the shore there began to reach us such vocal sounds of morning as the crowing of cocks, the lowing of cattle, and the persistent murmur of human voices.

Similarly the buff-coloured bales in the steamer's stern gradually reddened, as did the grey tints in the beard of the large peasant where, sprawling his ponderous form over the deck, he was lying asleep with mouth open, nostrils distended with stertorous snores, brows raised as though in astonishment, and thick moustache intermittently twitching.

Someone amid the piles of bales was panting as he fidgeted, and as I glanced in that direction I encountered the gaze of a pair of small, narrow, inflamed eyes, and beheld before me the ragged-mittenlike face, though now it looked even thinner and greyer than it had done on the previous evening. Apparently its owner was feeling cold, for he had hunched his chin between his knees, and clasped his hirsute arms around his legs, as his eyes stared gloomily, with a hunted air, in my direction. Then wearily, lifelessly he said:

140

" Yes, you have found me. And now you can thrash me if you wish to do so—you can give me a blow, for I gave *you* one, and, consequently, it's your turn to do the hitting."

Stupefied with astonishment, I inquired in an undertone:

" It was you, then, that hit me? "

" It was so, but where are your witnesses? "

The words came in hoarse, croaked, suppressed accents, with a separation of the hands, and an upthrow of the head and projecting ears which had such a comical look of being crushed beneath the weight of the battened-down cap. Next, thrusting his hands into the pockets of his pea-jacket, the man repeated in a tone of challenge:

" Where, I say, are your witnesses? You can go to the devil! "

I could discern in him something at once helpless and froglike which evoked in me a strong feeling of repulsion; and since, with that, I had no real wish to converse with him, or even to revenge myself upon him for his cowardly blow, I turned away in silence.

But a moment later I looked at him again, and saw that he was seated in his former posture, with his arms embracing his knees, his chin resting upon them, and his red, sleepless eyes gazing lifelessly at the barge which the steamer was towing between wide ribbons of foaming water—ribbons sparkling in the sunlight like mash in a brewer's vat.

And those eyes, that dead, alienated expression, the gay cheerfulness of the morning, and the clear radiance of the heavens, and the kindly tints of the two banks, and the vocal sounds of the June day, and the bracing freshness of the air, and the whole scene around us served but to throw into the more tragic relief.

*

Just as the steamer was leaving Sundir the man threw himself into the water—in the sight of everybody he sprang overboard. Upon that all shouted, jostled their neighbours as they rushed to the side, and fell to scanning the river where from bank to bank it lay wrapped in blinding glitter.

The whistle sounded in fitful alarm, the sailors threw lifebelts overboard, the deck rumbled like a drum under the crowd's surging rush, steam hissed affrightedly, a woman vented an hysterical cry, and the captain bawled from the bridge the imperious command:

" Avast heaving lifebelts! By now the fool will have got one! Damn you, calm the passengers! "

141

An unwashed, untidy priest with timid, staring eyes thrust back his long, dishevelled hair, and fell to repeating, as his fat shoulder jostled all and sundry, and his feet tripped people up:

"A *muzhik*, is it, or a woman? A *muzhik*, eh?"

By the time that I had made my way to the stern the man had fallen far behind the stern of the barge, and his head looked as small as a fly on the glassy surface of the water. However, towards that fly a fishing-boat was already darting with the swiftness of a water beetle, and causing its two oars to show quiveringly red and grey, while from the marshier of the two banks there began hastily to put out a second boat which leapt in the steamer's wash with the gaiety of a young calf.

Suddenly there broke into the painful hubbub on the steamer's deck a faint, heartrending cry of "A-a-ah!"

In answer to it a sharp-nosed, black-bearded, well-dressed peasant muttered with a smack of his lips:

"Ah! That is him shouting. What a madman he must have been! And an ugly customer too, wasn't he?"

The peasant with the curly beard rejoined in a tone of conviction engulfing all other utterances:

"It is his conscience that is catching him. Think what you like, but never can conscience be suppressed."

Therewith, constantly interrupting one another, the pair betook themselves to a public recital of the tragic story of the fair-haired young fellow, whom the fishermen had now lifted from the water, and were conveying towards the steamer with oars that oscillated at top speed.

The bearded peasant continued:

"As soon as it was seen that he was but running after the soldier's wife——"

"Besides," the other peasant interrupted, "the property was not to be divided after the death of the father."

With which the bearded *muzhik* eagerly recounted the history of the murder done by the brother, the nephew, and a son, while the spruce, spare, well-dressed peasant interlarded the general buzz of conversation with words and comments cheerfully and stridently delivered, much as though he were driving in stakes for the erection of a fence.

"Every man is drawn most in the direction whither he finds it easiest to go."

"Then it will be the Devil that will be drawing him, since the direction of Hell is always the easiest."

" Well, *you* will not be going that way, I suppose? You don't altogether fancy it? "

" Why should I? "

" Because you have declared it to be the easiest way."

" Well, I am not a saint."

" No, ha-ha! you are not."

" And you mean that——? "

" I mean nothing. If a dog's chain be short, *he* is not to be blamed."

Whereupon, setting nose to nose, the pair plunged into a quarrel still more heated as they expounded in simple, but often curiously apposite, language opinions intelligible to themselves alone. The one peasant, a lean fellow with lengthy limbs, cold, sarcastic eyes, and a dark, bony countenance, spoke loudly and sonorously, with frequent shrugs of the shoulders, while the other peasant, a man stout and broad of build who until now had seemed calm, self-assured, of demeanour, and a man of settled views, breathed heavily, while his oxlike eyes glowed with an ardour causing his face to flush patchily, and his beard to stick out from his chin.

" Look here, for instance," he growled as he gesticulated and rolled his dull eyes about. " How can that be? Does not even God know wherein a man ought to restrain himself? "

" If the Devil be one's master, God doesn't come into the matter."

" Liar! For who was the first who raised his hand against his fellow? "

" Cain."

" And the first man who repented of a sin? "

" Adam."

" Ah! You see! "

Here there broke into the dispute a shout of " They are just getting him aboard! " and the crowd, rushing away from the stern, carried with it the two disputants—the sparer peasant lowering his shoulders, and buttoning up his jacket, as he went, while the bearded peasant, following at his heels, thrust his head forward in a surly manner as he shifted his cap from the one ear to the other.

With a ponderous beating of paddles against the current the steamer heaved to, and the captain shouted through a speaking-trumpet, with a view to preventing a collision between the barge and the stern of the vessel:

" Put her over! Put her o-o-over! "

143

Soon the fishing-boat came alongside, and the half-drowned man, with a form as limp as a half-empty sack, and water exuding from every stitch, and his hitherto haggard face grown smooth and simple-looking, was hoisted on board.

Next, on the sailors laying him upon the hatchway of the baggage hold, he sat up, leaned forward, smoothed his wet hair with the palms of his hands, and asked dully, without looking at anyone:

" Have they also recovered my cap? "

Someone among the throng around him exclaimed reprovingly:

" It is not about your cap that you ought to be thinking, but about your soul."

Upon this he hiccuped loudly and freely, like a camel, and emitted a stream of turgid water from his mouth. Then, looking at the crowd with lack-lustre eyes, he said in an apathetic tone:

" Let me be taken elsewhere."

In answer the boatswain sternly bade him stretch himself out, and this the young fellow did, with his hands clasped under his head, and his eyes closed, while the boatswain added brusquely to the onlookers:

" Move away, move away, good people. What is there to stare at? This is not a show. . . . Hi, you *muzhik*! Why did you play us such a trick, damn you? "

The crowd, however, was not to be suppressed, but indulged in comments.

" He murdered his father, didn't he? "

" What? *That* wretched creature? "

As for the boatswain, he squatted upon his heels, and proceeded to subject the rescued man to a course of strict interrogation.

" What is the destination marked on your ticket? "

" Perm."

" Then you ought to leave the boat at Kazan. And what is your name? "

" Yakov."

" And your surname? "

" Bashkin—though we are known also as the Bukolov family."

" Your family has a *double* surname, then? "

With the full power of his trumpet-like lungs the bearded peasant (evidently he had lost his temper) broke in:

" Though his uncle and his brother have been sentenced to penal servitude, and are travelling together on that barge, *he*

144

—well, *he* has received his discharge! That is only a personal matter, however. In spite of what judges may say, one ought never to kill, since conscience cannot bear the thought of blood. Even *nearly* to become a murderer is wrong."

By this time more and more passengers had collected as they awakened from sleep and emerged from the first- and second-class cabins. Among them was the mate, a man with a black moustache and rubicund features who inquired of someone amid the confusion: " You are not a doctor, I suppose? " and received the astonished, high-pitched reply: " No, sir, nor ever have been one."

To this someone added with a drawl:

" Why is a doctor needed? Surely the man is a fellow of no particular importance? "

Over the river the radiance of the summer daylight had gathered increased strength, and, since the date was a Sunday, bells were sounding seductively from a hill, and a couple of women in gala apparel who were following the margin of the river waved handkerchiefs towards the steamer, and shouted some greeting.

Meanwhile the young fellow lay motionless, with his eyes closed. Divested of his pea-jacket, and wrapped about with wet, clinging underclothing, he looked more symmetrical than previously—his chest seemed better developed, his body plumper, and his face more rotund and less ugly.

Yet though the passengers gazed at him with compassion or distaste or severity or fear, as the case might be, all did so without ceremony, but, rather, as though he had not been a living man at all.

For instance, a gaunt gentleman in a grey frock-coat said to a lady in a yellow straw hat adorned with a pink ribbon:

" At our place, in Riazan, when a certain master-watchmaker went and hanged himself to a ventilator, he first of all stopped every watch and clock in his shop. Now, the question is, *why* did he stop them? "

" An abnormal case indeed! "

On the other hand, a dark-browed woman who had her hands hidden beneath her shawl stood gazing at the rescued man in silence, and with her side turned towards him. As she did so tears were welling in her grey-blue eyes.

Presently two sailors appeared. One of them bent over the young fellow, touched him on the shoulder, and said:

" Hi! You are to get up."

145

Whereupon the young fellow rose, and was removed else-whither.

*

When, after an interval, he reappeared on deck he was clean and dry, and clad in a cook's white jumper and a sailor's blue serge trousers. Clasping his hands behind his back, hunching his shoulders, and bending his head forward, he walked swiftly to the stern, with a throng of idlers—at first one by one, and then in parties of from three to a dozen—following in his wake.

The man seated himself upon a coil of rope, and, craning his neck in wolf-like fashion to eye the bystanders, frowned, let fall his temples upon hands thrust into his flaxen hair, and fixed his gaze upon the barge.

Standing or sitting about in the hot sunshine, people stared at him without stint. Evidently they would have liked, but did not dare, to engage him in conversation. Presently the big peasant also arrived on the scene, and, after glancing at all present, took off his hat, and wiped his perspiring face. Next, a grey-headed old man with a red nose, a thin wisp of beard, and watery eyes cleared his throat, and in honeyed tones took the initiative.

"Would you mind telling us how it all happened?" he began.

"Why should I do so?" retorted the young fellow without moving.

Taking a red handkerchief from his bosom, the old man shook it out and applied it cautiously to his eyes. Then he said through its folds in the quiet accents of a man who is determined to persevere:

"Why, you say? For the reason that the occasion is one when all ought to know the tru——"

Lurching forward, the bearded peasant interposed with a rasp:

"Yes, do you tell us all about it, and things will become easier for you. For a sin always needs to be made known."

While, like an echo, a voice said in bold and sarcastic accents:

"It would be better to seize him and tie him up."

Upon this the young fellow raised his brows a little, and retorted in an undertone:

"Let me bide."

"The rascal!" the crowd commented, while the old man, neatly folding and replacing his handkerchief, raised a hand as dry as a cock's leg, and remarked with a sharp, knowing smile:

" Possibly it is not merely out of idle curiosity that folk are making this request."

" Go and be damned to you! " the young fellow exclaimed with a grim snap. Whereupon the big peasant bellowed out in blustering fashion:

" What? Then you will not tell us at least your destination? "

Whereafter the same speaker continued to hold forth on humanity, God, and the human conscience—staring wildly around him as he did so, and waving his arms about, and growing ever more frantic, until really it was curious to watch him.

At length the crowd grew similarly excited, and took to encouraging the speaker with cries of " True! That is so! "

As for the young fellow, he listened awhile in silence, without moving. Then, straightening his back, he rose, thrust his hands into the pockets of his trousers, and, swaying his body to and fro, began to glare at the crowd with greenish eyes which were manifestly lightening to a vicious gleam. At length, thrusting forth his chest, he cried hoarsely:

" So you ask me whither I am bound? I am bound for the brigands' lair, for the brigands' lair, where, unless you first take and put me in fetters, I intend to cut the throat of every man that I meet. Yes, a hundred murders will I commit, for all folk will be the same to me, and not a soul will I spare. Aye, the end of my tether is reached, so take and fetter me whilst you can."

His breath was issuing with difficulty, and as he spoke his shoulders heaved, and his legs trembled beneath him. Also, his face had turned grey and become distorted with tremors.

Upon this the crowd broke into a gruff, ugly, resentful roar, and edged away from the man. Yet, in doing so, many of its members looked curiously like the man himself in the way that they lowered their heads, caught at their breath, and let their eyes flash. Clearly the man was in imminent danger of being assaulted.

Suddenly he recovered his subdued demeanour—he, as it were, thawed in the sunlight: until, as suddenly, his legs gave way beneath him, and, narrowly escaping injury to his face from the corner of a bale, he fell forward upon his knees as though felled with an axe. Thereafter, clutching at his throat, he shouted in a strange voice, and crowding the words upon one another:

" Tell me what I am to do. Is all of it my fault? Long

I lay in prison before I was tried and told to go free. yet——"

Tearing at his ears and cheeks, he rocked his head to and fro as though seeking to rend it from its socket. Then he continued:

"Yet I am *not* free. Nor is it in my power to say what will become of me. For me there remains neither life nor death."

"Aha!" exclaimed the big peasant; and at the sound the crowd drew back as in consternation, while some hastened to depart altogether. As for the remainder (numbering a dozen or so), they herded sullenly, nervously, involuntarily into a group as the young fellow continued in distracted tones and with trembling head:

"Oh that I could sleep for the next ten years! For then could I prove myself, and decide whether I am guilty or not. Last night I struck a man with a faggot. As I was walking about I saw asleep a man who had angered me, and thereupon thought, 'Come! I should like to deal him a blow, but can I actually do it?' And strike him I did. Was it my fault? Always I keep asking myself, 'Can I, or can I not, do a thing?' Aye, lost, lost am I!"

Apparently this outburst caused the man to reach the end of his power, for presently he sank from knees to heels—then on to his side, with hands clasping his head, and his tongue finally uttering the words, "Better had you kill me!"

A hush fell, for all now stood confounded and silent, with, about them, a greyer, a more subdued, look which made all more resemble their fellows. In fact, to all had the atmosphere become oppressive, as though everyone's breast had had clamped into it a large, soft clod of humid, viscid earth. Until at last someone said in a low, shamefaced, but friendly, tone:

"Good brother, we are not your judges."

To which someone else added with an equal measure of gentleness:

"Indeed, we may be no better than you."

"We pity you, but we must not judge you. Only pity is permitted."

As for the well-dressed peasant, his loud, triumphant utterance was:

"Let God judge him, but men suffer him. Of judging of one another there has been enough."

And a fifth man remarked to a friend as he walked away:

" What are we to make of this? To judge by the book, the young fellow is at once guilty and not guilty."

" Bygones ought to be bygones. Of all courses that is the best."

" Yes, for we are too quick. What good can that do? "

" Aye, what? "

At length the dark-browed woman stepped forward. Letting fall her shawl to her shoulders, straightening hair streaked with grey under a bright blue scarf, and deftly putting aside a skirt-tail, she so seated herself beside the young fellow as to screen him from the crowd with the height of her figure. Then, raising a kindly face, she said civilly, but authoritatively, to the bystanders:

" Do all of you go away."

Whereupon the crowd began to depart—the big peasant saying as he went:

" There! Just as I foretold has the matter turned out. Conscience *has* asserted itself."

Yet the words were spoken without self-complacency—rather, thoughtfully, and with a sense of awe.

As for the red-nosed old man, who was walking like a shadow behind the last speaker, he opened his snuff-box, peered therein with his moist eyes, and drawled to no one in particular:

" How often does one see a man play with conscience, yes, even though he be a rogue! He erects that conscience as a screen to his knaveries and tricks and wiles, and masks the whole with a cloud of words. Yes, *we* know how it is done, even though folk may stare at him, and say to one another, ' How fervently his soul is glowing!' Aye, all the time that he is holding his hand to his heart he will be dipping the other hand into your pocket."

The lover of proverbs, for his part, unbuttoned his jacket, thrust his hands under his coat-tails, and said in a loud voice:

" There is a saying that you can trust any wild beast, such as a fox or a hedgehog or a toad, but not——"

" Quite so, dear sir. The common folk are exceedingly degenerate."

" Well, they are not developing as they ought to do."

" No, they are over-cramped," was the big peasant's rasped-out comment. " They have no room for *growth*."

" Yes, they *do* grow, but only as regards beard and moustache, as a tree grows to branch and sap."

With a glance at the purveyor of proverbs the old man

149

assented by remarking: "Yes, true it is that the common folk are cramped." Whereafter he thrust a pinch of snuff into his nostrils, and threw back his head in anticipation of the sneeze which failed to come. At length, drawing a deep breath through his parted lips, he said as he measured the peasant again with his eyes:

"My friend, you are of a sort calculated to last."

In answer the peasant nodded.

"*Some* day," he remarked, "we shall get what we want."

In front of us, now, was Kazan, with the pinnacles of its churches and mosques piercing the blue sky, and looking like garlands of exotic blooms. Around them lay the grey wall of the Kremlin, and above them soared the grim Tower of Sumbek.

Here one and all were due to disembark.

I glanced towards the stern once more. The dark-browed woman was breaking off morsels from a wheaten scone that was lying in her lap, and saying as she did so:

"Presently we will have a cup of tea, and then keep together as far as Christopol."

In response the young fellow edged nearer to her, and thoughtfully eyed the large hands which, though inured to hard work, could also be very gentle.

"I have been trodden upon," he said.

"Trodden upon by whom?"

"By all. And I am afraid of them."

"Why so?"

"Because I am."

Breathing upon a morsel of the scone, the woman offered it him with the quiet words:

"You have had much to bear. Now, shall I tell you my history, or shall we first have tea?"

*

On the bank there was now to be seen the frontage of the gay, wealthy suburb of Uslon, with its brightly-dressed, rainbow-tinted women and girls tripping through the streets, and the water of its foaming river sparkling hotly, yet dimly, in the sunlight.

It was a scene like a scene beheld in a vision.

A WOMAN

THE wind is scudding over the steppe, and beating upon the rampart of the Caucasian heights until their backbone seems to be bellying like a huge sail, and the earth to be whirling and whizzing through unfathomable depths of blue, and leaving behind it a rack of wind-torn clouds which, as their shadows glide over the surface of the land, seem ever to be striving to keep in touch with the onrush of the gale, and, failing to maintain the effort, dissolving in tears and despondency.

The trees too are bending in the attitude of flight—their boughs are brandishing their foliage as a dog worries a fleece, and littering the black soil with leaves among which runs a constant, querulous hissing and rustling. Also, storks are uttering their snapping cry, sleek rooks cawing, steppe grass-hoppers maintaining their tireless chirp, sturdy, well-grown husbandmen uttering shouts like words of command, the threshing-floors of the rolling steppe diffusing a rain of golden chaff, and eddying whirlwinds catching up stray poultry feathers, dried onion-strips, and leaves yellowed with the heat, to send them dancing again over the trim square of the little Cossack hamlet.

Similarly does the sun keep appearing and disappearing as though he were pursuing the fugitive earth, and ever and anon halting through weariness before his decline into the dark, shadowy vista where the snowclad peaks of the western mountains are rearing their heads, and fast-reddening clouds are reminding one of the surface of a ploughed field.

At times those clouds part their bulk to reveal in blinding splendour the silvery saddle of Mount Elburz, and the crystal fangs of other peaks—all, apparently, striving to catch and detain the scudding vapours. And to such a point does one come to realise the earth's flight through space that one can scarcely draw one's breath for the tension, the rapture, of the thought that with the rush of that dear and beautiful earth oneself is keeping pace towards, and ever tending towards, the region where, behind the eternal, snow-clad peaks, there lies a boundless ocean of blue—an ocean beside which there may lie

153

stretched yet other proud and marvellous lands, a void of azure amid which one may come to descry far-distant, many-tinted spheres of planets as yet unknown, but sisters, all, to this earth of ours.

Meanwhile from the steppe slow, ponderous grey oxen with sharp horns are drawing an endless succession of waggon-loads of threshed grain through rich, black, sootlike dust. Patiently the beasts' round eyes regard the earth, while on the top of each load there lolls a Cossack who, with face sunburnt to the last pitch of swarthiness, and eyes reddened with exposure to the wind, and beard matted, seemingly solidified, with dust and sweat, is clad in a shirt drab with grime, and has a shaggy Persian cap thrust to the back of his head. Occasionally, also, he may be seen riding on the pole in front of his team, and being buffeted from behind by the wind which inflates his shirt. And as sleek and comfortable as the carcasses of the bullocks are these Cossacks' frames—in proportion their eyes are sluggishly intelligent, and in their every movement is the deliberate air of men who know precisely what they have to do.

" *Tsob, tsobé !* " such fellows shout to their teams. This year they are reaping a splendid harvest.

Yet though these folk, one and all, look fat and prosperous, their mien is dour, and they speak reluctantly, and through their teeth. Possibly this is because they are over-weary with toil. However that may be, the full-fed country people of the region laugh but little, and seldom sing.

In the centre of the hamlet soars the red brick church of the place—an edifice which, with its five pinnacles, its belfry over its porch, and its yellow plaster window-mouldings, looks like an edifice that has been fashioned of meat, and cemented with grease. Nay, its very shadow seems so richly heavy as to be the shadow of a fane erected by men endowed with a plethora of this world's goods to a god otiose in his grandeur. Ranged around the building in ring fashion, the hamlet's squat white huts stand girdled with belts of plaited wattle, shawled in the gorgeous silken scarves of gardens, and crowned with a flowered brocade-work of reed-thatched roofs. In fact, they resemble a bevy of buxom *babi*,[1] as over and about them wave silver poplar trees, with quivering, lacelike leaves of acacias, and dark-leaved chestnuts (the leaves of the latter like the palms of human hands) which rock to and fro as though they would fain seize and detain the driving clouds. Also, from court to

[1] Peasant women.

154

court scurry Cossack women who, with skirt-tails tucked up to
reveal muscular legs bare to the knee, are preparing to array
themselves for the morrow's festival, and, meanwhile, chattering
to one another, or shouting to plump infants which may be
seen bathing in the dust like sparrows, or picking up handfuls
of sand, and tossing them into the air.

Sheltered from the wind by the churchyard wall, there may
be seen also, as they sprawl on the dry, faded herbage, a score
of " strollers for work "—that is to say, of folk who, a com-
munity apart, consist of " nowhere people," of dreamers who
live constantly in expectation of some stroke of luck, some
kindly smile from fortune, and of wastrels who, intoxicated with
the abundant bounty of the opulent region, have fallen passive
victims to the Russian craze for vagrancy. These folk tramp
from hamlet to hamlet in parties of two or three, and, while
purporting to seek employment, merely contemplate that employment lethargically, express astonishment at the plenitude
which it produces, and then decline to put their hands to toil
save when dire necessity renders it no longer possible to satisfy
hunger's pangs through the expedients of mendicancy and theft.
Dull, or cowed, or timid, or furtive of eye, these folk have lost
all sense of the difference between that which constitutes honesty
and that which does not.

The morrow being the Feast of the Assumption, these people
have, in the present instance, gathered from every quarter of
the country, for the reason that they hope to be provided
with food and drink without first being made to earn their
entertainment.

For the most part they are Russians from the central provinces
—vagabonds whose faces are blackened, and heads blanched,
with the unaccustomed sunshine of the South, but whose bodies
are clad merely in rags tossed and tumbled by the wind. True,
the wearers of those rags declare themselves to be peaceful,
respectable citizens whom toil and life's buffetings have exhausted, and compelled to seek temporary rest and prayer;
yet never does a creaking, groaning, ponderous grain waggon,
with its Cossack driver, pass them by without their according
the latter a humble, obsequious salute as, with straw in mouth,
and omitting, always, to raise his cap, the man glances at them
askance and with contempt, or, more frequently, does not even
descry these tattered, grimy hulks between whom and himself
there is absolutely nothing in common.

Lower even, and more noticeably, more pretentiously, than

the rest does a certain "needy" native of Tula named Konev salute each Cossack. A hardbitten *muzhik* as sunburnt as a stick of ergot, he has a black beard distributed irregularly over a lean face, a fawning smile, and eyes deep-sunken in their sockets.

Most of these persons I have met for the first time to-day; but Konev is an old acquaintance of mine, for he and I have more than once encountered one another on the road between Kursk and the province of Ter. An "artelni," that is to say, a member of a workman's union, he cultivates his fellows' good graces for the reason that he is also an arrant coward, and accustomed, everywhere save in his own village (which lies buried among the sands of Alexin), to assert that:

"Certainly, this countryside is rich, yet I cannot hit things off with its inhabitants. In my own part of the country folk are more spiritual, more truly Russian, by far than here—they are folk with whom the natives of this region are not to be compared, since in the one locality the population has a human soul, whereas in the other locality it is a flint-stone."

And with a certain quiet reflectiveness he loves also to recount a marvellous example of unlooked-for enrichment. He will say to you:

"Maybe you do not believe in the virtue of horseshoes? Yet *I* tell *you* that once, when a certain peasant of Efremov found a horseshoe, the next three weeks saw it befall that that peasant's uncle, a tradesman of Efremov, was burnt to death with all his family, and the property devolved to the peasant. Did you ever hear of such a thing? What is going to happen *cannot* be foretold, for at any moment fortune may pity a man, and send him a windfall."

As Konev says this his dark, pointed eyebrows will go shooting up his forehead, and his eyes come protruding out of their sockets, as though he himself cannot believe what he has just related.

Again, should a Cossack pass him without returning his salute, he will mutter as he follows the man with his eyes:

"An overfed fellow, that—a fellow who can't even look at a human being! The souls of these folk, I tell you, are *withered.*"

On the present occasion he has arrived on the scene in company with two women. One of them, aged about twenty, is gentle-looking, plump, and glassy of eye, with a mouth perpetually half-open, so that the face looks like that of an imbecile: and though the exposed teeth of its lower portion may seem to be set in a smile, you will perceive, should you peer into the motionless eyes under the overhanging brows, that she has recently been weeping in the terrified, hysterical fashion of a person of weak intellect.

" I have come here with that man and other strangers "—thus I heard her narrate in low, querulous tones as with a stumpy finger she rearranged the faded hair under her yellow and green scarf.

A fat-faced youth with high cheek-bones and the small eyes of a Mongol here nudged her, and said carelessly:

" You mean, rather, that your own man has cast you off. Probably he was the only man you ever saw."

" Aye," Konev drawled thoughtfully as he felt in his wallet. " Nowadays folk need think little of deserting a woman, since in this year of grace women are no good at all."

Upon this the woman frowned—then blinked her eyes timidly, and would have opened her lips to reply but that her companion interrupted her by saying in a brisk, incisive tone:

" Do not listen to those rascals ! "

*

The woman's companion, some five or six years her senior, has a face exceptional in the constant change and movement of its great dark eyes as at one moment they withdraw themselves from the street of the Cossack hamlet, to gaze fixedly and gravely towards the steppe where it lies scoured with the scudding breeze, and at another moment fall to scanning the faces of the persons around her, and, at another, frown anxiously, or send a smile flitting across her comely lips as she bends her head until her features are concealed. Next, the head is raised again, for the eyes have taken on another phase, and become dilated with interest, while a sharp furrow is forming between the slender eyebrows, and the finely moulded lips and trim mouth have compressed themselves together, and the thin nostrils of the straight nose are snuffing the air like those of a horse.

In fact, in the woman there is something non-peasant in its origin. For instance, let one but watch her sharply clicking feet as, in walking, they peep from under her blue skirt, and one will perceive that they are not the splayed feet of a villager, but, rather, feet arched of instep, and at one time accustomed to the wearing of boots. Or as the woman sits engaged in embroidering a blue bodice with a pattern of white peas, one will perceive that she has long been accustomed to plying the needle, so dexterously, swiftly do the small, sunburnt hands fly in and out under the tumbled material, eagerly though the wind may strive to wrest it from her. Again, as she sits bending over her work, one will descry through a rent in her bodice a small, firm bosom which might almost have been that of a virgin, were it not for the fact that a projecting teat proclaims that she is a woman preparing to suckle an infant. In short, as she sits among her companions she looks like a fragment of copper flung into the midst of some rusty old scrap-iron.

Most of the people in whose society I wander neither rise to great heights nor sink to great depths, but are as colourless as dust, and wearisomely insignificant. Hence is it that whenever I chance upon a person whose soul I can probe and explore for thoughts unfamiliar to me and words not hitherto heard I congratulate myself, seeing that though it is my desire to see life grow more fair and exalted, and I yearn to bring about that end, there constantly reveals itself to me merely a vista of sharp angles and dark spaces and poor crushed, defrauded people. Yes, never do I seek to project a spark of my own fire into the darkness of my neighbour's soul but I see that spark disappear, become lost, in a chaos of dumb vacuity.

Hence the woman of whom I have just spoken particularly excites my fancy, and leads me to attempt divinations of her past, until I find myself evolving a story which is not only of vast complexity, but has got painted into it merely the colours of my own hopes and aspirations. It is a story necessarily illusory, necessarily bound to make life seem even worse than before. Yet it is a grievous thing *never* to distort actuality, *never* to envelop actuality in the wrappings of one's imagination. . . .

Closing his eyes, and picking his words with difficulty, a tall, fair peasant drawls in thick, gluelike tones:

" ' Very well,' I said: and off we set. On the way I said again: ' Gubin, though you may not like to be told so, you are no better than a thief.' "

The o's uttered by this peasant are uniformly round and firm—they roll forward as a cart-wheel trundles along a hot, dusty country road.

The youth with the high cheek-bones fixes the whites of his porcine eyes (eyes the pupils of which are as indeterminate as the eyes of a blind man) upon the woman in the green scarf. Then, having, like a calf, plucked and chewed some stalks of

the withered grass, he rolls up the sleeves of his shirt, bends
one fist into the crook of the elbow, and says to Konev with
a glance at the well-developed muscle:

" Should you care to hit me? "

" No, you can hit yourself. Hit yourself over the head.
Then, perhaps, you'll grow wiser."

Stolidly the young fellow looks at Konev, and inquires:

" How do you know me to be a fool? "

" Because your personality tells me so."

" Eh? " cries the young fellow truculently as he raises himself to a kneeling posture. " How know you *what* I am? "

" I have been told what you are by the Governor of your
province."

The young fellow opens his mouth, and stares at Konev.
Then he asks:

" To what, province do I belong? "

" If you yourself have forgotten to what province you belong,
you had better try and loosen your wits."

" Look here. If I were to hit you, I——"

The woman who has been sewing drops her work to shrug
one rounded shoulder as though she were cold, and ask con-
ciliatorily:

" Well, *what* province do you belong to? "

" I? " the young fellow re-echoes as he subsides on to his
heels. " I belong to Penza. Why do you ask? "

" Oh, never mind why."

Presently, with a strangely youthful laugh, the woman adds
in a murmur:

" I ask because I too belong to that province."

" And to which canton? "

" To that of Penza." In the woman's tone is a touch of
pride.

The young fellow squats down before her, as before a wood
fire, stretches out his hands, and says in an ingratiating voice:

" What a fine place is our cantonal town! What churches
and shops and stone houses there are in it! In fact, one shop
sells a machine on which you can play anything you like, any
sort of a tune! "

" As well as, probably, the fool," comments Konev in an
undertone, though the young fellow is too enthralled with the
memory of the amenities of his cantonal capital to notice the
remark. Next, smacking his lips, and chewing his words, he
continues in a murmur:

" In those stone houses——"

Here the woman drops her sewing a second time to inquire:
" Is there a convent there? "

" A convent? "

And the young fellow pauses uncouthly to scratch his neck.
Only after a while does he answer:

" A convent? Well, I do not know, for only once, to tell
the truth, have I been in the town, and that was when some
of us famine folk were set to a job of roadmaking."

" Well, well! " gasps Konev as he rises and takes his departure.

The vagabonds, huddled against the churchyard wall, look
like litter driven thither by the steppe wind, and as liable to
be whirled away again whenever the wind shall choose. Three
of the party are sleeping, and the remainder either mending
their clothing, or killing fleas, or lethargically munching bread
collected at the windows of the Cossacks' huts. I find the sight
of them weary me as much as does the young fellow's fatuous
babble. Also, I find that whenever the elder of the two
women lifts her eyes from her work, and half smiles, the faint
half-smile in question vexes me intensely. Consequently I end
by departing in Konev's wake.

Guarding the entrance of the churchyard, four poplar trees
stand erect save when, as the wind harries them, they bow
alternately to the arid, dusty earth and towards the dim vista
of tow-coloured steppe and snowcapped mountain peaks. Yet
oh, how that steppe, bathed in golden sunshine, draws one to
itself and its smooth desolation of sweet, dry grasses as the
parched, fragrant expanse rustles under the soughing wind!

" You ask about that woman, eh? " queries Konev, whom
I find leaning against one of the poplar trunks, and embracing
it with an arm.

" Yes. From where does she hail? "

" From Riazan, she says. Another story of hers is that her
name is Tatiana."

" Has she been with you long? "

" No. In fact, it was only this morning, some thirty *versts*
from here, that I overtook her and her companion. However, I have seen her before, at Maikop-on-Laba, during the
season of hay harvest, when she had with her an elderly, smooth-
faced *muzhik* who *might* have been a soldier, and *certainly* was
either her lover or an uncle, as well as a bully and a drunkard
of the type which, before it has been two days in a place, starts
about as many brawls. At present, however, she is tramping with

none but this female companion, for, after that the ' uncle ' had drunk away his very belly-band and reins, he was clapped in gaol. The Cossack, you know, is an awkward person to deal with."

Although Kanev speaks without constraint, his eyes are fixed upon the ground in a manner suggestive of some disturbing thought. And as the breeze ruffles his dishevelled beard and ragged pea-jacket it ends by robbing his head of his cap, of the tattered, peakless clout which, with rents in its lining, so closely resembles a *tchepchik* [1] as to communicate to the picturesque features of its wearer an appearance comically feminine.

" Ye-es," expectorating, and drawling the words between his teeth, he continues. " She is a remarkable woman, a regular, so to speak, high-stepper. Yet it must have been the Devil himself that blew this young oaf with the bloated jowl on to the scene. Otherwise I should soon have fixed up matters with her. The cur that he is ! "

" But once you told me that you had a wife already? "

Darting at me an angry glance, he turns away with a mutter of :

" *Am* I to carry my wife about with me in my wallet? "

Here there comes limping across the square a moustachioed Cossack. In one hand he is holding a bunch of keys, and in the other hand a battered Cossack cap, peak in front. Behind him, sobbing and applying his knuckles to his eyes, there is creeping a curly-headed urchin of eight, while the rear is brought up by a shaggy dog whose dejected countenance and lowered tail would seem to show that he too is in disgrace. Each time that the boy whimpers more loudly than usual the Cossack halts, awaits the lad's coming in silence, cuffs him over the head with the peak of the cap, and, resuming his way with the gait of a drunken man, leaves the boy and the dog standing where they are—the boy lamenting, and the dog wagging its tail as its old black muzzle sniffs the air. Somehow I discern in the dog's mien of holding itself prepared for anything that may turn up a certain resemblance to Konev's bearing, save that the dog is older in appearance than is the vagabond.

" You mentioned my wife, I think? " presently he resumes with a sigh. " Yes, I know, but not *every* malady proves mortal, and I have been married nineteen years ! "

The rest is well-known to me, for all too frequently have I heard it and similar tales. Unfortunately, I cannot now take the trouble to stop him; so once more I am forced to let his complaints come oozing tediously into my ears.

[1] Woman's mob cap.

"The wench was plump," says Konev, "and panting for love; so we just got married, and brats began to come tumbling from her like bugs from a bunk."

Subsiding a little, the breeze takes, as it were, to whispering.

"In fact, I could scarcely turn round for them. Even now seven of them are alive, though originally the stud numbered thirteen. And what was the use of such a gang? For, consider. My wife is forty-two, and I am forty-three. *She* is elderly, and *I* am what you behold. True, hitherto I have contrived to keep up my spirits; yet poverty is wearing me down, and when, last winter, my old woman went to pieces I set forth (for what else could I do?) to tour the towns. In fact, folk like you and myself have only one job available—the job of licking one's chops, and keeping one's eyes open. Yet, to tell you the truth, I no sooner perceive myself to be growing superfluous in a place than I spit upon that place, and clear out of it."

Never to this sturdy, inveterate rascal does it seem to occur to insinuate that he has been doing work of any kind, or that he in the least cares to do any: while at the same time all self-pity is eschewed in his narrative, and he relates his experiences much as though they are the experiences of another man, and not of himself.

Presently, as the Cossack and the boy draw level with us, the former, fingering his moustache, inquires thickly:

"Whence are you come?"

"From Russia."

"All such folk come from there."

Thereafter, with a gesture of disdain, this man of the abnormally broad nose, eyes floating in fat, and flaxen head shaped like a flounder's, resumes his way towards the porch of the church. As for the boy, he wipes his nose, and follows him, while the dog sniffs at our legs, yawns, and stretches itself by the churchyard wall.

"Did you see?" mutters Konev. "Oh yes, I tell you that the folk here are far less amiable than our own folk in Russia. . . . But hark! What is that?"

To our ears there have come from behind the corner of the churchyard wall a woman's scream and the sound of dull blows. Rushing thither, we behold the fair-headed peasant seated on the prostrate form of the young fellow from Penza, and methodically, gruntingly delivering blow after blow upon the young fellow's ears with his ponderous fists, while counting the blows as he does so. Vainly, at the same time, the woman from

Riazan is prodding the assailant in the back, whilst her female companion is shrieking, and the crowd at large has leapt to its feet, and, collected into a knot, is shouting gleefully, " *That's* the way! *That's* the way!"

"Five!" the fair-headed peasant counts.

"Why are you doing this?" the prostrate man protests.

"Six!"

"Oh dear!" ejaculates Konev, dancing with nervousness. "Oh dear, oh dear!"

The smacking, smashing blows fall in regular cadence as, prone on his face, the young fellow kicks, struggles, and puffs up the dust. Meanwhile a tall, dour man in a straw hat is rolling up a shirt-sleeve, and alternately bending and stretching a long arm, whilst a lithe, white-headed young stripling is hopping, sparrow-like, from one onlooker to another, and exclaiming in suppressed, cautious tones:

"Stop it, pray stop it, or we shall be arrested for creating a disturbance!"

Presently the tall man strides towards the fair-headed peasant, deals him a single blow which knocks him from the back of the young fellow, and, turning to the crowd, says with an informing air:

" *That's* how we do it in Tambov."

"Brutes! Villains!" screams the woman from Riazan as she bends over the young fellow. Her cheeks are livid, and as she wipes the flushed face of the beaten youth with the hem of her gown her dark eyes are flashing with dry wrath, and her lips quivering so painfully as to disclose a set of fine, level teeth.

Konev, pecking up to her, says with an air of advice:

"You had better take him away, and give him some water."

Upon this the fair-headed *muzhik*, rising to his knees, stretches a fist towards the man from Tambov, and exclaims:

"Why should he have gone and bragged of his strength, pray?"

"Was that a good reason for thrashing him?"

"And who are *you*?"

"Who am *I*?"

"Yes, who are *you*?"

"Never mind. See that I don't give you another swipe!"

Upon this the onlookers plunge into a heated debate as to who was actually the beginner of the disturbance, while the lithe young fellow continues to wring his hands, and cry imploringly:

"*Don't* make so much noise about it! Remember that we are in a strange land, and that the folk hereabouts are strict."

So queerly do his ears project from his head that he would seem to be able, if he pleased, to fold them right over his eyes.

Suddenly from the roseate heavens comes the vibrant note of a bell; whereupon the hubbub ceases, and at the same moment a young Cossack with a face studded with freckles, and, in his hands, a cudgel, makes his appearance among the crowd.

"What does all this mean?" he inquires not uncivilly.

"They have been beating a man," the woman from Riazan replies. As she does so she looks comely in spite of her wrath.

The Cossack glances at her—then smiles.

"And where is the party going to sleep?" he inquires of the crowd.

"Here," someone ventures.

"Then you must not—someone might break into the church. Go, rather, to the Ataman,[1] and you will be billeted among the huts."

"It is a matter of no consequence," Konev remarks as he paces beside me. "Yet——"

"They seem to be taking us for robbers," is my interruption.

"As is everywhere the way," he comments. "It is but one thing more laid to our charge. Caution decides always that a stranger is a thief."

In front of us walks the woman from Riazan, in company with the young fellow of the bloated features. He is downcast of mien, and at length mutters something which I cannot catch, but in answer to which she tosses her head, and says in a distinct, maternal tone:

"You are too young to associate with such brutes."

The bell of the church is slowly beating, and from the huts there keep coming neat old men and women who make the hitherto deserted street assume a brisk appearance, and the squat huts take on a welcoming air.

In a resonant, girlish voice there meets our ears:

"Ma-am! Ma-amka! Where is the key of the green box? I want my ribands!"

While in answer to the bell's summons the oxen low a deep echo.

The wind has fallen, but reddish clouds still are gliding over the hamlet, and the mountain peaks blushing until they seem,

[1] Cossack headman or mayor.

thawing, to be sending streams of golden, liquid fire on to the steppes, where, as though cast in stone, a stork, standing on one leg, is listening, seemingly, to the rustling of the heat-exhausted herbage.

*

In the forecourt of the Ataman's hut we are deprived of our passports, while two of our number, found to be without such documents, are led away to a night's lodging in a dark store-house in a corner of the premises. Everything is executed quietly enough, and without the least fuss, purely as a matter of routine; yet Konev mutters, as dejectedly he contemplates the darkening sky:

" What a surprising thing, to be sure ! "

" What is ? "

" A passport. Surely a decent, peaceable man ought to be able to travel *without* a passport? So long as he be harmless, let him——"

" *You* are not harmless," with angry emphasis the woman from Riazan interposes.

Konev closes his eyes with a smile, and says nothing more.

Almost until the vigil service is over are we kept kicking our heels about that forecourt, like sheep in a slaughter-house. Then Konev, myself, the two women, and the fat-faced young fellow are led away towards the outskirts of the village, and allotted an empty hut with broken-down walls and a cracked window.

" No going out will be permitted," says the Cossack who has conducted us thither. " Else you will be arrested."

" Then give us a morsel of bread," Konev says with a stammer.

" Have you done any work here? " the Cossack inquires.

" Yes—a little."

" For me? "

" No. It did not so happen."

" When it does so happen I will give you some bread."

And like a water-butt the fat, kindly-looking man goes rolling out of the yard.

" What else was to be expected? " grumbles Konev with his eyebrows elevated to the middle of his forehead. " The folk hereabouts are knaves. Ah, well ! "

As for the women, they withdraw to the darkest corner of the hut, and lie down, while the young fellow disappears after probing the walls and floor, and returns with an armful of straw which he strews upon the hard, beaten clay. Then he stretches himself thereon with hands clasped behind his battered head.

165

" See the resourcefulness of that fellow from Penza! " comments Konev enviously. " Hi, you women! There is, it would seem, some straw about."

To this comes from the women's corner the acid reply:

" Then go and fetch some."

" For you? "

" Yes, for us."

" Then I must, I suppose."

Nevertheless Konev merely remains sitting on the window-sill, and discoursing on the subject of certain needy folk who do but desire to go and say their prayers in church, yet are banded into barns.

" Yes, and though you may say that folk, the world over, have a soul in common, *I* tell *you* that this is not so—that, on the contrary, we Russian strangers find it a hard matter here to get looked upon as respectable."

With which he slips out quietly into the street, and disappears from view.

The young fellow's sleep is restless—he keeps tossing about, with his fat arms and legs sprawling over the floor, and grunting, and snoring. Under him the straw makes a crackling sound, while the two women whisper together in the darkness, and the reeds of the dry thatch on the roof rustle (the wind is still drawing an occasional breath), and ever and anon a twig brushes against an outside wall. The scene is like a scene in a dream.

Out of doors the myriad tongues of the pitch-black, starless night seem to be debating something in soft, sad, pitiful tones which ever keep growing fainter: until when the hour of ten has been struck on the watchman's gong, and the metal ceases to vibrate, the world grows quieter still, much as though all living things, alarmed by the clang in the night, have concealed themselves in the invisible earth or the equally invisible heavens.

I seat myself by the window, and watch how the earth keeps exhaling darkness, and the darkness enveloping, drowning the grey, blurred huts in black, tepid vapour, though the church remains invisible—evidently something stands interposed between it and my viewpoint. And it seems to me that the wind, the seraph of many pinions which has spent three days in harrying the land, must now have whirled the earth into a blackness, a denseness, in which, exhausted, and panting, and scarcely moving, it is helplessly striving to remain within the encompassing, all-pervading obscurity where, helpless and weary in like degree, the wind has sloughed its thousands of wing-feathers—feathers white and blue and golden of tint, but also broken, and smeared with dust and blood.

And as I think of our petty, grievous human life, as of a drunkard's tune on a sorry musical instrument, or as of a beautiful song spoilt by a witless, voiceless singer, there begins to wail in my soul an insatiable longing to breathe forth words of sympathy with all mankind, words of burning love for all the world, words of appreciation of, for example, the sun's beauty as, enfolding the earth in his beams, and caressing and fertilising her, he bears her through the expanses of blue. Yes, I yearn to recite to my fellow-men words which shall raise their heads. And at length I find myself compounding the following jejune lines:

> To our land we all are born
> In happiness to dwell.
> The sun has bred us to this land
> Its fairness to excel.
> In the temple of the sun
> We high priests are, divine.
> Then each of us should claim his life,
> And cry, " This life is mine! "

Meanwhile from the women's corner there comes a soft, intermittent whispering: and as it continues to filter through the darkness I strain my ears until I succeed in catching a few of the words uttered, and can distinguish at least the voices of the whisperers.

The woman from Riazan mutters firmly, and with assurance:

" Never ought you to show that it hurts you."

And with a sniff, in a tone of dubious acquiescence, her companion replies:

" Ye-es—so long as one can bear it."

" Ah, but never mind. *Pretend*. That is to say, when he beats you, make light of it, and treat it as a joke."

" But what if he beats me very much indeed? "

" Continue still to make light of it, still to smile at him kindly."

" Well, *you* can never have been beaten, for you do not seem to know what it is like."

" Oh, but I have, my dear—I *do* know what it is like, for my experience of it has been large. Do not be afraid, however. *He* won't beat you."

A dog yelps, pauses a moment to listen, and then barks more angrily than ever. Upon that other dogs reply, and for a moment or two I am annoyed to find that I cannot overhear the women's conversation. In time, however, the dogs cease their uproar, for want of breath, and the suppressed dialogue filters once more to my ears.

" Never forget, my dear, that a *muzhik's* life is a hard one. Yes, for us plain folk life is hard. Hence one ought to make nothing of things, and let them come easy to one."

" Mother of God ! "

" And particularly should a woman so face things; for upon her everything depends. For one thing, let her take to herself, in place of her mother, a husband or a sweetheart. Yes, try that, and see. And though, at first, your husband may find fault with you, he will afterwards take to boasting to other *muzhiks* that he has a wife who can do everything, and remain ever as bright and loving as the month of May. ' Never does she give in; never *would* she give in—no, not if you were to cut off her head ! ' "

" Indeed ? "

" Yes. And see if that will not come to be your opinion as much as mine."

Again, to my annoyance, the dialogue is interrupted—this time by the sound of uncertain footsteps in the street without. Thus the next words of the women's conversation escape me. Then I hear:

" Have you ever read ' The Vision of the Mother of God '? "

" N-no, I have not."

" Then you had better ask some older woman than myself to tell you about it, for it is a good book to become acquainted with. Can you read ? "

" No, I cannot. But tell me, *yourself*, what the vision was? "

" Listen, and I will do so." ·

From outside the window Konev's voice softly inquires:

" Is that our lot in there? Yes? Thank God, then, for I had nearly lost my way, after stirring up a lot of dogs, and being forced to use my fists upon them. Here, you! Catch hold! "

With which, handing me a large water-melon, he clambers through the window with a great clattering and disturbance.

" I have managed also to get a good supply of bread," he continues. " Perhaps you believe that I stole it? But no. Indeed, *why* should one steal when one can beg—a game at which I am particularly an old hand, seeing that always, on any occasion, I can make up to people? It happened like this. When I went out I saw a fire glowing in a hut, and folk seated at supper. And since, wherever many people are present, *one* of them at least has a kind heart, I ate and drank my fill, and then managed to make off with provender for you as well. Hi, you women!"

There follows no answer.

"I believe those daughters of whores must be asleep," he comments. "Hi, women!"

"What is it?" drily inquires the woman from Riazan.

"Should you like a taste of water-melon?"

"I should, thank you."

Thereupon Konev begins to make his way towards the voice.

"Yes, bread, soft wheaten bread such as you——"

Here the other woman whines in beggar fashion:

"And give *me* a taste, too."

"Oh, yes, I will. But where the devil are you?"

"And a taste of melon as well?"

"Yes, certainly. Hullo! Who is this?"

From the woman from Riazan comes a cry of pain.

"Mind how you step, wretch!" she exclaims.

"All right, but you needn't make so much noise about it. You see how dark it is, and I——"

"You ought to have struck a match, then."

"I possess but a quarter of a match, for matches are not over-plentiful, and even if I did catch hold of you no great harm can have been done. For instance, when your husband used to beat you he must have hurt you far worse than I. By the way, *did* he beat you?"

"What business is that of yours?"

"None; only, I am curious to know. Surely a woman like you——"

"See here. Do not dare to touch me, or I——"

"Or you what?"

There ensues a prolonged altercation amid which I can hear epithets of increasing acerbity and opprobrium being applied; until the woman from Riazan exclaims hoarsely:

"Oh, you coward of a man, take that!"

Whereupon follows a scrimmage amid which I can distinguish slappings, gross chuckles from Konev, and a muffled cry from the younger woman of:

"Oh, do not so behave, you wretch!"

Striking a match, I approach the spot, and pull Konev away. He is in no way abashed, but merely cooled in his ardour as, seated on the floor at my feet, and panting and expectorating, he says reprovingly to the woman:

169

" When folk wish merely to have a game with you, you ought not to let yourself lose your temper. Fie, fie! "

" Are you hurt? " the woman inquires quietly.

" What do you suppose? You have cut my lip, but that is the worst damage."

" Then if you come here again I will lay the whole of your face open."

" Vixen! What bumpkinish stupidity! "

Konev turns to myself.

" And as for you, you go catching at the first thing you find, and have torn my coat."

" Then do not insult people.

" *Insult* people, fool? The idea of anyone insulting a woman like *that*! "

Whereafter, with a mean chuckle, the fellow goes on to discourse upon the ease with which peasant women err, and upon their love of deceiving their husbands.

" The impudent rascal! " comments the woman from Penza sleepily.

After a while the young fellow springs to his feet, and grates his teeth. Then, reseating himself, and clutching at his head, he says gloomily:

" I intend to leave here to-morrow, and go home. I do not care *what* becomes of me."

With which he subsides on to the floor as though exhausted.

" The blockhead! " is Konev's remark.

Amid the darkness a black shape rises. It does so as soundlessly as a fish in a pond, glides to the door, and disappears.

" That was she," remarks Konev. " What a strong woman! However, if you had not pulled me away, I should have got the better of her. By God I should! "

" Then follow her, and make another attempt."

" No," after a moment's reflection he rejoins. " Out there she might get hold of a stick, or a brick, or some such thing. However, *I'll* get even with her. As a matter of fact, you wasted your time in stopping me, for she detests me like the very devil."

And he renews his wearisome boastings of his conquests: until suddenly he stops as though he has swallowed his tongue.

All becomes quiet; everything seems to have come to a halt, and to be pressing close in sleep to the motionless earth. I too grow drowsy, and have a vision amid which my mind returns to the donations which I have received that day, and sees them swell and multiply and increase in weight until I feel their bulk pressing upon me like a tumulus of the steppes. Next, the coppery notes of a bell jar in my ears, and, struck at random intervals, go floating away into the darkness.

It is the hour of midnight.

Soon scattered drops of rain begin to patter down upon the dry thatch of the hut and the dust in the street outside, while a cricket continues chirping, as though it were hurriedly relating a tale. Also, I hear filtering forth into the darkness a softly gulped, eager whispering.

" Think," says one of the voices, " what it must mean to have to go tramping about without work, or only with work for another to do! "

The young fellow who has been so soundly thrashed replies in a dull voice:

" I know nothing of you."

" More softly, more softly! " urges the woman.

" What is it you want? "

" I want *nothing*. It is merely that I am sorry for you as a man yet young and strong. You see—well, I have not lived with my eyes shut. That is why I say, come with me."

" But come whither? "

" To the coast, where I know there to be beautiful plots of land for the asking. You yourself can see how good the land hereabout is. Well, *there* land better still is to be obtained."

" Liar! "

" More softly, more softly! " again urges the woman. " Moreover, I am not bad-looking, and can manage things well, and do any sort of work. Hence you and I might live quite peacefully and happily, and come, eventually, to have a place of our own. Yes, and I could bear and rear you a child. Only see how fit I am. Only feel this breast of mine."

The young fellow snorts, and I begin to find the situation oppressive, and to long to let the couple know that I am *not* asleep. Curiosity, however, prevents me, and I continue listening to the strange, arresting dialogue.

" Wait a little," whispers the woman with a gasp. " Do not play with me, for I am not that sort of woman. Yes, I mean what I say. Let be! "

Rudely, roughly the young fellow replies:

" Then don't run after me. A woman who runs after a man, and plays the whore with him, is——"

" Less noise, please—less noise, I beg of you, or we shall be heard, and I shall be put to shame! "

" Doesn't it put you to shame to be offering yourself to me like this? "

A silence ensues, save that the young fellow goes on snorting and fidgeting, and the raindrops continue to fall with the same reluctance, the same indolence, as ever. Then once more the woman's voice is heard through the pattering.

" Perhaps," says the voice, " you have guessed that I am seeking a husband? Yes, I *am* seeking one—a good, steady *muzhik*."

" But I am *not* a good, steady *muzhik*."

" Fie, fie! "

" What? " he sniggers. " A husband for *you*? The impudence of you! A ' husband '! Go along! "

" Listen to me. I am tired of tramping."

" Then go home."

This time there ensues a long pause. Then the woman says very softly:

" I have neither home nor kindred."

" A lie! " ejaculates the young fellow.

" No, by God it is not a lie! The Mother of God forget me if it is! "

In these last words I can detect the note of tears. By this time the situation has become intolerable, for I am yearning to rise and kick the young fellow out of the hut, and then to have a long and earnest talk with his companion. " Oh that I could take her to my arms," I reflect, " and cherish her as I would a poor lost child! "

After a while the sounds of a new struggle between the pair are heard.

" Don't put me off like that! " growls the young fellow.

" And don't you make any attempt upon me! I am not the sort of woman to be forced."

The next moment there arises a cry of pain and astonishment.

" What was that for? What was that for? " the woman wails.

With an answering exclamation I spring to my feet, for my feelings have become those of a wild beast.

At once everything grows quiet again, save that someone crawls over the floor and, in leaving the hut, jars the latch of the crazy, single-hinged portal.

" It was not my fault," grumbles the young fellow. " It all

came of that stinking woman offering herself to me. Besides, the place is full of bugs, and I cannot sleep."

" Beast! " pants someone in the vicinity.

" Hold your tongue, bitch! " is the fellow's retort.

By now the rain has ceased, and such air as filters through the window seems increasedly stifling. Momentarily the hush grows deeper, until the breast feels filled with a sense of oppression, and the face and eyes as though they were glued over with a web. Even when I step into the yard I find the place to be like a cellar on a summer's day, when the very ice has melted in the dark retreat, and the latter's black cavity is charged with hot, viscous humidity.

Somewhere near me a woman is gulping out sobs. For a moment or two I listen: then I approach her, and come upon her seated in a corner with her head in her hands, and her body rocking to and fro as though she were doing me obeisance.

Yet I feel angry, somehow, and remain standing before her without speaking: until at length I ask:

" Are you mad? "

" Go away," is, after a pause, her only reply.

" I heard all that you said to that young fellow."

" Oh, did you? Then what business is it of yours? Are you my brother? "

Yet she speaks the words absent-mindedly rather than angrily. Around us the dim, blurred walls are peering in our direction with sightless eyes, while in the vicinity a bullock is drawing deep breaths.

I seat myself by her side.

" Should you remain much longer in that position," I remark, " you will have a headache."

There follows no reply.

" Am I disturbing you? " I continue.

" Oh no; not at all." And, lowering her hands, she looks at me. " Whence do you come? "

" From Nizhni Novgorod."

" Oh, from a long way off! "

" Do you care for that young fellow? "

Not for a moment or two does she answer; and when she does so she answers as though the words have been rehearsed.

" Not particularly. It is that he is a strong young fellow who has lost his way, and is too much of a fool (as you too must have seen) to find it again. So I am very sorry for him. A good *muzhik* ought to be well placed."

A WOMAN

On the bell of the church there strikes the hour of two. Without interrupting herself, the woman crosses her breast at each stroke.

" Always," she continues, " I feel sorry when I see a fine young fellow going to the dogs. If I were able, I would take all such young men, and restore them to the right road."

" Then you are not sorry *for yourself?* "

" Not for myself? Oh yes: for myself as well."

" Then why flaunt yourself before this booby, as you have been doing? "

" Because I might reform him. Do you not think so? Ah, you do not know me."

A sigh escapes her.

" He hit you, I think? " I venture.

" No, he did not. And in any case you are not to touch him."

" Yet you cried out? "

Suddenly she leans towards me, and says:

" Yes, he *did* strike me—he struck me on the breast, and would have overpowered me had it not been that I cannot, I will not, do things heartlessly, like a cat. Oh, the brutes that men can be! "

Here the conversation undergoes an interruption through the fact that someone has come out to the hut door, and is whistling softly, as for a dog.

" There he is! " whispers the woman.

" Then had I not best send him about his business? "

" No, no! " she exclaims, catching at my knees. " No need is there for that, no need is there for that! "

Then with a low moan she adds:

" O Lord, how I pity our folk and their lives! O God our Father! "

Her shoulders heave, and presently she bursts into tears, with a whisper, between the pitiful sobs, of:

" How, on such a night as this, one remembers all that one has ever seen, and the folk that ever one has known! And oh, how wearisome, wearisome it all is! And how I should like to cry throughout the world—But to cry what? I know not —I have no message to deliver."

That feeling I can understand as well as she, for all too often has it seemed to crush my soul with voiceless longing.

Then, as I stroke her bowed head and quivering shoulder, I ask her who she is: and presently, on growing a little calmer, she tells me the history of her life.

A WOMAN

She is, it appears, the daughter of a carpenter and bee-keeper. On her mother's death, this man married a young woman, and allowed her, as stepmother, to persuade him to place the narrator, Tatiana, in a convent, where she (Tatiana) lived from the age of nine till adolescence, and, meanwhile, was taught her letters, and also a certain amount of manual labour: until, later, her father married her off to a friend of his, a well-to-do ex-soldier who was acting as forester on the convent's estate.

As the woman relates this I feel vexed that I cannot see her face—only a dim, round blur amid which there looms what appears to be a pair of closed eyes. Also, so complete is the stillness that she can narrate her story in a barely audible whisper: and I gain the impression that the pair of us are sitting plunged in a void of darkness where life does not exist, yet where we are destined to begin life.

"However, the man was a libertine and a drunkard, and many a riotous night did he spend with his cronies in the porter's lodge of the convent. Also, he tried to arouse a similar taste in myself: and though for a time I resisted the tendency, I at length, on his taking to beating me, yielded. Only for one man, however, had I really a liking: and with him it was, and not with my husband, that I first learnt the meaning of spouse-hood. . . . Unfortunately, my lover himself was married; and in time his wife came to hear of me, and procured my husband's dismissal. The chief reason was that the lady, a person of great wealth, was herself handsome, albeit stout, and did not care to see her place assumed by a nobody. Next, my husband died of drink; and as my father had long been dead, and I found myself alone, I went to see and consult my stepmother. All that she said, however, was: 'Why come to *me*? Go and think things out for yourself.' And I too then reflected: 'Yes, *why* should I have gone to her?' and repaired to the convent. Yet even there there seemed to be no place left for me, and eventually old Mother Taisia, who had once been my governess, said: 'Tatiana, do you return to the world; for there, and only there, will you have a chance of happiness. . . .' So to the world I returned —and still am roaming it."

"Your quest of happiness is not following an easy road!"

"It is following the road that it best can."

By now the darkness has ceased to keep spread over us, as it were, the stretched web of a heavy curtain, but has grown thinner and more transparent with the tension, save that, in

175

places (for instance, in the window of the hut), it still lies in thick folds or clots as it peers at us with its sightless eyes.

Over the hummock-like roofs of the huts rise the church's steeple and the poplar-trees; while hither and thither on the wall of the hut the cracks and holes in the crumbling plaster have caused the wall to resemble the map of an unknown country.

Glancing at the woman's dark eyes, I perceive them to be shining as pensively, innocently as the eyes of a young maiden.

" You are indeed a curious woman! " I remark.

" Perhaps I am," she replies as she moistens her lips with a slender, almost feline tongue.

" What are you really seeking? "

" I have considered the matter, and know, at last, my mind. It is this. I hope some day to fall in with a good *muzhik* with whom to go in search of land. Probably land of the kind I mean is to be found in the neighbourhood of New Athos,[1] for I have been there already, and know of a likely spot for the purpose. And there we shall set our place in order, and lay out a garden and an orchard, and prepare as much plough land as we may need for our working."

Her words are now firmer, more assured.

" And when we have put everything in order other folk may join us; and then, as the oldest settlers in the place, we shall hold the position of honour. And thus things will continue until a new village, really a fine settlement, will have become formed—a settlement of which my husband will be selected the warden until such time as I shall have made of him a *barin*[2] outright. Also, children may one day play in that garden, and a summer-house be built there. Ah, how delightful such a life appears! "

In fact, she has planned out the future so thoroughly that already she can describe the new establishment in as much detail as though she has long been a resident in it.

" Yes, I yearn indeed for a nice home! " she continues. " Oh that such a home could fall to my lot! But the first requisite, of course, is a *muzhik*."

Her gentle face and eyes peer into the waning night as though they aspire to caress everything upon which they may light.

---

[1] A monastery in the Caucasus, built on the reputed site of a cave tenanted by Simeon the Canaanite.

[2] Gentleman or squire.

A WOMAN

And all the while I am feeling sorry for her—sorry almost to tears. To conceal the fact I murmur:

" Should I myself suit you? "

She gives a faint laugh.

" No."

" Why not? "

" Because the ideas in your mind are different from mine."

" How do you know what my ideas are? "

She edges away from me a little—then says drily:

" Because I can see them in your eyes. To be plain, I could never consent."

With a finger tapping upon the mouldy, gnarled old oaken stump on which we are sitting, she adds:

" The Cossacks, for instance, live comfortably enough: yet I do not like them."

" What in them is it that displeases you? "

" Somehow they repel me. True, much of everything is theirs; yet also they have ways which alienate me."

Unable any longer to conceal from her my pity, I say gently:

" Never, I fear, will you discover what you are seeking."

She shakes her head protestingly.

" And never ought a woman to be discouraged," she retorts. " Woman's proper round is to wish for a child, and to nurse it, and, when it has been weaned, to get herself ready to have another one. That is how woman should live. She should live as pass spring and summer, autumn and winter."

I find it a pleasure to watch the play of the woman's intellectual features; and though, also, I long to take her in my arms, I feel that my better plan will be to seek once more the quiet, empty steppe, and, bearing in me the recollection of this woman, to resume my lonely journey towards the region where the silver wall of the mountains merges with the sky, and the dark ravines gape at the steppe with their chilly jaws. At the moment, however, I cannot so do, for the Cossacks have temporarily deprived me of my passport.

" What are you yourself seeking? " she asks suddenly as again she edges towards me.

" Simply nothing. My one desire is to observe how folk live."

" And are you travelling alone? "

" I am."

" Even as am I. O God, how many lonely people there are in the world! "

By this time the cattle are awakening from slumber, and,

with their soft lowings, reminding one of a pipe which I used to hear played by a certain blind old man. Next, four times, with unsteady touch, the drowsy watchman strikes his gong—twice softly, once with a vigour that clangs the metal again, and a fourth time with a mere tap of the iron hammer against the copper plate.

" What sort of lives do the majority of folk lead? "

" Sorry lives."

" Yes, that is what I too have found."

A pause follows. Then the woman says quietly:

" See, dawn is breaking, yet never this night have my eyes closed. Often I am like that; often I keep thinking and thinking until I seem to be the only human being in the world, and the only human being destined to re-order it."

" Many folk live unworthy lives. They live them amid discord, abasement, and wrongs innumerable, wrongs born of want and stupidity."

And as the words leave my lips my mind loses itself in recollections of all the dark and harrowing and shameful scenes that I have beheld.

" Listen," I say. " You may approach a man with nothing but good in your heart, and be prepared to surrender both your freedom and your strength: yet still he may fail to understand you aright. And how shall he be blamed for this, seeing that never may he have been shown what is good? "

She lays a hand upon my shoulder, and looks straight into my eyes as she parts her comely lips.

" True," she rejoins—" But, dear friend, it is also true that goodness never bargains."

Together she and I seem to be drifting towards a vista which is coming to look, as it sloughs the shadow of night, ever clearer and clearer. It is a vista of white huts, silvery trees, a red church, and dew-bespangled earth. And as the sun rises he reveals to us clustered, transparent clouds which, like thousands of snow-white birds, go gliding over our heads.

" Yes," she whispers again as gently she gives me a nudge. " As one pursues one's lonely way one thinks and thinks—but of what? Dear friend, you have said that no one really cares what is the matter. Ah, *how* true that is! "

Here she springs to her feet, and, pulling me up with her, glues herself to my breast with a vehemence which causes me momentarily to push her away. Upon this, bursting into tears, she tends towards me again, and kisses me with lips so dry as almost to cut me—she kisses me in a way which penetrates to my very soul.

"You have been oh, so good!" she whispers softly. As she speaks the earth seems to be sinking under my feet.

Then she tears herself away, glances around the courtyard, and darts to a corner where, under a fence, a clump of herbage is sprouting.

"Go now," she adds in a whisper. "Yes, go."

Then, with a confused smile, as, crouching among the herbage as though it had been a small cave, she rearranges her hair, she adds:

"It has befallen so. Ah, me! May God grant unto me His pardon!"

Astonished, feeling that I must be dreaming, I gaze at her with gratitude, for I sense an extraordinary lightness to be present in my breast, a radiant void through which joyous, intangible words and thoughts keep flying as swallows wheel across the firmament.

"Amid a great sorrow," she adds, "even a small joy becomes a great felicity."

Yet as I glance at the woman's bosom, whereon moist beads are standing like dewdrops on the outer earth; as I glance at that bosom, whereon the sun's rays are finding a roseate reflection, as though the blood were oozing through the skin, my rapture dies away, and turns to sorrow, heartache, and tears. For in me there is a presentiment that before the living juice within that bosom shall have borne fruit it will have become dried up.

Presently, in a tone almost of self-excuse, and one wherein the words sound a little sadly, she continues:

"Times there are when something comes pouring into my soul which makes my breasts ache with the pain of it. What is there for me to do at such moments save reveal my thoughts to the moon, or, in the daytime, to a river? O God in Heaven! And afterwards I feel as ashamed of myself! . . . Do not look at me like that. Why stare at me with those eyes, eyes so like the eyes of a child?"

"*Your* face, rather, is like a child's," I remark.

"What? Is it so stupid?"

"Something like that."

As she fastens up her bodice she continues:

"Soon the time will be five o'clock, when the bell will ring for Mass. To Mass I must go to-day, for I have a prayer to offer to the Mother of God. . . Shall you be leaving here soon?"

179

" Yes—as soon, that is to say, as I have received back **my** passport."

" And for what destination? "

" For Alatyr. And you? "

She straightens her attire, and rises. As she does so I perceive that her hips are narrower than her shoulders, and that throughout she is well-proportioned and symmetrical.

" I? As yet I do not know. True, I had thought of proceeding to Naltchik, but now, perhaps, I shall not do so, for all my future is uncertain."

Upon that she extends to me a pair of strong, capable arms, and proposes with a blush:

" Shall we kiss once more before we part? "

She clasps me with the one arm, and with the other makes the sign of the cross, adding:

" Good-bye, dear friend, and may Christ requite you for all your words, for all your sympathy! "

" Then shall we travel together? "

At the words she frees herself, and says firmly, nay, sternly:

" Not so. Never would I consent to such a plan. Of course, had you been a *muzhik*—— But no. Even then what would have been the use of it, seeing that life is to be measured, not by a single hour, but by years? "

And, quietly smiling me a farewell, she moves away towards the hut, whilst I, remaining seated, lose myself in thoughts of her. Will she ever overtake her quest in life? Shall I ever behold her again?

The bell for early Mass begins, though for some time past the hamlet has been astir, and humming in a sedate and non-festive fashion.

I enter the hut to fetch my wallet, and find the place empty. Evidently the whole party has left by the gap in the broken-down wall.

I repair, next, to the Ataman's office, where I receive back my passport before setting out to look for my companions in the square.

In similar fashion to yesterday those " folk from Russia " are lolling alongside the churchyard wall, and also have seated among them, leaning his back against a log, the fat-jowled youth from Penza, with his bruised face looking even larger and uglier than before, for the reason that his eyes are sunken amid purple protuberances.

Presently there arrives a newcomer in the shape of an old

man with a grey head adorned with a faded velvet skull-cap, a pointed beard, a lean, withered frame, prominent cheekbones, a red, porous-looking, cunningly hooked nose, and the eyes of a thief.

Him a flaxen-haired youth from Orel joins with a similar youth in accosting.

" Why are *you* tramping? " inquires the former.

" And why are *you*? " the old man retorts in nasal tones as, looking at no one, he proceeds to mend the handle of a battered metal teapot with a piece of wire.

" We are travelling in search of work, and therefore living as we have been commanded to live."

" By *whom* commanded? "

" By God. Have you forgotten? "

Carelessly, but succinctly, the old man retorts:

"Take heed lest upon you, some day, God vomit all the dust and litter which you are raising by tramping His earth!"

" How? " cries one of the youths, a long-eared stripling. " Were not Christ and His Apostles also tramps? "

" Yes, *Christ*," is the old man's meaning reply as he raises his sharp eyes to those of his opponent. " But what are you talking of, you fools? With whom are you daring to compare yourselves? Take care lest I report you to the Cossacks! "

I have listened to many such arguments, and always found them distasteful, even as I have done discussions regarding the soul. Hence I feel inclined to depart.

At this moment, however, Konev makes his appearance. His mien is dejected, and his body perspiring, while his eyes keep blinking rapidly.

" Has any one seen Tanka—that woman from Riazan? " he inquires. " No? Then the bitch must have bolted during the night. The fact is that, overnight, someone gave me a drop or two to drink, a mere dram, but enough to lay me as fast asleep as a bear in winter-time. And in the meantime she must have run away with that Penza fellow."

" No, *he* is here," I remark.

" Oh, he is, is he? Well, as what has the company registered itself? As a set of ikon-painters, I should think! "

Again he begins to look anxiously about him.

" Where can she have got to? " he queries.

" To Mass, maybe."

" *Of* course! Well, I am greatly smitten with her. Yes, my word I am! "

Nevertheless, when Mass comes to an end, and, to the sound of a merry peal of bells, the well-dressed local Cossacks file out of church, and distribute themselves in gaudy streams about the hamlet, no Tatiana makes her appearance.

"Then she *is* gone," says Konev ruefully. "But *I'll* find her yet! *I'll* come up with her!"

That this will happen I do not feel confident. Nor do I desire that it should.

*

Five years later I am pacing the courtyard of the Metechski Prison in Tiflis, and, as I do so, trying to imagine for what particular offence I have been incarcerated in that place of confinement.

Picturesquely grim without, the institution is, inwardly, peopled with a set of cheerful, but clumsy, humourists. That is to say, it would seem as though, "by order of the authorities," the inmates are presenting a stage spectacle in which they are playing, willingly and zealously, but with a complete lack of experience, imperfectly comprehended rôles as prisoners, warders, and gendarmes.

For instance, to-day, when a warder and a gendarme came to my cell to escort me to exercise, and I said to them, "May I be excused exercise to-day? I am not very well, and do not feel like, etcetera, etcetera," the gendarme, a tall, handsome man with a red beard, held up to me a warning finger.

"No one," he said, "has given you permission to feel, or not to feel, like doing things."

To which the warder, a man as dark as a chimney-sweep, with large blue "whites" to his eyes, added stutteringly:

"To *no one* here has permission been given to feel, or not to feel, like doing things. You hear that?"

So to exercise I went.

In this stone-paved yard the air is as hot as in an oven, for overhead there lours only a small, flat patch of dull, drab-tinted sky, and on three sides of the yard rise high grey walls, with, on the fourth, the entrance-gates, topped by a sort of look-out post.

Over the roof of the building there comes floating the dull roar of the turbulent river Kura, mingled with shouts from the hucksters of the Avlabar Bazaar (the town's Asiatic quarter) and, as a cross *motif* thrown into these sounds, the sighing of the wind and the cooing of doves. In fact, to be here is like being in a drum which a myriad drumsticks are beating.

Through the bars of the double line of windows on the second and the third stories peer the murky faces and towsled heads of some of the inmates. One of the latter spits his furthest into the yard—evidently with the intention of hitting myself: but all his efforts prove vain. Another one shouts with a mordant expletive:

" Hi, you! Why do you keep tramping up and down like an old hen? Hold up your head! "

Meanwhile the inmates continue to intone in concert a strange chant which is as tangled as a skein of wool after serving as a plaything for a kitten's prolonged game of sport. Sadly the chant meanders, wavers, to a high, wailing note. Then, as it were, it soars yet higher towards the dull, murky sky, breaks suddenly into a snarl, and, growling like a wild beast in terror, dies away to give place to a refrain which coils, trickles forth from between the bars of the windows until it has permeated the free, torrid air.

As I listen to that refrain, long familiar to me, it seems to voice something intelligible, and agitates my soul almost to a sense of agony. . . .

Presently, while pacing up and down in the shadow of the building, I happen to glance towards the line of windows. Glued to the framework of one of the iron window-squares I can discern a blue-eyed face. Overgrown with an untidy sable beard it is, as well as stamped with a look of perpetually grieved surprise.

" That must be Konev," I say to myself aloud.

Konev it is—Konev of the well-remembered eyes. Even at this moment they are regarding me with puckered attention.

I throw around me a hasty glance. My own warder is dozing on a shady bench near the entrance. Two more warders are engaged in throwing dice. A fourth is superintending the pumping of water by two convicts, and superciliously marking time for their lever with the formula, " Mashkam, dashkam! Dashkam, mashkam! "

I move towards the wall.

" Is that you, Konev? " is my inquiry.

" It is," he mutters as he thrusts his head a little further through the grating. " Yes, Konev *I* am, but who *you* are I have not a notion."

" What are you here for? "

" For a matter of base coin, though, to be truthful, I am here accidentally, without genuine cause."

The warder rouses himself, and, with his keys jingling like a set of fetters, utters drowsily the command:

"Do not stand still. Also, move further from the wall. To approach it is forbidden."

"But it is so hot in the middle of the yard, sir!"

"Everywhere it is hot," retorts the man reprovingly, and his head subsides again. From above comes the whispered query:

"Who *are* you?"

"Well, do you remember Tatiana, the woman from Riazan?"

"*Do* I remember her?" Konev's voice has in it a touch of subdued resentment. "*Do* I remember her? Why, I was tried in court together with her!"

"Together with *her*? Was she too sentenced for the passing of base coin?"

"Yes. Why should she not have been? She was merely the victim of an accident, even as I was."

As I resume my walk in the stifling shade I detect that from the windows of the basement there is issuing a smell of, in equal parts, rotten leather, mouldy grain, and dampness. To my mind there recur Tatiana's words, "Amid a great sorrow even a small joy becomes a great felicity," and, "I should like to build a village on some land of my own, and create for myself a new and better life."

And to my recollection there recur also Tatiana's face and yearning, hungry breast. As I stand thinking of these things there come dropping on to my head from above the low-spoken, ashen-grey words:

"The chief conspirator in the matter was her lover, the son of a priest. He it was who engineered the plot. He has been sentenced to ten years' penal servitude."

"And she?"

"Tatiana Vasilievna? To the same, and I also. I leave for Siberia the day after to-morrow. The trial was held at Kutair. In Russia I should have got off with a lighter sentence than here, for the folk in these parts are, one and all, evil, barbaric scoundrels."

"And Tatiana, has she any children?"

"How could she have while living such a rough life as this? Of course not! Besides, the priest's son is a consumptive."

"Indeed sorry for her am I!"

"So I expect." And in Konev's tone there would seem to be a touch of meaning. "The woman was a fool—of that there

184

can be no doubt; but also she was comely, as well as a person out of the common in her pity for folk."

" Was it then that you found her again? "

" When? "

" On that Feast of the Assumption? "

" Oh no. It was only during the following winter that I came up with her. At the time she was serving as governess to the children of an old officer in Batum whose wife had left him."

Something snaps behind me—something sounding like the hammer of a revolver. However, it is only the warder closing the lid of his huge watch before restoring the watch to his pocket, giving himself a stretch, and yawning to the utmost extent of his jaws.

" You see, she had money, and, but for her restlessness, might have lived a comfortable life enough. As it was, her restlessness——"

" Time for exercise is up! " shouts the warder.

" Who *are* you? " adds Konev hastily. " Somehow I seem to remember your face; but I cannot place it."

Yet so stung am I with what I have heard that I move away in silence: save that just as I reach the top of the steps I turn to cry:

" Goodbye, mate, and give her my greeting! "

" What are you bawling for? " blusters the warder. . . .

The corridor is dim, and filled with an oppressive odour. The warder swings his keys with a dry, thin clash, and I, to dull the pain in my heart, strive to imitate him. But the attempt proves futile; and as the warder opens the door of my cell he says severely:

" In with you, ten-years man! "

Entering, I move towards the window. Between some grey spikes on a wall I can just discern the boisterous current of the Kura, with *sakli* [1] and houses glued to the opposite bank, and the figures of some workmen on the roof of a tanning shed. Below, with his cap pushed to the back of his head, is pacing backwards and forwards a sentry.

Wearily my mind recalls the many scores of Russian folk whom it has seen perish to no purpose. And as it does so it feels crushed, as in a vice, beneath the burden of great and inexorable sorrow with which all life is dowered.

[1] Warehouses.

IN A MOUNTAIN DEFILE

In a mountain defile near a little tributary of the Sunzha there was being built a workman's *barraque*, a low, long edifice which reminded one of a large coffin-lid.

The building was approaching completion, and, meanwhile, a score of carpenters were employed in fashioning thin planks into doors of equal thinness, knocking together benches and tables, and fitting window-frames into the small window-squares.

Also, to assist these carpenters in the task of protecting the *barraque* from tribesmen's nocturnal raids, the shrill-voiced young student of civil engineering who had been set in charge of the work had sent to the place, as watchman, an ex-soldier named Paul Ivanovitch, a man of the Cossack type, and myself.

Yet whereas we were out-at-elbows, the carpenters were sleek, respectable, monied, well-clad fellows. Also, there was something dour and irritating about them, since, for one thing, they had failed to respond to our greeting on our first appearance, and eyed us with nothing but dislike and suspicion. Hence, hurt by their chilly attitude, we had withdrawn from their immediate neighbourhood, constructed a causeway of stepping-stones to the eastern bank of the rivulet, and taken up our abode beneath the chaotic grey mists which enveloped the mountain side in that direction.

Also, over the carpenters there was a foreman—a man whose bony frame, clad in a white shirt and a pair of white trousers, looked always as though it were ready-attired for death. Moreover, he wore no cap to conceal the yellow patch of baldness which covered most of his head, and, in addition, his nose was squat and grey, his neck and face had over them skin of a porous, pumice-like consistency, his eyes were green and dim, and upon his features there was stamped a dead and disagreeable expression. To be candid, however, behind the dark lips lay a set of fine, close teeth, while the hairs of the grey beard (a beard trimmed after the Tartar fashion) were thick and, seemingly, soft.

Never did this man put a hand actually to the work: always

he kept roaming about with the large, rigid-looking fingers of his hands tucked into his belt, and his fixed and expressionless eyes scanning the *barraque*, the men, and the work as his lips vented some such lines as:

> O God our Father, bound hast Thou
> A crown of thorns upon my brow!
> Listen to my humble prayer!
> Lighten the burden which I bear!

" What on earth can be in the man's mind? " once remarked the ex-soldier with a frowning glance at the singer.

As for our duties, my mates and I had nothing to do, and soon began to find the time tedious. For his part, the man with the Cossack physiognomy scaled the mountain side; whence he could be heard whistling and snapping twigs with his heavy feet, while the ex-soldier selected a space between two rocks for a shelter of ace-rose boughs, and, stretching himself on his stomach, fell to smoking strong mountain tobacco in his large meerschaum pipe as dimly, dreamily he contemplated the play of the mountain torrent. Lastly, I myself selected a seat on a rock which overhung the brook, dipped my feet in the coolness of the water, and proceeded to mend my shirt.

At intervals the defile would convey to our ears a dull echo of sounds so wholly at variance with the locality as muffled hammer-blows, a screeching of saws, a rasping of planes, and a confused murmur of human voices.

Also, a moist breeze blew constantly from the dark-blue depths of the defile, and caused the stiff, upright larches on the knoll behind the *barraque* to rustle their boughs, and distilled from the rank soil the voluptuous scents of ace-rose and pitch-pine, and evoked in the trees' quiet gloom a soft, crooning, somnolent lullaby.

About a *sazhen* [1] below the level of the *barraque* there coursed noisily over its bed of stones a rivulet white with foam. Yet though of other sounds in the vicinity there were but few, the general effect was to suggest that everything in the neighbourhood was speaking or singing a tale of such sort as to shame the human species into silence.

On our own side of the valley the ground lay bathed in sunshine—lay scorched to the point of seeming to have spread over it a tissue-cloth old-gold in colour, while from every side arose the sweet perfume of dried grasses, and in dark clefts there could be seen sprouting the long, straight spears and fiery,

[1] Fathom.

190

reddish, cone-shaped blossoms of that bold, hardy plant which is known to us as saxifrage—the plant of which the contemplation makes one long to burst into music, and fills one's whole body with sensuous languor.

Laced with palpitating, snow-white foam, the beautiful rivulet pursued its sportive way over tessellated stones which flashed through the eddies of the glassy, sunlit, amber-coloured water with the silken sheen of a patchwork carpet or costly shawl of Cashmir.

Through the mouth of the defile one could reach the valley of the Sunzha, whence, since men were there, building a railway to Petrovsk on the Caspian Sea, there kept issuing and breaking against the crags a dull rumble of explosions, of iron rasped against stone, of whistles of works locomotives, and of animated human voices.

From the *barraque* the distance to the point where the defile debouched upon the valley was about a hundred paces, and as one issued thence one could see, away to the left, the level steppes of the Cis-Caucasus, with a boundary wall of blue hills, topped by the silver-hewn saddle of Mount Elburz behind it. True, for the most part the steppes had a dry, yellow, sandy look, with merely here and there dark patches of gardens or black poplar-clumps which rendered the golden glare more glaring still; yet also there could be discerned on the expanse farm buildings shaped like lumps of sugar or butter, with, in their vicinity, toylike human beings and diminutive cattle—the whole shimmering and melting in a mirage born of the heat.

And at the mere sight of those steppes with their embroidery of silk under the blue of the zenith one's muscles tightened, and one felt inspired with a longing to spring to one's feet, close one's eyes, and walk for ever with the soft, mournful song of the waste crooning in one's ears.

To the right also of the defile lay the winding valley of the Sunzha, with more hills; and above those hills hung the blue sky, and in their flanks were clefts which, full of grey mist, kept emitting a ceaseless din of labour, a sound of dull explosions as a great, puissant force attained release.

Yet almost at the same moment would that hurly-burly so merge with the echo of our defile, so become buried in the defile's verdure and rock-crevices, that once more the place would seem to be singing only its own gentle, gracious song.

And, should one turn to glance up the defile, it could be seen to grow narrower and narrower as it ascended towards the mists, and the latter to grow thicker and thicker until the whole defile was swathed in a dark blue pall. Higher yet there could be discerned the brilliant gleam of blue sky. Higher yet one could distinguish the ice-capped peak of Kara Dagh, floating and dissolving amid the, from here, invisible sunlight. Highest of all brooded again the serene, steadfast peace of heaven.

Also, everything was bathed in a strange tint of bluish grey: to which circumstance must have been due the fact that always one's soul felt filled with restlessness, one's heart stirred to disquietude, and fired as with intoxication, and charged with incomprehensible thoughts, and conscious as of a summons to set forth for some unknown destination.

*

The foreman of the carpenters shaded his eyes to gaze in our direction; and as he did so he drawled and rasped out in tedious fashion:

> Some shall to the left be sent,
> And in the pit of Hell lie pent.
> While others, holding palm in hand,
> Shall on God's right take up their stand.

" *Did* you hear that? " the ex-soldier growled through clenched teeth. " ' Palm in hand ' indeed! Why, the fellow must be a Mennonite or a Molokan, though the two, really, are one, and absolutely indistinguishable, as well as equally foolish. Yes, ' palm in hand ' indeed! "

Similarly could I understand the ex-soldier's indignation, for, like him, I felt that such dreary, monotonous singing was altogether out of place in a spot where everything could troll a song so delightful as to lead one to wish to hear nothing more, to hear only the whispering of the forest and the babbling of the stream. And especially out of place did the terms " palm " and " Mennonite " appear.

Yet I had no great love for the ex-soldier. Somehow he jarred upon me. Middle-aged, squat, square, and bleached with the sun, he had faded eyes, flattened-out features, and an expression of restless moroseness. Never could I make out what really he wanted, what really he was seeking. For instance, once, after reviewing the Caucasus from Khassav-Urt to Novorossisk, and from Batum to Derbent, and, during the review, crossing the mountain range by three different routes at least, he remarked with a disparaging smile:

" I suppose the Lord God made the country."

192

" You do not like it, then? "

" How should I? Good for nothing is what I call it."

Then, with a further glance at me, and a twist of his sinewy neck, he added:

" However, not bad altogether are its forests."

A native of Kaluga, he had served in Tashkend, and, in fighting with the Chechintzes of that region, been wounded in the head with a stone. Yet as he told me the story of this incident he smiled shamefacedly, and, throughout, kept his glassy eyes fixed upon the ground.

" Though I am ashamed to confess it," he said, " once a woman chipped a piece out of me. You see, the women of that region are shrieking devils—there is no other word for it; and when we captured a village called Akhal-Tiapa a number of them had to be cut up, so that they lay about in heaps, and their blood made walking slippery. Just as our company of the reserve entered the street something caught me on the head. Afterwards I learnt that a woman on a roof had thrown a stone, and, like the rest, had had to be put out of the way."

Here, knitting his brows, the ex-soldier went on in more serious vein:

" Yet all that folk used to say about those women, about their having beards to shave, turned out to be so much gossip, as I ascertained for myself. I did so by lifting the woman's skirt on the point of my bayonet, when I perceived that, though she was lean, and smelt like a goat, she was quite as regular as, as——"

" Things must have been indeed terrible on that expedition! " I interposed.

" I do not know for certain, since, though men who took an actual part in the expedition's engagements have said that they were so (the Chechintze is a vicious brute, and never gives in), I myself know but little of the affair, since I spent my whole time in the reserve, and never once did my company advance to the assault. No, it merely lay about on the sand, and fired at long range. In fact, nothing *but* sand was to be seen thereabouts; nor did we ever succeed in finding out what the fighting was for. True, if a piece of country be good, it is in our interest to take it; but in the present case the country was poor and bare, with never a river in sight, and a climate so hot that all one thought of was one's mortal need of a drink. In fact, some of our fellows died of thirst outright. Moreover, in those parts there grows a sort of millet called *dzhugar*—

193

millet which not only has a horrible taste, but proves absolutely delusive, since the more one eats of it, the less one feels filled."

As the ex-soldier told me the tale colourlessly and reluctantly, with frequent pauses between the sentences (as though either he found it difficult to recall the experience or he were thinking of something else), he never once looked me straight in the face, but kept his eyes shamefacedly fixed upon the ground.

Unwieldily and unhealthily stout, he always conveyed to me the impression of being charged with a vague discontent, a sort of captious inertia.

"Absolutely unfit for settlement is this country," he continued as he glanced around him. "It is fit only to do nothing in. For that matter, one doesn't *want* to do anything in it, save to live with one's eyes bulging like a drunkard's; for the climate is too hot, and the place smells like a chemist's shop or a hospital."

Nevertheless, for the past eight years had he been roaming this "too hot" country, as though fascinated!

"Why not return to Riazan?" I suggested.

"Nothing would there be there for me to do," he replied through his teeth, and with an odd division of his words.

My first encounter with him had been at the railway station at Armavir, where, purple in the face with excitement, he had been stamping like a horse, and, with distended eyes, hissing, or, rather, snarling, at a couple of Greeks:

"*I*'ll tear the flesh from your bones!"

Meanwhile the two lean, withered, ragged, identically similar denizens of Hellas had been baring their sharp white teeth at intervals, and saying apologetically:

"What has angered you, sir?"

Finally, regardless of the Greeks' words, the ex-soldier had beat his breast like a drum, and shouted in accents of increased venom:

"Now, where are you living? In Russia, do you say? Then who is supporting you there? Aha-a-a! Russia, it is said, is a good foster-mother. I expect you say the same."

And, lastly, he had approached a fat, greyheaded, bemedalled gendarme, and complained to him:

"Everyone curses us born Russians, yet everyone comes to live with us—Greeks, Germans, Serbs, and the lot. And while they get their livelihood here, and eat and drink their fill, they continue to curse us. A scandal, is it not?"

*

194

The third member of our party was a man of about thirty who wore a Cossack cap over his left ear, and had a Cossack forelock, rounded features, a large nose, a dark moustache, and a *retroussé* lip. When the volatile young engineering student first brought him to us and said, " Here is another man for you," the newcomer glanced at me through the lashes of his elusive eyes—then plunged his hands into the pockets of his Turkish overalls. Just as we were departing, however, he withdrew one hand from the left trouser-pocket, passed it slowly over the dark bristles of his unshaven chin, and asked in musical tones:

" Do you come from Russia? "

" Whence else, I should like to know? " snapped the ex-soldier gruffly.

Upon this the newcomer twisted his right-hand moustache — then replaced his hand in his pocket. Broad-shouldered, sturdy, and well-built throughout, he walked with the stride of a man who is accustomed to cover long distances. Yet with him he had brought neither wallet nor gripsack, and somehow his supercilious, *retroussé* upper lip and thickly fringed eyes irritated me, and inclined me to be suspicious of, and even actively to dislike, the man.

Suddenly, while we were proceeding along the causeway by the side of the rivulet, he turned to us, and said, as he nodded towards the sportively coursing water:

" Look at the matchmaker! "

The ex-soldier hoisted his bleached eyebrows, and gazed around him for a moment in bewilderment. Then he whispered:

" The fool! "

But, for my own part, I considered that what the man had said was apposite: that the rugged, boisterous little river did indeed resemble some fussy, lighthearted old lady who loved to arrange *affaires du cœur* both for her own private amusement and for the purpose of enabling other folk to realise the joys of affection amid which she was living, and of which she would never grow weary, and to which she desired to introduce the rest of the world as speedily as possible.

Similarly, when we arrived at the *barraque* this man with the Cossack face glanced at the rivulet, and then at the mountains and the sky, and, finally, appraised the scene in one pregnant, comprehensive exclamation of " *Slavno !* " [1]

The ex-soldier, who was engaged in ridding himself of his

[1] " How splendid! "

knapsack, straightened himself, and asked with his arms set akimbo:

"*What* is it that is so splendid?"

For a moment or two the newcomer merely eyed the squat figure of his questioner—a figure upon which hung drab shreds as lichen hangs upon a stone. Then he said with a smile:

"Cannot you see for yourself? Take that mountain there, and that cleft in the mountain: are they not good to look at?"

And as he moved away, the ex-soldier gaped after him with a repeated whisper of:

"The fool!"

To which presently he added in a louder, as well as a mysterious, tone:

"I have heard that occasionally they send fever patients hither for their health."

The same evening saw two sturdy women arrive with supper for the carpenters; whereupon the clatter of labour ceased, and therefore the rustling of the forest and the murmuring of the rivulet became the more distinct.

Next, deliberately, and with many coughs, the ex-soldier set to work to collect some twigs and chips for the purpose of lighting a fire. After which, having arranged a kettle over the flames, he said to me suggestively:

"You too should collect some firewood, for in these parts the nights are dark and chilly."

I set forth in search of chips among the stones which lay around the *barraque*, and, in so doing, stumbled across the newcomer, who was lying with his body resting on an elbow, and his head on his hand, as he conned a manuscript spread out before him. As he raised his eyes to gaze vaguely, inquiringly into my face, I saw that one of his eyes was larger than the other.

Evidently he divined that he interested me, for he smiled. Yet so taken aback by this was I that I passed on my way without speaking.

Meanwhile the carpenters, disposed in two circles around the *barraque* (a circle to each woman), partook of a silent supper.

Deeper and deeper grew the shadow of night over the defile. Warmer and warmer, denser and denser, grew the air, until the twilight caused the slopes of the mountains to soften in outline, and the rocks to seem to swell and merge with the bluish-blackness which overhung the bed of the defile, and the superimposed heights to form a single apparent whole, and the scene in general to resolve itself into, become united into, one compact bulk.

Quietly then did tints hitherto red extinguish their tremulous glow—softly there flared up, dusted purple in the sunset's sheen, the peak of Kara Dagh. Vice versa, the foam of the rivulet now blushed to red, and, seemingly, assuaged its vehemence—flowed with a deeper, a more pensive, note; while similarly the forest hushed its voice, and appeared to stoop towards the water while emitting ever more powerful, intoxicating odours to mingle with the resinous, cloyingly sweet perfume of our wood fire.

The ex-soldier squatted down before the little blaze, and rearranged some fuel under the kettle.

" Where is the other man? " said he. " Go and fetch him."

I departed for the purpose, and, on my way, heard one of the carpenters in the neighbourhood of the *barraque* say in a thick, unctuous, sing-song voice:

" A great work is it indeed! "

Whereafter I heard the two women fall to drawling in low, hungry accents:

> With the flesh I'll conquer pain;
> The spirit shall my lust restrain;
> All-supreme the soul shall reign;
> And carnal vices lure in vain.

True, the women pronounced their words distinctly enough; yet always they prolonged the final " u " sound of the stanza's first and third lines until, as the melody floated away into the darkness, and, as it were, sank to earth, it came to resemble the long-drawn howl of a wolf.

In answer to my invitation to come to supper, the newcomer sprang to his feet, folded up his manuscript, stuffed it into one of the pockets of his ragged coat, and said with a smile:

" I had just been going to resort to the carpenters. For they would have given us some bread, I suppose? Long is it since I tasted anything."

The same words he repeated on our approaching the ex-soldier; much as though he took a pleasure in their phraseology.

" You suppose that they would have given us bread? " echoed the ex-soldier as he unfastened his wallet. " Not they! No love is lost between them and ourselves."

" Whom do you mean by ' ourselves '? "

" Us here—you and myself—all Russian folk who may happen to be in these parts. From the way in which those fellows keep singing about palms I should judge them to be sectarians of the sort called Mennonites."

" Or Molokans, rather? " the other man suggested as he seated himself in front of the fire.

" Yes, or Molokans. Molokans or Mennonites, they're all one. It is a German faith, and though such fellows love a Teuton, they do not exactly welcome *us*."

Upon this the man with the Cossack forelock took a slice of bread which the ex-soldier cut from a loaf, with an onion and a pinch of salt. Then, as he regarded us with a pair of good-humoured eyes, he said, balancing his food on the palms of his hands:

" There is a spot on the Sunzha, near here, where those fellows have a colony of their own. Yes, I myself have visited it. True, those fellows are hard enough, but at the same time, to speak plainly, *no one* in these parts has any regard for us, since only too many of the sort of Russian folk who come here in search of work are not over-desirable."

" Where do you yourself come from? " The ex-soldier's tone was severe.

" From Kursk, we might say."

" From Russia, then? "

" Yes, I suppose so. But I have no great opinion even of myself."

The ex-soldier glanced distrustfully at the newcomer. Then he remarked:

" What you say is cant, sheer Jesuitism. It is fellows like *those*, rather, that ought to have a poor opinion of themselves."

To this the other made no reply—merely he put a piece of bread into his mouth. For a moment or two the ex-soldier eyed him frowningly. Then he continued:

" You seem to me to be a native of the Don country? "

" Yes, I have lived on the Don as well."

" And also served in the army? "

" No. I was an only son."

" Of a *miestchanin*? " [1]

" No, of a merchant."

" And your name——? "

" Is Vasili."

The last reply came only after a pause, and reluctantly: wherefore, perceiving that the Kurskan had no particular

[1] A member of the small commercial class.

198

desire to discuss his own affairs, the ex-soldier said no more on the subject, but lifted the kettle from the fire.

The Molokans also had kindled a blaze behind the corner of the *barraque*, and now its glow was licking the yellow boards of the structure until they seemed almost to be liquescent, to be about to dissolve and flow over the ground in a golden stream.

Presently, as their fervour increased, the carpenters, invisible amid the obscurity, fell to singing hymns—the basses intoning monotonously, " Sing, thou Holy Angel! " and voices of higher pitch responding, coldly and formally:

> Sing ye!
> Sing glory unto Christ, thou Angel of Holiness!
> Sing ye!
> Our singing will we add unto Thine,
> Thou Angel of Holiness!

And though the chorus failed altogether to dull the splashing of the rivulet and the babbling of the by-cut over a bed of stones, it seemed out of place in this particular spot—it aroused resentment against men who could not think of a lay more a-tune with the particular living, breathing objects around us.

Gradually darkness enveloped the defile until only over the mouth of the pass, over the spot where, gleaming a brilliant blue, the rivulet escaped into a cleft that was overhung with a mist of a deeper shade, was there not yet suspended the curtain of the Southern night.

Presently the gloom caused one of the rocks in our vicinity to assume the guise of a monk who, kneeling in prayer, had his head adorned with a pointed skull-cap, and his face buried in his hands. Similarly, the stems of the trees stirred in the fire-light until they developed the semblance of a file of friars entering, for early Mass, the porch of their chapel-of-ease.

To my mind there then recurred a certain occasion when, on just such a dark and sultry night as this, I had been seated tale-telling under the boundary-wall of a row of monastic cells in the Don country. Suddenly I had heard a window above my head open, and someone exclaim in a kindly, youthful voice:

" The Mother of God be blessed for all this goodly world of ours! "

And though the window had closed again before I had had time to discern the speaker, I had known that there was resident in the monastery a friar who had large eyes, and a limp, and just such a face as had Vasili here: wherefore in all probability it had been he who had breathed the benediction upon mankind at large, for the reason that moments there are when all humanity seems to be one's own body, and in oneself there seems to beat the heart of all humanity. . . .

Vasili consumed his food deliberately as, breaking off morsels from his slice, and neatly parting his moustache, he placed the morsels in his mouth with a curious stirring of two globules which underlay the skin near the ears.

The ex-soldier, however, merely nibbled at his food—he ate but little, and that lazily. Then he extracted a pipe from his breast pocket, filled it with tobacco, lit it with a faggot taken from the fire, and said as he set himself to listen to the singing of the Molokans:

"They are filled full, and have started bleating. Always folk like them seek to be on the right side of the Almighty."

"Does that hurt you in any way?" Vasili asked with a smile.

"No, but I do not respect them—they are less saints than humbugs, than prevaricators whose first word is God, and second word rouble."

"How do you know that?" cried Vasili amusedly. "And even if their first word *is* God, and their second word rouble, we had best not be too hard upon them, since if they chose to be hard upon *us*, where should *we* be? Yes, we have only to open our mouths to speak a word or two for ourselves, and we should find every fist at our teeth."

"Quite so," the ex-soldier agreed as, taking up a square of scantling, he examined it attentively.

"Whom *do* you respect?" Vasili continued after a pause.

"I respect," the ex-soldier said with some emphasis, "only the Russian people, the true Russian people, the folk who labour on land whereon labour is hard. Yet who are the folk whom you find *here*? In this part of the world the business of living is an easy one. Much of every sort of natural produce is to be had, and the soil is generous and light—you need but to scratch it for it to bear, and for yourself to reap. Yes, it is indulgent to a fault. Rather, it is like a maiden. Do but touch her, and a child will arrive."

"Agreed," was Vasili's remark as he drank tea from a tin mug. "Yet to this very part of the world is it that I should like to transport every soul in Russia."

"And why?"

"Because here they could earn a living."

"Then is not that possible in Russia?"

" Well, why are you yourself here? "

" Because I am a man lacking ties."

" And why are you lacking ties? "

" Because it has been so ordered—it is, so to speak, my lot."

" Then had you not better consider *why* it is your lot? "

The ex-soldier took his pipe from his mouth, let fall the hand which held it, and smoothed his plain features in silent amazement. Then he exclaimed in uncouth, querulous tones:

" Had I not better consider *why* it is my lot, and so forth? Why, damn it, the causes are many. For one thing, if one has neighbours who neither live nor see things as oneself does, but are uncongenial, what does one do? One just leaves them, and clears out—more especially if one be neither a priest nor a magistrate. Yet *you* say that I had better consider why this is my lot. Do you think that *you* are the only man able to consider things, possessed of a brain? "

And in an access of fury the speaker replaced his pipe, and sat frowning in silence. Vasili eyed his interlocutor's features as the firelight played red upon them, and, finally, said in an undertone:

" Yes, it is always so. We fail to get on with our neighbours, yet lack a charter of our own, so, having no roots to hold us, just fall to wandering, troubling other folk, and earning dislike."

" The dislike of whom? " gruffly queried the ex-soldier.

" The dislike of everyone, as you yourself have said."

In answer the ex-soldier merely emitted a cloud of smoke which completely concealed his form. Yet Vasili's voice had in it an agreeable note, and was flexible and ingratiating, while enunciating its words roundly and distinctly.

A mountain owl, one of those splendid brown creatures which have the crafty physiognomy of a cat, and the sharp grey ears of a mouse, made the forest echo with its obtrusive cry. A bird of this species I once encountered among the defile's crags, and as the creature sailed over my head it startled me with the glassy eyes which, as round as buttons, seemed to be lit from within with menacing fire. Indeed, for a moment or two I stood half-stupefied with terror, for I could not conceive what the creature was.

" Whence did you get that splendid pipe? " next asked Vasili as he rolled himself a cigarette. " Surely it is a pipe of old German make? "

" You need not fear that I stole it," the ex-soldier responded as he removed it from his lips and regarded it proudly. " It was given me by a woman."

To which, with a whimsical wink, he added a sigh.

" Tell me how it happened," said Vasili softly. Then he flung up his arms, and stretched himself with a despondent cry of:

" Ah, these nights here! Never again may God send me such bad ones! Try to sleep as one may, one never succeeds. Far easier, indeed, is it to sleep during the daytime, provided that one can find a shady spot. During such nights I go almost mad with thinking, and my heart swells and murmurs."

The ex-soldier, who had listened with mouth agape and eyebrows raised even higher than usual, responded to this:

" It is the same with me. If one could only—— What did you say? "

This last was addressed to myself, who had been about to remark, " The same with me also," but on seeing the pair exchanging a strange glance (as though involuntarily they had surprised one another), had left the words unspoken. My companions then set themselves to a mutually eager questioning with respect to their respective identities, past experiences, places of origin, and destinations, even as though they had been two kinsmen who, meeting unexpectedly, had discovered for the first time their bond of relationship.

Meanwhile the black, fringed boughs of the pine-trees hung stretched over the flames of the Molokans' fire as though they would catch some of the fire's glow and warmth, or seize it altogether, and put it out. And when, at times, their red tongues projected beyond the corner of the *barraque*, they made the building look as though it had caught alight, and extended their glow even to the rivulet. Constantly the night was growing denser and more stifling; constantly it seemed to embrace the body more and more caressingly, until one bathed in it as in an ocean. Also, much as a wave removes dirt from the skin, so the softly vocal darkness seemed to refresh and cleanse the soul. For it is on such nights as that that the soul dons its finest raiment, and trembles like a bride at the expectation of something glorious.

" You say that she had a squint? " presently I heard Vasili continue in an undertone, and the ex-soldier slowly reply:

" Yes, she had one from childhood upwards—she had one from the day when a fall from a cart caused her to injure her eyes. Yet, if she had not always gone about with one of her eyes shaded, you would never have guessed the fact. Also, she was so neat and practical! And her kindness—well, it was kindness as inexhaustible as the water of that rivulet there; it was kindness of the sort that wished well to all the world, and to all animals, and to every beggar, and even to myself! So at last there gripped my heart the thought, ' Why should I not try a soldier's luck? She is the master's favourite—true; yet none the less the attempt shall be made by me.' However, this way or that, always the reply was ' No '; always she put out at me an elbow, and cut me short."

Vasili, lying prone upon his back, twitched his moustache, and chewed a stalk of grass. His eyes were fully open, and for the second time I perceived that one of them was larger than the other. The ex-soldier, seated near Vasili's shoulder, stirred the fire with a bit of charred stick, and sent sparks of gold flying to join the midges which were gliding to and fro over the blaze. Ever and anon night moths subsided into the flames with a plop, crackled, and became changed into lumps of black. For my own part, I constructed a couch on a pile of pine boughs, and there lay down. And as I listened to the ex-soldier's familiar story I recalled persons whom I had on one and another occasion remembered, and speeches which on one and another occasion had made an impression upon me.

" But at last," the ex-soldier continued, " I took heart of grace, and caught her in a barn. Pressing her into a corner, I said: ' Now let it be yes or no. Of course it shall be as you wish, but remember that I am a soldier with a small stock of patience.' Upon that she began to struggle and exclaim: ' What do you want? What do you want? ' until, bursting into tears like a girl, she said through her sobs: ' Do not touch me. I am not the sort of woman for you. Besides, I love another— not our master, but another, a workman, a former lodger of ours. Before he departed he said to me: " Wait for me until I have found you a nice home, and returned to fetch you "; and though it is seventeen years since I heard speech or whisper of him, and maybe he has since forgotten me, or fallen in love with someone else, or come to grief, or been murdered, you, who are a man, will understand that I must bide a little while longer.' True, this offended me (for in what respect was I any worse than the other man?); yet also I felt sorry for her, and grieved that I should have wronged her by thinking her frivolous when all the time there had been *this* at her heart. I drew back, therefore—I could not lay a finger upon her, though she was in

my power. And at last I said: ' Good-bye! I am going away.'
' Go,' she replied. ' Yes, go for the love of Christ!' . . . Wherefore, on the following evening I settled accounts with our master,
and at dawn of a Sunday morning packed my wallet, took with
me this pipe, and departed. ' Yes, take the pipe, Paul Ivanovitch,' she said before my departure. ' Perhaps it will serve to
keep you in remembrance of me—you whom henceforth I shall
regard as a brother, and whom I thank.' . . . As I walked
away I was very nigh to tears, so keen was the pain in my
heart. Aye, keen it was indeed!"

" You did right," Vasili remarked softly after a pause.
" Things must always so befall. Always must it be a case
either of ' Yes?' ' Yes,' and of folk coming together, or of
' No?' ' No,' and of folk parting. And invariably the one
person in the case grieves the other. Why should that be?"

Emitting a cloud of grey smoke, the ex-soldier replied thoughtfully:

" Yes, I know I did right; but that right was done only at
a great cost."

" And always that too is the case," Vasili agreed. Then he
added:

" Generally such fortune falls to the lot of people who have
tender consciences. He who values himself also values his
fellows: but, unfortunately a man all too seldom values even
himself."

" To whom are you referring? To you and myself?"

" To our Russian folk in general."

" Then you cannot have very much respect for Russia."
The ex-soldier's tone had taken on a curious note. He seemed
to be feeling both astonished at and grieved for his companion.

The other, however, did not reply; and after a few moments
the ex-soldier softly concluded:

" So now you have heard my story."

By this time the carpenters had ceased singing around the
barraque, and let their fire die down until quivering on the wall
of the edifice there was only a fiery-red patch, a patch barely
sufficient to render visible the shadows of the rocks; while
beside the fire there was seated only a tall figure with a black
beard which had, grasped in its hands, a heavy cudgel, and, lying
near its right foot, an axe. The figure was that of a watchman
set by the carpenters to keep an eye upon ourselves, the
appointed watchmen; though the fact in no way offended us.

Over the defile, in a ragged strip of sky, there were gleaming stars, while the rivulet was bubbling and purling, and from the obscurity of the forest there kept coming to our ears, now the cautious, rustling tread of some night animal, and now the mournful cry of an owl, until all nature seemed to be instinct with a secret vitality the sweet breath of which kept moving the heart to hunger insatiably for the beautiful.

Also, as I lay listening to the voice of the ex-soldier, a voice reminiscent of a distant tambourine, and to Vasili's pensive questions, I conceived a liking for the men, and began to detect that in their relations there was dawning something good and human. At the same time, the effect of some of Vasili's dicta on Russia was to arouse in me mingled feelings which impelled me at once to argue with him and to induce him to speak at greater length, with more clarity, on the subject of our mutual fatherland. Hence always I have loved that night for the visions which it brought to me—visions which still come back to me like a dear, familiar tale.

I thought of a student of Kazan whom I had known in the days of the past, of a young fellow from Viatka who, pale-browed, and sententious of diction, might almost have been brother to the ex-soldier himself. And once again I heard him declare that " before all things must I learn whether or not there exists a God: pre-eminently must I make a beginning there."

And I thought, too, of a certain accoucheuse named Velikova who had been a comely, but reputedly gay, woman. And I remembered a certain occasion when, on a hill overlooking the river Kazan and the Arski Plain, she had stood contemplating the marshes below, and the far blue line of the Volga; until, suddenly turning pale, she had, with tears of joy sparkling in her fine eyes, cried under her breath, but sufficiently loudly for all present to hear her:

" Ah, friends, how gracious and how fair is this land of ours! Come, let us salute that land for having deemed us worthy of residence therein! "

Whereupon all present, including a deacon-student from the Ecclesiastical School, a Morduine from the Foreign College, a student of veterinary science, and two of our tutors, had done obeisance. At the same time I recalled the fact that subsequently one of the party had gone mad, and committed suicide.

Again, I recalled how once, on the Piani Bor [1] by the river Kama, a tall, sandy young fellow with intelligent eyes and

[1] Liquor Wharf.

the face of a ne'er-do-weel had caught my attention. The day had been a hot, languorous Sunday on which all things had seemed to be exhibiting their better side, and telling the sun that it was not in vain that he was pouring out his brilliant potency, and diffusing his living gold; while the man of whom I speak had, dressed in a new suit of blue serge, a new cap cocked awry, and a pair of brilliantly polished boots, been standing at the edge of the wharf, and gazing at the brown waters of the Kama and the emerald expanse beyond them and the silver-scaled pools left behind by the tide. Until, as the sun had begun to sink towards the marshes on the other side of the river, and to become dissolved into streaks, the man had smiled with increasing rapture, and his face had glowed with creasing eagerness and delight; until finally he had snatched the cap from his head, flung it, with a powerful throw, far out into the russet waters, and shouted: " Kama, O my mother, I love you, and never will desert you ! "

And the last, and also the best, recollection of things seen before the night of which I speak was the recollection of an occasion when, one late autumn, I had been crossing the Caspian Sea on an old two-masted schooner laden with dried apricots, plums, and peaches. Sailing on her also she had had some hundred fishermen from the Bozhi Factory, men who, originally forest peasants of the Upper Volga, had been well-built, bearded, healthy, goodhumoured, animal-spirited young fellows, youngsters tanned with the wind, and salted with the sea water, youngsters who, after working hard at their trade, had been rejoicing at the prospect of returning home, and careering about the deck like youthful bears as ever and anon lofty, sharp-pointed waves had seized and tossed aloft the schooner, and the yards had cracked, and the taut-run rigging had whistled, and the sails had bellied into globes, and the howling wind had shaved off the white crests of billows, and partially submerged the vessel in clouds of foam.

And seated on the deck with his broad back resting against the mainmast there had been one young giant in particular. Clad in a white linen shirt and a pair of blue serge trousers, and innocent alike of beard and moustache, this young fellow had had full, red lips, blue, boyish, and exceedingly translucent eyes, and a face intoxicated *in excelsis* with the happiness of youth; while leaning across his knees as they had rested sprawling over the deck there had been a young female trimmer of fish, a wench as massive and tall as the young man himself, and a wench whose face had become tanned to roughness with the sun and wind, eyebrows dark, full, and as large as the wings of a swallow, breasts as firm as stone, and teats around which, as they projected from the folds of a red bodice, there had lain a pattern of blue veins.

The broad, iron-black palm of the young fellow's long, knotted hand had been resting on the woman's left breast, with the arm bare to the elbow; while in his right hand, as he had sat gazing pensively at the woman's robust figure, there had been grasped a tin mug from which some of the red liquor had scattered stains over the front of his linen shirt.

Meanwhile around the pair there had been hovering some of the youngster's comrades, who, with coats buttoned to the throat, and caps gripped to prevent their being blown away by the wind, had employed themselves with scanning the woman's figure with envious eyes, and viewing her from either side. Nay, the shaggy green waves themselves had been stealing occasional glimpses at the picture as clouds had swirled across the sky, gulls had uttered their insatiable scream, and the sun, dancing on the foam-flecked waters, had vested the billows, now in tints of blue, now in natural tints as of flaming jewels.

In short, all the passengers on the schooner had been shouting and laughing and singing, while the great bearded peasants had also been paying assiduous court to a large leathern bottle which had lain ensconced on a heap of peach-sacks, with the result that the scene had come to have about it something of the antique, legendary air of the return of Stepan Razin from his Persian campaign.

At length the buffeting of the wind had caused an old man with a crooked nose set on a hairy, faun-like face to stumble over one of the woman's feet; whereupon he had halted, thrown up his head with non-senile vigour, and exclaimed:

" May the devil fly away with you, you shameless hussy! Why lie sprawling about the deck like this? See, too, how exposed you are! "

The woman had not stirred at the words—she had not even opened an eye: only over her lips there had passed a faint tremor. Whereas the young fellow had straightened himself, deposited his tin mug upon the deck, and cried loudly as he laid his disengaged hand upon the woman's breast:

" Ah, you envy me, do you, Yakim Petrov? Never mind, though: you have done no great harm. But run no risks; do not look for needless trouble, for your day for sucking sugar-plums is past."

Whereafter, raising both his hands, the young fellow had softly let them sink again upon the woman's bosom as he added triumphantly:

" These breasts could feed all Russia ! "

Then, and only then, had the woman smiled a long, slow smile. And as she had done so everything in the vicinity had seemed to smile in unison, and to rise and fall in harmony with her bosom—yes, the whole vessel, and the vessel's freight. And at the moment when a particularly large wave had struck the bulwarks, and besprinkled all on board with spray, the woman had opened her dark eyes, looked kindly at the old man, and at the young fellow, and at the scene in general—then set herself to re-cover her bosom.

" Nay," the young fellow had cried as he interposed to remove her hands. " There is no need for that, there is no need for that. Let them *all* look."

*

Such the memories that came back to my recollection that night. Gladly I would have recounted them to my companions, but, unfortunately, these had, by now, succumbed to slumber. The ex-soldier, resting in a sitting posture, and snoring loudly, had his back prised against his wallet, his head sloped sideways, and his hands clasped upon his knees, while Vasili was lying on his back with his face turned upwards, his hands clasped behind his head, his dark, finely moulded brows raised a little, and his moustache erect. Also, he was weeping in his sleep—tears were coursing down his brown, sunburnt cheeks; tears which, in the moonlight, had in them something of the greenish tint of a chrysolite or sea water, and which, on such a manly face, looked strange indeed!

Still the rivulet was purling as it flowed, and the fire crackling; while bathed in the red glow of the flames there was sitting, bent forward, the dark, stonelike figure of the Molokans' watchman, with the axe at his feet reflecting the radiant gleam of the moon in the sky above us.

All the earth seemed to be sleeping as ever the waning stars seemed to draw nearer and nearer. . . .

The slow length of the next day was dragged along amid an inertia born of the moist heat, the song of the river, and the intoxicating scents of forest and flowers. In short, one felt inclined to do nothing, from morn till night, save roam the defile without the exchanging of a word, the conceiving of a desire, or the formulating of a thought.

At sunset, when we were engaged in drinking tea by the fire, the ex-soldier remarked:

" I hope that life in the next world will exactly resemble life in this spot, and be just as quiet and peaceful and immune from work. Here one needs but to sit and melt like butter, and suffer neither from wrong nor anxiety."

Then, as carefully he withdrew his pipe from his lips, and sighed, he added:

" Aye! If I could but feel sure that life in the next world will be like life here, I would pray to God: ' For Christ's sake take my soul at the earliest conceivable moment.' "

" What might suit *you* would not suit *me*," Vasili thoughtfully observed. " I would not always live such a life as this. I might do so for a time, but not in perpetuity."

" Ah, but never have you worked hard," grunted the ex-soldier.

In every way the evening resembled the previous one: there were to be observed the same luscious flooding of the defile with dove-coloured mist, the same flashing of the silver crags in the roseate twilight, the same rocking of the dense, warm forest's soft, leafy tree-tops, the same softening of the rocks' outlines in the gloom, the same gradual uplift of shadows, the same chanting of the " matchmaking " river, the same routine on the part of the big, sleek carpenters around the *barraque*— a routine as slow and ponderous in its course as the movements of a drove of wild boars.

More than once during the off hours of the day had we sought to make the carpenters' acquaintance, to start a conversation with them, but always their answers had been given reluctantly, in monosyllables, and never had a discussion seemed likely to get under way without the whiteheaded foreman shouting to the particular member of the gang concerned: " Hi, you, Pavlushka! Get back to work, there! " Indeed, he, the foreman, had outdone all in his manifestations of dislike for our friendship, and as monotonously as though he had been minded to rival the rivulet as a songster he had hummed his pious ditties, or else raised his snuffling voice to sing them with an ever-importunate measure of insistence, so that all day long those ditties had been coursing their way in a murky, melancholy-compelling flood. Indeed, as the foreman had stepped cautiously on thin legs from stone to stone during his ceaseless inspection of the work of his men he had come to seem to have for his object the describing of an invisible, circular path, as a means of segregating us more securely than ever from the society of the carpenters.

Personally, however, I had no desire to converse with him, for his frozen eyes chilled and repelled me; and from the moment when I had approached him, and seen him fold his hands behind him, and recoil a step as he inquired with suppressed sternness, " What do you want? " there had fallen away from me all further ambition to learn the nature of the songs which he sang.

The ex-soldier gazed at him resentfully—then said with an oath:

" The old wizard and pilferer! Take my word for it that a lump of piety like that has got a pretty store put away somewhere."

Whereafter, as he lit his pipe and squinted in the direction of the carpenters, he added with stifled wrath: ·

" The airs that the ' elect ' give themselves—the sons of bitches! "

" It is always so," commented Vasili with a resentment equal to the last speaker's. " Yes, no sooner, with us, does a man accumulate a little money than he sticks his nose in the air, and falls to thinking himself a real *barin*."

" Why is it that you always say ' With us,' and ' Among us,' and so on? "

" Among us Russians, then, if you like it better."

" I do like it better. For you are not a German, are you, nor a Tartar? "

" No. It is merely that I can see the faults in our Russian folk."

Upon that (not for the first time) the pair plunged into a discussion which had come so to weary them that now they spoke only indifferently, without effort.

" The word ' faults ' is, I consider, an insult," began the ex-soldier as he puffed at his pipe. " Besides, you don't speak consistently. Only this moment I observed a change in your terms."

" To what? "

" To the term ' Russians.' "

" What should you prefer? "

A new sound floated into the defile as from some point on the steppe the sound of a bell summoning folk to the usual

Saturday vigil service. Removing his pipe from his mouth, the ex-soldier listened for a moment or two. Then, at the third and last stroke of the bell, he doffed his cap, crossed himself with punctilious piety, and said:

" There are not very many churches in these parts."

Whereafter he threw a glance across the river, and added venomously:

" Those devils *there* don't cross themselves, the accursed Serbs! "

Vasili looked at him, twisted a left-hand moustache, smoothed it again, regarded for a moment the sky and the defile, and sank his head.

" The trouble with me," he remarked in an undertone, " is that I can never remain very long in one place—always I keep fancying that I shall meet with better things elsewhere, always I keep hearing a bird singing in my heart, ' Do you go further, do you go further.' "

" That bird sings in the heart of *every* man," the ex-soldier growled sulkily.

With a glance at us both, Vasili laughed a subdued laugh.

" ' In the heart of *every* man '? " he repeated. " Why, such a statement is absurd. For it means, does it not, that every one of us is an idler, every one of us is constantly waiting for something to turn up—that, in fact, no one of us is any better than, or able to do any better than, the folk whose sole utterance is ' Give unto us, pray give unto us '? Yes, if that be the case, it is an unfortunate case indeed! "

And again he laughed. Yet his eyes were sorrowful, and as the fingers of his right hand lay upon his knee they twitched as though they were longing to grasp something unseen.

The ex-soldier frowned and snorted. For my own part, however, I felt troubled for, and sorry for, Vasili. Presently he rose, broke into a soft whistle, and moved away by the side of the stream.

" His head is not quite right," muttered the ex-soldier as he winked in the direction of the retreating figure. " Yes, I tell you that straight, for from the first it was clear to me. Otherwise, what could his words in depreciation of Russia mean, when of Russia nothing the least hard or definite can be said? Who really knows her? What is she in reality, seeing that each of her provinces is a soul to itself, and no one could state which of the two Holy Mothers stands nearest to God—the Holy Mother of Smolensk, or the Holy Mother of Kazan? "

For a while the speaker sat scraping greasy deposit from the bottom and sides of the kettle; and all that while he grumbled as though he had a grudge against someone. At length, however, he assumed an attitude of attention, with his neck stretched out as though to listen to some sound.

" Hist! " was his exclamation.

What then followed, followed as unexpectedly as when, like an evil bird, a summer whirlwind suddenly sweeps up from the horizon, and discharges a bluish-black cloud in torrents of rain and hail, until everything is overwhelmed, and battered to mud.

That is to say, with much din of whistling and other sounds there now came pouring into the defile, and began to ascend the trail beside the stream, a straggling procession of some thirty workmen with, gleaming dully in the hands of their leading files, flagons of *vodka*, and, suspended on the backs and shoulders of others, wallets and bags of bread and other comestibles, and, in two instances, poised on the heads of yet other processionists, large black cauldrons the effect of which was to make their bearers look like mushrooms.

" A *vedro* [1] and a half to the cauldron! " whispered the ex-soldier with a computative grunt as he gained his feet.

" Yes, a *vedro* and a half," he repeated. As he spoke the tip of his tongue protruded until it rested on the under-lip of his half-opened mouth. In his face there was a curiously thirsty, gross expression, and his attitude, as he stood there, was that of one who had just received a blow, and was about to cry out in consequence.

Meanwhile the defile rumbled like a barrel into which heavy weights are being dropped, for one of the newcomers was beating an empty tin pail, and another one whistling in a manner the tossed echoes of which drowned even the rivulet's murmur as nearer and nearer came the mob of men, a mob clad variously in black, grey, or russet, with sleeves rolled up, and heads, in many cases, bare save for their own towsled, dishevelled locks, and bodies bent with fatigue, or carried stumblingly along on legs bowed outwards. Meanwhile, as the dull, polyphonous roar of voices swept through the neck of the defile, a man shouted in broken, but truculent, accents:

" I say no! Fiddlesticks! Not a man is there who could drink more than a *vedro* of ' blood-and-sweat ' in a day."

" A man could drink a lake of it."

[1] 2¾ gallons.

" No, a *vedro* and a half. That is the proper reckoning."

" Aye, a *vedro* and a half." And the ex-soldier, as he repeated the words, spoke both as though he were an expert in the matter and as though he felt for the matter a touch of respect. Then, lurching forward like a man pushed by the scruff of the neck, he crossed the rivulet, intercepted the crowd, and became swallowed up in its midst.

Around the *barraque* the carpenters (the foreman ever glimmering among them) were hurriedly collecting tools. Presently Vasili returned—his right hand thrust into his pocket, and his left holding his cap.

" Before long those fellows will be properly drunk!" he said with a frown. " Ah, that *vodka* of ours! It is a perfect curse!" Then to me: " Do *you* drink? "

" No," I replied.

" Thank God for that! If one does not drink one will never really get into trouble."

For a moment he gazed gloomily in the direction of the newcomers. Then he said without moving, without even looking at me:

" You have remarkable eyes, young fellow. Also, they seem familiar to me—I have seen them somewhere before. Possibly that happened in a dream, though I cannot be sure. Where do you come from? "

I answered, but, after scanning me perplexedly, he shook his head.

" No," he remarked. " I have never visited that part of the country, or indeed, been so far from home."

" But this place is further still? "

" Further still? "

" Yes—from Kursk."

He laughed.

" I must tell you the truth," he said. " I am not a Kurskan at all, but a Pskovian. The reason why I told the ex-soldier that I was from Kursk was that I neither liked him nor cared to tell him the whole truth—he was not worth the trouble. And as for my real name, it is Paul, not Vasili—Paul Nikolaev Silantiev, and is so marked on my passport (for a passport, and a passport quite in order, I have got)."

" And why are you on your travels? "

" For the reason that I am so—I can say no more. I look back from a given place, and wave my hand, and am gone again as a feather floats before the wind."

" Silence! " a threatening voice near the *barraque* broke in.
" I am the foreman here."

The voice of the ex-soldier replied:

" What workmen are these of yours? They are mere sectarians, fellows who are for ever singing hymns."

To which someone else added:

" Besides, old devil that you are, aren't you bound to finish
all building work before the beginning of a Sunday? "

" Let us throw their tools into the stream."

" Yes, and start a riot," was Silantiev's comment as he
squatted before the embers of the fire.

Around the *barraque*, picked out against the yellow of its
framework, a number of dark figures were surging to and fro
as around a conflagration. Presently we heard something
smashed to pieces—at all events, we heard the cracking and
scraping of wood against stone, and then the strident, hilarious
command:

" Hold on there! *I*'ll soon put things to rights! Carpenters,
just hand over the saw! "

Apparently there were three men in charge of the proceedings:
the one a red-bearded *muzhik* in a seaman's blouse; the second
a tall man with hunched shoulders, thin legs, and long arms
who kept grasping the foreman by the collar, shaking him, and
bawling, " Where are your lathes? Bring them out! " (while
noticeable also was a broad-shouldered young fellow in a ragged
red shirt who kept thrusting pieces of scantling through the
windows of the *barraque*, and shouting, " Catch hold of these!
Lay them out in a row! "); and the third the ex-soldier himself.
The last-named, as he jostled his way among the crowd, kept
vociferating, viciously, virulently, and with a curious system
of division of his syllables:

" Aha-a, ra-abble, secta-arians. Yo-ou would have nothing
to say to me, you Se-erbs! Yet *I* say to *you*: Go along, my
chickens, for the re-est of us are ti-ired of you, and come to
sa-ay so! "

" What does he want? " asked Silantiev quietly as he lit a
cigarette. " *Vodka?* Oh, *they*'ll give him *vodka!* . . . Yet are
you not sorry for fellows of that stamp? "

Through the blue tobacco-smoke he gazed into the glowing
embers: until at last he took a charred stick, and collected
the embers into a heap glowing red-gold like a bouquet of fiery
poppies: and as he did so his handsome eyes gleamed with

214

just such a reverent affection, such a prayerful kindliness, as must have lurked in the eyes of primeval, nomadic man in the presence of the dancing, beneficent source of light and heat.

"At least *I* am sorry for such fellows," Vasili continued. "Aye, the very thought of the many, many folk who have come to nothing! The very thought of it! Terrible, terrible!"

A touch of daylight was still lingering on the tops of the mountains, but in the defile itself night was beginning to loom, and to lull all things to sleep—to incline one neither to speak oneself nor to listen to the dull clamour of those others on the opposite bank, where even to the murmur of the rivulet the distasteful din seemed to communicate a note of anger.

There the crowd had lit a huge bonfire, and then added to it a second one which, crackling, hissing, and emitting coils of bluish-tinted smoke, had fallen to vying with its fellow in lacing the foam of the rivulet with muslin-like patterns in red. As the mass of dark figures surged between the two flares an hilarious voice shouted to us the invitation:

"Come over here, you! Don't be backward! Come over here, I say!"

Upon which followed a clatter as of the smashing of a drinking-vessel, while from the red-bearded *muzhik* came a thick, raucous shout of:

"These fellows needed to be taught a lesson!"

Almost at the same moment the foreman of the carpenters broke his way clear of the crowd, and, carefully crossing the rivulet by the stepping-stones which we had constructed, squatted down upon his heels by the margin, and with much puffing and blowing fell to rinsing his face, a face which in the murky firelight looked flushed and red.

"I think that someone has given him a blow," hazarded Silantiev *sotto voce*.

And when the foreman rose to approach us this proved to be the case, for then we saw that dripping from his nose, and meandering over his moustache and soaked white beard, there was a stream of dark blood which had spotted and streaked his shirt-front.

"Peace to this gathering!" he said gravely as, pressing his left hand to his stomach, he bowed.

"And we pray your indulgence," was Silantiev's response, though he did not raise his eyes as he spoke. "Pray be seated."

Small, withered, and, for all his blood-stained shirt, scrupulously clean, the old man reminded me of certain pictures of old-time hermits, and the more so since either pain or shame or the gleam of the firelight had caused his hitherto dead eyes to gather life and grow brighter—aye, and sterner. Somehow, as I looked at him, I felt awkward and abashed.

A cough twisted his broad nose. Then he wiped his beard on the palm of his hand, and his hand on his knee; whereafter, as he stretched forth the pair of senile, dark-coloured hands, and held them over the embers, he said:

" How cold the water of the rivulet is! It is absolutely icy."

With a glance from under his brows Silentiev inquired:

" Are you very badly hurt? "

" No. Merely a man caught me a blow on the bridge of the nose, where the blood flows readily. Yet, as God knows, he will gain nothing by his act, whereas the suffering which he has caused me will go to swell my account with the Holy Spirit."

As the man spoke he glanced across the rivulet. On the opposite bank two men were staggering along, and drunkenly bawling the tipsy refrain:

> In the du-u-uok let me die,
> In the au-autumn time!

" Aye, long is it since I received a blow," the old man continued, scanning the two revellers from under his hand. " Twenty years it must be since last I did so. And now the blow was struck for nothing, for no real fault. You see, I have been allowed no nails for the doing of the work, and have been obliged to make use of wooden clamps for most of it, while battens also have not been forthcoming: and, this being so, it was through no remissness of mine that the work could not be finished by sunset to-night. I suspect, too, that, to eke out its wages, that rabble has been thieving, with the eldest leading the rest. And that, again, is not a thing for which I can be held responsible. True, this is a Government job, and some of those fellows are young, and young, hungry fellows such as they will (may they be forgiven!) steal, since everyone hankers to get something in return for a very little. But, once more, how is that my fault? Yes, that rabble must be a regular set of rascals! Just now they deprived my eldest son of a saw, of a brand-new saw; and thereafter they spilt my blood, the blood of a greybeard! "

Here his small, grey face contracted into wrinkles, and, closing his eyes, he sobbed a dry, grating sob.

Silantiev fidgeted—then sighed. Presently the old man

looked at him, blew his nose, wiped his hand upon his trousers, and said quietly:

" Somewhere, I think, I have seen you before."

" That is so. You saw me one evening when I visited your settlement for the mending of a thresher."

" Yes, yes. That is where I *did* see you. It *was* you, was it not? Well, do you still disagree with me? "

To which the old man added with a nod and a smile:

" See how well I remember your words! You are, I imagine, still of the same opinion? "

" How should I not be? " responded Silantiev dourly.

" Ah, well! Ah, well! "

And the old man stretched his hands over the fire once more —discoloured hands the thumbs of which were curiously bent outwards, and splayed, and, seemingly, unable to move in harmony with the fingers.

The ex-soldier shouted across the river:

" The land here is easy to work, and makes the people lazy. Who would care to live in such a region? Who would care to come to it? Much rather would I go and earn a living on difficult land."

The old man paid no heed, but said to Silantiev—said to him with an austere, derisive smile:

" Do you *still* think it necessary to struggle against what has been ordained of God? Do you *still* think that long-suffering is bad, and resistance good? Young man, your soul is weak indeed: and remember that it is only the soul that can over-come Satan."

In response Silantiev rose to his feet, shook his fist at the old man, and shouted in a rough, angry voice, a voice that was not his own:

" All that I have heard before, and from others besides yourself. The truth is that I hold all you father-confessors in abhorrence. Moreover " (this last was added with a violent oath), " it is not Satan that needs to be resisted, but such devil's ravens, such devil's vampires, as *you*."

Which said, he kicked a stone away from the fire, thrust his hands into his pockets, and turned slowly on his heel, with his elbows pressed close to his sides. Nevertheless the old man, still smiling, said to me in an undertone:

" He is proud, but that will not last for long."

" Why not? "

" Because I know in advance that——"

Breaking off short, he turned his head upon his shoulder, and sat listening to some shouting that was going on across the river. Everyone in that quarter was drunk, and, in particular, someone could be heard bawling in a tone of challenge:

" Oh? *I*, you say? A-a-ah! Then take that! "

Silantiev, stepping lightly from stone to stone, crossed the river. Then he mingled—a conspicuous figure (owing to his apparent handlessness)—with the crowd. Somehow, on his departure, I felt ill at ease.

Twitching his fingers as though performing a conjuring trick, the old man continued to sit with his hands stretched over the embers. By this time his nose had swollen over the bridge, and bruises risen under his eyes which tended to obscure his vision. Indeed, as he sat there, sat mouthing with dark, bestreaked lips under a covering of hoary beard and moustache, I found that his bloodstained, disfigured, wrinkled, as it were " antique " face reminded me more than ever of those of great sinners of ancient times who abandoned this world for the forest and the desert.

" I have seen many proud folk," he continued with a shake of his hatless head and its sparse hairs. " A fire may burn up quickly, and continue to burn fiercely, yet, like these embers, become turned to ashes, and so lie smouldering till dawn. Young man, there you have something to think of. Nor are they merely my words. They are the words of the Holy Gospel itself."

Ever descending, ever weighing more heavily upon us, the night was as black and hot and stifling as the previous one had been, albeit as kindly as a mother. Still the two fires on the opposite bank of the rivulet were aflame, and sending hot blasts of vapour across a seeming brook of gold.

Folding his arms upon his breast, the old man tucked the palms of his hands into his armpits, and settled himself more comfortably. Nevertheless, when I made as though to add more twigs and shavings to the embers he exclaimed imperiously:

" There is no need for that."

" Why is there not? "

" Because that would cause the fire to be seen, and bring some of those men over here."

Again, as he kicked away some boughs which I had just broken up, he repeated:

" There is no need for that, I tell you."

Presently there approached us through the shimmering firelight on the opposite bank two carpenters with boxes on their backs, and axes in their hands.

" Are all the rest of our men gone? " inquired the foreman of the newcomers.

" Yes," replied one of them, a tall man with a drooping moustache and no beard.

" Well, ' shun evil, and good will result.' "

" Aye, and we likewise wish to depart."

" But a task ought not to be left unfinished. At dinner-time I sent Olesha to say that none of those fellows had better be released from work; but released they have been, and now the result is apparent! Presently, when they have drunk a little more of their poison, they will fire the *barraque*."

Every time that the first of the two carpenters inhaled the smoke of my cigarette he spat into the embers, while the other man, a young fellow as plump as a female baker, sank his towsled head upon his breast as soon as he sat down, and fell asleep.

Next, the clamour across the rivulet subsided for awhile. But suddenly I heard the ex-soldier exclaim in drunken, singsong accents which came from the very centre of the tumult:

" Hi, do you answer me! How comes it that you have no respect for Russia? Is not Riazan a part of Russia? What *is* Russia, then, I should like to know? "

" A tavern," the foreman commented quietly: whereafter, turning to me, he added more loudly:

" I say this of such fellows: that a tavern—— But what a noise those roisterers are making, to be sure! "

The young fellow in the red shirt had just shouted:

" Hi, there, soldier! Seize him by the throat! Seize him, seize him! "

While from Silantiev had come the gruff retort:

" What? Do you suppose that you are hunting a pack of hounds? "

" Here, answer me! " was the next shouted utterance—it came from the ex-soldier: whereupon the old man remarked to me in an undertone:

" It would seem that a fight is brewing."

Rising, I moved in the direction of the uproar. As I did so I heard the old man say softly to his companions:

" He too is gone, thank God! "

Suddenly there surged towards me from the opposite bank a crowd of men. Belching, hiccuping, and grunting, they seemed to be carrying or dragging in their midst some heavy weight. Presently a woman's voice screamed, " Ya-av-sha!" and other voices raised mingled shouts of " Throw him in!" " Give him a thrashing!" and " Drag him along!"

The next moment we saw Silantiev break out of the crowd, straighten himself, swing his right fist in the air, and hurl himself at the crowd again. As he did so the young fellow in the red shirt raised a gigantic arm, and there followed the sound of a muffled, grisly blow. Staggering backwards, Silantiev slid silently into the water, and lay there at my feet.

" That's right!" was the comment of someone.

For a moment or two the clamour subsided a little, and during that moment or two one's ears once more became laved with the sweet sing-song of the river. Shortly afterwards someone threw into the water a huge stone, and someone else laughed in a dull way.

As I was bending to look at Silantiev some of the men jostled me. Nevertheless I continued to struggle to raise him from the spot where, half in, and half out of, the water, he lay with his head and breast resting against the stepping-stones.

" You have killed him!" next I shouted—not because I believed the statement to be true, but because I had a mind to frighten into sobriety the men who were impeding me.

Upon this someone exclaimed in a faltering, sobered tone: " Surely not? "

As for the young fellow in the red shirt, he passed me by with a braggart, resentful shout of:

" Well? He had no right to insult me. Why should he have said that I was a nuisance to the whole country? "

And someone else shouted:

" Where is the ex-soldier? Who is the watchman here? "

" Bring a light," was the cry of a third.

Yet all these voices were more sober, more subdued, more restrained than they had been, and presently a little *muzhik* whose poll was swathed in a red handkerchief stooped and raised Silantiev's head. But almost as instantly he let it fall again, and, dipping his hands into the water, said gravely:

" You have killed him. He is dead."

At the moment I did not believe the words; but presently, as I stood watching how the water coursed between Silantiev's legs, and turned them this way and that, and made them stir as though they were striving to divest themselves of the shabby old boots, I realised with all my being that the hands which

were resting in mine were the hands of a corpse. And, true enough, when I released them they slapped down upon the surface like wet dish-clouts.

Until now about a dozen men had been standing on the bank to observe what was toward, but as soon as the little *muzhik's* words rang out these men recoiled, and, with jostlings, began to vent, in subdued, uneasy tones, cries of:

" Who was it first struck him? "

" This will lose us our jobs."

" It was the soldier that first started the racket."

" Yes, that is true."

" Let us go and denounce him."

As for the young fellow in the red shirt, he cried:

" I swear on my honour, mates, that the affair was only a quarrel."

" To hit a man with a bludgeon is more than a quarrel."

" It was a stone that was used, not a bludgeon."

" The soldier ought to——"

A woman's high-pitched voice broke in with a plaintive cry of:

" Good Lord! Always something happens to us! "

As for myself, I felt stunned and hurt as I seated myself upon the stepping-stones; and though everything was plain to my sight, nothing was plain to my understanding, while in my breast a strange emptiness was present, save that the clamour of the bystanders aroused me to a certain longing to outshout them all, to send forth my voice into the night like the voice of a brazen trumpet.

Presently two other men approached us. In the hand of the first was a torch which he kept waving to and fro to prevent its being extinguished, and whence, therefore, he kept strewing showers of golden sparks. A fair-headed little fellow, he had a body as thin as a pike when standing on its tail, a grey, stonelike countenance that was deeply sunken between the shoulders, a mouth perpetually half-agape, and round, owlish-looking eyes.

As he approached the corpse he bent forward with one hand upon his knee to throw the more light upon Silantiev's bruised head and body. That head was resting turned upon the shoulder, and no longer could I recognise the once handsome Cossack face, so buried was the jaunty forelock under a clot of black-red mud, and concealed by a swelling which had made its appearance above the left ear. Also, since the mouth and moustache had been bashed aside, the teeth lay bared in a twisted, truly horrible smile, while, as the most horrible point of all, the left eye was hanging from its socket, and, become hideously large, gazing, seemingly, at the inner pocket of the flap of Silantiev's pea-jacket, whence there was protruding a white edging of paper.

Slowly the torch holder described a circle of fire in the air, and thereby sprinkled a further shower of sparks over the poor mutilated face, with its streaks of shining blood. Then he muttered with a smack of the lips:

" You can see for yourselves who the man is."

As he spoke a few more sparks descended upon Silantiev's scalp and wet cheeks, and went out, while the flare's reflection so played in the ball of Silantiev's eye as to communicate to it an added appearance of death.

Finally the torch holder straightened his back, threw his torch into the river, expectorated after it, and said to his companion as he smoothed a flaxen poll which, in the darkness, looked almost greenish:

" Do you go to the *barraque*, and tell them that a man has been done to death."

" No; I should be afraid to go alone."

" Come, come! Nothing is there to be afraid of. Go, I tell you."

" But I would much rather not."

" Don't be such a fool! "

Suddenly there sounded over my head the quiet voice of the foreman.

" *I* will accompany you," he said. Then he added disgustedly as he scraped his foot against a stone:

" How horrible the blood smells! It would seem that my very foot is smeared with it."

With a frown the fair-headed *muzhik* eyed him, while the foreman returned the *muzhik's* gaze with a scrutiny that never wavered. Finally the elder man commented with cold severity:

" All the mischief has come of *vodka* and tobacco, the devil's drugs."

Not only were the pair strangely alike, but both of them strangely resembled wizards, in that both were short of stature, as sharp-finished as gimlets, and as green-tinted by the darkness as tufts of lichen.

" Let us go, brother," the foreman said. " Go we with the Holy Spirit."

And, omitting even to inquire who had been killed, or even to glance at the corpse, or even to pay it the last salute demanded of custom, the foreman departed down the stream, while in his wake followed the messenger, a man who kept stumbling as he picked his way from stone to stone. Amid the gloom the pair moved as silently as ghosts.

The narrow-chested, fair-headed little *muzhik* then raked me with his eyes: whereafter he produced a cigarette from a tin box, snapped-to the lid of the box, struck a match (illuminating once more the face of the dead man), and applied the flame to the cigarette. Lastly he said:

" This is the sixth murder which I have seen one thing and another commit."

" One thing and another commit? " I queried.

The reply came only after a pause; when the little *muzhik* asked: " What did you say? I did not quite catch it."

I explained that human beings, not inanimate entities, murdered human beings.

" Well, be they human beings or machinery or lightning or anything else, they are all one. One of my mates was caught in some machinery at Bakhmakh. Another one had his throat cut in a brawl. Another one was crushed against the bucket in a coal mine. Another one was——"

Carefully though the man counted, he ended by erring in his reckoning to the extent of making his total " five." Accordingly he re-computed the list—and this time succeeded in making the total amount to " seven."

" Never mind," he remarked with a sigh as he blew his cigarette into a red glow which illuminated the whole of his face. " The truth is that I cannot always repeat the list correctly, just as I should like. Were I older than I am, I too should contrive to get finished off: for old-age is a far from desirable thing. Yes, indeed! But, as things are, I am still alive, nor, thank the Lord, does anything matter very much."

Presently, with a nod towards Silantiev, he continued:

" Even now *his* kinsfolk or his wife may be looking for news of him, or a letter from him. Well, never again will he write, and as likely as not his kinsfolk will end by saying to themselves: ' He has taken to bad ways, and forgotten his family.' Yes, good sir."

By this time the clamour around the *barraque* had ceased, and the two fires had burnt themselves out, and most of the men dispersed. From the smooth yellow walls of the *barraque* dark, round knot-holes were gazing at the rivulet like eyes. Only in a single window without a frame was there visible a

223

faint light, while at intervals there issued thence fragmentary, angry exclamations such as:

" Look sharp there, and deal! "

" Clubs will be the winners."

" Ah! Here is a trump!"

" Indeed? What luck, damn it! "

The fair-headed *muzhik* blew the ashes from his cigarette, and observed:

" No such thing is there at cards as luck—only skill."

At this juncture we saw approaching us softly from across the rivulet a young carpenter who wore a moustache. He halted beside us, and drew a deep breath.

" Well, mate? " the fair-headed *muzhik* inquired.

" Would you mind giving me something to smoke? " the carpenter asked. The obscurity caused him to look large and shapeless, though his manner of speaking was bashful and subdued.

" Certainly. Here is a cigarette."

" Christ reward you! To-day my wife forgot to bring my tobacco, and my grandfather has strict ideas on the subject of smoking."

" Was it he who departed just now? "

" It was."

As the carpenter inhaled a whiff he continued:

" I suppose that man was beaten to death? "

" He was—to death."

For a while the pair smoked in silence. The hour was past midnight.

Over the defile the jagged strip of sky which roofed it looked like a river of blue flowing at an immense height above the night-enveloped earth, and bearing the brilliant stars on its smooth current.

Quieter and quieter was everything growing: more and more was everything becoming part of the night. . . .

One might have thought that nothing particular had happened.

KALININ

WHISTLING from off the sea, the wind was charged with moist, salt spray, and dashing foaming billows ashore with their white manes full of snakelike, gleaming black ribands of seaweed, and causing the rocks to rumble angrily in response, and the trees to rustle with a dry, agitated sound as their tops swayed to and fro, and their trunks bent earthwards as though they would fain reeve up their roots, and betake them whither the mountains stood veiled in a toga of heavy, dark mist.

Over the sea the clouds were hurrying towards the land as ever and anon they rent themselves into strips, and revealed fathomless abysses of blue wherein the autumn sun burned uneasily, and sent cloud-shadows gliding over the puckered waste of waters, until, the shore reached, the wind further harried the masses of vapour towards the sharp flanks of the mountains, and, after drawing them up and down the slopes, relegated them to clefts, and left them steaming there.

There was about the whole scene a louring appearance, an appearance as though everything were contending with everything, as now all things turned sullenly dark, and now all things emitted a dull sheen which almost blinded the eyes. Along the narrow road, a road protected from the sea by a line of wave-washed dykes, some withered leaves of oak and wild cherry were scudding in mutual chase of one another: with the general result that the combined sounds of splashing and rustling and howling came to merge themselves into a single din which issued as a song with a rhythm marked by the measured blows of the waves as they struck the rocks.

" Zmiulan, the King of the Ocean, is abroad! " shouted my fellow traveller in my ear. He was a tall, round-shouldered man of childishly chubby features and boyishly bright, transparent eyes.

" *Who* do you say is abroad? " I queried.

" King Zmiulan."

Never having heard of the monarch, I made no reply.

The extent to which the wind buffeted us might have led one to suppose that its primary object was to deflect our steps, and turn them in the direction of the mountains. Indeed, at times its pressure was so strong that we had no choice but to halt, to turn our backs to the sea, and, with feet planted apart, to prise ourselves against our sticks, and so remain, poised on three legs, until we were past any risk of being overwhelmed with the soft incubus of the tempest, and having our coats torn from our shoulders.

At intervals such gasps would come from my companion that he might well have been standing on the drying-board of a bath. Nor, as they did so, was his appearance aught but comical, seeing that his ears, appendages large and shaggy like a dog's, and indifferently shielded with a shabby old cap, kept being pushed forward by the wind until his small head bore an absurd resemblance to a china bowl, and that, to complete the resemblance, his long and massive nose, a feature grossly disproportionate to the rest of his diminutive face, might equally well have passed for the spout of the receptacle indicated.

Yet a face out of the common it was, like the whole of his personality. And this was the fact which had captivated me from the moment when I had beheld him participating in a vigil service held in the neighbouring church of the monastery of New Athos. There, spare, but with his withered form erect, and his head slightly tilted, he had been gazing at the Crucifix with a radiant smile, and moving his thin lips in a sort of whispered, confidential, friendly conversation with the Saviour. Indeed, so much had the man's smooth, round features (features as beardless as those of a Skopetz,[1] save for two bright tufts at the corners of the mouth) been instinct with intimacy, with a consciousness of actually being in the presence of the Son of God, that the spectacle, transcending anything of the kind that my eyes had before beheld, had led me, with its total absence of the customary laboured, servile, pusillanimous attitude towards the Almighty which I had generally found to be the rule, to accord the man my whole interest, and, as long as the service had lasted, to keep an eye upon one who could thus converse with God without rendering Him constant obeisance, or again and again making the sign of the cross, or invariably making it to the accompaniment of groans and tears which had always hitherto obtruded itself upon my notice.

Again had I encountered the man when I had had supper at the workmen's *barraque*, and then proceeded to the monas-

[1] A member of the *Skoptzi*, a non-Orthodox sect the members of which " do make of themselves eunuchs for the Lord's sake."

tery's guest-chamber. Seated at a table under a circle of light falling from a lamp suspended from the ceiling, he had gathered around him a knot of pilgrims and their women, and was holding forth in low, cheerful tones that yet had in them the telling, incisive note of the preacher, of the man who frequently converses with his fellow men.

"One thing it may be best always to disclose," he was saying, "and another thing to conceal. If aught in ourselves seems harmful or senseless, let us put to ourselves the question, ' Why is this so? ' Contrariwise ought a prudent man never to thrust himself forward and say, ' How discreet am I! ' while he who makes a parade of his hard lot, and says, ' Good folk, see ye and hear how bitter my life is,' also does wrong."

Here a pilgrim with a black beard, a brigand's dark eyes, and the wasted features of an ascetic rose from the further side of the table, straightened his virile frame, and said in a dull voice:

"My wife and one of my children were burnt to death through the falling of an oil lamp. On *that* ought I to keep silence? "

No answer followed. Only someone muttered to himself, "What? Again? ": until the first speaker, the speaker seated near the corner of the table, launched into the oppressive lull the unhesitating reply:

"That of which you speak may be taken to have been a punishment by God for sin."

"What? For a sin committed by one three years of age (for, indeed, my little son was no more)? The accident happened of his pulling down a lamp upon himself, and of my wife seizing him, and herself being burnt to death. She was weak, too, for but eleven days had passed since her confinement."

"No. What I mean is that in that accident you see a punishment for sins committed by the child's father and mother."

This reply from the corner came with perfect confidence. The black-bearded man, however, pretended not to hear it, but spread out his hands as though parting the air before him, and proceeded hurriedly, breathlessly to detail the manner in which his wife and little one had met their deaths. And all the time that he was doing so one had an inkling that often before had he recounted his narrative of horror, and that often again would he repeat it. His shaggy black eyebrows, as he delivered his speech, met in a single strip, while the whites of his eyes grew bloodshot, and their dull, black pupils never ceased their nervous twitching.

Presently the gloomy recital was once more roughly, unceremoniously broken in upon by the cheerful voice of the Christ-loving pilgrim.

" It is not right, brother," the voice said, ' to blame God for untoward accidents, or for mistakes and follies committed by ourselves."

" But if God be God, He is responsible for *all* things."

" Not so. Concede to yourself the faculty of reason."

" Pah! What avails reason if it cannot make me understand? "

" Cannot make you understand *what*? "

" The main point, the point why *my* wife had to be burnt rather than my neighbour's? "

Somewhere an old woman commented in spitefully distinct tones:

" Oh ho, ho! This man comes to a monastery, and starts railing as soon as he gets there!"

Flashing his eyes angrily, the black-bearded man lowered his head like a bull. Then, thinking better of his position, and contenting himself with a gesture, he strode swiftly, heavily towards the door. Upon this the Christ-loving pilgrim rose with a swaying motion, bowed to everyone present, and set about following his late interlocutor.

" It has all come of a broken heart," he said with a smile as he passed me. Yet somehow the smile seemed to lack sympathy.

With a disapproving air someone else remarked:

" That fellow's one thought is to enlarge and to enlarge upon his tale."

" Yes, and to no purpose does he do so," added the Christ-loving pilgrim as he halted in the doorway. " All that he accomplishes by it is to weary himself and others alike. Such experiences are far better put behind one."

Presently I followed the pair into the forecourt, and near the entrance-gates heard a voice say quietly:

" Do not disturb yourself, good father."

" Nevertheless " (the second voice was that of the porter of the monastery, Father Seraphim, a strapping Vetlugan) "a spectre walks here nightly."

" Never mind if it does. As regards myself, no spectre would touch me."

Here I moved in the direction of the gates.

" Who comes there? " Seraphim inquired as he thrust a hairy and uncouth, but infinitely kindly, face close to mine. " Oh, it is the young fellow from Nizhni Novgorod! You are wasting your time, my good sir, for the women have all gone to bed."

With which he laughed and chuckled like a bear.

Beyond the wall of the forecourt the stillness of the autumn night was the languid inertia of a world exhausted by summer, and the withered grass and other objects of the season were exhaling a sweet and bracing odour, and the trees looking like fragments of cloud where motionless they hung in the moist, sultry air. Also, in the darkness the half-slumbering sea could be heard soughing as it crept towards the shore, while over the sky lay a canopy of mist, save at the point where the moon's opal-like blur could be descried over the spot where that blur's counterfeit image glittered and rocked on the surface of the dark waters.

Under the trees there was set a bench whereon I could discern there to be resting a human figure. Approaching the figure, I seated myself beside it.

" Whence, comrade? " was my inquiry.

" From Voronezh. And you? "

A Russian is never averse to talking about himself. It would seem as though he is never sure of his personality, as though he is ever yearning to have that personality confirmed from some source other than, extraneous to, his own ego. The reason for this must be that we Russians live diffused over a land of such vastness that, the more we grasp the immensity of the same, the smaller do we come to appear in our own eyes: wherefore, traversing, as we do, roads of a length of a thousand versts, and constantly losing our way, we come to let slip no opportunity of restating ourselves, and setting forth all that we have seen and thought and done.

Hence, too, must it be that in conversations one seems to hear less of the note of " I am I " than of the note of " Am I really and truly myself? "

" What may be your name? " next I inquired of the figure on the bench.

" A name of absolute simplicity—the name of Alexei Kalinin."

" You are a namesake of mine, then."

" Indeed? Is that so? "

With which, tapping me on the knee, the figure added:

" Come, then, namesake. ' I have mortar, and you have water, so together let us paint the town.' "

Murmuring amid the silence could be heard small, light waves that were no more than ripples. Behind us the busy clamour of the monastery had died down, and even Kalinin's cheery voice seemed subdued by the influence of the night—it seemed to have in it less of the note of self-confidence.

"My mother was a wet-nurse," he went on to volunteer, "and I her only child. When I was twelve years of age I was, owing to my height, converted into a footman. It happened thus. One day, on General Stepan (my mother's then employer) happening to catch sight of me, he exclaimed: 'Evgenia, go and tell Fedor' (the ex-soldier who was then serving the General as footman) 'that he is to teach your son to wait at table. The boy is at least tall enough for the work.' And for nine years I served the General in this capacity. And then, and then—oh, *then* I was seized with an illness. . . . Next I obtained a post under a merchant who was then mayor of our town, and stayed with him twenty-one months. And next I obtained a situation in an hotel at Kharkov, and held it for a year. And after that I kept changing my places, for, steady and sober though I was, I was beginning to lack taste for my profession, and to develop a spirit of the kind which deemed all work to be beneath me, and considered that I had been created to serve only myself, not others."

Along the high road to Sukhum which lay behind us there were proceeding some invisible travellers whose scraping of feet as they walked proclaimed the fact that they were not over-used to journeying on foot. Just as the party drew level with us a musical voice hummed out softly the line " Alone will I set forth upon the road," with the word " alone " plaintively stressed. Next, a resonant bass voice said with a sort of indolent incisiveness:

"*Aphon* or *aphonia* means loss of speech to the extent of, to the extent of—oh, to *what* extent, most learned Vera Vasilievna? "

" To the extent of total loss of power of articulation," replied a voice feminine and youthful of *timbre*.

Just at that moment we saw two dark, blurred figures, with a paler figure between them, come gliding into view.

" Strange indeed is it that, that——"

" That what? "

" That so many names proper to these parts should also be so suggestive. Take, for instance, Mount Nakopioba. Certainly folk hereabouts seem to have " amassed " things, and to have known how to do so." [1]

" For my part, I always fail to remember the name of Simon the Canaanite. Constantly I find myself calling him ' the Cainite.' "

" Look here," interrupted the musical voice in a tone of chastened enthusiasm. " As I contemplate all this beauty, and inhale this restfulness, I find myself reflecting: ' How would it be if I were to let everything go to the devil, and take up my abode here for ever? ' "

At this point all further speech became drowned by the sound of the monastery's bell as it struck the hour. The only utterance that came borne to my ears was the mournful fragment—

> Oh, if into a single word
> I could pour my inmost thoughts!

To the foregoing dialogue my companion had listened with his head tilted to one side, much as though the dialogue had deflected it in that direction: and now, as the voices died away into the distance, he sighed, straightened himself, and said:

" Clearly those people were educated folk. And see too how, as they talked of one thing and another, there cropped up the old and ever-persistent point."

" To what point are you referring? "

My companion paused a moment before he replied. Then he said:

" Can it be that you did not hear it? Did you not hear one of those people remark, ' I have a mind to surrender everything '? "

Whereafter, bending forward, and peering at me as a blind man would do, Kalinin added in a half-whisper:

" More and more are folk coming to think to themselves: ' Now must I forsake everything.' In the end I myself came to think it. For many a year did I increasingly reflect: ' Why should I be a servant? What will it ever profit me? Even if I should earn twelve, or twenty, or fifty roubles a month, to what will such earnings lead, and where will the man in me come in? Surely it would be better to do nothing at all, but just to gaze into space (as I am doing now), and let my eyes stare straight before me? ' "

" By the way, what were you talking to those people about? "

" Which people do you mean? "

[1] The verb *nakopit* means to amass, to heap up.

" The bearded man and the rest, the company in the guest-chamber? "

" Ah, *that* man I did not like—I have no fancy at all for fellows who strew their grief about the world, and leave it to be trampled upon by every chance-comer. For how can the tears of my neighbour benefit *me*? True, every man has his troubles; but also has every man such a predilection for his particular woe that he ends by deeming it the most bitter and remarkable grief in the universe—you may take my word for that."

Suddenly the speaker rose to his feet, a tall, lean figure.

" Now I must seek my bed," he remarked. " You see, I shall have to leave here very early to-morrow."

" And for what point? "

" For Novorossisk."

Now, the day being a Saturday, I had drawn my week's earnings from the monastery's pay-office just before the vigil service. Also, Novorossisk did not really lie in my direction. Thirdly, I had no particular wish to exchange the monastery for any other lodging. Nevertheless, despite all this, the man interested me to such an extent (of persons who genuinely interest one there never exist but two, and, of them, oneself is always one) that straightway I observed:

" I too shall be leaving here to-morrow."

" Then let us travel together."

*

At dawn, therefore, we set forth to foot the road in company. At times I mentally soared aloft, and viewed the scene from that vantage-point. Whenever I did so I beheld two tall men traversing a narrow track by a seashore—the one clad in a grey military overcoat and a hat with a broken crown, and the other in a drab *kaftan* and a plush cap. At their feet the boundless sea was splashing white foam, salt-dried ribands of seaweed were strewing the path, golden leaves were dancing hither and thither, and the wind was howling at, and buffeting, the travellers as clouds sailed over their heads. Also, to their right there lay stretched a chain of mountains towards which the clouds kept wearily, nervelessly tending, while to their left there lay spread a white-laced expanse over the surface of which a roaring wind kept ceaselessly driving transparent columns of spray.

On such stormy days in autumn everything near a seashore

looks particularly cheerful and vigorous, seeing that, despite the soughing of wind and wave, and the swift onrush of cloud, and the fact that the sun is only occasionally to be seen suspended in abysses of blue, and resembles a drooping flower, one feels that the apparent chaos has lurking in it a secret harmony of mundane, but imperishable, forces—so much so that in time even one's puny human heart comes to imbibe the prevalent spirit of revolt, and, catching fire, to cry to all the universe, " I love you! "

Yes, at such times one desires to taste life to the full, and so to live that the ancient rocks shall smile, and the sea's white horses prance the higher, as one's mouth acclaims the earth in such a pæan that, intoxicated with the laudation, it shall unfold its riches with added bountifulness, and display more and more manifest beauty under the spur of the love expressed by one of its creatures, expressed by a human being who feels for the earth what he would feel for a woman, and yearns to fertilise the same to ever-increasing splendour.

Nevertheless words are as heavy as stones, and after felling Fancy to the ground, serve but to heap her grey coffin-lid, and cause one, as one stands contemplating the tomb, to laugh in sheer self-derision. . . .

Suddenly, plunged in dreams as I walked along, I heard through the plash of the waves and the sizzle of the foam the unfamiliar words:

" Hymen, Demon, Igamon, and Zmiulan. Good devils are these, not bad."

" How does Christ get on with them? " I asked.

" Christ? He does not enter into the matter."

" Is He hostile to them? "

" Is He *hostile* to them? How could He be? Devils of that kind are devils to themselves—devils of a decent sort. Besides, to no one is Christ hostile." . . . .
. . . .[1]

As though unable any longer to brave the assault of the billows, the path suddenly swerved towards the bushes on our right, and, in doing so, caused the cloud-wrapped mountains to shift correspondingly to our immediate front, where the masses of vapour were darkening as though rain were probable.

Kalinin's discourse proved instructive as with his stick he from time to time knocked the track clear of clinging tendrils.

" The locality is not without its perils," once he remarked.

[1] In the Russian this hiatus occurs as marked.

" For hereabouts there lurks malaria. It does so because long ago Maliar of Kostroma banished his evil sister, Fever, to these parts. Probably he was paid to do so, but the exact circumstances escape my memory."

So thickly was the surface of the sea streaked with cloud-shadows that it bore the appearance of being in mourning, of being decked in the funeral colours of black and white. Afar off Gudaout lay lashed with foam, while constantly objects like snowdrifts kept gliding towards it.

" Tell me more about those devils," at length I said.

" Well, if you wish. But what exactly am I to tell you about them? "

" All that you may happen to know."

" Oh, I know *everything* about them."

To this my companion added a wink. Then he continued:

" I say that I know *everything* about those devils for the reason that for my mother I had a most remarkable woman, a woman cognisant of each and every species of proverb, ana-thema, and item of hagiology. You must know that, after spreading my bed beside the kitchen stove each night, and her own bed on the top of the stove (for, after her wet-nursing of three of the General's children, she lived a life of absolute ease, and did no work at all)——"

Here Kalinin halted, and, driving his stick into the ground, glanced back along the path before resuming his way with firm, lengthy strides.

" I may tell you that the General had a niece named Valentina Ignatievna. And she too was a most remarkable woman."

" Remarkable for what? "

" Remarkable for *everything*."

At this moment there came floating over our heads through the damp-saturated air a cormorant—one of those voracious birds which so markedly lack intelligence. And somehow the whistling of its powerful pinions awoke in me an unpleasant reminiscent thought.

" Pray continue," I said to my fellow traveller.

" And each night, as I lay on the floor (I may mention that never did I climb on to the stove, and to this day I dislike the heat of one), it was her custom to sit with her legs dangling over the edge of the top, and tell me stories. And though the room would be too dark for me to see her face, I could yet see the things of which she would be speaking. And at times, as these tales came floating down to me, I would find them so

236

horrible as to be forced to cry out, ' Oh, Mamka, Mamka, *don't*! . . .' To this hour I have no love for the bizarre, and am but a poor hand at remembering it. And as strange as her stories was my mother. Eventually she died of an attack of blood-poisoning, and, though but forty, had become grey-headed. Yes, and so terribly did she smell after her death that everyone in the kitchen was constrained to exclaim at the odour."

" Yes, but what of the devils? "

" You must wait a minute or two."

Ever, as we proceeded, clinging, fantastic branches kept closing in upon the path, so that we appeared to be walking through a sea of murmuring verdure. And from time to time a bough would flick us as though to say, " Speed, speed, or the rain will be upon you! "

If anything, however, my companion slackened his pace as in measured, sing-song accents he continued:

" When Jesus Christ, God's Son, went forth into the wilderness to collect His thoughts, Satan sent devils to subject Him to temptation. Christ was then young: and as He sat on the burning sand in the middle of the desert He pondered upon one thing and another, and played with a handful of pebbles which He had collected. Until presently from afar there descried Him the devils Hymen, Demon, Igamon, and Zmiulan—devils of equal age with the Saviour.

" Drawing near unto Him, they said, ' Pray suffer us to sport with Thee.' Whereupon Christ answered with a smile, ' Pray be seated.' Then all of them did sit them down in a circle, and proceed to business. Which business was to see whether or not any member of the party could so throw a stone into the air as to prevent it from falling back upon the burning sand. . . . .[1]

" Christ Himself was the first to throw a stone; whereupon His stone became changed into a six-winged dove, and fluttered away towards the Temple of Jerusalem. And, next, the impotent devils strove to do the same: until at length, when they saw that Christ could not in any wise be tempted, Zmiulan, the senior of the devils, cried:

" ' O Lord, we will tempt Thee no more: for of a surety do we avail not, and, though we be devils, never shall do so! '

" ' Aye, never shall ye! ' Christ did agree. ' And therefore I will now fulfil that which from the first I did conceive. That ye be devils I know right well. And that, while yet afar off,

---

[1] In the original Russian this hiatus occurs as given.

ye did, on beholding me, have compassion upon me I know right well. While also ye did not in any wise seek to conceal from me the truth as concerning yourselves. Hence shall ye, for the remainder of your lives, be *good* devils; so that at the last shall matters be rendered easier for you. Do thou, Zmiulan, become King of the Ocean, and send the winds of the sea to cleanse the land of foul air. And do thou, Demon, see to it that the cattle shall eat of no poisonous herb, but that all herbs of the sort be covered with prickles. Do thou, Igamon, comfort, by night, all comfortless widows who shall be blaming God for the death of their husbands. And do thou, Hymen, as the youngest devil of the band, choose for thyself wherein shall lie thy charge.'

" ' O Lord,' replied Hymen, ' I do love but to laugh.'

" And the Saviour replied:

" ' Then cause thou folk to laugh. Only, mark thou, see to it that they laugh not *in church*.'

" ' Yet even in church would I laugh, O Lord,' the devil objected.

" Jesus Christ Himself laughed.

" ' God go with you! ' at length He said. ' Then let folk laugh even in church—but *quietly*.'

" In such wise did Christ convert those four evil devils into devils of goodness."

Soaring over the green, bushy sea were a number of old oaks. On them the yellow leaves were trembling as though chilled, and here and there a sturdy hazel was doffing its withered garments, and elsewhere a wild cherry was quivering, and elsewhere an almost naked chestnut was politely rendering obeisance to the earth.

" Did you find that story of mine a good one? " my companion inquired.

" I did, for Christ was so good in it."

" Always and everywhere He is so," Kalinin proudly rejoined. " But do you also know what an old woman of Smolensk used to sing concerning Him? "

" I do not."

Halting, my strange traveller chanted in a feignedly senile and tremulous voice, as he beat time with his foot:

> In the heavens a flow'r doth blow,
> It is the Son of God.
> From it all our joys do flow,
> It is the Son of God.

KALININ

In the sun's red rays He dwells—
He, the Son of God.
His light our every ill dispels.
Praised be the Son of God!

Each successive line seemed to inspire Kalinin's voice with added youthfulness, until, indeed, the concluding words, "The One and Only God," issued in a high, agreeable tenor.

Suddenly a flash of lightning blazed before us, while dull thunder crashed among the mountains, and sent its hundred-voiced echoes rolling over land and sea. In his consternation Kalinin opened his mouth until a set of fine, even teeth became bared to view. Then, with repeated crossings of himself, he muttered:

"O dread God, O beneficent God, O God who sittest on high, and on a golden throne, and under a gilded canopy, do Thou now punish Satan, lest he overwhelm me in the midst of my sins!"

Whereafter, turning a small and terrified face in my direction, and blinking his bright eyes, he added with hurried diction:

"Come, brother! Come! Let us run on ahead, for thunderstorms are my bane. Yes, let us run with all possible speed, run *anywhere*, for soon the rain will be pouring down, and these parts are full of lurking fever."

Off, therefore, we started, with the wind smiting us behind, and our kettles and teapots jangling, and my wallet, in particular, thumping me about the middle of the body as though it had been wielding a large, soft fist. Yet a far cry would it be to the mountains, nor was any dwelling in sight, while ever and anon branches caught at our clothes, and stones leapt aloft under our tread, and the air grew steadily darker, and the mountains seemed to begin gliding towards us.

Once more from the black cloud-masses heaven belched a fiery dart which caused the sea to scintillate with blue sapphires in response, and, seemingly, to recoil from the shore as the earth shook, and the mountain defiles emitted a gigantic scrunching sound of their rock-hewn jaws.

"O Holy One! O Holy One! O Holy One!" screamed Kalinin as he dived into the bushes.

In the rear the waves lashed us as though they had a mind to arrest our progress; from the gloom to our front came a sort of scraping and rasping; long black hands seemed to wave over our heads; just at the point where the mountain crests

239

lay swathed in their dense coverlet of cloud there rumbled once more the deafening iron chariot of the thunder-god; more and more frequently flashed the lightning as the earth rang, and rifts cleft by the blue glare disclosed, amid the obscurity, great trees that were rustling and rocking and, to all appearances, racing headlong before the scourge of a cold, slanting rain.

The occasion was a harassing, but bracing, one, for as the fine bands of rain beat upon our faces our bodies felt filled with a heady vigour of a kind to fit us to run indefinitely—at all events to run until this storm of rain and thunder should be outpaced, and clear weather be reached again.

Suddenly Kalinin shouted: " Stop! Look!"

This was because the fitful illumination of a flash had just shown up in front of us the trunk of an oak tree which had a large black hollow let into it like a doorway. So into that hollow we crawled as two mice might have done—laughing aloud in our glee as we did so.

" Here there is room for *three* persons," my companion remarked. " Evidently it is a hollow that has been burnt out —though rascals indeed must the burners have been to kindle a fire in a living tree!"

However, the space within the hollow was both confined and redolent of smoke and dead leaves. Also, heavy drops of rain still bespattered our heads and shoulders, and at every peal of thunder the tree quivered and creaked until the strident din around us gave one the illusion of being afloat in a narrow caïque. Meanwhile at every flash of the lightning's glare we could see slanting ribands of rain cutting the air with a network of blue, glistening, vitreous lines.

Presently the wind began to whistle less loudly, as though now it felt satisfied at having driven so much productive rain into the ground, and washed clean the mountain tops, and loosened the stony soil.

" U-oh! U-oh!" hooted a grey mountain owl just over our heads.

" Why, surely it believes the time to be night!" Kalinin commented in a whisper.

" U-oh! U-u-u-oh!" hooted the bird again, and in response my companion shouted:

" You have made a mistake, my brother!"

By this time the air was feeling chilly, and a bright grey fog had streamed over us, and wrapped a semi-transparent veil about the gnarled, barrel-like trunks with their outgrowing shoots and the few remaining leaves still adhering.

Far and wide the monotonous din continued to rage—it did so until conscious thought began almost to be impossible. Yet even as one strained one's attention, and listened to the rain lashing the fallen leaves, and pounding the stones, and bespattering the trunks of the trees, and to the murmuring and splashing of rivulets racing towards the sea, and to the roaring of torrents as they thundered over the rocks of the mountains, and to the creaking of trees before the wind, and to the measured thud-thud of the waves; as one listened to all this the thousand sounds seemed to combine into a single heaviness of hurried clamour, and involuntarily one found oneself striving to dis-unite them, and to space them even as one spaces the words of a song.

Kalinin fidgeted, nudged me, and muttered:

" I find this place too close for me. Always I have hated confinement."

Nevertheless he had taken far more care than I to make himself comfortable, for he had edged himself right into the hollow, and, by squatting on his haunches, reduced his frame to the form of a ball. Moreover, the rain-drippings scarcely or in no wise touched him, while, in general, he appeared to have developed to the full an aptitude for vagrancy as a permanent condition, and for the allowing of no unpleasant circumstance to debar him from invariably finding the most convenient vantage-ground at a given juncture. Presently, in fact, he continued:

" Yes; despite the rain and cold and everything else, I consider life to be not quite intolerable."

" Not quite intolerable in what? "

" Not quite intolerable in the fact that at least I am bound to the service of no one save God. For if disagreeablenesses *have* to be endured, at all events they come better from Him than from one's own species."

" 'Then you have no great love for your own species? "

" One loves one's neighbour as the dog loves the stick." To which, after a pause, the speaker added:

" For *why* should I love him? "

It puzzled me to cite a reason off-hand, but, fortunately, Kalinin did not wait for an answer—rather, he went on to ask:

" Have you ever been a footman? "

" No," I replied.

" Then let me tell you that it is peculiarly difficult for a footman to love his neighbour."

" Wherefore? "

" Go and be a footman: *then* you will know. In fact, it is never the case that, if one serves a man, one can love that man. . . . How steadily the rain persists! "

Indeed, on every hand there was in progress a trickling and a splashing—a sound as though the weeping earth were venting soft, sorrowful sobs over the departure of summer before winter and its storms should arrive.

" How come you to be travelling the Caucasus? " I asked at length.

" Merely through the fact that my walking and walking has brought me hither," was the reply. " For that matter, *everyone* ends by heading for the Caucasus."

" Why so? "

" Why *not*, seeing that from one's earliest years one hears of nothing but the Caucasus, the Caucasus? Why, even our old General used to harp upon the name, with his moustache bristling, and his eyes protruding, as he did so. And the same as regards my mother, who had visited the country in the days when, as yet, the General was in command but of a company. Yes, everyone tends hither. And another reason is the fact that the country is an easy one to live in, a country which enjoys much sunshine, and produces much food, and has a winter less long and severe than our own winter, and therefore presents pleasanter conditions of life."

" And what of the country's people? "

" What of the country's people? Oh, so long as you keep yourself to yourself they will not interfere with you."

" And why will they not? "

Kalinin paused, stared at me, smiled condescendingly, and, finally, said:

" What a dullard you are to ask about such simple things! Were you never given any sort of an education? Surely by this time you ought to be able to understand *something*? "

Then, with a change of subject, and subduing his tone to one of snuffling supplication, he added in the sing-song chant of a person reciting a prayer:

" 'O Lord, suffer me not to become bound unto the clergy, the priesthood, the diaconate, the *tchinovstvo*,[1] or the *intel-*

[1] The official class.

242

ligentsia!' This was a petition which my mother used often to repeat."

The raindrops now were falling more gently, and in finer lines and more transparent network, so that one could once more descry the great trunks of the blackened oaks, with the green and gold of their leaves. Also, our own hollow had grown less dark, and there could be discerned its smoky, satin-bright walls. From those walls Kalinin picked a bit of charcoal with finger and thumb, saying:

" It was shepherds that fired the place. See where they dragged in hay and dead leaves! A shepherd's life hereabouts must be a truly glorious one!"

Lastly, clasping his head as though he were about to fall asleep, he sank his chin between his knees, and relapsed into silence.

Presently a brilliant, sinuous little rivulet which had long been laving the bare roots of our tree brought floating past us a red and fawn leaf.

" How pretty," I thought, " that leaf will look from a distance when reposing on the surface of the sea! For, like the sun when he is in solitary possession of the heavens, that leaf will stand out against the blue, silky expanse like a lonely red star."

After awhile my companion began, catlike, to purr to himself a song. Its melody, the melody of " the moon withdrew behind a cloud," was familiar enough, but not so the words, which ran:

> O Valentina, wondrous maid,
> More comely thou than e'er a flow'r!
> The nurse's son doth pine for thee,
> And yearn to serve thee every hour!

" What does that ditty mean? " I inquired.

Kalinin straightened himself, gave a wriggle to a form that was as lithe as a lizard's, and passed one hand over his face.

" It is a certain composition," he replied presently. " It is a composition that was composed by a military clerk who afterwards died of consumption. He was my friend his life long, and my only friend, and a true one, besides being a man out of the common."

" And who was Valentina? "

" My one-time mistress." Kalinin spoke unwillingly.

" And he, the clerk—was he in love with her? "

" Oh dear no! "

Evidently Kalinin had no particular wish to discuss the

subject, for he hugged himself together, buried his face in his hands, and muttered:

" I should like to kindle a fire, were it not that everything in the place is too damp for the purpose."

The wind shook the trees, and whistled despondently, while the fine, persistent rain still whipped the earth.

> I but humble am, and poor,
> Nor fated to be otherwise,

sang Kalinin softly as, flinging up his head with an unexpected movement, he added meaningly:

" Yes, it is a mournful song, a song which could move to tears. Only to two persons has it ever been known: to my friend the clerk and to myself. Yes, and to *her*, though I need hardly add that at once she forgot it."

And Kalinin's eyes flashed into a smile as he added:

" I think that, as a young man, you had better learn forth-with where the greatest danger lurks in life. Let me tell you a story."

And upon that a very human tale filtered through the silken, monotonous swish of the downpour, with, for listeners to it, only the rain and myself.

" Lukianov was *never* in love with her," he narrated. " Only I was that. All that Lukianov did in the matter was to write, at my request, some verses. When she first appeared on the scene (I mean Valentina Ignatievna) I was just turned nineteen years of age; and the instant that my eyes fell upon her form I realised that in her alone lay my fate, and my heart almost stopped beating, and my vitality stretched out towards her as a speck of dust flies towards a fire. Yet all this I had to conceal as best I might: with the result that in the company's presence I felt like a sentry doing guard duty in the presence of his commanding officer. But at last, though I strove to pull myself together, to steady myself against the ferment that was raging in my breast, something happened. Valentina Ignatievna was then aged about twenty-five, and very beautiful—marvel-lous, in fact! Also, she was an orphan, since her father had been killed by the Chechentzes, and her mother had died of small-pox at Samarkand. As regards her kinship with the General, she stood to him in the relation of niece by marriage. Golden-locked, and as skin-fair as enamelled porcelain, she had eyes like emeralds, and a figure wholly symmetrical, though as slim as a wafer. For bedroom she had a little corner apartment situated next to the kitchen (the General possessed his own house, of course), while, in addition, they allotted her a bright little boudoir in which she disposed her curios and knick-knacks, from cut-glass bottles and goblets to a copper pipe and a glass ring mounted on copper. This ring, when turned, used to emit showers of·glittering sparks, though she was in no way afraid of them, but would sing as she made them dance:

> " Not for me the spring will dawn!
> Not for me the Bug will spate!
> Not for me love's smile will wait!
> Not for me, ah, not for me!

" Constantly would she warble this.

" Also, once she flashed an appeal at me with her eyes, and said:

" ' Alexei, please never touch anything in my room, for my things are too fragile.'

" Sure enough, in *her* presence *anything* might have fallen from my hands!

" Meanwhile her song about ' Not for me ' used to make me feel sorry for her. ' Not for you? ' I used to say to myself. ' Ought not *everything* to be for you? ' And this reflection would cause my heart to yearn and stretch towards her. Next, I bought a guitar, an instrument which I could not play, and took it for instruction to Lukianov, the clerk of the Divisional Staff, which had its headquarters in our street. In passing I may say that Lukianov was a little Jewish convert with dark hair, sallow features, and gimlet-sharp eyes, but beyond all things a fellow with brains, and one who could play the guitar unforgettably.

" Once he said: ' In life all things are attainable—nothing need we lose for want of trying. For whence does everything come? From the plainest of mankind. A man may not be *born* in the rank of a general, but at least he may attain to that position. Also, the beginning and ending of all things is woman. All that she requires for her captivation is poetry. Hence let me write you some verses, that you may tender them to her as an offering.'

" These, mind you, were the words of a man in whom the heart was absolutely single, absolutely dispassionate."

Until then Kalinin had told his story swiftly, with animation; but thereafter he seemed, as it were, to become extinguished. After a pause of a few seconds he continued—continued in slower, to all appearances more unwilling, accents:

"At the time I believed what Lukianov said, but subsequently I came to see that things were not altogether as he had represented—that woman is merely a delusion, and poetry merely fiddle-faddle, and that a man cannot escape his fate, and that, though good in war, boldness is, in peace affairs, but naked effrontery. In this, brother, lies the chief, the fundamental law of life. For the world contains certain people of high station, and certain people of low; and so long as these two categories retain their respective positions, all goes well; but as soon as ever a man seeks to pass from the upper category to the inferior category, or from the inferior to the upper, the fat falls into the fire, and that man finds himself stuck midway, stuck neither here nor there, and bound to abide there for the remainder of his life, for the remainder of his life. . . . Always keep to your own position, to the position assigned you by fate. . . . Will the rain *never* cease, think you?"

By this time, as a matter of fact, the raindrops were falling less heavily and densely than hitherto, and the wet clouds were beginning to reveal bright patches in the moisture-soaked firmament, as evidence that the sun was still in existence.

"Continue," I said.

Kalinin laughed.

"Then you find the story an interesting one," he remarked.

Presently he resumed:

"As I have said, I trusted Lukianov implicitly, and begged of him to write the verses. And write them he did—he wrote them the very next day. True, at this distance of time I have forgotten the words in their entirety, but at least I remember that there occurred in them a phrase to the effect that 'for days and weeks have your eyes been consuming my heart in the fire of love, so pity me, I pray.' I then proceeded to copy out the poem, and tremblingly to leave it on her table.

"The next morning, when I was tidying her boudoir, she made an unexpected entry, and, clad in a loose red dressing-gown, and holding a cigarette between her lips, said to me with a kindly smile as she produced my precious paper of verses:

"'Alexei, did *you* write these?'

"'Yes,' was my reply. 'And for Christ's sake pardon me for the same.'

"'What a pity that such a fancy should have entered your head! For, you see, I am engaged already—my uncle is intending to marry me to Doctor Kliachka, and I am powerless in the matter.'

LOLA FIELDING

" The very fact that she could address me with so much sympathy and kindness struck me dumb. As regards Doctor Kliachka, I may mention that he was a good-looking, blotchy-faced, heavy-jowled fellow with a moustache that reached to his shoulders, and lips that were for ever laughing and vociferating, ' Nothing has either a beginning or an end. The only thing really existent is pleasure.'

" Nay, even the General could, at times, make sport of the fellow, and say as he shook with merriment:

" ' A doctor-comedian is the sort of man that *you* are.'

" Now, at the period of which I am speaking I was as straight as a dart, and had a shock of luxuriant hair over a set of ruddy features. Also, I was living a life clean in every way, and maintaining a cautious attitude towards womenfolk, and holding prostitutes in a contempt born of the fact that I had higher views with regard to my life's destiny. Lastly, I never indulged in liquor, for I actually disliked it, and gave way to its influence only in days subsequent to the episode which I am narrating. Yes, and, last of all, I was in the habit of taking a bath every Saturday.

" The same evening Kliachka and the rest of the party went out to the theatre (for, naturally, the General had horses and a carriage of his own), and I, for my part, went to inform Lukianov of what had happened.

" He said: ' I must congratulate you, and am ready to wager you two bottles of beer that your affair is as good as settled. In a few seconds a fresh lot of verses shall be turned out, for poetry constitutes a species of talisman or charm.'

" And, sure enough, he then and there composed the piece about ' the wondrous Valentina.' What a tender thing it is, and how full of understanding! My God, my God! "

And, with a thoughtful shake of his head, Kalinin raised his boyish eyes towards the blue patches in the rain-washed sky.

" Duly she found the verses," he continued after a while, and with a vehemence that seemed wholly independent of his will. " And thereupon she summoned me to her room.

" ' What are we to do about it all? ' she inquired.

" She was but half-dressed, and practically the whole of her bosom was visible to my sight. Also, her naked feet had on them only slippers, and as she sat in her chair she kept rocking one foot to and fro in a maddening way.

" ' What are we to do about it all? ' she repeated.

" 'What am *I* to say about it,' at length I replied, ' save that I feel as though I were not really existing on earth? '

" ' Are you one who can hold your tongue? ' was her next question.

" I nodded—nothing else could I compass, for further speech had become impossible. Whereupon, rising with brows puckered, she fetched a couple of small phials, and, with the aid of ingredients thence, mixed a powder which she wrapped in paper, and handed me with the words:

" ' Only one way of escape offers from the Plagues of Egypt. Here I have a certain powder. To-night the doctor is to dine with us. Place the powder in his soup, and within a few days I shall be free!—yes, free for *you*! '

" I crossed myself, and duly took from her the paper, whilst a mist rose, and swam before my eyes, as I did so, and my legs became perfectly numb. What I next did I hardly know, for inwardly I was swooning. Indeed, until Kliachka's arrival the same evening I remained practically in a state of coma."

Here Kalinin shuddered—then glanced at me with drawn features and chattering teeth, and stirred uneasily.

" Suppose we light a fire? " he ventured. " I am growing shivery all over. But first we must move outside."

The torn clouds were casting their shadows wearily athwart the sodden earth and glittering stones and silver-dusted herbage. Only on a single mountain top had a blur of mist settled like an arrested avalanche, and was resting there with its edges steaming. The sea too had grown calmer under the rain, and was splashing with more gentle mournfulness, even as the blue patches in the firmament had taken on a softer, warmer look, and stray sunbeams were touching upon land and sea in turn, and, where they chanced to fall upon herbage, causing pearls and emeralds to sparkle on every leaf, and kaleidoscopic tints to glow where the dark-blue sea reflected their generous radiance. Indeed, so goodly, so full of promise, was the scene that one might have supposed autumn to have fled away for ever before the wind and the rain, and beneficent summer to have been restored.

Presently through the moist, squelching sound of our footsteps, and the cheerful patter of the rain-drippings, Kalinin's narrative resumed its languid, querulous course.

" When, that evening, I opened the door to the doctor I could not bring myself to look him in the face—I could merely hang my head: whereupon, taking me by the chin, and raising it, he inquired:

" ' Why is your face so yellow? What is the matter with you? '

" Yes, a kind-hearted man was he, and one who had never failed to tip me well, and to speak to me with as much consideration as though I had not been a footman at all.

" ' I am not in very good health,' I replied. ' I, I——'

" ' Come, come! ' was his interjection. ' After dinner I must look you over, and in the meanwhile do you keep up your spirits.'

" Then I realised that poison him I could not, but that the powder must be swallowed by myself—yes, by myself! Aye, over my heart a flash of lightning had gleamed, and shown me that now I was no longer following the road properly assigned me by fate.

" Rushing away to my room, I poured out a glass of water, and emptied into it the powder: whereupon the water thickened, fizzed, and became topped with foam. Oh, a terrible moment it was! . . . Then I drank the mixture. Yet no burning sensation ensued, and though I listened to my vitals, nothing was to be heard in that quarter, but, on the contrary, my head began to lighten, and I found myself losing the sense of self-pity which had brought me almost to the point of tears. . . . Shall we settle ourselves here? "

Before us a large stone, capped with green moss and climbing plants, was good-humouredly thrusting upwards a broad, flat face beneath which the body had, like that of the hero Sviatogov, sunken into the earth through its own weight until only the face, a visage worn with æons of meditation, was now visible. On every side, also, had oak-trees overgrown and encompassed the bulk of the projection, as though they too had been made of stone, with their branches drooping sufficiently low to brush the wrinkles of the ancient monolith. Kalinin seated himself on his haunches under the overhanging rim of the stone, and said as he snapped some twigs in half:

" This is where we ought to have been sitting whilst the rain was coming down."

" And so say I," I rejoined. " But pray continue your story."

" Yes, when you have put a match to the fire."

Whereafter, further withdrawing his spare frame under the stone, so that he might stretch himself at full length, Kalinin continued:

" I walked to the pantry quietly enough, though my legs

were tottering beneath me, and I had a cold sensation in my breast: when suddenly I heard the dining-room echo to a merry peal of laughter from Valentina Ignatievna, and the General reply to that outburst:

" ' Ah, that man! Ah, these servants of ours! Why, the fellow would do *anything* for a *piatak* [1]!'

" To this my beloved one retorted:

" ' Oh, uncle, uncle! Is it only a *piatak* that I am worth?'

" And then I heard the doctor put in:

" ' What was it you gave him?'

" ' Merely some soda and tartaric acid. To think of the fun that we shall have!'"

Here, closing his eyes, Kalinin remained silent for a moment, whilst the moist breeze sighed as it drove dense, wet mist against the black branches of the trees.

" At first my feeling was one of overwhelming joy at the thought that at least not *death* was to be my fate. For I may tell you that, so far from being harmful, soda and tartaric acid are frequently taken as a remedy against drunken head-ache. Then the thought occurred to me: 'But, since I am not a tippler, why should such a joke have been played upon *me*?' However, from that moment I began to feel easier, and when the company had sat down to dinner, and, amid a general silence, I was handing round the soup, the doctor tasted his portion, and, raising his head with a frown, inquired:

" ' Forgive me, but what soup is this?'

" ' Ah!' I inwardly reflected. 'Soon, good gentlefolk, you will see how your jest has miscarried.'

" Aloud I replied—replied with complete boldness:

" ' Do not fear, sir. I have taken the powder myself.'

" Upon this the General and his wife, who were still in ignorance that the jest had gone amiss, began to titter, but the others said nothing, though Valentina Ignatievna's eyes grew rounder and rounder, until in an undertone she murmured:

" ' Did you *know* that the stuff was harmless?'

" ' I did not,' I replied. 'At least, not at the moment of my drinking it.'

" Whereafter falling headlong to the floor, I lost conscious-ness."

Kalinin's small face had become painfully contracted, and grown old and haggard-looking. Rolling over on to his breast

[1] A silver five-kopeck piece, equal in value to 2½d.

before the languishing fire, he waved a hand to dissipate the smoke which was lazily drifting slant-wise.

" For seventeen days did I remain stretched on a sick-bed, and was attended by the doctor in person. One day, when sitting by my side, he inquired:

" ' I presume your intention was to poison yourself, you foolish fellow? '

" Yes, merely *that* was what he called me—a ' foolish fellow.' Yet indeed, what was I to him? Only an entity which might become food for dogs, for all he cared. Nor did Valentina Ignatievna herself pay me a single visit, and my eyes never again beheld her. Before long she and Dr. Kliachka were duly married, and departed to Kharkov, where he was assigned a post in the Tchuguerski Camp. Thus only the General remained. Rough and ready, he was, nevertheless, old and sensible, and for that reason, did not matter: wherefore I retained my situation as before. On my recovery, he sent for me, and said in a tone of reproof:

" ' Look here. You are not wholly an idiot. What has happened is that those vile books of yours have corrupted your mind ' (as a matter of fact, I had never read a book in my life, since for reading I have no love or inclination). ' Hence you must have seen for yourself that only in tales do clowns marry princesses. You know, life is like a game of chess. Every piece has its proper move on the board, or the game could not be played at all.' "

Kalinin rubbed his hands over the fire (slender, non-work-manlike hands they were), and winked and smiled.

" I took the General's words very seriously, and proceeded to ask myself: ' To what do those words amount? To this: that though I may not care actually to take part in the game, I need not waste my whole existence through a disinclination to learn the best use to which that existence can be put.' "

With a triumphant uplift of tone, Kalinin continued:

" So, brother, I set myself to *watch* the game in question: with the result that soon I discovered that the majority of men live surrounded with a host of superfluous commodities which do but burden them, and have in themselves no real value. What I refer to is books, pictures, china, and rubbish of the same sort. Thought I to myself: ' Why should I devote my life to tending and dusting such commodities while risking, all the time, their breakage? No more of it for me! Was it for the tending of such articles that my mother bore me amid the agonies of childbirth? Is it an existence of *this* kind that must be passed until the tomb be reached? No, no—a thousand times noe Rather will I, with your good leave, reject altogether the gam ! of life, and subsist as may be best for me, and as may happen to be my pleasure.' "

Now, as Kalinin spoke, his eyes emitted green sparks, and as he waved his hands over the fire, as though to lop off the red tongues of flame, his fingers twisted convulsively.

" Of course, not all at a stroke did I arrive at this conclusion; I did so but gradually. The person who finally confirmed me in my opinion was a friar of Baku, a sage of pre-eminent wisdom, through his saying to me: ' With nothing at all ought a man to fetter his soul. Neither with bond-service, nor with property, nor with womankind, nor with any other concession to the temptations of this world ought he to constrain its action. Rather ought he to live alone, and to love none but Christ. Only this is true. Only this will be for ever lasting.'

" And," added Kalinin with animation and inflated cheeks and flushed, suppressed enthusiasm, " many lands and many peoples have I seen, and always have I found (particularly in Russia) that many folk already have reached an understanding of themselves, and, consequently, refused any longer to render obeisance to absurdities. ' Shun evil, and you will evolve good.' That is what the friar said to me as a parting word—though long before our encounter had I grasped the meaning of the axiom. And that axiom I myself have since passed on to other folk, as I hope to do yet many times in the future."

At this point the speaker's tone reverted to one of querulous anxiety.

" Look how low the sun has sunk ! " he exclaimed.

True enough, that luminary, large and round, was declining into—rather, towards—the sea, while suspended between him and the water were low, dark, white-topped cumuli.

" Soon nightfall will be overtaking us," continued Kalinin as he fumbled in his *kaftan*. " And in these parts jackals howl when darkness is come."

In particular did I notice three clouds that looked like Turks in white turbans and robes of a dusky red colour. And as these cloud Turks bent their heads together in private converse, suddenly there swelled up on the back of one of the figures a hump, while on the turban of a second there sprouted forth a pale pink feather which, becoming detached from its base, went floating upwards towards the zenith and the now rayless, despondent, moonlike sun. Lastly the third Turk stooped forward over the sea to screen his companions, and as he did so developed a huge red nose which comically seemed to dip towards, and sniff at, the waters.

"Sometimes," continued Kalinin's even voice through the crackling and hissing of the wood fire, "a man who is old and blind may cobble a shoe better than cleverer men than he can order their whole lives."

But no longer did I desire to listen to Kalinin, for the threads which had drawn me, bound me, to his personality had now parted. All that I desired to do was to contemplate in silence the sea, while thinking of some of those subjects which at eventide never fail to stir the soul to gentle, kindly emotion. Howbeit, Kalinin's words continued dripping into my ear like belated raindrops.

"Nowadays everybody is a busybody. Nowadays everyone inquires of his fellow-man, 'How is your life ordered?' To which always there is added didactically, 'But you ought not to live as you are doing. Let *me* show you the way.' As though *anyone* can tell me how best my life may attain full development, seeing that no one can possibly have such a matter within his knowledge! Nay, let every man live as best he pleases, without compulsion. For instance, I have no need of *you*. In return, it is not *your* business either to require or to expect aught of *me*. And this I say though Father Vitali says the contrary, and avers that throughout should man war with the evils of the world."

In the vague, wide firmament a blood-red cluster of clouds was hanging, and as I contemplated it there occurred to me the thought, "May not those clouds be erstwhile righteous world-folk who are following an unseen path across that expanse, and dyeing it red with their good blood as they go, in order that the earth may be fertilised?"

To right and left of that strip of living flame the sea was of a curious wine tint, while further off, rather, it was as soft and black as velvet, and in the remote east sheet-lightning was flashing even as though some giant hand were fruitlessly endeavouring to strike a match against the sodden firmament.

Meanwhile Kalinin continued to discourse with enthusiasm on the subject of Father Vitali, the Labour Superintendent of the monastery of New Athos, while describing in detail the monk's jovial, clever features with their pearly teeth and contrasting black and silver beard. In particular he related how once Vitali had knitted his fine, almost womanlike eyes, and said in a bass which stressed its o's:

"On our first arrival here, we found in possession only prehistoric chaos and demoniacal influence. Everywhere had clinging weeds grown to rankness; everywhere one found one's feet entangled among bindweed and other vegetation of the sort. And *now* see what beauty and joy and comfort the hand of man has wrought!"

And, having thus spoken, the monk had traced a great circle with his eye and doughty hand, a circle which had embraced as in a frame the mount, and the gardens fashioned and developed by ridgings of the rock, and the downy soil which had been beaten into those ridgings, and the silver streak of waterfall playing almost at Vitali's feet, and the stone-hewn staircase leading to the cave of Simeon the Canaanite, and the gilded cupolas of the new church where they had stood flashing in the noontide sun, and the snow-white, shimmering blocks of the guest-house and the servants' quarters, and the glittering fishponds, and the trees of uniform trimness, yet a uniformly regal dignity.

"Brethren," the monk had said in triumphant conclusion, "wheresoever man may be, he will, an he so desire, be given power to overcome the desolation of the wilds."

"And then I pressed him further," Kalinin added. "Yes, I said to him: 'Nevertheless Christ, our Lord, was not like you, for He was homeless and a wanderer—He was one who utterly rejected your life of intensive cultivation of the soil'" (as he related the incident Kalinin gave his head sundry jerks from side to side which made his ears flap to and fro). "'Also, neither for the lowly alone nor for the exalted alone did Christ exist. Rather, He, like all great benefactors, was one who had no particular leaning. Nay, even when He was roaming the Russian Land in company with Saints Yuri and Nikolai, He always forbore to intrude Himself into the villages' affairs, just as, whenever His companions engaged in disputes concerning mankind, He never failed to maintain silence on the subject.' Yes, thus I plagued Vitali until he shouted at my head, 'Ah, impudence, you are a heretic!'"

By this time the air under the lee of the stone was growing smoky and oppressive, for the fire, with its flames looking like a bouquet compounded of red poppies or azaleas and blooms of an aureate tint, had begun fairly to live its beautiful existence, and was blazing, and diffusing warmth, and laughing its bright, cheerful, intelligent laugh. Yet from the mountains and the cloud-masses evening was descending, as the earth emitted profound gasps of humidity, and the sea intoned its vague, thoughtful, resonant song.

" I presume we are going to pass the night here? " Kalinin at length queried.

" No, for my intention is, rather, to continue my journey."

" Then let us make an immediate start."

" But my direction will not be the same as yours, I think? "

Previously to this, Kalinin had squatted down upon his haunches, and taken some bread and a few pears from his wallet; but now, on hearing my decision, he replaced the viands in his receptacle, snapped-to the lid of it with an air of vexation, and asked:

" Why did you come with me at all? "

" Because I wanted to have a talk with you—I had found you an interesting character."

" Yes, at least I am *that*: many like me do not exist."

" Pardon me; I have met several."

" Perhaps you have." After which utterance, doubtfully drawled, the speaker added more sticks to the fire.

Eventide was falling with tardy languor, but, as yet, the sun, though become a gigantic, dull red lentil in appearance, was not hidden, and the waves were still powerless to besprinkle his downward road of fire. Presently, however, he subsided into a cloud bank; whereupon darkness flooded the earth like water poured from an empty basin, and the great kindly stars shone forth, and the nocturnal profundity, enveloping the world, seemed to soften it even as a human heart may be rendered gentle.

" Good-bye! " I said as I pressed my companion's small, yielding hand: whereupon he looked me in the eyes in his open, boyish way, and replied:

" I wish I were going with you! "

" Well, come with me as far as Gudaout."

" Yes, I will."

So we set forth once more to traverse the land which I, so alien to its inhabitants, yet so at one with all that it contained, loved so dearly, and of which I yearned to fertilise the life in return for the vitality with which it had filled my own existence.

For daily the threads with which my heart was bound to the world at large were growing more numerous; daily my heart

was storing up something which had at its root a sense of love
for life, of interest in my fellow-man.

And as, that evening, we proceeded on our way, the sea was
singing its vespertinal hymn, and the rocks were rumbling as
the water caressed them, and on the furthermost edge of the
dark void there were floating dim white patches where the
sunset's glow had not yet faded, though already stars were
glowing in the zenith. Meanwhile every slumbering tree-top was
a-quiver, and as I stepped across the scattered rain-pools their
water gurgled dreamily, timidly under my feet.

Yes, that night I was a torch unto myself, for in my breast
a red flame was smouldering like a living beacon, and leading
me to long that some frightened, belated wayfarer should, as it
were, sight my little speck of radiancy amid the darkness.

THE DEAD MAN

ONE evening I was sauntering along a soft, grey, dusty track between two breast-high walls of grain. So narrow was the track that here and there tar-besmeared ears were lying, tangled and broken and crushed, in the ruts of the cart-way.

Field mice squeaked as a heavy ear first swayed—then bent forwards towards the sun-baked earth. A number of martins and swallows were flitting in the sky, and constituting a sign of the immediate proximity of dwellings and a river; though for the moment, as my eyes roved over the sea of gold, they encountered naught beyond a belfry rising to heaven like a ship's mast, and some trees which from afar looked like the dark sails of a ship. Yes, there was nothing else to be seen save the brocaded, undulating steppe where gently it sloped away south-westwards. And as was the earth's outward appearance, so was that of the sky—equally peaceful.

Invariably the steppe makes one feel like a fly on a platter. Invariably it inclines one to believe, when the centre of the expanse is reached, that the earth lies within the compass of the sky, with the sun embracing it, and the stars hemming it about as, half-blinded, they stare at the sun's beauty.

*

Presently the sun's huge, rosy-red disk impinged upon the blue shadows of the horizon before preparing to sink into a snow-white cloud-bank; and as it did so it bathed the ears of grain around me in radiance, and caused the cornflowers to seem the darker by comparison, and the stillness, the herald of night, to accentuate more than ever the burden of the earth's song.

Fanwise then spread the ruddy beams over the firmament; and, in so doing, they cast upon my breast a shaft of light like Moses' rod, and awoke therein a flood of calm, but ardent, sentiments which set me longing to embrace all the evening world, and to pour into its ear great, eloquent, and never previously voiced utterances.

Now, too, the firmament began to spangle itself with stars;

and since the earth is equally a star, and is peopled with human-kind, I found myself longing to traverse every road throughout the universe, and to behold, dispassionately, all the joys and sorrows of life, and to join my fellows in drinking honey mixed with gall.

Yet also there was upon me a feeling of hunger, for not since the morning had my wallet contained a morsel of food. Which circumstance hindered the process of thought, and intermittently vexed me with the reflection that, rich though is the earth, and much thence though humanity has won by labour, a man may yet be forced to walk hungry. . . .

Suddenly the track swerved to the right, and as the walls of grain opened out before me there lay revealed a steppe valley, with, flowing at its bottom, a blue rivulet, and, spanning the rivulet, a newly-constructed bridge which, with its reflection in the water, looked as yellow as though fashioned of rape. On the further side of the rivulet some seven white huts lay pressed against a small declivity that was crowned with a cattle-fold, and amid the silver-grey trunks of some tall black poplars whose shadows, where they fell upon the hamlet, seemed as soft as down a knee-haltered horse was stumping with swishing tail. And though the air, redolent of smoke and tar and hemp ensilage, was filled with the sounds of poultry cackling and a baby crying during the process of being put to bed, the hubbub in no way served to dispel the illusion that everything in the valley was but part of a sketch executed by an artistic hand, and cast in soft tints which the sun had since caused, in some measure, to fade.

In the centre of the semi-circle of huts there stood a brick-kiln, and next to it, a high, narrow red chapel which resembled a one-eyed watchman. And as I stood gazing at the scene in general a crane stooped with a faint and raucous cry, and a woman who had come out to draw water looked, as she raised bare arms to stretch herself upwards, as though, cloud-like, and white-robed from head to foot, she were about to float away altogether.

Also, near the brick-kiln there lay a patch of black mud, in the glistening, crumpled-velvet-blue substance of which two urchins of five and three were, breechless, and naked from the waist upwards, kneading yellow feet amid a silence as absorbed as though their one desire in life had been to impregnate the mud with the red radiance of the sun. And so much did this laudable task interest me, and engage my sympathy and attention, that I stopped to watch the strapping youngsters, seeing that even in mire the sun has a rightful place, for the reason that the deeper the sunlight's penetration of the soil, the better does that soil become, and the greater the benefit to the people dwelling on its surface.

Viewed from above, the scene lay, as it were, in the palm of one's hand. True, by no manner of means could such lowly farm cots provide me with a job, but at least should I, for that evening, be able to enjoy the luxury of a chat with the cots' kindly inhabitants. Hence, with, in my mind, a base and mischievous inclination to retail to those inhabitants tales of the marvellous kind of which I knew them to stand wellnigh as much in need as of bread, I resumed my way, and approached the bridge.

As I did so there arose from the ground-level an animated clod of earth in the shape of a sturdy individual. Unwashed and unshaven, he had hanging on his frame an open canvas shirt, grey with dust, and baggy blue breeches.

" Good evening," I said to the fellow.

" I wish you the same," he replied. " Whither are you bound? "

" First of all, what is the name of this river? "

" What is its name? Why, it is the Sagaidak, of course."

On the man's large, round head there was a shock of bristling, grizzled curls, while pendent to the moustache below it were ends like those of the moustache of a Chinaman. Also, as his small eyes scanned me with an air of impudent distrust I could detect that they were engaged in counting the holes and darns in my raiment. Only after a long interval did he draw a deep breath as from his pocket he produced a clay pipe with a cane mouthpiece, and, knitting his brows attentively, fell to peering into the pipe's black bowl. Then he said:

" Have you matches? "

I replied in the affirmative.

" And some tobacco? "

For awhile he continued to contemplate the sun where that luminary hung suspended above a cloud-bank before finally declining. Then he remarked:

" Give me a pinch of the tobacco. As for matches, I have some."

So both of us lit up; after which he rested his elbows upon the balustrade of the bridge, leant back against the central stanchions, and for some time continued merely to emit and inhale blue coils of smoke. Then his nose wrinkled, and he expectorated.

" Muscovite tobacco is it? " he inquired.

" No—Roman, Italian."

" Oh! " And as the wrinkles of his nose straightened themselves again he added: " Then *of course* it is good tobacco."

To enter a dwelling in advance of one's host is a breach of decorum; wherefore I found myself forced to remain standing where I was until my interlocutor's tale of questions as to my precise identity, my exact place of origin, my true destination, and my real reasons for travelling should tardily win its way to a finish. Greatly the process vexed me, for I was eager, rather, to learn what the steppe settlement might have in store for my delectation.

" Work? " the fellow drawled through his teeth. " Oh no, there is no work to be got here. How could there be at this season of the year? "

Turning aside, he spat into the rivulet.

On the further bank of the latter a goose was strutting importantly at the head of a string of round, fluffy, yellow goslings, whilst driving the brood were two little girls—the one a child but little larger than the goose itself, dressed in a red frock, and armed with a switch, and the other one a youngster absolutely of a size with the bird, pale of feature, plump of body, bowed of leg, and grave of expression.

" Ufim! " came at this moment in the strident voice of a woman unseen, but incensed: upon which my companion bestowed upon me a sidelong nod, and muttered with an air of appreciation:

" *There's* lungs for you! "

Whereafter he fell to twitching the toes of a chafed and blackened foot, and to gazing at their nails. His next question was:

" Are you, maybe, a scholar? "

" Why do you ask? "

" Because, if you are, you might like to read the Book over a corpse."

And so proud, apparently, was he of the proposal that a faint smile crossed his flaccid countenance.

" You see, it would be work," he added with his brown eyes veiled, " whilst, in addition, you would be paid ten kopecks for your trouble, and allowed to keep the shroud."

" And should also be given some supper, I suppose? "

" Yes—and should also be given some supper."

" Where is the corpse lying? "

" In my own hut. Shall we go there? "

Off we set. *En route* we heard once more a strident shout of:

" Ufi-i-im! "

As we proceeded shadows of trees glided along the soft road
to meet us, while behind a clump of bushes on the further bank
of the rivulet some children were shouting at their play. Thus,
what with the children's voices, and the purling of the water,
and the noise of someone planing a piece of wood, the air seemed
full of tremulous, suspended sound. Meanwhile my host said
to me with a drawl:

" Once we did have a reader here. An old woman she was,
a regular old witch who at last had to be removed to the town
for amputation of the feet. They might well have cut off her
tongue too whilst they were about it, since, though useful
enough, she could rail indeed! "

Presently a black puppy, a creature of about the size of
a toad, came ambling, three-legged fashion, under our feet.
Upon that it stiffened its tail, growled, and snuffed the air with
its tiny pink nose.

Next there popped up from somewhere or another a barefooted young woman. Clapping her hands, she bawled:

' Here, you Ufim, how I have been calling for you, and
calling for you! "

" Eh? Well, I never heard you."

" Where were you, then? "

By way of reply my conductor silently pointed in my direction
with the stem of his pipe. Then he led me into the forecourt of
the hut next to the one whence the young woman had issued,
whilst she proceeded to project fresh volleys of abuse, and
fresh expressions of accentuated non-amiability.

In the little doorway of the dwelling next to hers we found
seated two old women. One of them was as rotund and dishevelled as a battered leathern ball, and the other one was a
woman bony and crooked of back, swarthy of skin, and irritable
of feature. At the women's feet lay, lolling out a rag-like tongue,
a shaggy dog which, red and pathetic of eye, could boast of a
frame nearly as large as a sheep's.

First of all Ufim related in detail how he had fallen in with
myself. Then he stated the purpose for which, he conceived,
it was possible that I might prove useful. And all the time that
he was speaking two pairs of eyes contemplated him in silence;

until, on the completion of his recital, one of the old women gave a jerk to a thin, dark neck, and the other old dame invited me to take a seat whilst she prepared some supper.

Amid the tangled herbage of the forecourt, a spot overgrown with mallow and bramble shoots, there was standing a cart which, lacking wheels, had its axle-points dark with mildew. Presently a herd of cattle was driven past the hut, and over the hamlet there seemed to arise and drift and float a perfect wave of sound. Also, as evening descended, I could see an ever-increasing number of grey shadows come creeping forth from the forecourt's recesses, and overlaying and darkening the turf.

" One day all of us must die," remarked Ufim with *empressement* as he tapped the bowl of his pipe against a wall.

The next moment the barefooted, red-cheeked young woman showed herself at the gate, and asked in tones rather less vehement than recently:

" Are you coming, or are you not? "

" Presently," replied Ufim. " One thing at a time."

For supper I was given a hunch of bread and a bowl of milk: whereupon the dog rose, laid its aged, slobbering muzzle upon my knee, and gazed into my face with its dim eyes as though it were saying, " May I too have a bite? "

Next, like an eventide breeze among withered herbage there floated across the forecourt the hoarse voice of the crook-backed old woman.

" Let us pray," she said. " O God, take away from us all sorrow, and receive therefor requitement in twofold measure ! "

As she recited the prayer with a mien as dark as fate the supplicant rolled her long neck from side to side, and nodded her ophidian-shaped head in accordance with a sort of regular, lethargic rhythm. Next I heard sink to earth at my feet some senile words uttered in a sort of sing-song.

"Some folk need work just as much as they wish, and others need do no work at all. Yet *our* folk have to work beyond their strength, and to work without any recompense for the toil which they undergo."

Upon this the smaller of the old crones whispered:

" But the Mother of God will recompense them. She recompenses everyone."

Then a dead silence fell—a weighty silence, a silence seemingly fraught with matters of import, and inspiring in one an assurance that presently there would be brought forth impressive reflections, there would reach the ear words of mark.

THE DEAD MAN

" I may tell you," at length the crook-backed old woman remarked as she attempted to straighten herself, " that though my husband was not without enemies, he also had a particular friend named Andrei, and that when failing strength was beginning to make life difficult for us in our old home on the Don, and folk took to reviling and girding at my husband, Andrei came to us one day, and said: ' Yakov, let not your hands fail you, for the earth is large, and in all parts has been given to men for their use. If folk be cruel, they are so through stupidity and prejudice, and must not be judged for being so. Live your own life. Let theirs be theirs, and yours yours, so that, dwelling in peace, while yielding to none, you shall in time overcome them all.' "

" That is what Vasil too used to say. He used to say: ' Let theirs be theirs, and ours ours.' "

" Aye, never a good word dies, but, wheresoever it be uttered, flies thence through the world like a swallow."

Ufim corroborated this with a nod.

" True indeed ! " he remarked. " Though also it has been said that a good word is Christ's, and a bad word the priest's."

One of the old women shook her head vigorously at this, and croaked :

" The badness lies not in any word of a priest, but in what you yourself have just said. You are greyheaded, Ufim, yet often you speak without thought."

Presently Ufim's wife reappeared, and, waving her hands as though she were brandishing a sieve, began to vent renewed volleys of virulent abuse.

" My God," she cried, " what sort of a man is *that*? Why, a man who neither speaks nor listens, but for ever keeps baying at the moon like a dog ! "

" *Now* she's started ! " Ufim drawled.

Westward there were arising, and soaring skyward, clouds of such a similarity to blue smoke and blood-red flame that the steppe seemed almost to be in danger of catching fire thence. Meanwhile a soft evening breeze was caressing the expanse as a whole, and causing the grain to bend drowsily earthward as golden-red ripples skimmed its surface. Only in the eastern quarter whence night's black, sultry shadow was stealthily creeping in our direction had darkness yet descended.

At intervals there came vented from the window above my head the hot odour of a dead body: and whenever that happened the dog's grey nostrils and muzzle would quiver, and its eyes blink pitifully as it gazed aloft. Glancing at the heavens, Ufim remarked with conviction:

" There will be no rain to-night."

" Do you keep such a thing as a Psalter here? " I inquired.

" Such a thing as a what? "

" As a Psalter, a book? "

No answer followed.

Faster and faster the southern night went on descending, and wiping the land clean of heat, as though that heat had been dust. Upon me there came a feeling that I should like to go and bury myself in some sweet-smelling hay, and sleep there until sunrise.

" Maybe Panek has one of those things? " hazarded Ufim after a long pause. " At any rate he has dealings with the Molokans."

After that the company held further converse in whispers. Then all save the more rotund of the old women left the fore-court, while its remaining occupant said to me with a sigh:

" You may come and look at him if you wish."

Small and gentle looked the woman's meekly lowered head as, folding her hands across her breast, she added in a whisper:

" O purest Mother of God! O Thou of spotless chastity! "

In contrast to her expression, that on the face of the dead man was stern and, as it were, fraught with importance where thick grey eyebrows lay parted over a large nose, and the latter curved downwards towards a moustache which divided intro-spective, partially closed eyes from a mouth that was set half-open. Indeed, it was as though the man were pondering something of annoyance, so that presently he would make shift to deliver himself of a final and urgent injunction. The blue smoke of a meagre candle quivered, meanwhile, over his head, though the wick diffused so feeble a light that the death blurs under the eyes and in the cheek furrows lay un-effaced, and the dark hands and wrists, disposed, lumplike, on the front of the greyish-blue shroud, seemed to have had their fingers twisted in a manner which even death had failed to rectify. And ever and anon, streaming from door to window, came a draught variously fraught with the odours of worm-wood, mint, and corruption.

Presently the old woman's whispering grew more animated and intelligible, while constantly, amid the wheezed mutterings, sheet lightning cut the black square of the window space with menacing flashes, and seemed, with their blue glare, as it shot through the tomblike hut, to cause the candle's flickering flame to undergo a temporary extinction, a temporary withdrawal, and the grey bristles on the dead man's face to gleam like the scales of a fish, and his features to gather themselves into a grim frown. Meanwhile, like a stream of cold, bitter water dripping upon my breast, the old woman's whispered soliloquy maintained its uninterrupted flow.

At length there recurred, somehow, to my mind the words which, impressive though they be, never can assuage sorrow —the words:

" Weep not for me, Martha, nor gaze into the tomb, for, lo, I am risen! "

Nay, and never would *this* man rise again. . . .

Presently the bony old woman returned with a report that nowhere among the huts could a Psalter be found, but only a book of another kind. Would *it* do?

The other book turned out to be a grammar of the Church-Slavonic dialect, with the first pages torn out, and beginning with the words, " *Drug, drugi, druzhe.*" [1]

" What, then, are we to do? " vexedly asked the smaller of the dames when I had explained to her that a grammar could work no benefit to a corpse. As she put the query her small, childlike face quivered with disappointment, and her eyes swelled and overflowed with tears.

" My man has lived his life," she said with a sob, " and now he cannot even be given proper burial! "

And, similarly, when next I offered to recite over her husband each and every prayer and psalm that I could contrive to recall to my recollection, on condition that all present should meanwhile leave the hut (for I felt that, since the task would be one novel to me, the attendance of auditors might hinder me from mustering my entire stock of petitions), she so disbelieved me, or failed to understand me, that for long enough she could only stand tottering in the doorway as, with twitching nose, she drew her sleeve across her worn, diminutive features.

Nevertheless she did, at last, take her departure.

*

Low over the steppe stray flashes of summer lightning still gleamed against the jet-black sky as they flooded the hut with their lurid shimmer: and each time that the darkness of the sultry night swept back into the room the candle flickered, and

[1] " A friend, of a friend, O friend."

the corpse's prone figure seemed to open its half-closed eyes, and to glance at the shadows which palpitated on its breast, and danced over the white walls and ceiling.

Similarly did I glance from time to time at *him*, yet glance with a guarded eye, and with a feeling in me that when a corpse is present anything may happen: until finally I rallied conscience to my aid, and recited under my breath:

" Pardon Thou all who have sinned, whether they be men, or whether they, being not men, do yet stand higher than the beasts of the field."

However, the only result of the recitation was to bring to my mind a thought directly at variance with the import of the words, the thought that " it is not sin that is hard and bitter to ensue, but righteousness."

" Sins wilful and of ignorance," I continued. " Sins known and unknown. Sins committed through imprudence and evil example. Sins committed through frowardness and sloth.

" Though to *you*, brother," mentally I added to the corpse, " none of this, of course, applies."

Again, glancing at the blue stars where they hung glittering in the fathomless obscurity of the sky, I reflected:

" Who in this house is looking at them save myself? "

Presently, with a pattering of claws over the beaten clay of the floor, there entered the dog. Once or twice it paced the length of the room. Then, with a sniff at my legs, and a grumble to itself, it departed as it had come. Perhaps the creature felt too old to bay a dirge to its master after the manner of its kind. In any case, as it vanished through the doorway, the shadows —so I fancied—sought to slip out after it, and, floating in that direction, fanned my face with a breath as of ice, while the flame of the candle flickered the more, as though it too were seeking to wrest itself from the candlestick, and go floating upwards to join the band of stars, a band of luminaries which it might well have deemed to be of a brilliance as small and as pitiful as its own. And I, for my part, since I had no wish to see what light there was disappear, followed the struggles of the tiny flame with a tense anxiety which made my eyes ache. Oppressed and uneasy all over as I stood by the dead man's shoulder, I strained my ears and listened, listened ever, to the silence encompassing the hut.

Eventually drowsiness began to steal over me, and proved a feeling hard to resist. Yet still with an effort did I contrive to recall the beautiful prayers of Saints Makari Veliki,

Chrysostom, and Damarkin, while at the same time something resembling a swarm of mosquitos started to hum in my head the words wherein the Sixth Precept issues its injunction to " all persons about to withdraw to a couch of rest."

And next, to escape falling asleep, I fell to reciting the *kondak* [1] which begins:

" O Lord, refresh my soul thus grievously made feeble with wrong doing."

Still engaged in this manner, suddenly I heard something rustle outside the door. Then a dry whisper articulated:

" O God of Mercy, receive unto Thyself also my soul! "

Upon that the fancy occurred to me that probably the old woman's soul was as grey and timid as a linnet, and that when it should fly up to the throne of the Mother of God, and the Mother should extend to that little soul her tender, white, and gracious hand, the newcomer would tremble all over, and flutter her gentle wings until well nigh death should supervene.

And then the Mother of God would say to Her Son:

" Son, pray see the fearfulness of Thy people on earth, and their estrangement from joy! O Son, is that well? "

And He would make answer to Her——

He would make answer to Her, and say I know not what.

*

And suddenly, so I fancied, a voice answered mine out of the brooding hush, as though it too were reciting a prayer. Yet so complete, so profound, was the stillness that the voice seemed far away, submerged, unreal—a mere phantom of an echo, of the echo of my own voice: until, on my desisting from my recital, and straining my ears yet more, the sound seemed to approach and grow clearer as shuffling footsteps also advanced in my direction, and there came a mutter of:

" Nay, it *cannot* be so! "

" Why is it that the dogs have failed to bark? " I reflected, rubbing my eyes, and fancying, as I did so, that the dead man's eyebrows twitched, and his moustache stirred in a grim smile.

Presently a deep, hoarse, rasping voice vociferated in the forecourt:

" What do you say, old woman? Yes, that he must die I knew all along, so you can cease your chattering. Men like him

[1] Hymn for the end of the day.

keep up to the last, then lay them down to rise no more. ، ، ،
Who is with him? A stranger? A-ah! "

And, the next moment, a bulk so large and shapeless that
it might well have been the darkness of the night embodied
stumbled against the outer side of the door, grunted, hiccuped,
and, lurching head foremost into the hut, grew wellnigh to
the ceiling. Then it waved a gigantic hand, crossed itself in
the direction of the candle, and, bending forward until its
forehead almost touched the feet of the corpse, queried under
its breath:

" How now, Vasil? "

Thereafter the figure vented a sob, whilst a strong smell of
vodka arose in the room, and from the doorway the old woman
said in an appealing voice:

" Pray give *him* the book, Father Demid."

" No indeed! Why should I? I intend to do the reading
myself."

And a heavy hand laid itself upon my shoulder, while a
great hairy face bent over mine, and inquired:

" A young man, are you not? A member of the clergy, too,
I suppose? "

So covered with tufts of auburn hair was the enormous
head above me—tufts the sheen of which even the semi-obscurity
of the pale candle-light failed to render inconspicuous—that
the mass, as a whole, resembled a mop. And as its owner
lurched to and fro he made me lurch responsively by
now drawing me towards himself, now thrusting me away.
Meanwhile he continued to suffuse my face with the hot, thick
odour of spirituous liquor.

" Father Demid! " again essayed the old woman with an
imploring wail, but he cut her short with the menacing
admonition:

" How often have I told you that you must not address a
deacon as ' Father '? Go to bed! Yes, be off with you, and let
me mind my affairs myself! *Go*, I say! But first light me
another candle, for I cannot see a single thing in front of
me."

With which, throwing himself upon a bench, the deacon
slapped his knee with a book which he had in his hands, and
put to me the query:

" Should you care to have a dram of *gorielka* [1]? "

" No," I replied، " At all events, not here."

---

[1] Another name for *vodka*.

270

" Indeed? " the deacon cried, unabashed. " But come, a bottle of the stuff is here, in my very pocket."

" This is no place in which to be drinking."

For a moment the deacon said nothing. Then he muttered:

" True, true. So let us adjourn to the forecourt. . . . Yes, what you say is no more than the truth."

" Had you not better remain seated where you are, and begin the reading? "

" No, I am going to do no such thing. *You* shall do the reading. To-night I, I—well, I am not very well, for I have been drinking a little."

And, thrusting the book into my stomach, he sank his head upon his breast, and fell to swaying it ponderously up and down.

" Folk die," was his next utterance, " and the world remains as full of grief as ever. Yes, folk die even before they have seen a little good accrue to themselves."

" I see that your book is not a Psalter," here I interposed after an inspection of the volume.

" You are wrong."

" Then look for yourself."

He grabbed the book by its cover, and, by dint of holding the candle close to its pages, discovered, eventually, that matters were as I had stated.

This took him aback completely.

" What can the fact mean? " he exclaimed. " Oh, *I* know what has happened. The mistake has come of my being in such a hurry. The other book, the true Psalter, is a fat, heavy volume, whereas this one is——"

For a moment he seemed sobered by the shock. At all events he rose and, approaching the corpse, said, as he bent over the bed with his beard held back:

" Pardon me, Vasil, but what is to be done? "

Then he straightened himself again, threw back his curls, and, drawing a bottle from his pocket, and thrusting the neck of the bottle into his mouth, took a long draught, with a whistling of his nostrils as he did so.

" Well? " I said.

" Well, I intend to go to bed—my idea is to drink and enjoy myself awhile."

" Go, then."

" And what of the reading? "

" Who would wish you to mumble words which you would not be comprehending as you uttered them? "

The deacon reseated himself upon the bench, leaned forward, buried his face in his hands, and remained silent.

Fast the July night was waning. Fast its shadows were dissolving into corners, and allowing a whiff of fresh, dewy morningtide to enter at the window. Already was the combined light of the two candles growing paler, with their flames looking like the eyes of a frightened child.

"You have lived your life, Vasil," at length the deacon muttered, "and though once I had a place to which to resort, now I shall have none. Yes, my last friend is dead. O Lord, where is Thy justice?"

For myself, I went and took a seat by the window, and, thrusting my head into the open air, lit a pipe, and continued to listen with a shiver to the deacon's wailings.

"Folk used to gird at my wife," he went on, "and now they are gnawing at me as pigs might gnaw at a cabbage. That is so, Vasil. Yes, that is so."

Again the bottle made its appearance. Again the deacon took a draught. Again he wiped his beard. Then he bent over the dead man once more, and kissed the corpse's forehead.

"Good-bye, friend of mine!" he said. Then to myself he added with unlooked-for clarity and vigour:

"My friend here was but a plain man—a man as inconspicuous among his fellows as a rook among a flock of rooks. Yet no rook was he. Rather, he was a snow-white dove, though none but I realised the fact. And now he has been withdrawn from the 'grievous bondage of Pharaoh.' Only I am left. Verily, after my passing, shall my soul torment and vomit spittle upon his adversaries!"

"Have you known much sorrow?"

The deacon did not reply at once. When he did so he said dully:

"All of us have known much sorrow. In some cases we have known more than was rightfully our due. I, certainly, have known much. But go to sleep, for only in sleep do we recover what is ours."

And he added as he tripped over his own feet, and lurched heavily against me:

"I have a longing to sing something. Yet I feel that I had best not, for song at such an hour awakens folk, and starts them bawling. . . . But beyond all things would I gladly sing."

With which he buzzed into my ear:

THE DEAD MAN

To whom shall I sing of my grief?
To whom resort for relief?
To the One in whose ha-a-and——

At this point the sharp bristles of his beard so tickled my neck as to cause me to edge further away.

"You do not like me?" he queried. "Then go to sleep, and to the devil too!"

"It was your beard that was tickling me."

"Indeed? Ought I to have shaved for your benefit before I came?"

He reflected awhile—then subsided on to the floor with a sniff and an angry exclamation of:

"Read, you, whilst I sleep. And see to it that you do not make off with the book, for it belongs to the church, and is very valuable. Yes, *I* know you hard-ups! Why do you go roaming about as you do—what is it you hope to gain by your tramping? . . . However, tramp as much as you like. Yes, be off, and tell people that a deacon has come by misfortune, and is in need of some good person to take pity upon his plight. . . . Diomid Kubasov my name is—that of a man lost beyond recall."

With which he fell asleep. Opening the book at random, I read the words:

"A land unapportioned that shall produce a nourisher of humanity, a being that shall put forth the bounty of his hand to feed every creature."

"A nourisher of humanity." Before my eyes that "nourisher" lay outspread, a nourisher overlaid with dry and fragrant herbage. And as I gazed, in the haze of a vision, upon that nourisher's dark and enigmatical face, I saw also the thousands of men who have seamed this earth with furrows, to the end that dead things should become things of life. And in particular there uprose before me a picture strange indeed. In that picture I saw marching over the steppe, where the expanse lay bare and void—yes, marching in circles that increasingly embraced a widening area—a gigantic, thousand-handed being in whose train the dead steppe gathered unto itself vitality, and became swathed in juicy, waving verdure, and studded with towns and villages. And ever, as the being receded further and further into the distance, could I see him sowing with tireless hand that which had in it life, and was part of himself, and human, as, with thoughts intent upon the benefiting of humanity, he summoned all men to put forth the mysterious force that is in them, and thus to conquer death, and eternally and invincibly to convert dead things into things of life, while traversing in company the road of death towards that which has no knowledge of death, and ensuring that, in swallowing up mankind, the jaws of death should not close upon death's victims.

And this caused my heart to beat with emotions the pulsing wings of which at once gladdened me and cooled my fervour. And how greatly, at that moment, did I feel the need of someone able to respond to my questions without passion, yet with truth, and in the language of simplicity! For beside me there lay but a man dead and a man drunken, while without the threshold there was stationed one who had far outlived her span of years. No matter, however. If not to-day, then to-morrow, should I find a fellow-creature with whom my soul might commune.

Mentally I left the hut, and passed on to the steppe, that I might contemplate thence the little dwelling in which alone, though lost amid the earth's immensity, the windows were not blind and black as in its fellow huts, but showed, burning over the head of a dead human being, the fire which humanity had conquered for humanity's benefit.

And that heart which had ceased to beat in the dead man—had everything conceived in life by that heart found due expression in a world poverty-stricken of heart-conceived ideas? I knew that the man just passed away had been but a plain and insignificant mortal, yet as I reflected upon even the little that he had done his labour loomed before me as greater than prowess of larger magnitude. Yes, to my mind there recurred the immature, battered ears of corn lying in the ruts of the steppe track, the swallows traversing the blue sky above the golden, brocaded grain, the kite hovering in the void over the landscape's vast periphery. . . .

And along with these thoughts there struck upon my ears a whistling of pinions as the shadow of a bird flitted across the brilliant, dew-bespangled green of the forecourt, and five cocks crowed in succession, and a flock of geese announced the fact of their awakening, and a cow lowed, and the gate of the cattle-pen creaked.

And with that I fell to thinking how I should like *really* to go out on to the steppe, and there to fall asleep under a warm, dry bank.

As for the deacon, he was still slumbering at my feet—slumbering with his breast, the breast of a prize-fighter, turned uppermost, and his fine, golden shock of hair falling like a nimbus around his head and hot, fat, flushed red features and gaping mouth and ceaselessly twitching moustache. In passing, I had noticed that his hands were long, and that they were set upon shovel-shaped wrists.

Next I found myself imagining the scene as the powerful figure of this man embraced a woman. Probably her face would become lost to sight in his beard, until nothing of her features remained visible. Then, when the beard began to tickle her, she would throw back her head, and laugh. And the children that such a man might have begotten!

All this only made it the more painful and disagreeable to me to reflect that the breast of a human being of such a type should be bearing a burden of sorrow. Surely naught but joy should have been present therein!

Meanwhile the old woman's gentle face was still peering at me through the doorway, and presently the first beam of sunlight came glancing through the window-space. Above the rivulet's silky glimmer a transparent mist lay steaming, while trees and herbage alike were passing through that curiously inert stage when at any moment (so one fancied) they might give themselves a shake, and burst into song, and in keys intelligible to the soul alone set forth the wondrous mystery of their existence.

" What a good man he is! " the old woman whispered plaintively as she gazed at the deacon's gigantic frame. Whereafter, as though reading aloud from a book invisible to my sight, she proceeded quietly and simply to relate the story of his wife.

" You see," she went on, " his lady committed a certain sin with a certain man; and folk remarked this, and, after setting the husband on to the couple, derided him—yes, him, our Demid!—for the reason that he persisted in forgiving the woman her fault. At length the jeers made her take to her room, and him to liquor, and for two years past he has been drinking, and soon is going to be deprived of his office. One who scarcely drank at all, my poor husband, used to say: ' Ah, Demid, yield not to these folk, but live your own life, and let theirs be theirs, and yours yours.' "

With the words tears welled from the old woman's dim, small eyes, and became merged with the folds and wrinkles on her grief-stained cheeks. And in the presence of that little head, a head shaking like a dead leaf in the autumn time, and of those kindly features so worn with age and sorrow, my eyes fell, and I felt smitten with shame to find that, on searching my soul for at least a word of consolation to offer to the poor fellow-mortal before me, I could discover none that seemed suitable.

But at length there recurred to my mind some strange words which I had encountered in I know not what antique volume —words which ran:

" Let not the servants of the Gods lament, but, rather, rejoice, in that weeping and lamentation grieve both the Gods and mankind."

Thereafter I muttered confusedly:

" It is time that I was going."

" What? " was her hasty exclamation, an exclamation uttered as though the words had affrighted her. Whereafter, with quivering lips, she began hesitantly and uncertainly to fumble in her bodice.

" No, I have no need of money," I interposed. " Only, if you should be so willing, give me a piece of bread."

" You have no need of money? " she re-echoed dubiously.

" No, none. For that matter, of what use could it be to me? "

" Well, well! " she said after a thoughtful pause. " Then be it as you wish, and—and I thank you."

*

The sun, as he rose and ascended towards the blue of the firmament, was spreading over the earth a braggart, peacock-like tail of beams. And as he did so I winked at him, for by experience I knew that some two hours later his smiles would be scorching me with fire. Yet for the time being he and I had no fault to find with one another. Wherefore I set myself to search for a bank whence I might sing to him, as to the Lord of Life:

> O Thou of intangible substance,
> Reveal now that substance to me!
> Enwrap me within the great vestment
> Of light which encompasseth Thee!
> That, with Thy uprising, my substance
> May come all-prevailing to be!

*

" Let us live our lives unto ourselves. Let theirs be theirs, and ours ours."

This book, designed by
William B. Taylor
is a production of
Edito-Service S.A., Geneva

Printed in France